D1035379

GOLD MINE
MASSACRE

Center Point
Large Print

Also by William W. Johnstone and available from Center Point Large Print:

The Trail West
Rising Fire
Pray for Death
Rope Burn
Too Soon to Die
Hang Them Slowly
Dig Your Own Grave
The Range Detectives
Trigger Warning
Evil Never Sleeps
Ride the Savage Land
Hang Him Twice

GOLD MINE MASSACRE

The Jensen Brand

WILLIAM W. JOHNSTONE
WITH J. A. JOHNSTONE

CENTER POINT LARGE PRINT
THORNDIKE, MAINE

This Center Point Large Print edition
is published in the year 2021 by arrangement with
Kensington Publishing Corp.

Following the death of William W. Johnstone, the Johnstone family is working with a carefully selected writer to organize and complete Mr. Johnstone's outlines and many unfinished manuscripts to create additional novels in all of his series like The Last Gunfighter, Mountain Man, and Eagles, among others. This novel was inspired by Mr. Johnstone's superb storytelling.

The text of this Large Print edition is unabridged.
In other aspects, this book may vary
from the original edition.
Printed in the United States of America
on permanent paper.
Set in 16-point Times New Roman type.

ISBN: 978-1-64358-948-0

The Library of Congress has cataloged this record under Library of Congress Control Number: 2021932379

CHAPTER 1

Denise Nicole Jensen's head snapped around as she heard screams coming from somewhere along the main street of Big Rock, Colorado. Denny had just stepped out the front door of Goldstein's Emporium and had three paper-wrapped bundles in her arms. Since the packages didn't have anything breakable in them, she didn't hesitate to toss them into the back of the wagon parked in front of the store and bound down the steps from the high porch and run toward the commotion.

She was a sight to behold—a tall, well-built young woman in a man's soft flannel shirt and denim trousers that hugged the curves of her legs and hips. Wheat-colored curls cascaded to her shoulders and down her back from under the brown Stetson with its strap taut under her fine chin.

She carried a holstered Colt .38 Lightning on her right hip. In these modern and enlightened times, early in the twentieth century, fewer and fewer men carried guns on a daily basis, especially in town, and practically no women did. But as the daughter of Smoke Jensen, Denny was no ordinary woman.

Smoke was famous throughout the West— throughout the whole country, really—as one of the fastest men with a gun who had ever lived on the frontier. Maybe *the* fastest.

Early in his adventurous career, he'd had a reputation as a gunfighter, even as an outlaw, although the charges leveled against him had been bogus ones whipped up by his enemies. In the past two and a half decades, since marrying Sally Reynolds, he had gained a different sort of reputation, that of one of the most successful ranchers in Colorado.

During that time, he and Sally had also had two children, the twins Denise Nicole and Louis Arthur, along with several unofficially adopted siblings who had been part of the family for a while before striking out on their own.

Denny and Louis had spent most of their childhood in Europe with Sally's parents. The medical problems Louis had been born with had required the attention of the best doctors in Europe. But they had visited their parents often, and in young adulthood had returned to the Sugarloaf, the Jensen ranch, to stay.

Louis was back east, with his new wife and stepson, while he attended law school. Denny, a Western girl at heart despite having spent so much time across the Atlantic, was just fine with staying on the Sugarloaf, which, in the back of her mind, she already planned on running one of these days, when her father was ready to take it easy.

Knowing Smoke Jensen, that might be a long time yet!

Denny had been mixed up in a number of scrapes and adventures of her own since returning to Colorado. She had inherited Smoke's natural ability for gun handling, and she didn't mind using a gun when she had to.

It might be one of those times, judging by the frightened cries coming from up ahead somewhere.

She slowed as she saw four men in the street in front of the bank. Each had a bandanna tied around the lower half of his face and wore a long duster and a pulled-down hat. They brandished guns, and two of them had taken hostages. One man had his left arm wrapped around the neck of a middle-aged woman, while another had picked up a boy about eight years old and held the boy in front of himself like a human shield.

The other two men carried canvas bank bags in their left hands. All four bank robbers—no doubt what they were—backed slowly toward horses tied at a nearby hitch rack.

"Jeremy!" A woman sobbed on the boardwalk. She held out her arms toward the boy, who was kicking his legs and waving his arms frantically as the outlaw clutched him.

The kid's mother, thought Denny as she skidded to a halt in the dusty street. She didn't recognize the woman, but plenty of people she didn't know lived in Big Rock.

Such as the man who stood on the sidewalk beside the bank's open doors, his hands lifted halfway to show that he wasn't a threat. That was pretty obvious, anyway, given his expensive black suit, the fancy cravat, the glittering watch chain, the carefully shaven chin with a slight cleft in it, and the silver band on the flat-crowned black hat that sat on his sandy hair.

Denny knew a dude when she saw one, even though she barely glanced at the man. Nearly all of her attention was focused on the quartet of bank robbers.

Sheriff Monte Carson or some of his deputies ought to be there soon, but they might not arrive in time to stop the outlaws from fleeing. And when the outlaws lit out, they might take the hostages with them. That wouldn't be good, so somebody had to stop them.

As far as Denny could see, that was up to her.

"Hold it right there!" she called in a clear, powerful voice that was just a bit husky for a woman.

The four men stopped backing away, evidently surprised not only to be challenged but also because a woman was doing the challenging.

"You came to rob the bank in Big Rock?" Denny said. *"Big Rock?* Don't you know you could have run into Smoke Jensen here? Don't you know how many would-be bank robbers have wound up propped on boards in front of the undertaking parlor while folks pose for photographs with the carcasses?"

"Girl, you're loco!" shouted an outlaw as he jabbed his gun in her direction. "Shut up your yammerin'!"

"I ain't sure that's a girl," another said. "She's got long hair, but she's dressed like a man."

"Yeah, but she ain't a man," put in a third outlaw. "You can tell that by the way she fills out that shirt."

All four of them, in fact, were looking at Denny quite intently.

She wondered, fleetingly, if she should have unbuttoned her shirt before confronting them. That would have riveted their attention even more. *Nailed them right to the ground,* she thought.

That might have made what was coming a little easier.

"If you let that poor woman and the little boy go, you might just live through this," she said. "If you don't—"

"What are you gonna do?" sneered the man still holding the squirming boy.

Remembering what the boy's mother had called him, Denny said, quietly but intensely, "Jeremy, listen to me. You're going to be all right, but you need to stop wiggling around. Can you do that, Jeremy? Can you be very still?"

He stopped trying to get away from his captor. As soon as his arms and legs weren't waving around and his head wasn't jerking back and forth, Denny struck.

Her right hand swept down and up, moving too fast for the eye to follow. The Lightning's grips were smooth against her palm as the gun came level and she squeezed the trigger. The double-action revolver barked. The .38 slug hit the outlaw's right eyeball, popped it like a grape, and bored on into his brain. He dropped straight to the ground as if a giant had slammed a sledgehammer down on the top of his head.

The little boy tumbled free.

His feet hadn't hit the street by the time Denny pivoted slightly and fired again. Her target was the outlaw holding the female hostage. He twisted a little just as the bullet reached him, so instead of hitting the center of his throat and clipping his spine, as Denny had intended, it tore a bloody, painful tunnel through his neck. He let out a gurgling yell and staggered, but he didn't let go of the woman.

With the hostage still mostly in the way, Denny couldn't rush a third shot. As a heartbeat ticked past while she lined her sights, Denny knew the other two outlaws would have time to pull their triggers. She stood a good chance of dying, but at least she would save the hostages.

The Lightning spat flame again, and the slug

went in the bank robber's mouth as he opened it to howl a curse while pawing at the wound in his neck. As he let go of the hostage and crumpled, Denny expected to hear the roar of the other two outlaws' guns, steeled herself for the bullets that were about to smash into her.

She heard two shots slam out so fast they blended together, but she didn't feel anything hit her. One of the remaining bandits flipped backward like a bug flicked away by a finger, and the other swayed for a second before toppling like a tree. Neither of them moved once they hit the ground.

Denny looked over at the sidewalk. The dude she had seen earlier, the stranger with the fancy hatband, stood with a gun in his hand. A few wisps of powder smoke curled from the muzzle.

Knowing how close she had just come to dying, Denny couldn't speak for a second. Finding her voice again, she said, "That was some pretty good shooting. I'm obliged to you, Mister . . . ?"

The man slipped the revolver back into a cross-draw rig under his coat, smiled at her, pinched the brim of his hat, and said in a voice with a surprising hint of a Western drawl in it, "You're welcome, miss. The name's Morgan. Conrad Morgan."

CHAPTER 2

Running footsteps and labored breathing behind her made Denny look over her shoulder. She saw Sheriff Monte Carson approaching with a shotgun in his hands.

He came to a stop, gazed past her at the bodies sprawled in the street, and said, "Blast it, Denny, couldn't you have left at least *one* of 'em alive so I could question him?"

"Don't blame me for all of them, Sheriff. I only killed the two who had grabbed hostages." She nodded toward the boy named Jeremy, who was wrapped up in his sobbing mother's arms, and the middle-aged woman, who leaned against a hitch rack with a hand pressed to her bosom as she breathed deeply, trying to recover from her fright. Several strands of her graying brown hair had come loose from their pins and dangled around her pale face.

"Then who gunned down the other two?" Monte wanted to know.

"That would be me, Sheriff," the stranger said as he stepped down from the boardwalk and strolled in their direction. "My name is Conrad Morgan."

"New in town, aren't you?"

"Got off the train less than half an hour ago,"

Morgan confirmed with a smile and a nod. He was a handsome man probably in his late twenties.

As Denny looked at him, she realized she had been wrong to dismiss him so cavalierly in that quick glance earlier, just because he was well-dressed. His gaze was cool and steady, and he moved with an easy grace reminiscent of a big cat.

Denny recognized those attributes. She had seen them often enough in her own father.

Monte Carson nodded toward the dead outlaws and said to the newcomer, "You shot two of those fellas?"

"I had no choice. They were about to shoot this young woman." Morgan cocked his head slightly to the side as he looked at Denny and added, "Miss . . . ?"

"Jensen," she said.

"They were about to shoot Miss Jensen," Morgan continued. "So I did the only thing I could." He shrugged. "Unless you think I should have tried to merely wound them and spare their lives. But to my way of thinking, after they robbed the bank and then endangered innocent citizens, they forfeited any right to such consideration."

"Yeah, you did the right thing blowing holes in them," agreed Monte. "It's just that I would've liked to know if the four of them were the only ones trying to pull this robbery or if there might be more of their gang lurking around." The lawman shrugged and went on. "But if somebody's bound and determined to make trouble, I reckon I'll find out about it sooner or later." He shook his head ruefully. "I'm getting too old to be running up and down the street in the hot sun, though."

"Are you all right, Sheriff?" asked Denny with a note of concern in her voice. She knew he was one of her father's oldest and best friends, and he was like an uncle to her and her brother Louis.

"Oh, yeah, I'm fine," Monte replied with a wave of his hand. "Don't worry about me."

A man wearing spectacles stepped out of the bank. Slender, dark-haired, and dapper, Charles Barnhart was the bank president, which accounted for the look on his face when he saw the dead outlaws lying in the street, as well as the two canvas money bags they had dropped when Conrad Morgan shot them.

"Thank heavens," Barnhart said. "I was afraid they might have gotten away. Did you shoot them, Sheriff?"

"No, Miss Jensen and Mr. Morgan get the credit for that. Did they hurt anybody in there, Mr. Barnhart?"

The banker shook his head. "No, and I'm very thankful for that, as well. They just tied up me, the two tellers, and the three customers who were

14

in the bank when they came in. It took me a few minutes to work my bonds loose."

"Any of them call the others by name, or say anything else to indicate who they are?"

"Not that I recall. They just cursed and gave orders and waved their guns around."

Monte grunted. "I'll look through their pockets, maybe find something to tell me who they are. I can check the wanted posters in my office, too. And I'll want to talk to the other folks who were in there, but that can wait. Better see first about getting these four down to the undertaking parlor."

"I told them that's where they'd wind up," Denny said dryly.

The sheriff started to turn away, then paused. "Mr. Morgan, I didn't think to ask you what brings you to Big Rock?"

"I'm here on business," Conrad Morgan replied. He looked at the bank president. "Would you be Mr. Barnhart?"

"That's right. Have we met, sir?"

"No, but we've corresponded." Morgan held out his hand. "I'm Conrad Morgan. I was on my way into the bank to see about opening an account with you when those four holdup men came busting out."

"Mr. Morgan, of course." Barnhart shook the man's hand eagerly. "Come in, come in. After that disruption, it'll be a pleasure to do some actual banking business."

15

Monte Carson said, "Are you going to be around Big Rock for a while, Mr. Morgan, in case I need to talk to you again?"

"I certainly will, Sheriff. I'll be here for several weeks, at the very least."

"All right, thanks." Monte tucked the shotgun under his arm and headed toward the undertaker's.

Since the excitement was over, Denny turned away, too, intending to return to the wagon she had driven into town from the ranch. Before she could do that, the woman whose little boy had been taken hostage hurried over to her and thanked her profusely, finally giving in to the deep emotion she obviously felt and throwing her arms around Denny for a big hug of gratitude.

Denny didn't cotton to being fussed over like that, but she accepted the woman's thanks graciously. She might not always live up to her mother's standards of being ladylike, but she could be courteous, anyway.

The woman told her son to thank Denny, too, which he did by gravely shaking hands with her. Then he couldn't hold in his excitement any more as he burst out, "I never saw anybody draw and shoot like that before, Miss Jensen! Why, I bet not even your pa coulda killed those varmints any slicker!"

"Jeremy," his mother scolded, "don't be crude."

"Thanks, Jeremy," Denny smiled down at him. "I'm just glad I was able to help."

16

The woman put her arm around Jeremy's shoulder and led him away, but not before the little boy gazed back over his shoulder adoringly a couple of times. Denny just smiled at him and waited until he wasn't looking to chuckle.

She became aware of someone standing beside her, and her hand moved instinctively toward her gun as she looked around quickly, seeing Conrad Morgan.

"I thought you were going in the bank to talk business with Mr. Barnhart," she said as she relaxed.

"I am," he told her. The way his eyes twinkled with amusement told her that he had noticed her reaction. "But I told him I'd be there in a few minutes. I wanted to ask you a question first."

"All right," Denny said coolly as she hooked her thumbs into her gunbelt. "Go ahead and ask."

"You said your name is Jensen, and that boy mentioned your pa. Would your father happen to be Smoke Jensen?"

"You've heard of him?"

Morgan chuckled. "I imagine most red-blooded American boys have heard of Smoke Jensen. I remember reading dime novels about him when I was growing up. And there's a part of me that's still a red-blooded American boy. So . . . ?"

"Yes," Denny said. "My father is Smoke Jensen."

"And like father, like daughter, eh? I mean, the

lad was right. That was an amazingly fast draw you made, and remarkably accurate shooting under extreme pressure."

"I was lucky."

Morgan shook his head. "No, I've seen plenty of lucky shots. What you did wasn't luck. It was skill."

"You did some good shooting yourself," Denny pointed out. "Did you inherit that?"

"As a matter of fact, I did. *My* father is Frank Morgan." He pinched his hat brim again. "I'd better get to my business. Good day, Miss Jensen." He turned and his long-legged stride carried him toward the bank.

Denny stared after him, trying not to let her mouth sag open in surprise. *Frank Morgan is his father?* The man sometimes referred to as the Drifter?

And the man some folks called the Last Gunfighter.

CHAPTER 3

Conrad cocked his right ankle on his left knee and leaned back casually in the comfortable brown leather chair. He had his hat in his left hand, and his right hand toyed with the links of the silver band.

On the other side of the big desk, Charles Barnhart shuffled some papers in front of him. "I have your letters right here, Mr. Morgan. I'm very pleased that you've come to us for your banking needs."

"Well, your bank is the oldest, biggest, and most respectable in Big Rock," Conrad said. "Whenever I do business, I make it a habit to deal with the best. That's how my mother built the Browning Holdings into what they are today. It's my intention to continue that tradition."

"Yes, your mother was Vivian Browning, isn't that right? I remember hearing about her. She had a reputation as one of the shrewdest businesswomen in this country's history." Barnhart frowned slightly. "Now that I think about it, I would have sworn that your last name was Browning, as well . . ."

"My stepfather's name was Browning," Conrad replied, his tone cooling a little. "He helped raise me, and I used his name for a long time. But these days I go by my actual father's name."

Barnhart raised his hands, palms out, and said, "Yes, of course. My apologies, Mr. Morgan. I didn't mean to pry into your personal life. That's certainly no business of mine."

"Quite all right," Conrad said, flashing an easy smile that concealed the emotions the banker's comment had started stirring around inside him.

For a long time, Conrad had believed that the man married to his mother was actually his father. It had taken Vivian Browning's murder at the hands of an outlaw gang and Conrad's kidnapping and torture by those same desperadoes, for him to discover that his real father was Frank Morgan, a notorious gunfighter who had killed countless men from one end of the violent frontier to the other.

Frank Morgan had saved his son from almost certain death, but despite that, for several years Conrad had hated the man, blaming him at least partially for his mother's death.

Over time, the relationship between the two of them had thawed. Fate had thrown them together on several adventures, and during the course of those dustups, Conrad had come to learn just what a good man his father really was. When tragedy had caused Conrad to ride the gunfighter's trail, taking on the identity of a fast gun calling himself Kid Morgan, Frank had come to his aid on numerous occasions.

Finally, life had settled down a mite. Kid

20

Morgan had put away his guns, and Conrad had devoted his energies to running the vast business empire Vivian Browning had founded.

Trouble had eventually cropped up, drawing him and Frank together again, and Conrad had come to the realization that he wanted to do more than carry on his mother's legacy. He wanted to honor his real father, too, and he had done that by taking the Morgan name. Now and forevermore, he was Conrad Morgan.

None of that had anything to do with the business that had brought him to Big Rock, so he pushed those thoughts and memories aside and said to Charles Barnhart, "My new partner and I are going to need operating funds for a venture we're going into, here in the area, and so I decided to open an account in your bank with a deposit of, oh, let's say fifty thousand dollars."

Barnhart drew in a deep breath, and Conrad could tell that the man was trying hard not to stare at him across the desk. After a couple of seconds, Barnhart recovered enough from his surprise to say, "Yes, of course. Fifty, ah, fifty thousand dollars."

Conrad reached inside his coat and brought out a slip of paper. "I have a draft here from my bank in San Francisco in that amount. Will that be satisfactory, Mr. Barnhart?"

Barnhart barely suppressed his eagerness as he reached across the desk to take the draft when Conrad extended it to him. "Yes, more than satisfactory, Mr. Morgan." He looked at the draft, and his business sense reasserted itself. "Of course, the deposit will be provisional until such time as the other bank notifies us that it will honor this draft."

"Certainly," Conrad said with a casual wave of his hand. "We shouldn't be needing to draw on it for any large expenditures for a while. I brought along enough cash to cover our expenses until then."

Barnhart set the draft on the desk in front of him and brushed his fingertips over it as if he were caressing it. Then he looked up at Conrad and asked curiously, "You mentioned a partner . . ."

"Yes, a man named Axel Strom. He came in on the train with me and was taking care of getting our bags delivered to the hotel. Once that was done, he planned to come over here and say hello, too, unless we'd already concluded our business." Conrad chuckled. "Since our meeting was delayed by that little unpleasantness out in the street, I expect Axel will be here soon."

"Little unpleasantness," repeated Barnhart, shaking his head. "Those outlaws terrified everyone in here, and you and Miss Jensen could have been killed. I'd call that more than a little unpleasantness."

"I suppose it's a matter of what you're accustomed to."

"I, uh, I suppose." Barnhart cleared his throat. "Just out of curiosity, what sort of business venture are you and Mr. Strom planning to enter into in our area?"

"Mining," Conrad said.

"Gold mining?"

"That's right."

Barnhart looked a little confused. "Mining was certainly important at times in the area's past, but this is primarily cattle country now. There are some large cattle spreads. The largest is Mr. Jensen's Sugarloaf, as well as some ranches that specialize in raising fine horses. I believe that Mr. Jensen has an excellent horse herd, in addition to his cattle."

Conrad ran a finger along the silver band of his hat again. "Jensen's the big he-wolf around here, isn't he?"

Barnhart looked shocked by that comment, which would have been more likely to come from a Westerner rather than an eastern businessman, as he believed Conrad to be.

Conrad waved it off and went on. "I realize mining isn't a major industry in Eagle County these days, but that's about to change, Mr. Barnhart. We've done considerable research into the matter, and Mr. Strom and I found that many of the gold mines around here were still producing ore when they were shut down, just not in sufficient quantities to make the work of getting it out worthwhile. That's why their owners closed them."

"From what I know, that's true," said Barnhart, nodding. "You have to understand, Mr. Morgan, I came to Big Rock after the mining boom was over, so I'm not personally acquainted with all the details." .

"The process Mr. Strom utilizes can extract gold ore from the earth in a much more efficient manner," Conrad explained. "And, once the initial investment is recouped, it can continue to operate less expensively than traditional mining. With those two factors combined, mines that were closed because they weren't paying off enough can be reopened and made lucrative again. That's what we intend to do. That's why we've already purchased a number of such properties in the area."

"Oh," Barnhart said, looking impressed. "I wasn't aware of that. It does sound like you've thought everything through." He tapped the bank draft on the desk in front of him. "Then this fifty thousand dollars—"

"Will be used for machines and the men to run them," Conrad said. "And equipment to process the ore we take out of those mines."

"An operation such as this could transform the entire area. The entire state, perhaps."

Conrad smiled and leaned his head to the side to acknowledge Barnhart's statement. "There's no point to having goals and ambitions if they're not big ones."

As was customary in Western banks, Barnhart's desk wasn't in a separate office. It sat behind a wooden railing in a rear corner of the bank's lobby, not far from the massive door of the vault, and Conrad could hear everything that was going on inside the bank. He heard the front door open, followed by heavy footsteps, which made him look over his shoulder.

The man who had just come into the bank was tall, barrel-chested, broad-shouldered. He had the long, powerful arms and thick neck of someone who had done a lot of heavy physical labor in his life, and yet he wore an expensive gray tweed suit, and the stickpin in his cravat glittered from the diamond set into it. He didn't have a hat on and was bald except for a fringe of dark hair around his ears and the back of his head, as well as bushy eyebrows. A thick cigar jutted from his fleshy lips at a jaunty angle because of the way he had it clamped between his teeth.

Conrad lifted a hand in a signal to the newcomer, who came toward them with a stride that made it look as if he were prepared to stomp flat anything that got in his way. As the man came through the gate in the wooden railing, Conrad got to his feet. Charles Barnhart followed suit.

"Mr. Barnhart," Conrad said, "I'd like for you to meet my partner in this venture, Axel Strom."

CHAPTER 4

As skilled at handling a wagon team as she was at most jobs around the ranch, Denny didn't have to devote much actual thought to steering the horses along the road that led from Big Rock to the Sugarloaf Ranch. That freed up her mind to ponder what she knew about Frank Morgan.

She had never met the man, although she was aware that her father had crossed trails with him. She had heard Smoke talk about Morgan several times. He had even visited the Sugarloaf on more than one occasion and had given Smoke a hand in a couple of ruckuses.

Despite that, they weren't close friends. They shared the mutual respect that tough fighting men usually had for each other, but a certain wariness also existed between them. That was inevitable, since each of them carried around a reputation as top man with a gun. Denny suspected that the topic had been debated in countless saloons and bunkhouses all across the frontier.

Who is faster and deadlier on the draw, Smoke Jensen or Frank Morgan?

Denny knew what she believed was the answer to that question. And it wasn't just family loyalty that made her think Smoke was faster. She had seen him in action so many times that she had no doubts. Nobody could have ever been faster on the draw than Smoke Jensen at his peak.

And as far as she could tell, he hadn't slowed down a lick.

The little boy Jeremy, back there in town, had been wrong. Denny wasn't as fast or as good with a gun as her father. She knew that, and the knowledge didn't bother her. To be a hair less than the best was nothing to be ashamed of, when the best was the legendary Smoke Jensen.

Maybe Frank Morgan was just a hair less than the best, too.

She wondered how Conrad Morgan stacked up against *his* pa. Morgan's shooting had been fast and accurate when he drilled those two bank robbers, certainly, but Denny hadn't seen him make his draw.

What was he doing in Big Rock, anyway?

She had no answer to that as she wheeled the rig into the ranch yard and headed for the barn. The big double doors stood open. She drove inside and brought the wagon to a stop.

Wes "Pearlie" Fontaine stood up from the stool where he was mending some harness. He waved a hand in front of his face to clear away some of the billowing dust that the wagon wheels had stirred up. "You in a hurry, Denny? You drove in almost like somethin' was chasin' you."

The leathery, deeply tanned Pearlie had been the foreman of the Sugarloaf for many years

27

before turning that responsibility over to his old friend Calvin Woods. He remained on the ranch as a senior advisor of sorts. "Foreman *emeritus*" was how Denny's brother Louis referred to him.

Twenty-five years earlier, he had been a hired gun, working for one of Smoke's deadliest enemies in the early days of settlement in the valley. Realizing he had backed the wrong horse, he went over to Smoke's side and became one of his staunchest friends and allies in the process.

Monte Carson had followed that same progression, although he had become the sheriff in the newly founded town of Big Rock instead of going to work on the Sugarloaf.

Denny wrapped the reins around the wagon's brake lever and jumped lithely from the driver's box to the ground. "I was thinking about something, and I guess I was a little distracted," she explained.

"Deep thoughts'll do that to you," Pearlie agreed with a nod. "That's why I try to avoid 'em as much as I can. What was it you was mullin' over, if you don't mind me askin'?"

Instead of answering him directly, Denny asked a question of her own. "Pearlie, did you ever meet Frank Morgan?"

"The gunfighter?" Pearlie frowned in surprise. "Sure, I've met him. He was here at the Sugarloaf one Christmas when all Hades came to call, as has a habit of happenin' around here. Him and

Smoke have crossed trails a time or two besides that."

"Is he as fast with a gun as my father?"

Pearlie stared at her for a second, then asked, "What in blazes has got you puzzlin' over a thing like that?"

"I'm just curious. Is he? As fast as Smoke?"

Pearlie drew in a deep breath, then blew it out. "I'd plumb hate to have to live or die on the difference. I've seen Morgan in action. Not near as often as I've seen Smoke, of course, but when you've seen a man like Frank Morgan get down to some serious work with a shootin' iron, it's somethin' you ain't likely to ever forget."

Pearlie rasped his fingertips over his salt-and-pepper-stubbled chin. "When you're talkin' about men like your pa and Morgan, or Luke Short, Ben Thompson, Matt Bodine, Wes Hardin and the like . . . Men like that are at whole 'nother level when it comes to gun handlin'. They can do things that normal human bein's just can't. And on any given day, you can stack up any two of 'em against each other, and there just ain't no tellin' what's gonna happen. But whatever does happen, it'll be a sight to see, you can bet a hat on that."

He cleared his throat and looked vaguely embarrassed. "Here I am, yammerin' on, when you asked me a simple question. So I'll give you a simple answer. Smoke's the fastest I've ever seen. I believe in my heart he's the fastest that's

29

ever been. But if he ever had to go up against Frank Morgan, I'd be worried for him, because there's just that little difference between 'em. I purely would." Pearlie suddenly looked alarmed. "Dang it, girl, what's goin' on? Have you heard somethin'? Is Frank Morgan on the way here to have a showdown with Smoke?"

"No, not at all," Denny said quickly. "But I met a man in Big Rock, a stranger who just came into town on the train, who claimed to be Frank Morgan's son."

Pearlie looked very interested in that. "Really? Seems like I remember hearin' some stories about Morgan havin' a son. I can't recollect any of the details, though. What'd this hombre look like?"

"Like a dude," Denny replied with a laugh. "He was dressed in an expensive suit and wore a hat with a silver band. You know, flashy. I never would have taken him for the son of a famous gunfighter."

"Puny little fella, eh?"

"Oh, no, he was tall. Well-built, from what I could tell. And good-looking."

Pearlie cocked his head to the side, narrowed his eyes at her, and said, "You don't say."

Denny laughed again, took off her hat, and swatted him lightly on the arm with it. "Hush. I didn't mean anything by that. Men who look like that are always full of themselves. Not the sort who would interest me at all."

"What's he doin' in Big Rock?"

"I don't have any idea," she answered honestly. "He was on his way into the bank when—"

"When what?"

"Never mind," said Denny.

Her parents would find out about the bank robbery and the shooting and the four dead men soon enough. Her father probably wouldn't have much to say about it, other than making sure she was all right. More than likely, her mother would have a few choice words, though.

When she needed to, Sally Jensen could ride and shoot as well as most men and better than some, just like her daughter, but she also placed a value on a young woman being ladylike. Denny could manage ladylike if she put some effort into it—she had moved among the cream of European society for a long time and had managed to fit in very well—but it went against her nature, which was much more suited to riding the range and dealing with troublesome varmints.

She wouldn't go so far as to say that she believed she was a disappointment to her mother, but she also knew that Sally would be distressed by the idea of her swapping bullets with bank robbers. So she didn't fill Pearlie in on what had happened in town.

She said, "I'll get this team unhitched and put away."

"I'll take care of that," Pearlie volunteered. "You go on in and get outta this heat."

"Are you sure?"

"It'll do my old bones good to move around some. They stiffen up if I ain't workin'."

"Well, all right, then," Denny said. "Thank you. I'll see you at supper."

"Sure. Get Smoke to tell you more about Frank Morgan. He's probably heard plenty of stories, as well as meetin' the fella a few times."

Denny just nodded and left the barn, heading for the big ranch house.

She went inside and would have gone straight to her room to change her dusty clothes after the ride out from Big Rock, but her mother called to her from the parlor as she passed. Denny went into the room and found Smoke and Sally sitting in comfortable armchairs. They had been reading, each holding a leather-bound volume.

Denny frowned slightly. Normally at this time of day, Smoke would be out on the range somewhere, working with Cal and the other members of the crew. However, it was a pretty hot afternoon, and even though she didn't like to think about it, her father wasn't as young as he used to be. Neither of her parents were. There was nothing wrong with them slowing down a little.

As long as it was only a little. Not too much. Denny wasn't ready to consider the idea of her parents being *old*. Why, they were only in their early fifties and looked at least ten years younger than that.

"How was your trip to town, dear?" Sally asked. "Were you able to pick up those new curtains I ordered at Mr. Goldstein's store?"

"Oh, shoot," Denny said. "Yeah, I got them, but I walked off and left them in the back of the wagon. They're out in the barn. I'll go get them."

"Don't walk all the way back out there for that," Sally told her. "Someone can fetch them later."

"Pearlie's out there. He'll probably see them and bring them in. If he doesn't, I'll make sure I bring them in." Denny hesitated, then said to her father, "He told me to ask you about Frank Morgan."

Smoke's eyes had drifted back down to his book, but they lifted quickly at Denny's words. "Frank Morgan?" he repeated. "What about him?"

"I ran into a stranger in town who claimed to be Morgan's son."

"Conrad Browning?" Smoke asked sharply.

"Well, he introduced himself as Conrad Morgan. I'm sure he's the same one, though."

Smoke frowned. "What in blazes is Conrad Browning . . . or Morgan, or whatever he calls himself . . . doing in Big Rock?"

"He said he was there on business." Denny

33

paused again, then decided to plunge ahead. She had never had much luck at keeping anything important from her parents. "You might as well know that we met right after the two of us got through shooting it out with four outlaws who tried to rob the bank and take some hostages while they were getting away."

Sally didn't gasp. She was too coolheaded and in control of her emotions for that. But she did set her book aside and stand up. She moved quickly over to Denny and put a hand on her arm. "Are you all right?"

"Fine. Never better, in fact."

"And those owlhoots?" asked Smoke.

Denny shrugged. "They're at the undertakers. Innocent folks were in danger. I didn't have time *not* to kill them."

Smoke nodded solemnly, showing that he knew exactly what she meant.

"Was anyone else hurt?" Sally asked.

"No, ma'am. I accounted for two of the robbers, and Mr. Morgan got the other two."

"I'm not surprised," Smoke said as he put his book aside on the small table between their chairs, too.

"Why do you say that?" Denny asked him.

Smoke stood up. "Because Frank Morgan is the fastest man with a gun that I've ever seen, and you know the old saying about the apple not falling far from the tree."

Denny knew that saying, all right.

As the daughter of Smoke Jensen, she had heard it applied to her. She'd always taken it as a compliment.

Sally turned to her husband. "Remember how Frank helped us those times, Smoke?"

"I sure do. And now his son has stepped in to help Denny."

Grudgingly, Denny said, "He probably saved my life. I wasn't sure I could drop those other two before they got me. But I would have gotten them on my way down."

She hadn't had to tell her parents that. She could have ended the story without that detail. But that wouldn't have been fair to Conrad Morgan. She really did owe him her life.

"Well, that settles it," Sally said. "We have to have Mr. Morgan to supper, to thank him for what he's done. Is he staying at the hotel, Denny?"

"I don't have any idea. He was going into the bank the last time I saw him. But I suppose it's likely that's where he'll stay."

Sally nodded. "I'll send someone into town to find him and deliver the invitation, and then I'll talk to Inez about preparing something special for supper tonight. If he saved Denny's life, we owe Mr. Conrad Morgan a great deal."

CHAPTER 5

When the train had pulled into the Big Rock station earlier that afternoon, Conrad Morgan and Axel Strom weren't the only passengers to step down from the cars. Half a dozen others did, too, and among them was another stranger to Big Rock, an attractive young woman carrying a carpetbag.

She wore a dark green traveling outfit, and a hat of the same shade sat on her upswept dark brown hair. Her eyes were a lighter green. She was very pretty, medium height, and well-curved, the sort of young woman who would catch almost any man's attention. Young men would eye her and think of the possibilities; older men would look at her and sigh nostalgically for their lost youth.

Closer scrutiny would have revealed that her outfit was beginning to show some wear, although it was well cared for. The same was true of her shoes and carpetbag. Most men wouldn't notice that, however. They were more likely to be entranced by her smile and the twinkle in her eyes and the neat turn of her ankle.

They would probably miss the slight hardness around her mouth that showed her life had not always been an easy one.

She went into the depot and walked over to the ticket window. The man on the other side of the window, wearing a green eyeshade, a vest, and sleeve garters, leaned forward and asked, "Need a ticket, miss? Where are you headed?"

"Actually, I just came in on the train," she replied in a slightly husky voice that went well with her looks. "I was wondering if you could tell me where to find the office of a man named Jasper Dunlap?"

"Dunlap? The land agent?"

"I believe he also handles properties here in town."

"Yeah, that's right," the ticket agent said. "Well, sure. Just go out the front door there, turn right, go two blocks, turn right again, and his office will be just a couple doors down. You should be able to find it without much trouble."

"Thank you." The young woman started to turn away.

The ticket agent asked quickly, "Are you buyin' land in these parts?" Obviously, he was reluctant to see her go and would have liked to keep her talking.

Instead she just smiled, said, "We'll see," and headed out of the station lobby.

She stepped out into the hot sunshine, made a face for a second, then squared her shoulders and marched along the street, following the ticket agent's directions.

As she walked, she looked around Big Rock, what she could see of it from where she was.

It was a bustling, successful town, much larger than the frontier hamlet it must have been when it was founded. She saw a number of people on the boardwalks, even in the heat of the day. Quite a few wagons were parked in front of the businesses, and most of the hitch rails had at least a couple of horses tied to them.

She even saw three of the newfangled horseless carriage contraptions that were taking the big cities by storm.

In a few minutes she came to Jasper Dunlap's office, exactly where the ticket agent said it would be. It was the middle of three businesses in the block, with a ladies' clothing shop on one side and an empty storefront on the other. The front window of Dunlap's office could have used some cleaning. A few cobwebs were visible in the inside corners, through the glass.

The young woman opened the door and stepped inside. The room was sparsely furnished with an old, scarred desk, a couple of chairs, a dusty potted plant in a front corner, a filing cabinet, and a small table with a basin and a pitcher of water tucked in a rear corner.

The man behind the desk jerked upright and looked around, blinking. The young woman could tell that he had been dozing with his head down on the desk, and she had woken him by opening the door. As hot and stuffy as the room was, she couldn't blame him for nodding off.

She left the door open to let a little fresh air in, hot though it was. "Mr. Dunlap?" she said.

He cleared his throat and replied, "Yes. Yes, indeed. Jasper Dunlap, at your service, miss." With a grunt, he pushed himself to his feet. "What can I do for you?"

Dunlap was a thick-bodied, middle-aged man with oily dark curls and a thin mustache. His gray tweed suit had seen better days. The coat sleeves were starting to get shiny at the elbows. He'd been sweating as he napped. He pulled a handkerchief from his pocket and mopped his face with it.

"Excuse me. Bit of a heat wave we're having here."

"Yes, I know," said the young woman. "I just walked here from the train station."

"Quite unusual at this elevation." He put the handkerchief away and asked, "What brings you to my humble business?"

Humble is a good word for it, she thought. Clearly, Dunlap's enterprise wasn't a very lucrative one. But as long as he had what she needed, she didn't care about anything else.

"My name is Blaise Warfield," she said. "I wrote to you, inquiring about a property you have for sale."

"Miss Warfield! Yes, of course. I remember our correspondence quite well."

Blaise didn't believe he remembered it at all,

but she could tell he was racking his brain trying to recall the exchange. She also recognized the moment when it came back to him.

He came around the desk and said, "You were interested in the old Double or Nothing Saloon, isn't that right?"

"That's the one that was owned by Jess McChesney?"

"Old Jess, that's right," said Dunlap, nodding. "He passed away a year or so ago, and the building has been sitting vacant ever since."

"You own the property now?"

Dunlap brushed off his lapels, even though nothing was on them. "No heirs were ever located, so I picked it up when the sheriff auctioned it off. Purely as speculation, you understand. I'm not a saloon keeper."

"You thought you might be able to make a profit on it someday." Blaise didn't phrase it as a question, but Dunlap answered anyway.

"That's right. I buy and sell land and businesses. It's a risky way to make a living, but I find it rewarding."

Not too rewarding, thought Blaise as she glanced around the dingy office again.

As if reading her mind, Dunlap cleared his throat and changed the subject by saying, "What did you have in mind for the property?"

"If I buy it, I intend to open a saloon there."

"Oh." Dunlap frowned. "I thought you might

want it for something else. A shop of some sort—"

"No, it will be a saloon," Blaise said.

Dunlap hesitated, looked uncomfortable, then said, "Perhaps it's not in my own best interests as the potential seller, but I feel I have to tell you, Miss Warfield, that the Double or Nothing was never very successful. You see, there are two saloons in Big Rock that do most of the business. You have Longmont's, which is also a restaurant and caters to the classier folks, and you have the Brown Dirt Cowboy, which is where most of the cowboys, freighters, and railroad workers drink. The other saloons make do with the trade left over from those establishments, and they come and go on a pretty regular basis. So if you intend to open up the Double or Nothing as a saloon again, I'd advise you that it's a pretty risky venture."

Blaise had listened to him patiently. When he concluded, she said, "I appreciate your honesty, Mr. Dunlap, but almost everything in this world that's worth having carries some degree of risk with it."

"Certainly, but—"

"Why don't you just let me worry about my plans for the property?" she said coolly. "For now, would it be possible to take a look at it?"

"Of course." He paused. "You mean right now?"

"Yes, if we could."

He made a face, clearly not wanting to go out into the hot afternoon, but he also didn't want to lose a possible sale. So he forced a smile and said, "Let me get my hat."

CHAPTER 6

Axel Strom's hand pretty much engulfed Charles Barnhart's hand when the two men shook. Barnhart winced slightly from the force of Strom's grip, but he covered up the reaction quickly.

"Please sit down and join us, Mr. Strom," the banker invited as he stepped back. "Mr. Morgan and I were just discussing your business venture."

"Is that right?" Strom glanced over at Conrad as he pulled up another chair and sat down. "What did you tell him?"

"That we had purchased some of the mines around here that weren't operating any longer and hope to revive them with a new process."

"That's right." Strom put the cigar back in his mouth and rolled it from one side to the other, then added around it, "Hydraulic mining."

Barnhart nodded and repeated, "Hydraulic mining." He clasped his hands together on the desk. "Yes, I believe I've heard about it. It requires a great deal of heavy equipment, doesn't it?"

"Quite a bit," said Strom. "But we can pay for it, and the investment will be worth it once those mines start producing again."

Despite his rather brutish appearance, Strom

43

spoke like an educated man—which he was. Conrad knew some of the man's background— born in Prussia, educated at Heidelberg, immigrated to America as a young man because of some scandal, and two decades later had become a highly successful mining engineer with no trace remaining of a German accent. Strom had not invented the machinery necessary for hydraulic mining, but he had perfected several improvements to it that made it even more powerful and efficient.

Conrad didn't actually *like* the man, but when Strom had come to him with a proposal that they join forces to revitalize the mining industry around Big Rock, he had done enough research to confirm that the idea was more than feasible and held the potential for big returns. Conrad didn't have to enjoy someone's company in order to work with them and make money.

"Have you got the account set up?" Strom went on.

Barnhart pushed his chair back. "We will have, very soon," he said as he stood and picked up the bank draft from the desk. "I'll take this to my head teller and get the paperwork done. You gentlemen will be staying at the hotel here in town?"

"That's right," Conrad said.

"We can use that for your local address, then. Unless you plan to seek other accommodations . . . ?"

"The hotel will be fine," said Strom. "We'll be too busy to be doing much other than sleeping there."

"Just give me a few minutes." Barnhart left them and went over to the tellers' cages to speak to one of the men there.

Conrad looked over at Strom and asked, "Get the hotel rooms all right?"

"Sure. And while I was doing that, I heard gunfire. A man came running in a few minutes later to say that outlaws had tried to rob the bank, but some girl and a fancy-dressed stranger had stopped them. Killed them, in fact. I assume the stranger was you? I didn't see anybody else dressed that well getting off the train."

"I didn't have much choice in the matter," Conrad said. "They were threatening innocent people."

Strom grunted. "Including a pretty girl."

"As it turns out, that pretty girl turned out to be very good with a gun herself. Not surprising, since she's the daughter of Smoke Jensen."

Strom just looked at Conrad blankly for a couple of seconds, then shook his head. "Never heard of him."

"How is that possible?" Conrad asked, then grinned. "Never mind. I forgot that you didn't grow up in this country, reading our dime novels."

"Even after I got here, I had better things to do

with my time. Working to make money. Reading technical books."

"A man needs some entertainment, too."

Strom bit down on the cigar and growled, "I take my entertainment in other ways."

Conrad didn't press him on that. He didn't need to know the details of whatever Axel Strom found entertaining.

A few minutes later, Barnhart returned with documents for both men to sign. He gave them each a set of blank drafts, then said, "As I mentioned to Mr. Morgan, the deposit he made will be regarded as provisional until it's confirmed by the bank in San Francisco, but with the speed of telegraphic communication these days, I expect that to be no later than midday tomorrow. I hope that's acceptable, gentlemen."

"Fine," Strom said curtly.

"Is there anything else I can do for you?"

Conrad stood up and said, "I think we're ready to go. Thank you, Mr. Barnhart."

The banker shook hands with both of them again, and the two men took their leave.

Strom paused on the sidewalk outside and looked at the area in the street in front of the bank.

"This is where the shoot-out happened, eh?"

"That's right," Conrad said. "It really wasn't much. Over with very quickly."

"It doesn't take long for men to die," Strom said.

• • •

The building that had housed the Double or Nothing Saloon was on a side street, a block away from the main thoroughfare of Big Rock. While Blaise and Jasper Dunlap were on their way there, a short volley of gunfire erupted several blocks away.

Blaise looked over her shoulder.

Dunlap said, "Don't worry about that, Miss Warfield. It sounded to me like some cowboys letting off steam. Ah, here we are now. The former Double or Nothing Saloon."

The building was a frame structure of two stories. It looked solid enough from the outside, but Blaise needed to see the interior, too, and said as much to Jasper Dunlap.

He unlocked the front doors, opened them, and stepped aside to let Blaise go in. "We don't have a great deal of crime in Big Rock," he explained, "but with the business being closed and all, it was better to keep the place locked up so no tramps would decide to move in. From time to time we get men like that, being on the railroad and all."

"I understand," she said as she stepped across the threshold and moved into the big, shadowy room. The front windows had a thick layer of grime on them that they didn't let in a great deal of light.

She could see well enough, though, to make out the long bar on the right, the tables with chairs set upside down on them and canvas draped over

47

them, the piano and small dance floor at the back of the room, and the staircase past the bar that led to the second floor.

She nodded toward the stairs and said, "I suppose there are rooms for the girls up there."

Dunlap cleared his throat and shuffled his feet uncomfortably "Yes, there were a few ladies who, ah, lived and worked up there, I believe . . . not that I know that from personal experience, mind you—"

"It's all right, Mr. Dunlap," Blaise told him with a faint smile. "You don't need to be embarrassed. I know what goes on in saloons." She saw a new interest spark to life in his eyes.

Maybe he thought that she was interested in buying a saloon because she had worked in one herself—including upstairs. Some extra boldness lurked in his eyes as he said, "You can see for yourself that most of the furnishings are still here. There was a roulette wheel, but Emmett Brown, the owner of the Brown Dirt Cowboy, made me an offer for it and I took him up on it."

"What happened to all the liquor?"

"Mr. Brown bought it, as well. So you'd have to restock, but that shouldn't be too much of a problem, if you're really determined to operate a saloon."

She didn't respond to that. Instead she said, "The place needs a good cleaning and a fresh coat of paint."

"That would certainly improve its appearance, yes."

"Do you mind if I continue looking around?"

He held out a hand. "By all means."

Blaise spent the next ten minutes prowling around both floors of the building. She tested the stairs as she went up them, making sure that none of them sagged. Some of the rooms on the second floor still had narrow beds in them, with bare mattresses. Dusty, moth-eaten curtains hung on the windows. One of the rooms was larger, with enough space for a four-poster bed and perhaps a desk and dressing table. That would be her living quarters, she thought as she nodded slowly to herself.

Dunlap followed her around, watching her with a growing expression of lust on his face. In the West, respectable women had to be treated respectfully, but evidently he had decided that Blaise didn't fit into that category, even though he hoped to sell the property to her.

She went back downstairs and walked over to the piano. After striking a few keys, she laughed and said, "That's going to need tuning, too."

"I'm not sure how much the men who come into a saloon to drink and play cards will care about the music."

"*I* care, Mr. Dunlap. I want everyone who comes into Blaise's Place to be impressed."

"Blaise's Place?" Dunlap repeated as he cocked

an eyebrow. "You're not going to call it the Double or Nothing? That's still painted on the sign."

"I'll have it repainted. This is going to be a fresh start for the business."

And for me, too, she thought.

"You've made up your mind, then? You're going to buy the property?"

"I am." Blaise went over to the bar where she had set her carpetbag when she came in and opened it.

Dunlap's eyes widened as she began taking out bundles of greenbacks tied with string. Greed replaced lust on his face, at least for the moment.

When Blaise had placed four of the cash bundles on the bar, she said, "There's two thousand dollars."

"I believe the price we agreed on was two thousand, five hundred."

"That agreement was pending my inspection of the property," Blaise said sharply. "Getting it into the shape I want will cost more than I anticipated."

Dunlap spread his hands. "I shouldn't have to bear that expense—"

"Two thousand dollars," Blaise interrupted him. "Saying take it or leave it puts this arrangement on a more hostile footing, and I don't like being hostile when it's not necessary, so let's just say that this is my final offer."

50

Dunlap looked at her for a long moment that seemed longer in the heat and dust. Then he nodded and said, "You're right. We should keep everything friendly between us. No reason not to, is there?" He smiled. "All right. Two thousand it is. A few hundred dollars isn't really that much between, ah, friends, is it?"

He reached out and put his right hand on her left arm, rubbing it slowly back and forth. His thumb nudged gently against the swell of her bosom.

Blaise reached into the carpetbag again and instead of a bundle of cash, she held a derringer with a big enough barrel to show that it was a hefty caliber for such a small weapon. She pressed the muzzle to Dunlap's forehead, pulled back the hammer with her thumb, and said, "We're not friends, Mr. Dunlap. This is just a business deal. You'll be welcome in here as a customer any time you want to pay for a drink, but that's all."

Dunlap's hand jerked back. His eyes rolled up and threatened to cross as he tried to look at the derringer's barrel. He swallowed hard and said, "M-my apologies, Miss Warfield. It was an unwarranted assumption on my part and totally my fault."

"Indeed it was," agreed Blaise. She took the gun away from his head, stepped back, and used her other hand to push the money toward him.

"Do you have the bill of sale and the deed drawn up already?"

"Yes, I do."

"Then let's go back to your office and conclude our business, shall we?" Blaise smiled, but she didn't put the derringer back in her carpetbag. She slipped it into a pocket in the traveling outfit where it would be handy.

She didn't think she would need it, though. Jasper Dunlap had almost wet himself when she put the gun to his head. He hurried out of the saloon ahead of her, obviously eager to be done with her.

Blaise followed him out more slowly, taking a last look around.

Yes, she told herself, nodding. *This place will do nicely.*

CHAPTER 7

Conrad's room in the hotel was across the hall from Axel Strom's. When someone knocked on the door, he assumed it was Strom, so he opened it without hesitation.

As the door swung open, though, it was a reminder that a peaceful life had gotten him into some bad habits. Before the past couple of years, he never would have opened a door without knowing for sure who was on the other side.

And he'd have had a gun in his hand, too, or at least been carrying one where he could get to it in a hurry if he needed to.

As a matter of fact, his visitor *wasn't* Axel Strom, a discovery that reinforced the realization of his carelessness. Luckily, the stocky, red-headed young cowboy standing there with his hat in his hands didn't appear to be a threat. He wasn't even carrying a gun, as far as Conrad could see.

"Mr. Morgan?" the young puncher asked.

"That's right," Conrad said. He had taken off his coat, unbuttoned his vest, and loosened his cravat and collar. The window was wide open, but despite that, not much air moved in the room.

"My name is Orrie, Mr. Morgan, and I ride for Mr. Smoke Jensen of the Sugarloaf Ranch. Mrs.

53

Jensen asked me to deliver this to you, sir." He held out a small envelope.

Conrad saw *Mr. Conrad Morgan* written on the front of it in a flowing, elegant script. He took it and said, "Thank you, Orrie."

He started to reach into his pocket, but Orrie held up a hand and said, "No, sir, you don't need to give me nothin'. I'm not one of those fellas who delivers telegrams and suchlike." He smiled. "Besides, Cal—he's the foreman—said I could stop at the Brown Dirt Cowboy Saloon and have a beer on my way outta town. But just one."

"All right, Orrie. Then you have my thanks, and perhaps I can repay the favor someday." Conrad held out his hand. "It's good to meet you."

Orrie looked a mite surprised that a fine gent like Morgan would offer to shake hands with him, but he clasped Conrad's hand. "Likewise, Mr. Morgan." Then he clapped his hat back on his head and turned toward the stairs, enthusiasm in his step because he was on his way to get that beer.

Conrad chuckled as he closed the door. Even though he was less than a decade older than Orrie, he didn't feel like he had ever been as young as the puncher.

By the time he was Orrie's age, his mother had been murdered by outlaws and he had endured torture at the hands of her killers. The years since then had been filled with other tragedies

54

and great danger, although there had been some triumphs and moments of satisfaction, as well. Conrad usually felt as if his adventurous life had aged him beyond his years.

Instead of dwelling on that, he looked at the envelope in his hand. It was made of heavy, good-quality paper, and when he turned it over, he saw a dab of wax sealing the flap. He broke it open and took out a single, folded sheet of paper.

The paper had a delicate but very pleasant scent to it. The same elegant hand had written on it.

Dear Mr. Morgan,
My husband and I owe you a greater debt than we can ever repay for what you did for our daughter Denise today. In appreciation for that, we would like to invite you to join us for supper this evening at our ranch, the Sugarloaf. We can send a buggy for you, or if you would like, anyone at the hotel can tell you how to find the ranch. Any companions traveling with you are, of course, included in this invitation.

If it won't be possible for you to join us this evening, you will be welcome in our home at any time. We look forward to seeing you.

Sincerely,
Sally Jensen

Conrad had just folded the note and slipped it back in the envelope when another knock sounded on the door. He set the envelope on the dressing table and snagged the Colt from the cross-draw rig he had hung over the back of a chair earlier. When he opened the door this time, the gun was in his hand.

Orrie saw that, and his eyes widened a little in alarm. "I'm sorry," he blurted out. "I plumb forgot I was supposed to wait and get an answer from you before I headed back to the Sugarloaf. I was downstairs in the lobby and headed outta the hotel before I remembered."

Conrad smiled. "That's all right, Orrie. I was about to come and find you at the, ah, Brown Dirt Cowboy Saloon you mentioned. But since you're here, please tell Mrs. Jensen I'll be very pleased to join her and Mr. Jensen for supper tonight, and I'll be bringing my business partner, Mr. Axel Strom, with me, unless he's otherwise engaged."

Orrie's head bobbed up and down. "Got it. You'll be there, with that fella Mr. Storm."

"Strom," Conrad corrected.

"Strom. Got it. Much obliged, Mr. Morgan."

"And Mrs. Jensen won't need to send a buggy for us. We'll ride. There's a livery stable in town where we can rent some good mounts, isn't there?"

"Oh, sure. Patterson's Livery is the best in these parts." Orrie frowned dubiously. "But are you sure you want to ride that far?"

56

Conrad clapped a hand on the young cowboy's shoulder and said, "I'm certain. As a matter of fact, I'm anxious to get back on a horse again. It's been too long!"

"You should have had her send the buggy," Strom complained as he and Conrad rode along the trail that led from Big Rock to the Sugarloaf Ranch. It was early evening. The sun hadn't set, but it was low in the western sky and the day's heat had broken. A refreshing breeze blew out of the west.

Strom was on a big, sturdy bay gelding, a horse Conrad had picked out at the livery stable because it looked like it could handle Strom's weight. Conrad rode a rangy buckskin. He had a fondness for horses of that color.

"We're going to be traveling around all over this valley for a few weeks," Conrad pointed out, "and some places will be easier to get in and out of on horseback. So you might as well get used to the saddle."

"I've ridden before. I'm just not that fond of it." Strom shrugged. "But I suppose you're right. We're Western mining men now, aren't we?"

"We soon will be."

A speculative look appeared on Strom's face. "According to what I heard about him in town, this fellow Jensen has the largest, most successful ranch in this area. He might be looking to invest some money."

"We don't need any investors," said Conrad, with a slightly sharper note in his voice. "The Browning Holdings have enough to fund our operation."

The business empire known as the Browning Holdings had gotten its start in mining, as a matter of fact. The whole thing had its origins in the Henson Mining Company, founded by and named for Conrad's grandfather, Vivian Browning's father. After inheriting the company, Vivian had branched out into railroads, shipping, banking, freight lines, and numerous other enterprises. With her husband advising her and her own keen eye for businesses that could be successful, Vivian had built up the various holdings until, taken all together, they rivaled the operations of the tycoons who were much more famous.

The fact that the Browning Holdings hadn't become as notorious during the so-called Gilded Age as the others was a point of pride for Conrad. He figured it was better not to be noticed. Less chance of making enemies that way.

Anyway, he had made enough enemies in his life without even trying.

They came to another trail that turned off to the left from the one they were following. Two stone pillars flanked the entrance, with thick wooden beams extending even higher from them. Two wrought iron rails ran between the beams, and more wrought iron between those rails formed the words THE SUGARLOAF.

Strom looked up at the name and grunted. "Impressive."

"So is Miss Jensen."

"Your little partner in that shoot-out?" Strom frowned. "We came to Colorado to look for gold, not romance."

"I'm not looking for romance," Conrad said. "But it's a simple matter of objective fact that Miss Denise Jensen is spectacularly attractive."

Strom shrugged. "Women have their place, sure . . . but I never saw one as pretty as a pile of money."

"Then I feel sorry for you, Axel," drawled Conrad as he nudged his buckskin onto the trail leading to the ranch headquarters. "Clearly, you've just never met the right woman."

Strom didn't say anything in response to that as he rode alongside the younger man.

They had ridden more than a mile after leaving the main trail before they came in sight of the big, whitewashed ranch house, the long bunkhouse, the various outbuildings, and the big barns and sprawling corrals that made up the spread's headquarters. It was a beautiful, picturesque location, with mountains rearing up in several different directions, thick stands of trees, grassy fields, and a stream that wound its way through the valley.

If a person was going to settle down, thought Conrad, this wouldn't be a bad place to do it.

Several dogs ran from the barns, barking their greetings to the visitors.

Strom frowned. "I don't like dogs."

"Then that's another reason to feel sorry for you. I sometimes feel like they're God's greatest creation, and humanity usually isn't worthy of them."

"Loud, filthy creatures." Strom grimaced as the dogs ran around the horses in a big circle.

Conrad thought for a second that his partner was going to pull one of his feet from the stirrup and kick at them. Thankfully, a man stepped out of the barn and whistled to the dogs, and they dashed back to him.

Another man emerged from the ranch house onto its front porch, probably having heard the commotion from the dogs. He stood there with casual grace, his hands tucked into the back pockets of the jeans he wore. His hair was thick and ash blond, which meant that any gray in it was difficult to spot. He wasn't towering in height, but he gave an impression of size and power, probably because of his exceptionally broad shoulders.

He took his left hand from his pocket and raised it in a friendly gesture. "Welcome to Sugarloaf," he said as Conrad and Strom reined their horses to a stop in front of the house. "I'm Smoke Jensen."

CHAPTER 8

Earlier, Denny had taken a bath to rid herself of the dust from her trip to town, but when she dressed, she put on clean denim trousers, a white cotton shirt, and a brown vest of soft leather, as well as a nicer pair of brown boots.

She went downstairs and into the kitchen where her mother and Inez Sandoval, the cook and housekeeper, were preparing supper. Sally glanced around at her and then looked again.

"You could at least put on a dress, Denny," she said. "You're not a twelve-year-old tomboy anymore. And I know you're capable of looking like a lady. I've seen you put the *grandes dames* of European society to shame."

"But this is comfortable, and I think I look nice," Denny objected.

"But we're having company for supper."

"Yes . . . a man who, a couple of hours ago, was gunning down outlaws in the street."

"And saving your life in the process. Plus, he's the son of an old friend. Why, when we first met Frank Morgan that Christmas, before you were born, who knows what would have happened if he hadn't helped us? Also, Mr. Morgan is bringing his business partner with him, according to the message he sent back with Orrie, and we've never met the man, so of course we want to make a good impression."

Denny didn't want to upset her mother, and besides, whether she wanted to admit it or not, she knew Sally was right. "All right. I'll go change. But nothing too fancy."

"That's fine," Sally agreed.

When Denny came back down a short time later, she was wearing a simple light blue short-sleeved dress with white lace around the square-cut neckline and at the end of the sleeves.

Sally smiled in approval when she saw it. "There. You look very pretty and wholesome," she declared.

Wholesome wasn't exactly a word Denny would have used to describe herself, but if her mother wanted to think so, that was fine.

Anyway, just because she *looked* wholesome and innocent didn't mean that she *was*.

Denny found her father in the parlor and reminded him, "Pearlie told me to ask you about Frank Morgan. He said you'd probably have some stories to tell."

"Yes, I've seen him in action a few times," Smoke said. "He's fast with a gun, mighty fast. Or at least he was. I haven't crossed trails with him for a good number of years, so he might have slowed down."

"You haven't," Denny pointed out. "I would think that once your muscles learn how to draw and fire a gun, you never really forget it."

"That's true." Smoke smiled. "Time catches up to all of us, though, Denny. The nerves and the muscles just don't work like they once did. I know that's hard for you to grasp, as young as you are, but one of these days, you'll understand."

"Frank Morgan's still alive, isn't he?" she asked with a slight frown.

"As far as I know, and I think I would have heard about it if anything had happened to him. He and Monte Carson are old friends. They go back even further than Frank and I do. They found themselves on the same side a few times in the old range wars, when they were both hiring out their guns. They may have even been on opposite sides a time or two."

"So Morgan was a hired gun?"

Smoke rubbed his chin. "I reckon I misspoke a little there. Morgan was never really a hired gun in the same sense that Monte and Pearlie were, working for whoever was paying the highest fighting wages. Any time he got mixed up in some trouble, he fought because he believed he was on the right side. He might take expenses, or food and a place to sleep, but he had to be sure he was doing the right thing before he ever took his gun out of its holster. That didn't stop him from getting a reputation. All too often, fellas would show up, bound and determined to prove that they were faster than he was." A grim note entered Smoke's voice as he added, "They weren't. And that's a feeling I know all too well."

"So you're saying that Frank Morgan is basically a good man."

"A very good man," Smoke replied with a nod. "He and I aren't close, you understand. But he'd be welcome here anytime."

"Like his son."

"I don't really know anything about the boy," said Smoke. "And sons don't always turn out like their fathers. Right now, I'd say that you know Conrad Morgan better than any of us do."

"I only saw him for a few minutes . . . and they were pretty busy minutes."

"Well, you'll get to know him better this evening." Smoke lifted his head as the ranch dogs started barking outside. "That could be them now, I reckon. You want to come out and welcome them with me?"

"You go ahead," Denny told him. She couldn't have said why, but she didn't want to go outside to meet Conrad Morgan. It would be better if she waited for Smoke to bring him in.

She heard horses come up to the house, heard men talking, and then a few minutes later, Smoke led two men into the house. Denny recognized Conrad Morgan right away. He had changed his shirt, but he still wore the same dark suit and the hat with the fancy silver band, which he took off as he came in.

The man behind him was bigger and bulkier,

with a coarse look about him. He wore a homburg hat instead of the Western type of hat Conrad sported. He didn't take it off right away, but he did when he spotted Denny. That revealed a mostly bald head that reminded her of a chunk of hard rock.

Smoke said, "I don't know if you two were introduced formally earlier. I suspect not, since you were a mite busy at the time. This is my daughter, Denise Jensen. Denny, this is Conrad Morgan and his business partner, Axel Strom."

Conrad smiled and said, "It's nice to see you again, Miss Jensen. Especially since there are no guns going off this time."

"Yet," Strom said. He gave Denny a curt nod and added, "Miss Jensen."

"I'm not expecting any gunplay," said Smoke. "This is a new, modern century. The West is civilized now, or so my wife keeps informing me."

"I don't know if that's always true," said Conrad. "I've seen some parts of the West that are still pretty untamed."

"A lot of places are," Smoke agreed. "Why don't you gentlemen hang your hats over there?" He gestured toward a hat tree in the corner of the foyer.

The two men hung up their hats, then followed Smoke and Denny into the parlor.

"Have a seat, gentlemen," Smoke invited with

a wave of his hand toward the two comfortable armchairs flanking the fireplace, which was cold at that time of year, of course.

"As soon as Miss Jensen is seated," Conrad said.

Denny sat on the divan opposite the armchairs, and her father sat beside her. Conrad and Strom took their seats.

Smoke said, "Supper will be ready shortly. If you'd like something to drink before then, or a cigar . . . ?"

Conrad held up a hand. "We're fine. Aren't we, Axel?"

Strom said, "Sure."

Denny didn't want to jump to any conclusions, but she was getting the idea that the big man wasn't a very friendly sort.

Smoke said, "What brings you fellas to this part of the country? I assume you're in Colorado on business, since you were going into the bank when Denny saw you earlier?"

"That's right," Conrad replied. "We've bought some of the old abandoned mines in the area and plan to open them up again."

Smoke's forehead creased a little. Her father had a gold mine of his own, Denny knew, and it had been the source of much of his early success. But it hadn't been worked in years.

"The gold mines? I thought most of them around here had petered out."

"They have," said Strom, "if you're mining the old-fashioned way. We intend to use modern methods."

Smoke's frown deepened. He nodded slowly, then said, "I see." He changed the subject so abruptly that it took Denny by surprise. "Conrad—you don't mind if I call you Conrad?—how's your father doing these days?"

"That's fine, Mr. Jensen. Frank is doing quite well, as far as I know. The last time I saw him was a while back, down in Mexico, and he planned to stay there for a spell." Conrad smiled. "He said the warmth was good for his old bones. I've had a letter from him since then, letting me know that he was over in Texas, but he didn't say what he was doing." With a chuckle, he added, "Knowing my father, it could be almost anything."

"He's a good man, a mighty good man," Smoke said, nodding. "You call him Frank?"

"Well, you have to remember . . . I didn't find out he was my father until I was practically grown. I thought my stepfather was my real father. *He* was a good man, too, so I consider myself lucky to have had two such fellows in my life."

"Makes sense," Smoke agreed.

Sally came into the parlor then, which made the three men rise quickly to their feet. She looked around at them and smiled.

"Gentlemen, my wife Sally," Smoke said.

"Sally, this is Mr. Conrad Morgan and Mr. Axel Strom."

"It's a pleasure to meet you," Sally said as she took Conrad's hand. "I think the world of your father, you know."

"Yes, ma'am, so do I." Conrad smiled. "I have to admit, it wasn't always that way, but I've gotten fond of him over the years."

Sally turned to Strom and shook hands with him as well. "Welcome to our home, Mr. Strom," she told him.

"Thank you," he said with a little bow.

Denny could tell that he was making an effort to behave graciously, something that evidently didn't come naturally to him. Something about him also made her think he was about to click his shoe heels together, but if he felt that urge, he suppressed it.

"We're obliged to you for your hospitality," he said.

"Supper is ready," Sally went on, "so if you'll all follow me into the dining room . . ."

CHAPTER 9

It was a pleasant meal, and a delicious one—tender roast beef, potatoes, carrots, greens, and incredibly fluffy rolls, followed by peach cobbler.

Axel Strom wasn't exactly a sparkling conversationalist, but Conrad made up for that. He talked about growing up in Boston and then living in San Francisco for the past several years, where he supervised the operations of the various companies belonging to the Browning Holdings.

"I can't imagine what it must be like to own all those different businesses," Sally commented—even though, as Denny knew, Sally and Smoke had interests in a number of enterprises themselves. They were silent partners, though, and other than the Sugarloaf had no role in running any of them except occasionally.

"Well, I'm not the sole owner," Conrad said. "Actually, my mother left her estate equally to myself and my father, although Frank is more than happy for me to run things."

Smoke shook his head. "I can't imagine Frank Morgan sitting in an office wrangling paperwork."

"Neither can I," Conrad said. "He might last a day before he started throwing filing cabinets—and bookkeepers—out the window."

Denny said, "You don't seem to mind putting up with it, though."

Conrad shrugged. "Someone has to take care of those things. For a long time, I was content to let someone else do that while I did some drifting myself. Eventually I came to realize that I was shirking my responsibilities, and I didn't want to do that."

Smoke looked at Strom and asked, "How did the two of you come to team up in this new venture?"

"That was my idea. I knew that Morgan's company had a background in mining all over the country, so I approached him with a proposal."

"And it was a good one," Conrad added. "I had my engineers and geologists make an extensive study to confirm that, however, before I committed to the idea. It should prove quite lucrative for us *and* be good for this area, too. We'll be providing a considerable amount of employment, and we'll be needing to purchase a lot of supplies from the local businesses, as well, in addition to bringing in equipment on the railroad."

"I hope it all turns out as well as you think it's going to," Smoke said.

Conrad and Strom probably didn't notice it, but Denny detected just a faint hint of coolness in her father's tone, as if Smoke didn't fully approve of what he was hearing. He was too courteous to argue with guests, though, so once again he changed the subject by asking, "What were you and Frank doing down in Mexico?"

"Oh, just clearing up a little misunderstanding," Conrad replied with a wave of his hand, and Denny got the unmistakable sense that *he* was dodging the question.

There are too many secrets around this dinner table, she thought. She considered trying to shake things up with a few pointed questions, but she knew her mother wouldn't appreciate that, so she kept quiet.

Conrad changed that by asking her directly, "What about you, Miss Jensen?"

"What about me?" asked Denny, puzzled.

"What do you do with your time . . . when you're not battling bank robbers, that is?"

Smoke said, "Denny works out on the range a lot with the rest of the ranch crew."

Sally frowned at him for that blunt answer.

Conrad said, "So, you're a . . . cowgirl? Would that be the right term?"

"I'm a Jensen," Denny said. "I do what needs to be done, whatever it is." This handsome young man got under her skin a little, so she forged ahead boldly. "I figure I'll be running this ranch one of these days, so it's a good idea for me to know how everything about it works."

Smoke looked at her and raised an eyebrow.

"Don't look at me like that," she went on. "You're not going to run the Sugarloaf forever, and you know good and well Louis isn't going to take over for you."

"Just don't put me out to pasture yet," Smoke replied with a smile.

"Who's Louis?" asked Strom.

"My brother," Denny said. "He's back east in law school."

Conrad nodded. "A lawyer in the family. That's a good thing to have, in this day and age. Legal matters will just get more and more important in this new century of ours, I'm thinking."

"And whether that's good or bad is open to debate," Smoke responded. "But you're right, Denny, Louis isn't really cut out for running a ranch, especially a big spread like this one."

"But you shouldn't be looking that far into the future," Sally said, "because you never know when circumstances will change. For one thing, I'm sure that at some point you'll be getting married—"

"We don't know that," Denny interrupted. "I'm sure not planning on it right now."

"You should ask Brice about that," Smoke said dryly.

Conrad looked interested as he said, "Brice?"

"Brice Rogers," Denny said. "He's a friend of mine, I guess you'd say. But I can tell you one thing for sure—there's never been any talk of marriage between us. If anything, he's married to that job of his."

"What does he do?" asked Strom.

"He's a deputy United States marshal," Denny said.

At that moment, in the mountains forty miles northwest of the Sugarloaf ranch house, Brice Rogers was sliding down a steep talus slope studded with boulders, trying to keep his balance and stay upright as bullets whanged through the air all too close to his head.

Brice's feet got tangled up with each other, and he pitched forward, unable to control his slide any longer. He got his hands down in time to keep his head from crashing into the rocky mountainside. His momentum carried him forward. Over and over, he tumbled down the slope, grunting as the impacts from the rocks pounded his body.

His eyes had adjusted to the darkness well enough for him to see a scrubby bush looming up below him. As he rolled past it, his right hand shot out and closed around one of the branches. He stopped with a jolt that made pain explode all the way up his arm to his shoulder. But the joint didn't dislocate, and he was thankful for that.

Another slug kicked up gravel not far from him. He pulled himself over behind the bush and lay as flat as possible. The branches weren't thick enough to stop a bullet, so he knew he couldn't stay there. They obscured the sight of the men trying to kill him, though, that he had a chance to look around and seek some better cover.

A boulder jutted up about ten yards to his left as he lay facing back up the mountainside. To reach it, he would have to run across the slope and risk another slide.

But he couldn't stay where he was. He lay there breathing heavily as the shots searching for him came closer and closer. Then, when he had recovered for as long as he could risk, he gripped the bush tighter, clambered to his feet as quickly as he could, and broke into a run toward the boulder.

His booted feet slewed around crazily in the loose, sliding gravel, but his stubborn, straight-ahead drive kept him upright and moving. A slug whistled past his ear.

Close enough, he dived for the shelter of the upthrust slab of rock and landed hard enough to knock the breath out of him again. He lay there gasping.

Even with the shape he was in, he thought to reach down to the holster on his right hip and make sure his Colt was still there.

Empty.

Brice bit back a curse. As much tumbling around as he had done, of course the gun had fallen out of its holster. No telling where it had ended up on the steep, rocky slope. He'd probably never find it, even if it wouldn't have meant exposing himself to his enemies' fire to search for it.

A bullet whined off the boulder, making him wince.

To reach him with their shots, the men trying to kill him would have to either come down the slope after him or circle around for a mile or more to get below him.

They would be aware of that, too. After a few more shots, the guns abruptly fell silent. That stillness hung over the mountainside as the echoes rolled away, gradually diminishing.

Then a harsh voice called, "Marshal! You hear me, Marshal? No need for anybody to get hurt here! You come on out and throw down your gun, so we know you don't mean us no harm, and we'll let you go."

Considering that Lew Cudahy and his gang had just been doing their best to fill his hide full of holes a minute or so earlier, Brice wasn't inclined to believe that. But then, he seldom believed anything outlaws had to say.

"Forget it, Cudahy!" he shouted back. "The minute I step out into the open, you'd all blast me."

Brice heard faint, angry muttering above him. The outlaws were probably discussing what to do next . . . meaning, the best way to kill him.

He'd been on the trail of the Cudahy gang for a couple of weeks, ever since they had held up a train in western Kansas. Breaking into the mail car made it a federal crime, and that put Brice on the job. He had tracked them to their hideout in the mountains, a shack built under a beetling shelf of rock, then watched the place until three members of the gang had ridden out, leaving only Lew Cudahy and one other man behind. Brice had moved in on them, figuring he could get the drop on them, disarm them, and tie them up, then wait for the other three to return and take them by surprise.

That plan had gotten ruined almost right away. The three who had left had turned around and ridden back to the hideout for some reason, taking *him* by surprise instead. He'd been cut off from his horse and had to flee on foot, leading the outlaws on a pretty good chase. They had him pinned down, and it looked like it might be the end of the trail for him.

As that thought crossed his mind, he sighed and wished that he had told Denny Jensen how he really felt about her. Of course, that would have required *him* knowing for sure how he felt about her . . .

Denny was beautiful, no doubt about that, and smart and courageous and tough as nails, to boot. They had fought side by side on several occasions, saving each other's life at great risk to their own. That bond between fighting comrades would always be there.

And more than once, they had shared some pretty passionate kisses. Brice was too chivalrous, too much of a gentleman, to take things any further than that, although Denny had made it clear that she wouldn't object too much if he did. But other times she was a lot cooler and more standoffish, which made him believe that *she* didn't know how she truly felt any more than he did.

Did he just admire her and enjoy her company, or was he in love with her?

Brice didn't know, and it was sure as blazes not the best time to be worrying about it.

He pushed those thoughts out of his head and looked around the mountainside, trying to figure out his best move. A few more feet to his left was a smaller chunk of rock than the boulder behind which he had sought cover. If he could reach it without Cudahy and the other outlaws noticing him . . . and if it wasn't too heavy for him to budge . . . he might have an idea.

He eased in that direction, trying not to dislodge too much of the gravel. If they heard it sliding, they would know he was on the move. As long as they were arguing and he didn't make too much racket, he thought he had a chance.

He reached the rock, which was about three times the size of a man's head, and threw his arms around it. Straining, he tried first to pick it up, then gave up on that idea and settled for shoving it. The rock was dense and heavy and didn't want to move, but as Brice grunted with the effort, it shifted and then lurched downward.

That was all it took. The weight did the rest. The rock slid and rolled and began to pick up speed. As a rumble welled up from what was turning into a small avalanche below him, he scrambled back behind the slab where he had taken cover, tipped back his head, and let out a scream.

"Hear that?" cried one of the owlhoots. "He started a rock slide, and it's carryin' him away!"

Silent and motionless, Brice huddled against the rock slab and waited. The noise of the rock slide continued for a couple of minutes, then faded.

"Harkness, you and Johnny go down the slope," Lew Cudahy said into the silence that followed the rumbling. "The rest of us will get the horses and ride around to the bottom. I want to make sure that lawman's dead, even if we have to dig out his carcass from under a bunch of rocks."

"Damn it, Lew, that sounds like a lot of work," one of the other men protested.

"Never leave a wounded enemy behind you," said Cudahy. "I've made that a rule, and it's never backfired on me."

It's going to now, thought Brice.

If he could get just a little more luck on his side.

CHAPTER 10

When the meal was over, Smoke invited Conrad Morgan and Axel Strom into his study for brandy and cigars. Both men accepted.

Denny would have liked to join them. Knowing that both her parents would have frowned on that, she helped her mother and Inez clear the table.

"That young Mr. Morgan, he is a very handsome man, no?" Inez said with a smile.

"Why are you asking me?" Denny said.

"Because I could tell that he thinks you are a very pretty girl."

Denny scoffed. "Well, I barely noticed him, so I don't care what he thinks about me."

"I liked him," Sally said. "He's very polite. He reminds me a little of your father. But don't think I'm not fond of Brice, too."

Denny didn't respond to that. The prospects for her love life weren't something she wanted to discuss with her mother. She went into the parlor and sat there, reading, while she waited for Conrad Morgan and Axel Strom to conclude their visit. When they emerged from Smoke's study and moved toward the front door, she put aside her book, got up, and went into the foyer, as well.

"Good night, Miss Jensen," Conrad said as he retrieved his hat. "It was very nice to see you again, especially under more pleasant circumstances than this afternoon."

"Most things are better when folks aren't shooting at you," said Denny.

"That's been my experience, too," Conrad replied with a smile.

Strom got his hat and said to Smoke, "Please convey our appreciation to your wife for her hospitality, Mr. Jensen."

"I'll do that, Mr. Strom," Smoke said. "I'll have your horses brought from the barn."

Smoke and Strom stepped out of the house, but Conrad lingered at the door. His hat still in his hands, he looked at Denny. "Maybe if I rode back out here sometime, you'd be willing to show me around the ranch? From the way your father talked, you must know just about every foot of the range."

"I expect that I do," Denny agreed. She shrugged slightly. "I suppose we could take a ride around the place. You won't be doing any mining on the Sugarloaf, though, if that's what you're thinking."

"Oh, I know that. My investigation into the area revealed that your father had a working gold mine here on the ranch at one time, but I had a hunch he wouldn't want to sell it to us. Our conversation in his study just now confirmed that."

"You offered to buy it from him?"

"I brought up the subject," Conrad said carefully. "The discussion didn't get far enough for me to make an actual offer to him."

"I'm not surprised."

"Neither am I. Smoke seems very protective of this whole spread."

"As well he should be. He put a lot of time and effort—and blood and sweat—into building it up."

"It's a fine ranch," Conrad said as he put on his hat. "That's why I'd like to see more of it. Don't worry, I don't have any designs on it."

Denny laughed. "Wouldn't do you any good if you did. Jensens don't back down."

"I saw proof of that in town today. Good night, Miss Jensen."

"Good night, Mr. Morgan," Denny said. She returned Conrad's smile and watched as he turned away to cross the porch and join Smoke and Strom in front of the house, where one of the Sugarloaf's hands had brought the two rented horses.

The visitors swung up into their saddles, lifted hands in farewell, and rode away into the night. Denny stepped out onto the porch and rested her hands on the railing that ran along the front of it. Smoke climbed the steps and paused when he saw her standing there.

"Well, what did you think of them?" he asked.

Denny knew that he wasn't just being polite;

he actually valued her opinion. She said bluntly, "I don't like Strom. He didn't do or say anything wrong, but I don't think he wanted to be here. He's not interested in being friends. He came to Colorado to make money, and that's all."

"Nothing wrong with making money," Smoke said. "What about Conrad?"

"I couldn't really say. He seems genuinely nice, and I know you think highly of his father. And I certainly owe him for his help in town today. But he mentioned that he brought up buying your mine—"

"I put a stop to that conversation pretty quick. Anyway, I think that was mostly Strom's idea. I wouldn't be surprised if he pushed Conrad to bring it up."

"There's something I want to ask you," Denny said. "Earlier, when they mentioned they intended to make those mines profitable again by operating them in a different way, you changed the subject pretty quickly, as if it bothered you. Is something wrong with what they're planning?"

Smoke's face hardened in the light that came from inside the house. "They're talking about hydraulic mining. Do you know how that works, Denny?"

She shook her head. "I have no idea."

"Powerful equipment shoots a high-powered stream of water at the mountainside. It's strong enough to break up the rock into sediment, and it

82

washes all that down through long sluice boxes where any gold gets separated out because it's heavier than the rest. Back in the gold rush days in California, some fellas used sluice boxes like that, but they would shovel up the dirt and gravel and run it through there a little at a time.

"That hydraulic equipment creates so much sediment and pumps so much water that when it gets to the bottom of the sluice, it runs all over the place, causes flooding, and damages the plant and animal life. Plus it carves out huge craters that aren't good for anything else once all the gold's been extracted. Yeah, doing it that way makes it easier to turn a profit, but it's mighty hard on the landscape."

"I guess that doesn't matter to Mr. Morgan and Mr. Strom," Denny said.

"Maybe not. And they're not breaking any laws. But you can see why I wouldn't want to have anything to do with something like that on land that I own."

"I suppose so. Maybe Conrad Morgan's not as nice as he tries to pretend to be."

Smoke rubbed his chin and frowned in thought. "Maybe not. Or maybe he just doesn't realize what an impact an operation like that will have on this valley. But I can tell you one thing I'm pretty sure of. Axel Strom knows . . . and he doesn't care."

CHAPTER 11

Brice stayed where he was, with his back pressed against the rock slab, as he listened to the two outlaws carefully making their way down the slope above him.

He could tell by the sounds they made when one of them slipped and started to slide. The man yelled a curse.

His companion said, "Hold on, hold on. I got you, Johnny."

"Thanks," Johnny said. "If I ever started fallin' down this dang hill, I might not ever stop."

"Oh, you'd stop when you got to the bottom," said the other outlaw. "With a bunch of rocks piled on top of you, like that damn lawman."

"You reckon he's really dead?"

"From the sound of what happened, there's a mighty good chance of it."

You just go right on believing that, mister, thought Brice.

Faintly, he heard hoofbeats from somewhere above him and knew that Lew Cudahy and the other two outlaws had started on the circuitous route that would take them to the bottom of the slope, several hundred yards below him. Brice hoped that by the time they got there, he would have a surprise waiting for them.

Johnny and his pal were close. Lots of small rocks rattled and bounced past him, dislodged by their approach. Brice felt around beside him, closed his fingers around a stone a little larger than the size of a man's closed fist.

Harkness and Johnny were convinced he had gone down the slope with the rock slide. They didn't even glance toward the boulder where he had taken cover as they made their unsteady way past it. Brice let them go a few more feet before he raised up and swung the rock at the back of the nearest man's head.

Gravel grated under his feet as he made his move, but the warning came too late to help the outlaw. The rock, with all of Brice's strength behind it, smashed into his skull with a dull, crunching sound. The man pitched forward and landed face-first on the talus.

In a continuation of the same movement, Brice rammed into the other outlaw, tackling him and knocking him off his feet. He landed facedown, too, and started sliding. Brice was on top of him, riding him down the slope. They knocked more and more rocks loose, and suddenly, they were in the middle of another miniature avalanche.

The outlaw bucked up and tried to throw Brice off, but that just gave the lawman a chance to loop his arm around the man's neck and hang on tighter, squeezing as hard as he could. Between the choke hold and the pounding the man was taking from the rocks, he had gone limp by the time they finally slid to a stop.

Brice was only half-conscious himself. He had taken so much punishment over the past half hour that aches and pains threatened to swallow him whole. His pulse hammered crazily inside his skull, and he had to lie there for several minutes atop the unconscious—or dead—outlaw before he could summon the strength to move.

He pushed himself up, rolled to the side. As he lay there on his back, he heard something he identified as the bubbling and splashing of a stream flowing somewhere nearby. Rolling again, he came up on his hands and knees and crawled toward it, wincing from the pain of the rocks under his palms and knees.

Then he left the rocks behind for the welcome softness of grass. He was on the bank of a creek, the water right in front of him. He sprawled on his stomach and plunged his head in.

In the high country, snowmelt fed all the streams. The water was cold enough to take Brice's breath away. He stood it for several seconds, then pulled his head up and shook it so drops flew around him. He lay there panting. The icy water had braced him somewhat, but he was still battered and sore. It would have felt good to soak his whole body in the creek and let its icy chill numb him, but he didn't have time for that.

He didn't know how long it would be until

Cudahy and the others reached this spot, but he figured it was bound to happen soon.

He climbed to his feet and stumbled over to the man who had come down the slope in the rock slide with him. The outlaw hadn't budged since they came to a stop. He was half-buried in rocks. Brice looked around and spotted the barrel of the man's rifle sticking out from under the pile. He took hold of it and pulled it free, then checked it over as best he could in the darkness. He didn't think it was damaged too much to work.

Brice bent and felt for a pulse in the man's neck. He didn't find one. He took hold of the hombre's hair and lifted his head. The man's face was dark with blood from numerous cuts, and something seemed wrong about the shape of his forehead. Brice studied it in the moonlight and realized it was bashed in, more so than a man could suffer and still be alive.

With a sigh, he lowered the man's head, pretty sure he had killed the other outlaw, too, by stoving in his head with that rock. He didn't like killing, but sometimes lawbreakers gave him no choice.

All too often, manhunting was a case of kill or be killed.

Brice moved rocks around until he could reach the holster on the man's hip. He took the revolver from it, checked it over as well, and slipped the gun into his empty holster. He was still pretty done in, but he felt better being armed again.

It was a good thing he was, too. He heard horses approaching, turned, and quickly moved along the creek bank to a stand of trees where the shadows were thick under the branches. He eased back into them and waited.

The hoofbeats steadily got louder. Within minutes, three riders came into view, walking their mounts slowly along the stream as they came closer.

The man in the lead held up a hand in a signal to stop. "We should've come to the place where that avalanche wound up by now." He lifted his voice and called, "Johnny! Harkness!"

"I told you somethin' else happened, Lew," said one of the other men. "You heard that racket. It sounded like a second rock slide. That blasted lawman pulled some kind of trick!"

"Yeah, he might have, or else those two were clumsy and got caught in an avalanche of their own making," Cudahy said. He cursed bitterly, then went on. "I hate to leave those boys behind, but we'd better get out of here."

Even though he was outnumbered three to one, Brice wasn't going to just stand there in the shadows and let the outlaws get away. He stepped out into the open, bringing the rifle to his shoulder, and called, "Hold it right there! Get your hands up!"

"The marshal!" one of the men yelled. He clawed at the gun on his hip.

The light was too bad to try anything fancy. Brice cranked off five rounds as fast as he could work the rifle's lever, moving the barrel a little so the lead would spray across an arc along the creek bank.

The three outlaws returned his fire, Colt flame blooming like crimson flowers in the darkness. Brice heard bullets whistle past his ears, and more slugs thudded into the tree trunks just behind him. The blood in his veins seemed as icy as the water flowing in the creek as he stood his ground.

One of the men screamed, threw his arms in the air, and toppled off his horse. Another bent double in the saddle and let out a grunting cough of pain.

That left the leader, the man Brice was pretty sure was Lew Cudahy. As his companions were knocked out of the fight, he whirled his horse in an attempt to flee. The animal broke into a gallop. Brice fired again. Cudahy fell, landed on the grassy bank, and rolled over a couple of times before lying still.

Brice had shot him in the back, but considering that Cudahy had killed at least four innocent people that Brice knew of, he wasn't going to lose a lot of sleep over that fact.

The man who had doubled over on his horse slowly lost his grip and fell. The animal, skittish from the shooting and the smell of blood, danced away.

Brice levered another round into the rifle's chamber, then approached the fallen outlaws warily. The first one he came to was the man who had screamed and thrown his arms in the air. He lay motionless on his side. Brice pointed the rifle at him, put a boot against his shoulder, and pushed him over onto his back. The way the man's arm flopped limply told Brice he was dead. So did the large, dark stain on the front of his shirt.

He came next to the one who acted like he'd been shot in the belly. That man was still alive. Brice heard the rasp of his breathing as he approached.

The man must have heard his footsteps. He raised his head and gasped, "You . . . you've killed me . . . you son of a . . ." The grotesque rattle of his last breath coming from his throat prevented him from finishing the curse.

Brice prodded him in the side just to be sure, but the man didn't move or react. He was gone, all right.

That just left Lew Cudahy. Brice was turning toward him when another orange flash split the night and he felt the hammer blow of a bullet against his side.

Brice reeled back but managed to stay on his feet. He saw that Cudahy was propped up on his left hand while his right thrust out a revolver. The gun blasted again, but the shot missed, although it came close enough for Brice to hear the wind-rip of the slug as it passed by his ear.

He brought the Winchester up and fired. Cudahy's head jerked back. He dropped the gun and fell sideways so his head landed at the edge of the creek. He didn't move as the water washed over his face. Brice knew he had drilled the outlaw through the brain.

All five members of the gang were dead. He hadn't recovered the loot they had taken in the train robbery, but it was probably back at their hideout. All he had to do was get there. *After* he had loaded the carcasses on their horses so he could haul them in, too.

Of course, doing all that after he'd been shot wasn't going to be easy.

He grimaced as he pressed a hand to his side and felt the warm blood on his shirt around the rip that the bullet had left behind. He pulled the shirt up and gingerly explored the wound. The slug from Cudahy's gun had plowed a bloody furrow across his ribs on the left side. He took a deep breath. It stung, but he didn't feel the stabbing pain he would have felt inside if a rib was broken.

He could live without the blood he was losing, he told himself. But it would be a good idea to bind up the wound as tightly as he could, as soon as he could.

He spent the next quarter-hour looking through

the saddlebags on the outlaws' horses. In one he found a clean shirt and a flask of whiskey, and splashed whiskey on the wound. His breath hissed between his teeth as fiery pain bit into his side. He took a swig from the flask, as well, then got busy tearing strips from the clean shirt and bandaging the injury.

As he worked at that task, he mused about everything that had happened and realized that when he had been minutes away from death, thoughts of Denny Jensen and his feelings for her had been uppermost in his mind. He still wasn't certain how he felt about her, but one thing was for sure.

When he got back to Big Rock, he needed to have a long talk with her. It was past time that they got some things worked out.

CHAPTER 12

Denny didn't go into Big Rock for several days. She wondered what Conrad Morgan was doing but told herself that his actions were none of her business. He wouldn't be carrying out any mining operations on the Sugarloaf. More than likely, he and Strom were riding around the valley checking out the properties they had bought.

Pearlie announced one morning that he was taking the wagon into town to pick up some supplies and asked Denny if she wanted to accompany him.

"I will, but not on the wagon," she replied as an idea came to her. "I'm going to ride Rocket."

Pearlie gave her a dubious frown. "That loco black stallion? I ain't sure that's a good idea."

"I've been working with him," Denny argued. "He's doing better."

"You mean he hasn't gone crazy and tried to kill you this week?"

"He hasn't done that in a long time! At least a month."

Rocket was a sleek, powerfully muscled black stallion, a mustang that had been brought in with a bunch of wild horses captured in the hills in the far northern reaches of the Sugarloaf a year or so earlier. Rafael De Santos, who worked on the ranch as a wrangler and horse-breaker, had made a diligent effort with Rocket but had never proclaimed the stallion more than half-tamed, if that. At times he was docile and cooperative with a rider, but then, with no warning, he would bolt and run away or start bucking crazily.

Denny had felt an immediate connection with the horse, however, and had tried to ride him in the race held as part of the celebration of her brother Louis's wedding. That decision had backfired on her and put her in danger, but even so, she was convinced that Rocket was worth keeping. Smoke had talked about selling him as a stud or just letting him go back wild to the hills, but Denny hadn't given up on him and had insisted that she would work with him. She was convinced he had finally accepted her as the boss.

Pearlie rubbed his chin and frowned in thought, then said, "I ain't too comfortable about lettin' you take that devil horse without Smoke's say-so, but he's off on the south range today with Cal and the boys, so . . . Are you sure he won't go loco?"

"I honestly believe he won't."

"That ain't exactly the same thing as bein' sure." Pearlie sighed. "But all right, I reckon you can give it a try. You want me to throw a hull on him?"

"He's been around me more than anybody else. It would probably be better for me to saddle him."

Pearlie nodded. "Get to it, then, so we can be on our way."

A short time later, Denny rode Rocket alongside the wagon while Pearlie drove toward Big Rock. The black stallion had shown some spirit while Denny was getting the saddle on him, dancing back and forth a little in his stall, but once she was on his back, he hadn't given her any trouble. He responded instantly to her gentle touch on the reins and the pressure of her knees against his flanks.

"What do you think?" she asked Pearlie.

"He looks like he's behavin' himself." The former ramrod of the Sugarloaf sounded skeptical. "Ain't no tellin' how long he'll keep it up, though."

"Watch this," Denny said.

"Hold on there, girl—" began Pearlie, but his objection came too late.

Denny had already leaned forward in the saddle, dug her boot heels into Rocket's sides, and called out to the stallion. The big black horse instantly broke into a run and shot ahead of the wagon, leaving Pearlie in the dust.

As always, Denny felt a thrill go through her as the wind streamed over her face and tugged at her hat, which was kept on her head by the taut rawhide strap under her chin. She felt the smooth play of Rocket's powerful muscles as he ran. His stride was so easy and effortless that he seemed to glide over the ground, almost like she was sitting in a comfortable chair. The landscape flashed past her on both sides of the road.

Denny let the stallion run full-out for several hundred yards, then pulled back on the reins. That was the point at which, in the past, Rocket had refused to cooperate and had started to run even faster, ignoring all his rider's commands.

Today, however, he slowed gradually. Denny let him take his time about stopping. When his pace had dropped off to a walk, she reined him to a complete stop and turned in the road to watch the wagon rolling toward her.

Pearlie scowled as he came even with her, and she turned the stallion again to fall in alongside the vehicle once more.

"Givin' that critter his head was just askin' for trouble," he said.

"No, it was showing you that he's learned what he's supposed to do. You couldn't ask for anything better from him, could you?"

"No, I reckon not," Pearlie admitted grudgingly. A note of admiration came into his voice as he added, "That big varmint sure can run, can't he?"

Denny laughed. "Like the wind."

Rocket didn't give her any trouble the rest of the way into Big Rock. Pearlie brought the wagon to a stop in front of Goldstein's Mercantile, and Denny swung down from the saddle in front of the store and wrapped the reins around the hitch rail, tightening them with a practiced ease.

She was turning away from the stallion when a familiar voice said from the porch, "Good morning, Miss Jensen."

She looked up and saw Conrad Morgan standing there. He still wore the flat-crowned black hat with the silver band, but instead of the expensive suit he'd had on the last time she saw him, he was in jeans and a faded blue work shirt. His black boots showed signs of considerable wear, but she would have bet they were comfortable.

He wasn't wearing a gun. His shirtsleeves were rolled up a couple of turns, revealing muscular forearms. A few beads of sweat were on his forehead, and his shirt was stained dark in a few places. She could tell he'd been working. She looked at another wagon parked in front of the store and saw a number of heavy-looking crates in the back of it.

"You've been loading all that by yourself?" she asked.

"You know of any reason why I shouldn't?" he drawled.

Denny shook her head. "No, I suppose not. I just figured you'd hire people to do work like that."

He thumbed his hat back and said, "The sweat of honest labor is good for a man. Besides, I've spent most of my time in an office in recent months, and I like the feeling of getting out and moving around. It loosens up the muscles."

Denny thought about it and nodded. "I know the feeling. Sitting around fancy drawing rooms in England always got old in a hurry."

"You've spent time in England?"

"And France and Italy. Most of my childhood was spent in Europe, in fact." She pushed her own hat back a little. "I like it better here."

"So do I," said Conrad. "I've spent considerable time in Europe myself."

Pearlie jerked a thumb toward the mercantile's front doors. "I'm gonna go give Leo the list of things your ma and Inez wanted."

"That's fine. I'll be around. You'll be headed back to the ranch in an hour or so?"

"Yep, I expect that's about right." Pearlie went inside the store.

Conrad went down the steps at the end of the porch and said to Denny, "I need to be getting back to our camp—"

"You and Mr. Strom have a camp set up now?"

"That's right. Out at the old Bluejay Mine."

Denny frowned slightly and shook her head. "I've heard of the Bluejay Ranch. I didn't know there was a mine by that name."

"The owner stopped operating it a long time ago so that he could concentrate on raising cattle. The study our geologists made indicated a significant amount of ore remains on the property, though. Mr. Campbell, who owns the ranch, was willing to sell us the mine." Conrad smiled. "He warned us flat out that we're wasting our time. He says the rock is too hard and the yield is too low to make it worthwhile. I suppose we'll see."

"So that's going to be the first place you set up your equipment?"

"That's right. If you'd like to ride out there sometime and have a look at our setup, you'd be welcome."

Denny thought about giving voice to Smoke's objections to the hydraulic mining process. She was curious what Conrad was going to do to keep the operation from being so destructive . . . or if he was going to do anything. Maybe he didn't care, as long as the mine made plenty of money.

"Thanks," she said instead. "I'll think about it."

Conrad nodded, pulled his hat down, and untied the team. "I'll look forward to your visit," he told her, then climbed easily onto the driver's box.

Denny couldn't help but note the lithe grace with which he did so. She was thinking about that when someone called her name from behind her. The man had call twice before she noticed. When she did, she jumped a little and turned quickly to see who had hailed her.

Brice Rogers was walking toward her, accompanied by Sheriff Monte Carson.

Right away, Denny could tell from the stiff way Brice moved that something was wrong with him. He looked normal otherwise, a well-built young man of medium height with slightly wavy brown hair under his tan Stetson. He wasn't wearing his lawman's badge, but then, most deputy U.S. marshals usually didn't unless they were at some official ceremony.

Monte Carson was the one who had called Denny's name. As he and Brice came up to her, the sheriff went on. "Look who's back."

"I see that." Denny nodded to Brice. "We haven't seen you at the Sugarloaf in a while, Brice. Where have you been?"

"Where do you think he's been?" said Monte. "Chasing outlaws! He brought in the whole Lew Cudahy gang. All five of them, plus the loot from that train robbery they pulled over in Kansas."

"I'm afraid I don't keep up with the train robbery news," Denny said dryly.

"Just as well," Brice said. "It's not that interesting."

"No, but killing five owlhoots is," said Monte.

Denny looked at Brice. "So you brought them in dead instead of alive."

"They didn't give me much choice in the matter," he said with a shrug. "And I figured that was better than them dumping my body in some lonely ravine."

"Much better," Denny agreed. "But you're hurt, aren't you? I could tell by the way you were walking."

"One of them creased me on the side. It took a

few stitches to close up, so it's still a mite sore. But it's nothing to worry about."

Denny glanced over her shoulder and saw that Conrad Morgan was still sitting on his wagon. He hadn't moved the vehicle yet. He was watching the conversation she was having with Brice and looked curious.

She decided to satisfy his curiosity. She half turned, held out a hand toward Conrad, and said, "Brice, meet a newcomer to Big Rock. This is Conrad Morgan." She paused for a second, then added, "You might have heard of his father, Frank Morgan."

"The gunfighter?" Brice exclaimed in obvious surprise. Then he added, "I mean no offense—"

"And none taken," said Conrad, smiling. "It would be foolish of me to deny that my father has a reputation for his skill with a gun. Just like Denny wouldn't deny that her father is the famous Smoke Jensen."

Denny couldn't help but notice that he didn't call her "Miss Morgan" this time. Had he done that on purpose, since it was clear that she and Brice Rogers were friends and he wanted to put himself on that same footing?

Brice walked over to the wagon and held his hand up to Conrad.

"Deputy U.S. Marshal Brice Rogers, Mr. Morgan," he said. "It's a pleasure to meet you. What brings you to Big Rock?"

"Business," Conrad replied as he shook the young lawman's hand. "My partner and I are reopening some of the old mining properties here in the valley."

Brice's eyebrows rose. "Is that so? I wish you luck with it. Mining hasn't been a very big industry around here for a while, as I understand it. Its heyday had passed before I ever came to these parts."

"We're optimistic," Conrad said.

Denny put a hand on Brice's right arm. "You'll have to come out to the Sugarloaf and have dinner or supper with us soon. I'm sure my folks will be glad to see you."

He smiled at her. "Thanks. I'll do that. Chief Marshal Long told me to take some time off after that last job."

Monte Carson said, "I should think so, since you got shot. You need some time to recuperate."

"Oh, I'll be fine in another day or two," Brice said. "Even now, I reckon I can do anything I need to do—"

A sharply voiced cry of female dismay caused all of them to turn their heads and look toward the mercantile.

CHAPTER 13

A woman had just come out of the mercantile with a fairly high stack of paper-wrapped bundles in her arms that was teetering precariously. It was obvious she was about to drop the packages.

Conrad came to his feet and went from the driver's box of the wagon to the store's porch in one bound. He reached out to steady the stack of bundles, but the top one was already slipping off.

From the street beside the porch, Brice leaned over, reached out, and caught the package just before it hit the thick planks. Denny could tell from the way he winced that the sudden movement hurt his injured side.

"Got 'em?" Conrad said to the young woman. He still had both hands on the stack of packages, and his hands were very close to hers.

"Yes, thank you," she said. "I just couldn't keep them balanced."

Denny suppressed a disdainful sniff. The packages didn't look all that heavy, and keeping them balanced shouldn't have been *that* difficult of a job.

Conrad let go of them and reached down to take the one that Brice had caught. "That was a good catch, Marshal."

"Yes, it was," the young woman added. "Thank you, Marshal."

Brice nodded. "Glad to help, Miss . . . ?"

"Warfield," she replied. "Blaise Warfield."

"And it is *Miss* Warfield?" asked Conrad.

"Indeed it is," she replied, smiling. That put a dimple in the pretty brunette's cheek.

"You're new to Big Rock, aren't you?" Brice said. "I don't recall seeing you around town before."

Monte Carson said, "Miss Warfield bought the old Double or Nothing Saloon. She's fixing it up so she can open it again."

"That's right," Blaise Warfield said.

"We shouldn't be standing around talking like this," Conrad put in.

That's right, thought Denny. They had already fussed over Blaise Warfield enough. Nearly dropping a package wasn't some big catastrophe.

But Conrad went on. "Not while you're holding all those packages. Why don't we put them in the back of my wagon, and I'll drive you to your place, Miss Warfield? That'll save you from having to carry them all that way."

"You don't mind doing that, Mister . . . ?"

"Morgan. Conrad Morgan." Holding the package he had taken from Brice easily in one hand, he used the other hand to pinch the brim of his hat. "And I don't mind at all."

He stepped over to the driver's box, placed the

package behind the seat, and then turned back to take the rest of the stack from her. When he had set them down, he reached out to clasp the gloved hand Blaise extended to him and helped her step across the gap between the porch and the vehicle.

As she settled down on the seat and Conrad sat beside her, Blaise smiled sweetly at Denny. "I don't believe we've met, either."

"That's right, we haven't," Denny said, not bothering to keep the curtness out of her voice.

Conrad chuckled. "That's Miss Denise Nicole Jensen, Miss Warfield. Denny, better known."

"Like the boy's name?" said Blaise, still smiling.

"You can call me Miss Jensen," Denny grated.

"Then it's a pleasure to meet you, Miss Jensen."

"Denny's father is Smoke Jensen," Conrad said. "I expect you've heard of him."

Blaise's eyes widened slightly. "The famous gunman?"

Denny's jaw tightened even more than it already was. She jerked her head toward Conrad and said, "*His* father's a gunfighter, too."

"I'm surrounded by the offspring of famous people," Blaise said. "What about you, Marshal? Is your father famous? And I don't believe I caught your name."

"It's Brice Rogers, miss." Brice touched a finger to his hat brim and went on. "And no, my father's not famous at all, unless you count his reputation for growing some of the best corn in Iowa. He's a farmer."

"But you became a lawman."

Brice looked like he had started to shrug, then thought better of it because of the stiffness from his wound. "I never was that fond of plowing."

"You'd rather hunt outlaws? That seems a lot more dangerous."

"That depends on how you feel about following the hind end of a mule."

Blaise laughed lightly and musically at that comment.

There's more than one hind end of a mule around here right now, Denny thought as her frowning glance shuttled back and forth between Conrad and Brice. They both seemed pretty taken with Blaise Warfield.

It was true, Blaise looked nice in the midnight-blue dress she wore, and her brown curls were stylishly arranged on her head instead of stuffed under a Stetson, but she was opening a saloon, which made her just one step better than—

Denny stopped that thought short and for a second felt ashamed of herself for allowing it into her head in the first place. She had been raised not to look down on anyone for their place in the world, but rather to make up her mind about them based solely on their actions. Blaise Warfield hadn't done anything to deserve being judged. Well, other than a little flirting with Brice and Conrad.

And it was none of her business who either of those hombres flirted with, Denny told herself.

"We'd better get going," Conrad said as he unwrapped the wagon's reins from its brake lever. "I need to get these supplies back out to our camp, so if you'll tell me where your business is, Miss Warfield, I'll drop you off there."

"Of course. What sort of camp are you talking about?"

Denny didn't want to listen to Conrad's explanation all over again, so she turned and headed down the street, away from Goldstein's Mercantile. She heard Conrad turning the wagon around behind her.

Monte Carson caught up with her a moment later. She glanced over at him and asked, "Where's Brice? Following Miss Warfield with his tongue hanging out like a puppy?"

The sheriff let out a booming laugh. "No. As a matter of fact, he went on into the store to buy a box of cartridges from Leo. That's where he was headed when we ran into that little drawing-room comedy back there."

Denny frowned at him. "What do you mean by that?"

"You and her and Brice and the Morgan lad. I'd say sparks were flying, and not all of 'em were friendly."

"You're loco," muttered Denny. "I don't care what Brice Rogers or Conrad Morgan do, and

I just met the Warfield girl. None of it's any of my business." She bit her lip for a second. "But I'm sorry I was disrespectful, Sheriff. I shouldn't have called you loco."

"Oh, that's all right. Heat of the moment."

"No," Denny snapped. "No heat. I don't give a hoot about any of them."

Monte nodded slowly. He gestured toward one of the businesses they were approaching and asked, "Want to go into Longmont's and have a cup of coffee?"

"That actually sounds like a pretty good idea."

Longmont's was a saloon, but it was also a restaurant. The owner, Louis Longmont, was an old friend of Smoke's who had a reputation as a gambler and a gunman, although for more than two decades he had been content to live peacefully in Big Rock and cultivate a reputation as a saloon keeper and restaurateur.

In earlier times, though, he had fought alongside Smoke in some epic battles, and Smoke thought highly enough of the man to have named his son after him.

His establishment was sufficiently elegant that the respectable ladies of Big Rock didn't mind being seen there. Even a young, unmarried woman such as Denny could go into Longmont's without causing a scandal—especially if she was in the company of the local sheriff.

The place wasn't very busy at this hour of the

morning, since customers hadn't started coming in for lunch yet. Louis Longmont sat at a table in the rear with a cup of his excellent coffee by his hand and some papers spread out in front of him. Despite the early hour, he looked as dapper as always in a black suit, white shirt, and dark gray silk cravat.

He was as observant as ever, too, a habit left over from his gunfighting days. He spotted Denny and Monte Carson as they came in and lifted a hand in greeting, a gesture that doubled as an invitation for them to join him.

"Good morning," he said as he got to his feet. "Would you care for some coffee?"

"That's why we're here," said Monte. He grinned. "Well, that and to get Denny off the street before she starts a ruckus."

"Not another bank robbery, I hope," Longmont said as he cocked an immaculately plucked eyebrow. He signaled to the man behind the bar to bring two more cups and the coffeepot.

"Nope, no holdup this time," Monte replied as he thumbed back his hat. "Denny, Brice, and Conrad Morgan just met your new competition. I'm talking about Blaise Warfield."

"So I gathered, since no one else is in the process of opening a saloon in Big Rock at the moment," Longmont said. He motioned for them to sit down.

The barman filled their cups and then went back

behind the hardwood. Denny sipped the coffee and enjoyed its bracing effect. Working out on the range with the Sugarloaf crew had gotten her in the habit of taking her coffee the same way the cowboys did—hot, black, and strong enough to get up and walk around on its own hind legs.

"What do you know about her?" she asked as she set her cup down.

"Miss Warfield?" Longmont gathered up the papers, tapped them to square them up together, and set the stack aside. "Why do you think I would know anything more about her than anyone else in town?"

"Well, you're in the saloon business, too," said Denny. "And before you came to Big Rock, you spent a lot of time in . . . well . . ."

"Unsavory places?" Longmont asked. With a dry chuckle, he leaned back in his chair. "Denny, Miss Warfield is not much older than you. Which means that before I settled down in Big Rock, she would not have even been born, let alone working in the places I frequented."

"Well, blast it. That's true, I suppose." Denny sighed. "I didn't think long enough about that one, did I?"

Longmont frowned for a moment, then said, "I do know something about Miss Warfield, although I'm not sure I should be spreading gossip."

Denny edged forward in her chair. "Go ahead."

"Well . . . Monte, you remember when Jess McChesney passed away, you weren't able to locate any heirs to his estate."

"Sure," Monte nodded.

"Who's Jess McChesney?" asked Denny.

"He owned the Double or Nothing Saloon," Longmont explained. "Since he died with no heirs, Sheriff Carson auctioned off the property to take care of the taxes owing on it."

"And the Warfield girl bought it?"

Longmont shook his head. "No, Jasper Dunlap did."

Denny made a face. "That fella's slicker than snake oil."

"Indeed he is," Longmont agreed. "When Miss Warfield arrived in town recently, she purchased the property from Dunlap. I overheard him talking about it with some other men one evening, when he'd had a bit too much to drink." Longmont drew in a breath. "Evidently, Dunlap had the impression that since Miss Warfield was buying a saloon, she might be the sort of woman to, ah, welcome the advances of a gentleman."

"He tried to paw her," Denny said.

Longmont looked uncomfortable about having this conversation with the daughter of his old friend, but he nodded and said, "That was my understanding. And Miss Warfield did not take kindly to the attempt."

"She slapped his face."

Longmont shook his head. "No. She pulled a derringer from her bag, pressed it to his forehead, and threatened to blow his brains out."

"Good grief!" Monte Carson exclaimed. "This is the first I'm hearing about that."

Longmont shrugged. "Unsurprisingly, Dunlap wasn't too proud of letting a woman get the best of him like that. I doubt if he ever would have brought up the subject unless, as I said, he'd had too much to drink."

Denny leaned back in her chair. "So the new saloon girl's gun handy, is she?" Despite her instinctive dislike of Blaise Warfield, her voice held a note of admiration.

"She's not a saloon girl," Longmont pointed out. "She owns the place."

"And you'd better not be thinking about having some sort of shootout with her," Monte said.

Denny raised her hands. "Not me. I'm not looking for trouble. But from the sound of it, Blaise Warfield isn't the helpless little butterfly she was pretending to be a little while ago. Maybe somebody should warn Brice and Mr. Morgan."

"You want the job?"

She took another sip of coffee and shook her head. "Not me, Sheriff. As far as I'm concerned, those boys are on their own."

CHAPTER 14

The next couple of weeks were busy ones for Conrad. Although he had studied the hydraulic mining process and learned as much as he could about it before agreeing to Axel Strom's partnership proposal, he was still far from an expert.

Strom knew everything about it, though, and the refinements he had made on the equipment allowed it to produce a more powerful stream of water than ever before, to do an even better job of gouging dirt and rock out of the mountainsides and uncovering the valuable yellow metal it contained.

But even though Strom was responsible for getting the giant water tanks, pumps, hoses, and nozzles set up and operating correctly at the old Bluejay Mine, Conrad had his hands full making sure the horde of workers pouring into the valley were fed and housed and would have their wages forthcoming when it was time for payday. He left it up to Strom to hire the crew, since Strom had run hydraulic mining operations before.

However, the Browning Holdings included other mining interests, so it wasn't like Conrad was totally unfamiliar with the business. He knew that mining men were a rough bunch, overall, so he wasn't surprised to see the brawny, raucous individuals pouring into the valley to run the equipment and handle the sluices.

The head foreman, Strom's second in command, was a strapping Irishman named Seamus Burke. Conrad was in camp the day Burke arrived, driving a wagon with a dozen more miners crowded into the back.

"Hey, cowboy," Burke called as Conrad strode toward the mess tent. "Where'll I find Axel Strom?"

Conrad bristled slightly, unaccustomed to being addressed in such a disdainful manner. But then he reminded himself that he wasn't the arrogant, full-of-himself young man he had been a decade earlier, when he'd first come west and encountered his real father, Frank Morgan. And he *was* wearing range clothes, so he supposed it was a reasonable mistake for the big redheaded man to make.

Conrad turned and pointed up the slope. "The old diggings are about a hundred yards farther on. Mr. Strom will be up there."

The Irishman gave him a curt nod but didn't say thanks. He lifted the reins, then paused and said, "Maybe you'd better come along."

"Why's that?" asked Conrad.

Burke gestured toward the team pulling the wagon. "You're the mule wrangler around here, aren't you? You'll need to deal with this team of jackasses."

One of the men in the back of the wagon called out. "He appears to be well suited to that chore, aye, lads?"

The gibe brought several whoops of laughter from the joker's companions.

Again, Conrad started to react angrily but suppressed the impulse. Instead, he nodded and said mildly, "Sure, I'll come along." He motioned for the wagon to go ahead, up the trail toward the old mine.

The big Irishman got the mules moving again. Conrad walked alongside. The men in the back kept making rude comments about the stink of mules and their droppings, not addressing the words directly to Conrad although there was no doubt he was the one for whom they were intended.

He just smiled to himself as he walked along.

They came up to one of the massive water tanks on wheels that Strom was inspecting.

As Strom heard the wagon approaching and turned to look, Conrad announced, "We've got some new men here, Axel."

The big redhead on the driver's seat frowned at Conrad, clearly puzzled by the familiarity with which the man he had taken to be a mule wrangler spoke to Strom.

"Hello, Seamus," Strom said to the Irishman. "I see you've met Mr. Morgan."

"Morgan?" Burke repeated.

"That's right." Strom nodded toward Conrad. "This is my partner, Conrad Morgan."

Burke looked surprised but not particularly alarmed by his mistake. He told Strom, "No, we haven't met, not really." Burke's eyes narrowed slightly, giving them a piggish look. "Leastways, he didn't say who he was."

"Well, now you know. Conrad, this is Seamus Burke. He's the best man I know at bossing a crew like this."

"Pleased to meet you," Conrad said to the Irishman. "Now, if you fellas want to get down, I'll tend to that team—"

"No, that ain't necessary," Burke interrupted him. He turned his head and barked, "Flannery! Get your butt out of that wagon and see to these mules."

"Aye, Seamus, aye," muttered the man who had started the joking. As he climbed out of the wagon, he cast a scowl toward Conrad, as if *he* were the one who had caused the trouble.

Conrad saw that look but ignored it, saying instead, "I'm glad you're here, Mr. Burke. We have a lot of hard work ahead of us, and Axel speaks highly of you. I'm sure you'll do a fine job."

"Do my best," Burke replied with a surly note in his voice. "I always do."

"The mess tent's down below, in case you boys want a bite to eat." Conrad let his own voice harden a little. "After you've gotten started on whatever Mr. Strom needs you to do, of course."

With that, he lifted a hand in farewell to Strom, turned, and walked back down the slope. He hadn't exactly rubbed the fact that he was one of the bosses into Seamus Burke's face, but his words made it clear that was the case, anyway.

Conrad didn't care how surly any of the crew were, as long as they did the job.

Chip Runnels and Jack Denton were young cowboys, both in their early twenties, but despite their youth, they were experienced hands and had been riding for Seth Campbell's Bluejay Ranch for several years. They had been born too late to experience the excitement of the cattle drives, but they had heard older punchers spinning yarns about that era and felt that they were continuing a glorious, if grueling at times, tradition.

They were riding together through range along the western side of the spread, near the mountains that reared up to enclose the broad valley, when they reined in sharply at a sound that made them both frown in confusion.

"Is that thunder?" Runnels asked about the low but steadily growing rumble in the air.

"Can't be," replied Denton as he tipped his head back and looked around. "There ain't a cloud in the sky. Anyway, thunder booms and then stops. It don't just keep goin' like that."

It was true. The sound continued, and it got louder as the two cowboys listened.

"Can't be a train," said Runnels. "The tracks don't run anywhere near the old man's spread."

"Then what in blazes is it?"

Runnels shook his head. "I don't know, but it's comin' from somewhere on those slopes to the west, so I reckon we ought to go and find out."

"Mr. Campbell sold those old mine diggin's up there, didn't he? Maybe it's somethin' to do with that."

"Yeah, but I never heard such noises comin' from a mine. Maybe a dynamite blast every now and then, or a stamp mill runnin', but that don't sound like any stamp mill I ever heard. Anyway, whoever took it over ain't had time to build one."

"If the boss don't own that mine anymore, it's none of our business what they're doin," Denton pointed out.

"Maybe not, but ain't you curious? Don't you want to find out what's goin' on?"

"Well . . ." Denton made a face. "I reckon I do."

"Come on, then." Runnels heeled his horse into motion again, turning the animal's head toward the slopes about half a mile away.

Denton fell in alongside him, still looking a little reluctant to proceed. He would have rather headed for the ranch headquarters and reported to the boss, so Mr. Campbell could worry about whatever was making that terrible racket. But he wasn't going to act like a coward in front of his friend Chip.

The noise got louder as they neared the timbered slopes. Runnels pointed and said, "Look up yonder. See the smoke, Jack? There's some sort of fire burnin' up there!"

Forest fires were always a great fear on the range. If a blaze was burning on the mountainside, someone had to have set it, because there hadn't been any lightning.

"It's those blasted miners doin' it, whatever it is," Denton said. "I knew the boss shouldn't have sold that mine. Nothin' good comes from diggin' in the earth."

"What about growin' food?" asked Runnels as they rode. "You've got to dig in the earth to do that."

"Yeah, but not big holes. I've seen mines. They're more like . . . like big graves! Graves for giants!"

Runnels frowned. "You're loco! There ain't no such thing as giants. Next thing you know, you'll be tellin' me there's some sort of fire-breathin' dragon up there, like in the storybooks, and that's what's causin' the smoke."

"We don't know it ain't," muttered Denton.

The noise was loud enough that it seemed like it was shaking the earth under their horses' hooves. Maybe it was, or something was causing the earth to tremble, anyway. Both cowboys started to look even more worried. As they headed up the slope, it was all they could do not to whirl their horses around and rattle their hocks out of there.

Suddenly, the mounts began to struggle, their hooves slipping under them. Runnels and Denton tightened their reins as the unsteady footing made the animals skittish.

"What the devil!" Runnels cried. "Look at the ground, Jack! Where'd that water come from?"

Like the tide coming in, a surge of water several inches deep and yards wide had appeared with no warning, sweeping down the slope from somewhere up above. The horses continued to dance around nervously as the brown current flowed around their hooves. It was like a creek running down the mountain, but no creek had ever been there before.

"We'd better get outta here!" Denton said. "We're liable to wash away if we don't!"

The water wasn't that deep, but they had no way of knowing how much more of it was going to come flooding down the mountainside.

Besides, it wasn't just water. It was more like a tide of liquid mud, and that made the footing slicker and more treacherous for the horses. As Runnels jerked on the reins, trying to turn his mount, the horse suddenly screamed and fell. Runnels had to kick his feet free of the stirrups and leap frantically from the saddle to keep the horse from falling on him.

He landed facedown in the mud and started sliding. Seeing his friend in such a predicament might have been a comical sight to Denton if he hadn't realized that Runnels was sputtering and thrashing. He had gotten a faceful of the thin mud, and enough of it must have gone down his nose and throat that it threatened to choke him.

"Hang on, Chip, I'm comin'!" Denton called as he struggled to get his mount to cooperate.

He managed to turn the horse around, but as its legs slid crazily and it lurched back and forth, he realized that he might have a better chance on his feet, and so might the horse. He yanked his boots out of the stirrups, threw his left leg over the horse's back, and dropped to the ground, landing ankle deep in the sea of muck flowing down the slope.

Denton's feet almost went out from under him. He grabbed the trunk of a nearby sapling to steady himself and looked for Runnels. His friend had slid about fifty feet downhill before coming to a stop. He was thrashing around but seemed to be unable to pull his head up so he could breathe.

Denton sat down and let go of the sapling. By doing that, he was able to stay sitting mostly upright as he slid down the slope, too, instead of plunging face-first into the mud as Runnels had done.

He couldn't really steer himself very well, but he managed to get close enough to Runnels to reach out, grab him, and stop his slide. He braced himself as best he could, took hold of the other cowboy's shoulders, and heaved him up into a sitting position. Runnels's head flopped loosely. That made Denton fear that he had choked to the point of passing out already—if not worse.

Denton pawed at his friend's face, trying to wipe away as much of the mud as he could. A surge of relief went through him as Runnels suddenly coughed. Mud sprayed from his mouth and nose. He gasped for air, choked and spat, and blew some more.

Denton pounded him on the back, as he would have if Runnels had been underwater too long. Drowning in water and drowning in mud had to be sort of alike.

After a few minutes, Runnels was breathing heavily but fairly normally again. His face was completely coated with the brown mud. He managed to say, "What . . . what the hell . . . is all this?"

"I don't know, Chip, but it darned near killed you," said Denton. "Let's see if we can get back down to flatter ground, and then we'll figure out what to do next."

"I know what I'm gonna do next!" Runnels said as he pawed at his eyes in an attempt to clear away more of the mud. "I'm gonna kill whatever son of a buck is responsible for this!"

CHAPTER 15

Denny hadn't forgotten about Conrad Morgan's invitation to ride up to the Bluejay Mine and take a look at the hydraulic operation for herself. But after the encounter with Blaise Warfield in Big Rock, she had been annoyed enough with both Conrad and Brice Rogers to avoid them for a while.

She did, however, check in with Monte Carson whenever she was in town to make sure Brice was doing all right. Fawning over Blaise the way he had might have irritated Denny, but she still didn't want him to have trouble with that wound in his side.

According to Monte, Brice was doing fine.

"He claims to be good as new," the sheriff told Denny on one of her visits. "And he seemed to be getting around all right the last time I saw him."

"When was that?" Denny asked.

Monte hesitated. "Three or four days ago. He was, ah, having a beer . . ."

Monte's sudden change in attitude tipped Denny off to what was going on. She said, "You mean he was having a beer in Blaise Warfield's new saloon. I guess it must be open now."

"Yeah, that was the first night the place was open," Monte admitted. "I'm sure Brice was just there looking it over as a lawman. I mean, I was doing the same thing."

"Yes, I'm sure that's why he was at the Double or Nothing," Denny replied, her scathing tone of voice making it clear she didn't believe what she'd just said, at all.

"Actually, it's not the Double or Nothing. Miss Warfield changed the name. It's Blaise's Place now. She's got it cleaned up and looking nice. New sign and everything out front."

"Blaise's Place," repeated Denny. "Somebody's pretty full of herself."

"Now, don't say that. Louis calls his business Longmont's, you know. That's just a common way of naming a business."

"I suppose," Denny said. "Anyway, it's none of *my* business what she calls it. Or where Brice Rogers has himself a beer."

It was later that same day when she walked into her father's study and found Smoke leaning back in his chair behind the desk, frowning in thought.

"Something wrong?" Denny asked him.

"No, I was just thinking about something," Smoke said. "I'm curious how that mining operation is going. Figured I might ride up to Seth Campbell's ranch tomorrow and have a look."

Without really thinking about it, Denny said, "I'll come with you." The same idea had already been in her mind when she went in there.

124

Smoke cocked an eyebrow. "You're curious about it, too?"

"Well, when you were talking about it before, you made it sound like hydraulic mining might cause some trouble in the valley. If it is, we need to know about it, don't we?"

"They're not going to be doing any mining on the Sugarloaf," Smoke pointed out.

"Maybe not, but you've always felt sort of responsible for the whole valley, as well as the town, since you were one of the first settlers in these parts. Don't bother trying to deny it."

"Wasn't going to," he said. "When you've spilled blood for a place—your own blood, and others'—you can't help but care about it. If you want to come with me, be ready to ride in the morning."

"I will be," Denny said.

She didn't ride Rocket, instead saddling a sturdy chestnut mare she had used quite a few times as a saddle horse. Smoke rode a rangy gray gelding.

They went first to Seth Campbell's ranch house, since they would have to cut across the spread to reach the mine, and it was only good manners to let a man know when you were going to be on his range.

"I've been mighty curious about what's going on up there myself," Seth Campbell told them when Smoke had explained what they were

125

doing. Campbell was a compact, gray-haired man with a brush of a mustache. "I think I'll ride with you, Smoke, if that's all right."

"It's your spread, Seth," Smoke said. "I reckon you can ride wherever you want to."

"Give me a minute to throw a hull on a horse."

The three of them headed toward the western reaches of the ranch, where the mountains that marked the boundary of the valley reared toward the Colorado sky. Smoke and Campbell chatted about the cattle market as they rode. Denny tried to pay attention, since she wanted to learn as much as she could about running a ranch, but her thoughts kept straying.

There was no guarantee that Conrad Morgan would be at the mine when they got there. He might be in Big Rock or off at one of the other properties he and Strom owned.

It didn't matter whether he was there or not, Denny told herself. She had come along to check out the hydraulic mining, not to see Conrad Morgan again.

They were still a mile or so from the mine, according to Campbell, when the rancher suddenly said, "What in blazes is that racket?"

The three riders reined in and listened. A low, distinctive, steady rumbling came to their ears.

After a moment, Smoke said, "That's some sort of engine running."

"Like a train?" asked Campbell.

"No, I figure it's the equipment they're using to pump water into the mountain. You know how hydraulic mining works, don't you, Seth?"

"Well . . . not exactly. I know it has something to do with water. They've got some sort of giant sluice box, don't they?"

"That's only part of it," said Smoke. Quickly, he explained how the machinery created a high-powered stream of water to gouge out sediment and provide a steady flow through the sluices.

"Yeah, I can see how they'd need a big engine for that," Campbell said. "I didn't think about it being that noisy, though. That's liable to spook the cattle for miles around."

"The noise may not be the worst of it." Smoke heeled his horse into motion again. "Let's go have a look."

They came to a trail that wagons had carved out as they carried heavy equipment, men, and supplies to the mining camp.

Campbell frowned at the ruts. "I gave those fellas permission to cross my land, of course. No other way they can get to the old diggings. But I didn't realize they'd be making themselves a regular road."

"It's a big operation," Smoke said.

Campbell sighed. "I reckon I can live with it, as long as they don't do anything else."

They followed the wagon ruts. The trail rose at a slant as it entered the foothills on the western edge of the valley. As the slope grew steeper, the trail wound back and forth as it climbed toward the mine. The closer Denny, Smoke, and Campbell came, the louder the pounding rumble that filled the air.

The trail flattened out onto the broad, relatively level shoulder where the camp was located. Dozens of tents had been set up, including several large ones that probably functioned as a mess tent and storage areas; maybe a makeshift office for Conrad and Strom, as well.

The men had also built a couple of pole corrals to hold the mules used to haul the wagons full of equipment. Denny saw several large, circular tanks mounted on wheeled chassis. Those would hold the water used in the pumping operation, she guessed, in locations where there was no stream or lake to provide water. She spotted a couple of large machines, also on wheeled platforms, that reminded her of donkey engines, only on a smaller scale.

Those would be the pumps, she thought.

Canvas hoses as thick around as a man's waist were lying here and there.

The old mine tunnel was about fifty yards up the slope from the bench. One of the pumps sat at the base of the slope, along with a water tank. A hose connected the two, and another hose stretched up the hill and vanished into the tunnel. Another hose led back out of the dark, mouth-like opening and curved off to the north.

It must have taken a dozen or more men to wrestle those heavy hoses into place, Denny mused. That would be hard, dirty work.

Only a few men were in sight. All of them wore canvas trousers, flannel shirts, and work boots. As Denny, Smoke, and Campbell reined in, one of the men came over to them and asked with a suspicious frown on his face, "What are you folks doing here? Help you with something?"

"This used to be my mine," said Campbell. He waved a hand to take in the range to the east. "And that's still my ranch down there."

"Oh," the man said, nodding. "You're Campbell."

"*Mister* Campbell," the cattleman said.

"Sure. What can we do for you?"

"We just wanted to have a look at this mining you're doing."

Smoke said, "Where are Mr. Morgan and Mr. Strom?"

The man jerked a thumb at the tunnel. "Strom'll be up there. He keeps that big son of a gun of a pump humming."

They'd all had to raise their voices slightly to be heard over the pump's rumbling, so Denny wouldn't exactly call it humming.

"I don't know where Morgan is," the miner went on. He pointed at one of the large tents. "Could be in there. I haven't seen him for a while."

Campbell nodded. "Obliged to you." He rode toward the tunnel.

Smoke and Denny followed. Denny thought for a second that the man they'd been talking to was going to stop them, but then he shrugged and turned away. She made a face at the noise, which caused Smoke to grin.

He leaned toward her and said loudly, "If the racket bothers you, you can go look for Conrad."

"No, thanks," replied Denny. "I want to see what they're doing up here."

As they got closer, her eyes followed the curving path of the hose that emerged from the tunnel. It ran toward an area where the bench dropped off fairly sharply toward the valley. The end of the hose entered a large, enclosed, boxlike contraption that sat on short, thick wooden beams. That was the sluice, she realized. It ran on down the slope out of sight.

She pointed to it and said to Smoke, "How do they get the gold out after they run the water through there?"

"Gold's heavier than the rest of the dirt and rock," he said. "They have places inside the box built to catch it. Then they can lift the top and reach inside to clean it out. It's pretty simple. Fellas have been doing basically the same thing since the Gold Rush days. By using the pumps, they can run a lot more water and sediment through there."

She nodded, then recalled what Smoke had said. All that water and dirt had to go *somewhere* when it reached the bottom of the sluice. She wondered how they managed that part of it.

Campbell had reached the water tank and pump. The noise was making his horse skittish, so he dismounted and led the animal forward as a big man in work clothes, with his shirt sleeves rolled up, came out of the tunnel. Denny recognized Axel Strom from the man's visit to the Sugarloaf several weeks earlier.

Strom and Campbell spoke and shook hands. It was impossible to hear what they were saying to each other because of the noise from the pump. After a moment, they turned and walked over to Smoke and Denny.

"Good to see you again, Mr. Jensen!" said Strom, practically shouting. "You, too, Miss Jensen! Let's go back down to the mess tent so we can talk without yelling our heads off!"

Smoke smiled and nodded, and they turned their horses. She thought that Strom didn't seem quite so surly today. Maybe he was one of those men who was never really happy unless he was working.

As they went down the slope and the noise wasn't quite so bad, Smoke said, "I'd like to take a closer look at your setup, if you don't mind."

"Sure," Strom replied. "We'll find Morgan, and

he can show you around. I can't stay away from the tunnel for too long. We have a good crew and foreman, but I still like to keep a pretty close eye on things."

"I understand. I'm the same way myself."

They reached the flat and started toward one of the big tents. Smoke and Denny swung down from their saddles and led their horses like Campbell had done. The rumble from the pump was still too loud for conversation to be really comfortable. Denny hoped maybe the tent's canvas walls would muffle the roar, at least a little.

Before they reached the mess tent, Conrad Morgan walked out of one of the other tents. He paused for a second in apparent surprise as he spotted them, then started toward them, lifting a hand in greeting. He wasn't wearing a hat at the moment, and his fair hair shone in the sunlight.

At that moment, Denny spotted movement beyond Conrad. A couple of riders came up the wagon trail and over the edge of the bench to head toward the camp.

One of the newcomers suddenly leaned forward in his saddle and dug his heels into his horse's flanks. The animal leaped forward and charged toward the little group. Denny could see what was happening but couldn't hear the swift rataplan of hoofbeats, and evidently neither could Conrad.

He didn't show any signs of knowing that he was under attack . . .

Not even when the charging rider yanked a gun from his holster and flame spurted from the muzzle as he opened fire.

CHAPTER 16

Denny acted instinctively. She dropped the chestnut's reins and lunged forward, leaving her feet in a diving tackle aimed at Conrad. She crashed into him and wrapped her arms around him. Her momentum made both of them fall to the ground, landing in an ungainly sprawl as bullets whipped through the air above them.

If Denny had been wearing a handgun, she would have drawn it and returned the attacker's fire, but she had left the Sugarloaf without her usual Colt Lightning. Although she'd brought along a Winchester carbine, it was still in the saddle sheath.

Smoke was packing a .45, though, so as she jerked her head up to look around, she wasn't surprised to hear the revolver booming out a couple of shots.

The second rider had driven his mount up alongside his rash companion, and in a desperate move as Smoke opened fire, he rammed his horse's shoulder against the other animal. Both horses went down just as Smoke's shots rang through the air. The riders landed hard and rolled.

Seth Campbell had drawn his gun, too. He and Smoke ran toward the fallen men, passing Denny and Conrad along the way.

"Do bullets just naturally start flying wherever you happen to be?"

The coolly voiced question made her jerk her attention back to the man she had tackled. The man on whom she was still halfway sprawled, Denny realized to her chagrin.

"I reckon we're even now," she grated. "I just saved your life."

"I'm not so sure about that. It sounded to me like those shots were so high, they would have missed me anyway, even if you hadn't tackled me." Conrad grinned. "Not that I'm complaining, mind you."

"Oh!" With that disdainful exclamation, Denny pushed herself up onto hands and knees and then got to her feet, stepping away from Conrad. Her hat had fallen off when she tackled him, so she picked it up, slapped it against her jeans-clad thigh a couple of times, and settled it on her head.

He sat up, brushed himself off, and then smiled at her again as he said, "You're not going to give me a hand up?"

She ignored that impertinent question and turned her attention to Smoke and Campbell, who had reached the two men still lying on the ground. They covered the men with their guns as Campbell said in a loud, surprised voice, "Chip? Jack? Is that you? It's hard to tell with you boys coated in dried mud like that!"

"You know these hombres, Seth?" Smoke asked. "They look a mite familiar to me."

"You've seen 'em before on my ranch." Campbell gestured. "This one's Jack Denton, and the loco hombre who started shooting is Chip Runnels. They ride for the Bluejay, all right, even though I'm ashamed to admit it right now!"

Denny had walked up while the men were talking. She recognized them, too, although, as Campbell had said, they looked like they had been dipped completely in mud and then allowed to dry. Some of the muck was starting to flake off, though, revealing more of their features.

Jack Denton sat up first, shook his head, and groaned. "I'm sorry, Mr. Campbell. I didn't realize Chip was gonna go crazy like that. As soon as he hauled out his hogleg and started shootin', I did my best to stop him before he hurt anybody."

Campbell looked around at Denny. "*Did* he hurt anybody? Are you all right, Miss Denny?"

"I'm fine, and so is Mr. Morgan. Those shots went wild."

Smoke nodded. "That was quick thinking on your part, getting Conrad off his feet like that. Looked like he was the one the youngster was aiming at."

Chip Runnels pushed himself up and braced himself on one hand. He was breathing hard and could barely get the angry words out. "The varmint . . . had it comin'! . . . He tried to . . . drown us in mud!"

"I don't know what you're talking about,"

136

Conrad said. He had joined the group, too, along with Axel Strom.

Denton pointed. "Off over yonder at the edge of the valley there's practically a whole ocean of muddy water washin' down the hill. Once we were in it, we couldn't hardly get out. Chip almost choked to death on it."

Frowning, Campbell swung around to face Conrad and Strom. He had lowered his gun, but it was still in his hand. "What's the boy talking about?" he demanded. "Is he right? Are you flooding my range with mud?"

"Take it easy," Strom replied with a harsh note of anger in his voice, as well. "I don't know what these foolish cowpokes blundered into—"

"We have a holding pond for any overflow from the sluice box," Conrad said in a calm, steady tone.

Denny figured it was designed to smooth over hard feelings. Conrad was the businessman of the pair, accustomed to doing any slick talking that needed to be done.

Smoke said, "It sounds to me like that holding pond isn't big enough to handle the volume. Maybe you'd better take a look at it."

"And maybe you'd better let us run our own business," snapped Strom. Any semblance of affability he had summoned up earlier was gone. A dark scowl creased his forehead.

"Your business is supposed to be confined to

137

the property you bought from me," Campbell said. "I was willing to overlook the wagon ruts you left in my range because I understand you've got to be able to bring your equipment out here. But I won't stand for a bunch of mud spilling over onto my property."

"We're just getting underway," said Conrad, "and sometimes adjustments have to be made. I assure you, Mr. Campbell, we'll look into this, and we'll do whatever is necessary to make it right. Won't we, Axel?"

"Sure," Strom replied, but not very graciously. "Just give us a chance. It takes a few days to get everything lined up right and working the way it's supposed to."

Campbell's frown didn't go away, but after a moment he nodded and slipped his gun back into its holster. "I reckon that's reasonable enough. If you've done any permanent damage, though—"

"We'll reimburse you for it," Conrad said, ignoring the look that Strom gave him. "Don't worry about that."

The Bluejay cowboys struggled to their feet.

Runnels said, "When I was tryin' to get some air and all I could do was swallow mud, I sure figured *I* was gonna suffer some permanent damage. Mighty permanent!"

Campbell rounded on the young cowboys and asked, "What were you doing when you got messed up with that muck, anyway?"

"Tryin' to see what that terrible racket was," Denton explained. He waved a muddy hand toward the pump. "It was that thing."

"You'd better get used to it," Strom said. "We'll be here for a while." He turned and stalked off toward the mine tunnel.

Conrad said, "I'm very sorry for what's happened here." His voice hardened a little as he looked at Runnels and went on. "It wasn't very smart to come charging in here and start shooting, though. You could have hurt someone, or gotten killed yourself."

The young cowboy looked a little sheepish under the coating of mud. "Sorry," he muttered. "I reckon I lost my head. I didn't really mean to hurt anybody. I was just lettin' off steam because I was so mad about almost drownin' in that stuff. That's why I was shootin' high."

Campbell said, "From the way your horses got back up, they don't appear to be hurt. You check 'em out good and make sure they're not lame. Then get back to the ranch and start cleaning up." He sighed. "It's liable to take you a while to scrub all that off."

The cowboys walked away to catch their horses.

Conrad looked at Denny and said, "That was a little more excitement than you were counting on from your visit, I imagine."

"I didn't figure I'd have to tackle you, that's

for sure," she told him. She sniffed. "I'm still counting it as saving your life, whether that boy was trying to kill you or not. He could have gotten off a lucky shot."

"Or unlucky, depending on your perspective." Conrad turned to Smoke. "Do you still want a tour of the mine, Mr. Jensen?"

Smoke slid his Colt back into leather. "I think I'd rather take a look at that so-called holding pond of yours."

"I want to see that, too," Campbell growled.

Fifteen minutes later, Conrad, mounted on the same buckskin he had ridden out to the Sugarloaf, led the other three to a shallow pit about twenty yards across that had been dug out of the side of the mountain where the slope wasn't as steep. The lower side of it had been built up with earthworks and shored with horizontal logs sealed together with pitch.

The pond was almost full but not overflowing. However, thin mud flowed almost like water through a gap in the retaining wall, shooting out to splatter on the slope below. Clearly, a lot of it had escaped that way and spread out in a steadily widening fan shape as it washed on down the hill.

"There's the problem," Conrad said. "That wall just didn't get sealed well enough. We'll shut down the pumps and get to work repairing it."

140

"How will you do that when it's full of mud?" asked Smoke.

Conrad shook his head. "I hate to say it, but we'll have to let what's in there leak on out. We can't do anything to fix the problem while it's still full of water. Once the pumps are shut down, it shouldn't take long for the level to drop low enough to work on it. I'm truly sorry this happened, Mr. Campbell, but as my partner indicated, sometimes not everything functions perfectly right away. We'll take care of it. I give you my word on that."

Campbell leaned on his saddle horn, frowned in thought for a moment, and then said, "Well . . . it looks like an honest mistake. Seems to me like you ought to have a man watching this pond to make sure it doesn't spring another leak."

"That's a very good idea. We'll do that. I'm sorry for what happened to your men, but at least the problem was discovered early."

"Yeah, I reckon." Campbell shrugged. "And mud dries. If it had kept on doing that for weeks or months, it would have flooded the whole western side of my range and ruined it. No telling how many cows would've gotten bogged down. I've got a good, clear creek running through there, too, and if that runoff had gotten in there, it would have been fouled, maybe even blocked off."

"We'll make sure that doesn't happen," Conrad said.

"All right." Campbell paused, then added, "I'm obliged to you for taking care of it."

"Of course."

Denny said, "Even if you patch that leak, how are you going to keep the pond from overflowing? It has a lot of mud in it already."

"We'll have to keep an eye on it, like Mr. Campbell said, and shut down the pumps at regular intervals to let the level go down."

"But when the water soaks back into the ground, it's going to leave all the sediment from the tunnel behind. Won't that eventually fill up the space?"

"We'll have to remove it and dispose of it somehow," said Conrad. "I don't know exactly what the plan is regarding that, but it'll be dealt with, I'm sure." He smiled. "Those are good questions."

"I thought so," said Denny. "You sound surprised, Mr. Morgan. Did you think I was just another pretty face, like Blaise Warfield?"

"No, of course not," Conrad answered instantly, then a bit of a wild-eyed look came over his face as he realized he was venturing into dangerous territory. "I mean, certainly you're attractive, Miss Jensen, but I know that there's . . . ah . . . more to you than that. And it's probably unfair to Miss Warfield to think that just because she . . . because she's rather . . . um . . ."

"Let me give you some advice, son," Smoke

142

said. "If you really want to spend some time digging yourself a hole, you'd be making better use of your efforts by making that holding pond bigger, once you've got it drained."

CHAPTER 17

Anybody who had seen the inside of the old Double or Nothing Saloon a month earlier would be hard put to recognize the place. Blaise had spent long days cleaning, doing the work herself. She had some money left over from the funds she had brought with her to Big Rock, since she hadn't paid Jasper Dunlap as much for the property as they had agreed to originally, but she didn't want to spend that on anything she could do herself.

While the painters and carpenters she'd hired completed their work, she ordered a liquor supply from a wholesaler in Denver and had it brought in by train.

By the time that shipment reached Big Rock, Blaise had hired two men to work for her as bartenders. They loaded the crates of liquor into the back of a wagon and brought them to what had become Blaise's Place, as proclaimed by the new sign mounted above the awning over the boardwalk.

The time would come when she needed a piano player. She could sing fairly well and dance a little, and she knew she was attractive. She didn't mind wearing low-cut, spangled dresses. She had done that plenty of times in the past, after all.

She wasn't going to take men upstairs, though. That line was drawn pretty deeply in the sand. What was the point of owning your own business if you still had to degrade yourself like that?

She sent another telegram from the Western Union office in the train station, addressing it to an old friend who lived in San Francisco. Della would know some girls she could send to Big Rock.

Like the piano player, Blaise didn't have to have the soiled doves right away. She could open for business without them.

And that was what she did. She'd paid the local newspaperman to print up some flyers, and her bartenders tacked them up around town. As a result, she'd had a good crowd on hand the first night, good enough that both bartenders were kept busy.

Among the customers were the two lawmen, Sheriff Monte Carson and Deputy U.S. Marshal Brice Rogers. Blaise wasn't surprised to see the sheriff. Carson was responsible for keeping the peace in Big Rock, so naturally he would be interested in a new saloon opening up.

Brice Rogers was a different story. As a federal star-packer, he didn't really have any jurisdiction over local matters. His reasons for being there had to be different.

Blaise didn't mind flattering herself by assuming that *she* was the reason. She liked that idea. During her brief meeting with Denny Jensen, she hadn't liked the cowgirl, but she'd been able to tell that Denny was fond of Rogers. If the marshal was interested in Blaise, that would get under Denny's skin, for sure.

The thought had put a smile on Blaise's face. She'd made sure to pay plenty of attention to Brice Rogers that first night . . . and when he started showing up on a fairly regular basis, she never let him feel neglected.

On an evening a couple of weeks after opening, Brice wasn't in the saloon, but Blaise saw a number of already familiar faces. The tall, brawny Irishman who had come in with several similarly dressed companions was Seamus Burke, the foreman of the crew working at the Bluejay Mine for Conrad Morgan and Axel Strom. Conrad hadn't been in, and Blaise wouldn't have minded seeing him again. The miners were becoming regulars, though.

Only one of the bartenders was working at the moment. His name was Hank Lawdermilk. He set aside the rag he'd been using to wipe the bar and said, "Evening, Mr. Burke. The usual for you and your friends?"

"Aye," Burke replied. He tossed a coin on the hardwood. "An unopened bottle . . . and leave it."

Lawdermilk nodded and got a bottle of rye off the shelf behind the bar, then fetched down five glasses, sliding one each to the men. Burke used his teeth to pull the cork from the bottle and splashed liquor into the glasses.

Blaise was standing at the far end of the bar, watching the crowd.

Burke lifted his glass toward her and said, "Here's to you, Miss Warfield."

"Thank you, Mr. Burke," she told him. "You boys enjoy yourself this evening."

Burke threw back the rye, then licked his lips in appreciation. "Oh, we intend to, ma'am. We figure on enjoyin' ourselves very much, don't we, boys?"

The other miners downed their slugs and called out raucous agreement. Burke refilled the glasses.

Blaise kept a smile on her face, but worry lurked in her eyes. Given the boisterous mood the miners appeared to be in, trouble couldn't be ruled out. On the other hand, they might just drink themselves half blind and then stagger on out without starting anything.

She hoped that would be the case. Hank Lawdermilk was fairly tough, but he was middle-aged and not that big. He wouldn't be any match for five burly miners on a rampage.

Burke and the other miners continued drinking, gradually getting louder in their hilarity. Nobody crowded them, leaving them their own space at the bar. The other customers were mostly townsmen: gents who worked at the train station, the livery stables, the freight yards.

So far, very few cowboys from the surrounding

ranches had ventured into Blaise's Place. They were accustomed to drinking at the Brown Dirt Cowboy Saloon and must not have seen any reason to change that habit.

About an hour after Burke and his friends had come in, the batwing doors at the entrance swung back and four men dressed in range clothes sauntered in. Two of them were young, in their early twenties. Another was maybe a decade older than that, and the fourth man was longer in the tooth than any of them, a grizzled forty or so. From the looks of him, he probably had been cowboying for more than half his life. The newcomers paused, glanced warily at the group of miners, then moved to the other end of the bar.

Blaise heard Hank Lawdermilk ask them, "What'll it be, boys?"

The punchers ordered beers.

They talked quietly among themselves as they sipped from the mugs Lawdermilk filled, but they kept shooting looks at the miners, the two younger ones, especially.

Finally, one of them tipped his head back, drained the rest of the beer in his mug, and set it on the bar with a decisive thump. He turned toward the miners.

"Chip, what are you doin?" the old puncher asked.

"I just want to talk to these fellas for a minute, Asa," the cowboy called Chip replied.

"You know Mr. Campbell don't like trouble," warned Asa.

"Yeah, I know," Chip said, but he didn't sound like he cared. He hooked his thumbs into his belt and sauntered along the bar toward the miners.

Blaise felt her pulse speed up a little as she watched. At least none of the men appeared to be carrying guns. She had that to be thankful for, anyway.

"Hey, you," Chip said in an aggressive voice.

A couple of the miners moved aside so that it was Seamus Burke who turned to face the young puncher. Burke was their leader in town, as well as at the mine.

"Are you talkin' to me, boy?" he asked with a sneer on his face and in his voice.

"You work at that mine out on Mr. Campbell's ranch, don't you?"

"We work at the Bluejay *Mine*," snapped Burke. "It's not part of anybody's ranch anymore."

"Well, *we* ride for the Bluejay. The *ranch*. And you stinkin' miners almost killed me and Jack last week."

"Oh, no," Blaise said under her breath. She glanced around. All the work she had done cleaning and fixing the place up . . .

Burke stepped forward, his chest swelling from the deep, angry breath he took. He demanded, "What did you just call us?"

"You heard me," the cowboy said. Two of his

149

companions grabbed his arms, but he shook them off and stalked toward Burke. "I said you miners all stink worse 'n that mud you swamped us with."

"So you're one of the idiots who made that trouble and caused us all the extra work," Burke shot back at him. "If you damn cow nurses would just stay out of things that don't concern you—"

"You were floodin' the whole range with your filthy mud!"

"We're actually producing something worthwhile!" Burke countered.

Hank Lawdermilk held out both hands and made patting motions as he said, "Calm down now, fellas. There's no need for arguing. We're all friends here—"

"The hell we are!" Chip interrupted.

"How about a drink on the house?" Lawdermilk suggested. He glanced over at Blaise to confirm it was all right to make that offer.

She nodded quickly.

One of the other miners put a hand on Burke's shoulder. "Hear that, Seamus? I don't like these cowboys any more than you do, but I never turn down a free drink!"

"Yeah, I suppose you're right." Burke's hands had clenched into tight, malletlike fists. He relaxed them, sneered at Chip, and added, "You just run along, sonny. The grown men have drinkin' to do."

The grizzled cowhand said to Lawdermilk, "That offer go for us, too?"

"Sure," replied the bartender. He started setting out glasses and pulled another bottle from the shelf.

Chip backed off and rejoined his friends. About ten feet separated the two groups, and nobody else in the saloon was going to risk getting between them. Chip and Seamus Burke were on the near ends, closest to each other, but they faced the hardwood and picked up the fresh drinks that Hank Lawdermilk poured for them.

Chip was lifting his glass to his lips when he paused suddenly and looked over at Burke. "Hey, mister, no hard feelings, all right? In fact, I'll drink to you and your pards."

Burke looked surprised as he turned toward Chip. "Really?"

"Hell, no." Chip took a fast step to take him closer and flung the contents of his glass right in Seamus Burke's face.

CHAPTER 18

Brice Rogers was a block away when he heard the commotion from Blaise Warfield's saloon. Earlier in the evening, he had thought about stopping in there for a beer, but he'd decided against it. He figured he'd been spending too much time in Blaise's Place, even if it was nice enough for a saloon. And Miss Warfield was pleasant company, no doubt about that.

She'd been flirting with him, and he had been too receptive to it. He was just using it as a distraction to keep his mind off the problem of what to do about Denny Jensen.

So he had decided he would stop by Monte Carson's office and chew the fat with the local lawman.

The angry shouts couldn't be ignored, though. Brice turned the corner from the main street and hurried toward Big Rock's newest saloon. The faint catch in his side reminded him that he had been shot not all that long ago. The wound was fully healed, but it still twinged a little if he moved wrong or put too much of a strain on it.

He couldn't worry about that now, he told himself. As a lawman, he had a duty to keep the peace—and it sounded like Blaise's Place was anything but peaceful.

As he approached, a man came crashing out the batwings, going backward fast. He had been either hit hard enough to knock him through the entrance or thrown out the door. Unable to stop himself or catch his balance, he reached the edge of the boardwalk and fell into the street, landing hard on his back. He was dressed like a cowboy, but that was all Brice could tell about him in the light that spilled through the saloon's windows and entrance.

The man lifted his head and shook it like he was trying to clear the cobwebs from it, so maybe he wasn't hurt too badly.

Brice rushed past without paying any more attention to him and thrust the batwings aside.

As he stepped into the saloon, from the corner of his eye he spotted something flying through the air toward him. He ducked quickly as a chair flew over his head and struck the wall next to the door, bouncing off and clattering away.

Brice saw a knot of men slugging at each other in front of the bar. He put a hand on his gun, intending to break up the brawl before it did too much damage.

Before he could pull the iron, one of the combatants caught a wildly swung fist on the jaw. The blow spun him around and sent him reeling toward Brice. The man's eyes didn't focus for a second, then his vision cleared and he realized somebody was standing in front of him.

He howled a curse and aimed a roundhouse blow at the deputy marshal's head.

Brice barely took in the fact that the man attacking him wore canvas trousers, a flannel shirt, and laced-up work boots, and the thought flashed through his mind that the man was a miner, probably one of Conrad Morgan's crew.

Ducking, Brice let the knobby-knuckled fist sweep through the air above his head, missing by no more than a couple of inches. The man's momentum carried him forward into the hard left that Brice hooked into his belly. As the punch made the man double over and hot breath laden with whiskey fumes gusted from his mouth, Brice tagged him on the jaw with a right cross.

The man's head jerked to the side, and his knees buckled. Brice stepped back quickly to let him fall to the sawdust-littered floor, out cold.

The battle continued, four miners against three cowboys. As Brice watched, one of the miners crashed an empty bottle over a grizzled cowboy's head. The puncher tried to catch himself on the bar, but his grip failed him and he slid down it.

That made the odds four against two. One of the cowboys was young and wiry but didn't have much size to him. He and his companion didn't stand a chance against the burly miners. Brice reached for his gun again, knowing he needed to put a stop to the fight before someone was badly hurt or even killed.

Before Brice could draw the Colt, Blaise reached down to a shelf under the hardwood and pulled out a double-barreled shotgun. The barrels had been cut off to about half their normal length, which meant the weapon would be a real flesh-shredder at close range.

"Stop it!" she called, her slightly husky voice clear and powerful even over the commotion. "I'll shoot!"

"Look out, Seamus!" exclaimed one of the miners. "The saloon gal's got a scattergun!"

The tall, brawny, redheaded miner swung around. He was Seamus Burke, the foreman of Morgan's crew. Brice had seen the man and heard the name, although they hadn't actually met.

Burke lunged toward the bar and reached out as if he intended to take the shotgun away from Blaise. As she lifted the weapon to her shoulder and thumbed back both hammers, he stopped short like he'd run into an invisible wall.

Staring down the twin barrels of a cocked shotgun from two feet away would have that effect on most men.

"Take it easy, lass," Burke choked out. "Don't get too nervous there."

Everybody else had stopped fighting to watch the potentially deadly confrontation.

"I'm not the least bit nervous," said Blaise. "I have no reason to be. If I put a little more

155

pressure on these triggers, it's *your* head that will be blown off, not mine."

"You don't want to be doing that."

"No, I don't," she agreed. "It would make an unholy mess in here, and as much time and energy as I've put into cleaning the place already, I'd hate to have to do it again. But I will before I let your stupid battle do a lot of damage in here."

"I . . . I don't think there's been any real damage so far—"

"He's right about that," Brice said as he drew his gun and covered the miners and cowboys from the other side. "Looks like only one chair got thrown, and it didn't break when it hit the wall. You might need to touch up the paint a little."

Blaise glanced toward him. "Are you taking charge of these ruffians, Marshal?" she asked.

Brice saw gratitude in her eyes. "I'll cover them until Sheriff Carson gets here. I imagine he and his deputies will be along soon. Somebody's bound to have reported this fight to them by now."

Burke looked over his shoulder. "We're going to jail?"

"Don't you think you ought to?" Blaise said.

"Blast it, no, I don't!" Burke pointed at the young cowboy who was still on his feet. "He's the one who started it by throwin' that drink in my face!"

"You had it comin'," the cowhand said

breathlessly. "This is cattle country. We don't need a bunch of miners muckin' up the valley."

"You'd stand in the way of progress for some mangy cows?" Burke demanded.

"Both of you rein it in," Brice ordered. "Maybe Miss Warfield will ask the sheriff not to lock you up, providing you pay for the damage that's been done already and promise not to start any more ruckuses in here."

Blaise finally lowered the shotgun, but she kept it pointing in Seamus Burke's general direction. "That sounds reasonable. You broke a couple of bottles and nicked the paint on the wall. I'd say . . . five dollars ought to cover it."

"Five dollars!" Burke said. "Why, that's five times as much as—"

"You heard the lady," Brice interrupted. "If you ask me, you'll be getting off easy. The justice of the peace might lock you up for a week, or fine you twenty dollars, or both, for causing such a commotion." He gestured with the barrel of his gun. "Put the money on the bar there. And I want *all* of you to pitch in."

Grumbling, the miners and the cowboys dug out coins and rattled them on the hardwood until Blaise nodded and said, "That's good."

"All right," said Brice. "All of you get out. And don't come back tonight."

One of the miners asked, "Are you kickin' us out for good, Miss Blaise?"

She shook her head. "No, you'll be welcome back here in the future . . . as long as you don't start any more trouble."

"It wasn't us," Burke began. "It was that no-good—"

"Best get going while you still can," advised Brice. "Sheriff Carson might not be as agreeable about brawls in his town. You cowboys head out first, since it's one of yours who got knocked out into the street. Pick him up, put him on his horse, and head back to whatever spread you ride for."

Muttering, the two cowboys still standing helped the groggy older one to his feet, and they all went out of the saloon. A couple of minutes later, Brice heard hoofbeats outside.

"All right," he said to Burke and the other miners. "Load up that wagon you brought into town and move on."

Growling something that sounded like a curse but wasn't really audible, Burke led the others from the saloon, including the man Brice had knocked down when he first came in. Brice waited until they were gone before he pouched his iron.

Blaise had set the shotgun on the bar by that time.

He walked over to her, nodded to the double-barreled weapon, and asked, "Would you have really blown his head off?"

"I'm glad he didn't force us to find out."

Brice nodded. He was glad, too. He wouldn't have wanted Blaise to have to live with the fact that she'd killed a man.

She turned to the bartender. "Hank, bring Marshal Rogers a beer."

Brice started to say that wasn't necessary, then changed his mind and accepted the foamy mug that Hank Lawdermilk put in front of him. He'd exerted himself enough in the brief clash with the miner that the beer tasted good going down.

"Come sit with me, Marshal," Blaise invited. She gestured toward a table in the back of the room.

Brice had seen her sitting there on previous occasions, but she hadn't asked him to join her. "Don't mind if I do," he said honestly as he picked up the mug of beer and carried it over to the table, admiring the sway of Blaise's hips as he followed her.

They had been sitting there for a few minutes, chatting while Brice sipped his beer, when Sheriff Monte Carson pushed the batwings aside and came into the saloon. He spotted Brice and Blaise right away and headed toward the table.

"I heard there was some trouble here a while ago, Miss Warfield," the sheriff said as he paused beside the table and thumbed back his hat. "Sorry I didn't get here until now." He glanced around. "Looks like the fracas is over, though."

"It didn't really amount to that much, Sheriff,"

159

Blaise said. "Marshal Rogers and I were able to settle things down." She smiled sweetly. "We persuaded the men involved to be reasonable."

Nothing was much more persuasive than the yawning barrels of a shotgun. Maybe sometime Brice would tell Monte what had really happened. It was enough for the sheriff to know that things had been taken care of.

"Not too much damage, I hope?"

Blaise shook her head. "No. And the men involved were willing to chip in and cover the expense."

"Uh-huh. Well, I'm glad of that. I was handling some trouble at the Brown Dirt Cowboy. A sore loser at the poker table accused one of Emmett Brown's dealers of being a sharper. Some blood got spilled, but nobody died."

"Thank goodness," Blaise said.

"Anyway," Monte said, "you were here to take care of things, weren't you, Brice?"

"Just happenstance. Actually, I was on my way to your office when I heard the commotion and came to check it out."

"You were coming to see me on law business?"

Brice shook his head. "Not at all. Just figured on saying howdy, maybe buying you a beer. Might as well be here, I reckon." He waved a hand at one of the empty chairs. "Sit down and join us." For a split second, he thought Blaise didn't look happy about him asking Monte to join them.

But then she smiled brightly and said, "Yes, Sheriff, please do."

"It's been a troublesome enough evening that I don't mind if I do." Monte sat down.

Hank Lawdermilk brought him a beer in response to a signal from Blaise.

The sheriff took a swallow, then licked foam off his upper lip appreciatively. "You serve tasty beer, Miss Warfield. It appears that Blaise's Place has a good chance of being a success, if you keep on like you're going."

"Thank you, Sheriff. The business seems to be finding its customers."

"Those miners who work for Conrad Morgan and Axel Strom," Brice said. "They're getting to be regulars in here."

"There's nothing wrong with that, is there?" murmured Blaise.

"No, not at all," Brice answered. "Does Morgan ever come in?"

"I haven't seen him. Or Mr. Strom."

Brice didn't care where Axel Strom did his drinking. He had to admit, though, it pleased him to know that Conrad Morgan hadn't been showing up on a regular basis. It was none of his business who drank in Blaise's Place, of course . . . but for some reason, he was pleased anyway.

"Here's to plenty of customers and no more ruckuses," he said as he lifted his mug.

"I'll drink to that," the sheriff said.

CHAPTER 19

"When are you going to invite Conrad Morgan out here to have supper with us again?" Sally asked at the dinner table one evening as she, Smoke, and Denny were sitting down to eat. She was looking at Denny when she asked the question.

"What do you mean?" Denny responded. "Why should I be the one to invite him?"

"Well, I thought that since the two of you are both young, it might be better if the invitation came from you."

Denny shook her head. "I don't even know where he's spending his time these days. He and Mr. Strom have several mines operating, don't they? That's what I've heard in town."

Almost a month had passed since the confrontation at the Bluejay Mine. The pumps were still running, but as far as Denny knew, there hadn't been any more trouble other than a brawl in Big Rock between some members of Conrad's crew and a few cowboys who rode for Seth Campbell, including that young hothead Chip Runnels.

That fight had taken place in Blaise Warfield's new saloon. Denny knew it was petty of her, but when she'd heard the gossip about that, she had experienced a small amount of satisfaction, especially when she found out that no one had been hurt seriously.

She had been a little more worried when she heard rumors that Brice Rogers was involved in that battle . . .

Smoke leaned back in his chair, put his napkin in his lap, and said, "Conrad's at the old Spanish Peso Mine. Cal ran into some wagons on the main road the other day, and Conrad was with them. They were hauling in water tanks and pumps to get that mine back in operation. I figure they haven't had time to finish with that chore yet, so he's bound to be there supervising things."

"I don't guess I've ever heard of that one," said Denny.

"It's about a mile up Hammerhead Canyon. It operated for a while after that whole fiasco with Franklin Tilden and Fontana, but it never amounted to much."

Denny knew what her father was talking about. Fontana had been the first settlement in the valley, but it had dwindled away to nothing after Big Rock was founded. Pretty much the whole town was owned by Franklin Tilden, an ambitious, evil man who'd had his eye on controlling not only all the mines in the area but also the railroad. He had failed spectacularly because he had made a fatal mistake.

He had tried to kill Smoke Jensen.

That was all ancient history, having occurred several years before Denny and her brother Louis were born, so she wasn't surprised she had never heard of the Spanish Peso Mine.

"You should ride over there," Sally said.

"Maybe I will," Denny mused. She got a certain amount of satisfaction out of sparring with Conrad Morgan. He had a mocking, ironic humor about him at times, while Brice Rogers was just, well . . . earnest.

Inez brought the food in then, and the Jensens settled down to enjoy their supper. They didn't talk any more about inviting Conrad Morgan to dine with them.

After they had eaten, and Sally had gone to the kitchen to help Inez with the cleaning up, Smoke caught Denny's eye and said, "Come into my study. I want to talk to you for a minute."

"Sure," Denny said. She figured her father wanted to ask her opinion about something, more than likely something to do with the ranch's operation. Smoke had realized that Louis would never be running the Sugarloaf; Denny's brother was smart and tough in his own way but just not cut out for being in charge of a vast, successful ranch. Lately, Smoke had been sharing more of the details with Denny. It was unusual for a woman to be in charge, but it wasn't unheard of.

Anyway, Denny liked to believe that she wasn't an average woman.

"What is it?" she asked when they were both in the study. She casually tucked her hands into the hip pockets of the jeans she wore. "Something wrong?"

"No, not exactly," Smoke said. Equally nonchalant, he propped a hip on a front corner of the desk. "I wanted to talk to you about Conrad Morgan."

That took Denny by surprise, enough so that she took her hands out of her pockets and blurted, "Blast it! Don't tell me you've decided to try your hand at matchmaking, too, Pa!"

Smoke laughed. "Not hardly. Your mother will do a perfectly good job of that, if it ever needs to be done. I just wanted to say that if you do decide to ride up to Hammerhead Canyon and visit the Spanish Peso Mine . . . you'd better be packing that Colt Lightning of yours when you do. And a Winchester. At the very least."

"You think I'd be liable to run into trouble?" Denny asked with a frown.

"I don't know. Cal told me some other things he's heard recently. There have been several scrapes between the miners and the cowboys who work for the spreads around the mines."

"Like the one at the Bluejay that day?"

"That's right. I don't think the overflow and the flooding have been as bad at any of the other mines, so I reckon Conrad's trying to keep a closer eye on those things, but there's been *some* flooding and fouling of creeks, and the hard feelings are growing."

"I haven't heard about any shooting," said Denny with a frown.

"No, neither have I, but it could happen. Like I said right from the start, hydraulic mining is hard on the land, not just where the mine's located but in surrounding areas, too."

"So you're worried I might ride into a gunfight at the Spanish Peso."

Smoke shook his head. "Not really. But it's possible, and I'll feel better if I know you're being careful."

"*And* if you know I'm packing iron."

"That, too," Smoke said, tipping his head to the side in acknowledgment of her comment.

Denny thought about it for a moment, then nodded. "I probably would have worn my Colt anyway, but I'll be sure to now. It's supposed to be a new, peaceful century, though. The Wild West is over, isn't it?"

"Sometimes I feel like as long as there are Jensens around, the Wild West will never really be over," Smoke said.

A couple of days later, Denny saddled the chestnut mare and rode across the valley to Hammerhead Canyon. She knew roughly where it was, although she had never explored the canyon itself.

To get there, she had to cut through the range of a cattleman named Jock Pemberton. The man wasn't Smoke's friend, although as far as Denny knew there had never been any trouble between the two men. It was more a matter that circumstances had never led them to have much to do with each other.

She wasn't worried about riding across Pemberton's range. It wasn't like she was going to cut any fences or foul any water holes. Anyway, she only had to cut across one corner of the man's ranch to reach Hammerhead Canyon.

She had told her mother where she was going before she left the Sugarloaf. At one time, right after Denny and Louis had returned from England to live permanently in Colorado, Sally would have objected to Denny riding across the valley alone. During the past couple of years, however, she had learned that Denny could take care of herself.

And Denny was packing iron, just as Smoke had requested. In addition to the .38 caliber Colt Lightning holstered on her hip, she had an extra handgun, a Colt .45, in one of her saddlebags. And her Winchester carbine was snugged down in its saddle sheath under her left thigh.

She was pretty sure she had reached Pemberton's range when she spotted a long, high, rugged cliff running north and south in front of her, perhaps a half mile away. As she drew closer to it, she saw the dark mouth of a canyon cut into the cliff. She was confident that was her destination.

Within a couple hundred yards of the canyon, three men on horseback rode out of a stand of trees to her right and immediately spurred their horses and galloped to intercept her. Knowing they had seen her, she rode a short distance farther, then reined the chestnut to a stop and waited for them.

The men rode up and halted so that they were arranged in a line between her and the canyon mouth. Dust swirled up from their horses' hooves. Denny saw that they wore range clothes and were a little rougher looking than most cowboys in those parts. Beard stubble darkened their faces and they wore holstered guns, which was a little uncommon for typical punchers.

One of the men edged his horse a little ahead of the others and demanded, "Who in blazes are you, girl, and where do you think you're goin'?"

Denny could have told them she was Smoke Jensen's daughter. That would be enough to make most men in those parts back off, either because they were friends with Smoke—or because they didn't want to risk offending him.

She had a stubborn, contrary streak, though, so she snapped in return, "What business is it of yours?"

"This is Jock Pemberton's range," the man

replied, "and we ride for him. I don't recall hearin' anything about some girl havin' permission to go gallivantin' across the spread."

It was true that she *didn't* have permission, Denny reminded herself, and getting it would have been the proper thing to do. So she shouldn't be acting like she had such a burr under her saddle, and she knew it. "Sorry," she muttered. "I was just heading for Hammerhead Canyon, and this is the straightest way there."

Instead of mollifying the three men, her apology and explanation seemed to make them more tense.

One of the other men nudged his horse forward and said, "You're goin' to that blasted mine?"

Denny's natural orneriness surged up again. "What if I am? Again, what business is it of yours?"

"We have orders to keep folks away from the mine," the spokesman responded. "That includes girls, I reckon."

The third man snickered. "I didn't know gals like this would come out from town. I thought a fella had to go in and visit 'em there."

Denny drew in a sharp breath and squared her shoulders. They thought she was a soiled dove, did they? She was about to blast angry words at them, including a revelation of who she really was, but decided she wasn't going to dignify such a disgusting assumption. She said coldly,

"Get out of my way, or I'll ride around you."

"We've got our orders," the first man repeated. "Nobody goes in or out of Hammerhead Canyon."

Denny yanked the reins a little harder than she meant to as she turned the chestnut to the side, but she was mad. She kneed the horse into motion and started to ride around the trio.

The man closest to her ripped out a curse and lunged his horse forward. He reached for her reins as the two animals almost collided.

Denny backhanded him across the face, hard. He jerked away in surprise and pain and almost toppled out of his saddle, grabbing the horn to keep from doing so.

Denny dug her heels into the chestnut's flanks, and the horse leaped ahead.

"Get that little hellion!" yelled the leader.

Denny knew she had contributed to the flare-up of violence, but she wasn't going to let those men stop her. Their blood was up, and if they grabbed her, there was no telling what they might do. She didn't have any idea why Jock Pemberton had ordered them to block off Hammerhead Canyon, but, that didn't really matter.

She rode hard, trying to get away from them.

Unfortunately, the chestnut, while a good saddle mount with plenty of strength and stamina, didn't possess a lot of quickness. Cow ponies of the sort the men rode could turn on next to nothing and explode into action. Suddenly one of the men loomed up right beside her, crowding her, and she had to veer away from him.

That brought her within reach of the man galloping up on her other side. He leaned over in the saddle and snagged her reins, jerking them out of her hand.

Denny reached for her gun instead and pulled the Lightning from its holster. She figured they would let her go and back off if she fired a shot or two over their heads.

"Watch it!" yelled the man coming up behind them, the one she had struck. "She's got a gun!"

The man on Denny's right crowded in again, grabbed the wrist of her gun hand, and shoved that arm up so roughly that Denny felt a jolt of pain in her shoulder. Her finger clenched involuntarily on the trigger. The Lightning cracked, but the bullet went high in the air.

"C'mere, you wildcat!" the man grated as he tried to drag her out of her saddle.

Denny tried to get away from him, but he was too strong. She couldn't pull her wrist free from his grip. He leaned in and looped his other arm around her waist. She had only an instant to act, or else she would be his prisoner.

She stiffened her left hand, twisted toward him, and jabbed her fingers under his beard-stubbled chin into the hollow of his throat.

She had learned that tactic from a Chinese

man named Wang, who worked for her father's old friend Duff MacCallister, a rancher up in Wyoming. Denny had visited Sky Meadow, Duff's ranch, a couple of times with Smoke, and had learned several defensive techniques from Wang, who, according to Duff, had been a warrior priest as a young man in China.

This one worked very well. The cowboy who had grabbed her gagged and choked as his eyes practically bulged out of their sockets. He let go with the hand holding her wrist and the arm around her waist.

Unfortunately, he had already pulled her more than halfway out of the chestnut's saddle, and when he let go, Denny fell, plummeting to the ground with a startled cry. She landed hard enough to knock the breath out of her lungs, and she was stunned, barely able to lift her head.

When she did, she saw that the man who had been following the other two was practically on top of her, the hooves of his horse slashing at her as he was about to trample over her.

CHAPTER 20

The sudden death looming over her and the resulting jolt of fear racing along Denny's nerves forced her muscles to work. She rolled desperately to her left. Luck was with her.

The cowboy had spotted her in time and was trying to haul his horse aside. Those two things combined to make the flashing hooves miss Denny. The horse thundered past her, only a couple of feet away.

She came to a stop on her belly again. Lifting her head, she saw that the three cowboys had all reined in and were wheeling their mounts back toward her. Sunlight reflected on her gun, which lay on the ground about ten feet away. Panting with the effort, Denny scrambled up and lunged toward the Colt Lightning.

"She's goin' for her gun again," called one of the men.

"No little whore's gonna shoot me!" yelled another. He jerked his revolver from its holster as Denny reached the Colt and scooped it up.

A part of her still realized she wasn't completely in the right. Legally, she was trespassing.

But that didn't give these men the right to gun her down. If she had to shoot one or more of them to protect herself, she was going to do

173

it. That thought flashed through her head as she lifted the gun.

At that moment a rifle cracked somewhere close by and the cowboy who was about to throw down on her yelped in pain and dropped his gun.

Hoofbeats pounded nearby, and a man shouted, "Keep your hands away from those guns!"

Denny kept the Lightning ready as she climbed to her feet. She looked past the three cowboys and saw Conrad Morgan reining his buckskin saddle horse to a stop. He held a Winchester one-handed, and the rifle was steady as he aimed it at Jock Pemberton's men.

"I know you men," Conrad said as he shifted his left hand from the reins to the rifle. "You ride for the Slash P."

"That's right, mister, and this is Mr. Pemberton's range," said the cowboy who had spoken first to Denny. "That means you don't have any right to be pointin' that Winchester at us."

"I don't care who you are or where we are, I won't stand by and allow you to shoot a defenseless woman."

"She ain't defenseless!" said the cowboy who had yelped in pain a moment earlier.

Denny saw blood dripping from his fingers, blood that flowed from a wound on his forearm. The man pointed with his other hand and added, "The little whore's got a gun!"

174

Conrad shifted the Winchester's barrel and lifted the rifle as he said, "You call her that name again, and I'll blow you out of the saddle." His voice was like ice.

"Hold on, mister," the Slash P spokesman said hastily. He held out an empty hand in a conciliatory gesture. "Nobody else needs to get hurt here. You already winged Silas. And you, Silas, keep your blasted mouth shut! Don't you have the sense God gave a goose?"

The wounded cowboy muttered something that Denny couldn't make out, but he looked down at the ground and didn't say anything else.

A faint smile quirked the corners of Conrad's mouth. "You don't know it, Silas, but I just saved your life."

Silas looked up and demanded, "How in blazes do you figure that?"

"That young woman you were insulting and threatening to shoot is Miss Denise Jensen. Her father is Smoke Jensen."

All three cowboys stared at him and turned pale, especially Silas.

"Sm-Smoke Jensen?" he repeated. "You mean she . . . Her pa is . . . But he . . . he's—"

"Yes, he is," said Conrad. "Smoke Jensen is a man you don't want to have angry with you. In fact, even though Miss Jensen appears to be relatively unharmed . . . You *are* all right, Miss Jensen?"

"I'm fine," Denny said tightly. She was grateful for Conrad's help, but at the same time she didn't care for the idea of being in his debt again. *And* he had stolen the satisfaction of telling these proddy hombres that Smoke was her father.

"Even though Miss Jensen is unharmed," Conrad went on, "if I tell Smoke what happened here, he's liable to be on your trail anyway."

The leader of the trio shook his head vehemently. "There's no need to do that. Smoke Jensen don't need to know about this." He turned his head to look at Denny. "We're sorry, Miss Jensen. Plumb sorry. Truly."

"Don't grovel," Denny snapped. "My father doesn't fight my battles for me. This is between us."

Conrad said, "Are you sure that's the way you want it?"

"It is," Denny said.

The three cowboys looked a little relieved, even Silas.

But then Denny went on. "I want to know why these men tried to stop me from riding to Hammerhead Canyon."

Conrad's smile widened. "Were you coming to see me?"

"As a matter of fact, I was."

"I'm glad to hear it. You're always welcome." His features hardened again as he looked at the three Slash P punchers. "I received reports that some of Pemberton's men turned back a couple of wagons with supplies bound for the Spanish Peso Mine. Is that true?"

"The boss said we was to keep anybody from goin' in or out of that canyon," the spokesman answered in a surly voice. "This is Slash P range. It's up to him who has permission to cross it."

"That's true, but my men *have* permission. That was part of the deal I struck with Pemberton when I bought the Spanish Peso."

The spokesman shook his head. "Mr. Pemberton never owned that mine. You didn't buy it from him."

"No, but I made a separate deal with him paying for right-of-way through his land. You didn't know that, did you?"

"He never told us nothin' about that," the spokesman replied with a frown. "Just said for us to stop folks goin' in and out of the canyon. Reckon he, uh, must've changed his mind about the deal."

"I'll have to have a talk with your employer about that. In the meantime, I can show you the contract if you'd like, so you can see for yourself that by stopping people headed for the Spanish Peso, you're the ones who are in the wrong."

"You take that up with the boss. We're cowboys. We don't deal with contracts and suchlike."

Conrad nodded. "Fine. Then you'll have no objection to Miss Jensen riding on into the canyon with me?"

"Nope. And, uh, miss, again, we're sorry for the misunderstandin'."

Denny holstered her Colt and nodded.

"Next time, don't jump to conclusions about what sort of woman you're talking to," she told them. "In fact, maybe you'd better just assume she's respectable and conduct yourselves accordingly."

"Yes'm, that's good advice." The spokesman turned his horse and jerked his head at the other two. "Come on. Let's get back to the ranch. Silas, you need that arm tied up."

"I know," Silas said miserably. "It hurts like the dickens."

Denny watched the three of them ride off. Conrad slid his rifle back in its saddle sheath, then turned the buckskin and retrieved Denny's mount. The chestnut had stopped about fifty yards away and was cropping contentedly at some grass.

"I'm obliged to you," Denny said when Conrad rode back up, leading the horse. She took the reins when he held them out to her.

"I'm just glad I was already heading in this direction when I heard that shot. I might not have been able to get here in time, otherwise."

Denny swung up into the saddle and said, "They weren't going to shoot me."

"How do you know that? Silas certainly looked ready to blaze away."

"Because I would have shot him first," Denny

178

said. "You saw what happened in Big Rock, that day when you first came into town."

"That's true. You do seem to be quite skilled with a handgun. Of course, I wouldn't expect any less from one of Smoke Jensen's offspring."

Denny laughed. "You'd be a mite disappointed by my brother Louis, then. He's not much of a gun handler."

"I'm sure he has other abilities," Conrad said as they started riding toward the canyon mouth.

"He does. He's smart as a whip, and he's studying the law right now. When he comes back home, I expect he'll be the best lawyer in these parts."

"Does he plan to open a practice in Big Rock?"

"That's the idea," Denny said.

"I'll bear that in mind. I very well may need a good local attorney one of these days, since I plan to have business interests in this area for the foreseeable future."

Denny changed the subject. "That was a pretty impressive shot you made, winging that cowboy like that. You must be as good a hand with a rifle as you are with a revolver."

Conrad laughed out loud. "I probably shouldn't admit this, but there was a certain amount of luck in that shot. Actually, I was trying to do more than wound the man."

Denny looked over at him sharply. "You were trying to kill him?"

"He was pointing a gun at you," Conrad said with a shrug.

Denny was silent for a long moment, then said, "Some folks might have called that murder. I didn't have permission to be on Pemberton's range. And I drew and fired first. That was the shot you heard."

"I don't care," Conrad said. "I would have dealt with whatever the legal results were. I still wasn't going to let him hurt you."

Denny was silent again. She had heard the seriousness in Conrad's voice. She meant enough to him that he'd been willing to risk getting in trouble with the law. But would he have done the same for any woman . . . ?

Such as Blaise Warfield?

Denny put thoughts of Blaise out of her head. "You said you were already on your way out of the canyon. Where were you headed?"

"To do deliberately what you accomplished inadvertently. I wanted to draw out the guards Pemberton posted, so I could ask them why they stopped my supply wagons."

"If they stopped the wagons, how did you find out about it?"

"The drivers went back to Big Rock, where one of them got a saddle horse and rode the long way around to the far end of the canyon. There's enough of a trail that he was able to reach the mine that way and report to me what had happened, but wagons can't make it in over that trail. It's rough enough for a man on horseback."

"Then helping me interrupted the errand you were on."

Conrad shook his head. "Not really. The fear of your father those cowboys have gave me the leverage I needed to get answers out of them. I know now that Jock Pemberton has reneged on the deal I made with him. What I don't know is why, and I would have had to ask Pemberton about that, anyway." He shrugged again. "That can wait, though. I'd rather visit with you first."

"I don't want to be a bother—"

"No bother." He smiled over at her. "In case you haven't figured it out already, Denny, I enjoy spending time with you."

"And I enjoy spending time with you," she answered. That wasn't the coy sort of response that a lady should give a gentleman who had just said something flattering, but Denny wasn't what anybody would call coy by nature.

They rode up the canyon in companionable silence for several minutes. It was about a quarter of a mile wide, grassy and dotted with scrubby trees, with tall, sheer, rocky walls on both sides. There were no sharp bends, but it curved fairly often and they had just ridden around one of those curves when they came in sight of the camp and the mouth of the old mine tunnel to the left ahead of them.

CHAPTER 21

The tents and the equipment were identical to what Denny had seen at the Bluejay Mine on the other side of the valley. The pump wasn't running, so she figured they didn't have everything hooked up yet.

"Is Mr. Strom working here?" she asked.

"No, he's at one of the other properties. Seamus Burke is experienced enough to supervise the setup here, although Axel will inspect everything before we actually start operating the equipment."

"How are you going to run a sluice in here? You don't have a slope. The canyon floor's pretty much flat."

Conrad smiled. "You have a keen mind to think of that."

"I don't know how keen it is, but I like to think I have a practical streak."

"Since we don't have a natural slope, we'll build one. That's another thing that will require more time before this mine starts working again. We'll elevate one end of the sluice on a framework of timbers, and it'll lower gradually as it runs along the canyon."

"What about the water flow?"

"It'll be directed into a small side canyon where it won't cause problems for anyone."

Denny nodded. "Sounds like you've got it all thought out."

"That's the idea. We really don't want to stir up any trouble."

Denny hesitated, then said, "But from what I've heard, there's been trouble anyway, whether you intended it or not."

Conrad reined in and looked over at her, solemn again. "What have you heard?"

"There was a fight in town between some of your men and those cowboys from Mr. Campbell's ranch. No one was badly hurt, according to what Sheriff Carson told us . . . but they could have been."

Conrad nodded. "That's true. The fight happened in Miss Warfield's new saloon. When I heard about it, I rode in to make sure all the damages were taken care of."

"You did, did you?" asked Denny coolly.

"It was my responsibility, since members of my crew were involved."

Denny didn't press him for any more details on that. "We've heard other things about how the miners have clashed with cowboys from the spreads around here."

"Nothing serious," Conrad said, waving a hand in dismissal. Despite his words and gesture, Denny thought she saw a trace of worry lurking in his eyes. "Any time something new comes along, there's going to be a little resistance from people who are used to doing things a different way. We shouldn't let that stand in the way of progress, though."

"What some folks call progress, other folks see as ruining their livelihoods . . . and their lives."

"I suppose that's one reason the history books have so many wars in them."

"Probably," Denny agreed, "but we don't want a war in this valley."

"I assure you, neither do I." Conrad lifted his reins and went on. "Now, why don't I show you around?"

"That's fine." Denny hadn't come to debate history—or anything else—with Conrad Morgan.

Having seen the setup at the Bluejay Mine, she didn't really witness anything new at the Spanish Peso other than the difference in terrain that meant the sluice box had to be built in a different manner. The workers were just getting started on it, erecting the framework on which the sluice's upper end would rest. Conrad led her on up the canyon to the smaller side canyon where the water from the box would wind up.

"We'll angle the sluice's course here so that the water will flow into the canyon," he explained. "If we need to, we can set up an overflow tank here and use a smaller pump and a hose to direct the water even farther up in there. And if it becomes necessary, we'll erect a dam across the entrance and let that canyon fill up with water.

There's nothing up there but brush and rocks, so it won't hurt anything if it's flooded. I don't think it'll come to that, though. There are enough cracks in the rock for the water to drain off."

"I don't see how anybody could get upset about that," Denny commented.

"I certainly hope not." Conrad thumbed his hat back and rested his hands on the saddle horn. "Is there anything else you'd like to see?"

"No, I think you've given me a pretty good tour. But that's not the real reason I rode over here."

Conrad's eyebrows rose. "Oh? Then why did you come, if you don't mind me asking? Not that *I* mind you visiting for whatever reason, of course."

"My mother wanted me to invite you to our house for supper again."

"Your mother," Conrad repeated.

"That's right." Denny hesitated, then added, "And it's all right with me, too."

"In that case, I'd be happy to accept. How's tomorrow evening?"

"That'll be fine," Denny told him. She had checked with her mother before leaving the Sugarloaf, to make sure which evenings Sally considered acceptable.

They rode back toward the camp.

As they approached, Denny heard the swift rataplan of hoofbeats coming up Hammerhead

Canyon toward the Spanish Peso. "Somebody's in a hurry," she said. "That usually means trouble."

"I was just thinking the same thing," Conrad said with a look of concern on his face. "I'll go see if something's wrong. Maybe you'd better stay back—"

"You ought to know better than that by now!" Denny called over her shoulder to him as she heeled her chestnut into a run that carried her out ahead of him.

Conrad caught up to her before they reached the camp, so they rode in side by side.

The rapid hoofbeats they had heard earlier had come to a stop, but it wasn't hard to guess where they had come from. A man sat on a lathered horse in front of the large tent that would serve as the headquarters for the Spanish Peso's operation. Several members of the crew gathered around him. The air was full of questions as Conrad and Denny rode up, but the men fell silent at the arrival of their boss.

"What's going on here?" asked Conrad. "Dabney, what are you doing here? You're supposed to be working on the other side of the valley at the Bluejay."

The newcomer wore the rough clothes of a miner. He shifted uncomfortably in the saddle, indicating that he wasn't used to riding as hard as he had to in order to get there in a hurry. "There's trouble over there, Mr. Morgan. Bad trouble."

Conrad's face was like stone. "What is it?"

"The retaining wall on that overflow pond gave out entirely. The whole mess flooded down onto the range and wound up in the creek that runs through there. When those cowboys found out about it, they came chargin' up to the mine . . . and they came shootin'."

Grim trenches appeared in Conrad's cheeks. "Has anybody been hurt?"

Dabney said, "I honestly don't know. When those punchers galloped in and started blazin' away without any warning, all the boys jumped for cover. Some of 'em made it into the mine, while others hunkered down behind the equipment. We've got a few guns over there, so they tried to fight back." The man sleeved sweat off his forehead. "I happened to be down by the corrals to start with, so I threw a saddle on a horse and got out of there as fast as I could. I wasn't tryin' to run away, you understand. I figured the best thing to do was to fetch you."

"Nobody tried to get word to Mr. Strom?"

"I was the only one who got away," said Dabney, "and I thought I'd better find you."

Conrad nodded. "How long ago did all this happen?"

"The pond flooded sometime durin' the night. We didn't find it until first thing this mornin'.

187

Before we could even try to do anything about it, those kill-crazy cowboys showed up. That was about an hour ago. I wasn't completely sure where this mine was, but I was lucky enough to find it pretty quick."

"All right. Get down and rest yourself and that horse." Conrad turned his buckskin.

"What are you going to do?" Denny asked him.

"Get over there and try to settle things down before anybody gets killed." He added bleakly, "If that hasn't happened already."

"I'm coming with you."

Conrad glanced at her. "No, you're—"

"Listen to me," Denny said. "I know those cowboys a lot better than you do. At least, I know the type of men they are. And they'll just regard you as one of the enemy, while I'm Smoke Jensen's daughter. I hate to keep trading on that fact, but it might be useful in this situation."

Conrad studied her for a second, then jerked his head in a nod. "You're right about that. Come on." As he heeled his horse into motion, he added, "I'm obliged to you for your help, Denny."

"Save your thanks until we see if we can stop those fools from killing each other," she said as she urged her horse alongside his.

By the time they would reach the Bluejay Mine, at least two hours would have passed since the trouble started, Denny reflected as she and

Conrad pushed their mounts at a southwestward angle across the valley. They kept moving fast but tried not to wear the horses out.

With that much time passing, there was a good chance the shooting would be over when they got there. On the other hand, if the miners had been able to take cover, the attacking punchers might have settled down into a siege.

That was the best chance she and Conrad had for ending it without too much bloodshed.

For that reason, Denny was relieved when she heard the distant crackle of gunfire. "They're still at it. Maybe nobody's been killed yet."

"I hope so. If there are deaths to avenge on either side, it'll be just that much harder to get things settled down."

Denny looked over at her companion. "Maybe you shouldn't be doing what you're doing. Maybe hydraulic mining just doesn't mix with cattle country."

"It can if it's done properly," he insisted.

"Yeah, but that partner of yours seems to believe that doing it properly means making as much money as possible, and everybody else can go hang."

"I didn't know you studied mining and engineering in Europe," Conrad shot back at her with a chill in his voice.

"I didn't." Denny's reply was a little icy, too. "But I've got a practical streak, like I told you

189

before . . . and I'm a good enough judge of people to know that some folks can't be trusted."

"Like my partner?"

Denny just shrugged.

"And me," Conrad added.

"You said that, not me."

He was silent for a long moment, then said, "Let's just hope we get there in time."

"Same goes for me," Denny snapped.

The shots were louder. Their fairly steady rhythm told Denny that it wasn't an all-out gunfight going on. From the sound of it, the siege was still holding. That was good.

They came to the creek where the flood from the collapsed overflow pond had reached. Mud and gravel covered the far bank and had spilled into the stream. The creek was still flowing around the partial dam, but downstream the water was muddy, and the volume was diminished.

"That doesn't look too bad," Conrad said as he paused to study the scene. "We can clean the gravel out of the creek if it doesn't wash away on its own, and the grass will come back on the other side."

"Maybe it will," said Denny, "but it'll take a while, and in the meantime, Mr. Campbell's cows can't graze and drink here."

Conrad waved a hand. "He's got plenty of other range."

"That's not the point. This is *his* range, not yours."

Conrad's mouth had tightened into a grim line. One corner of it quirked in anger, but then he sighed and nodded. "You're right, of course. We've damaged his range, and we'll make it right, whatever that takes."

"What about all the other places in the valley where things like this can go wrong?"

"They haven't so far." Conrad lifted his reins. "Come on. I want to put a stop to this before anybody else gets hurt."

Denny agreed with that. They forded the creek and rode until they reached the wagon trail that climbed to the bench where the mine was located.

They were almost at the top when two men stepped out of the brush alongside the trail and leveled rifles at them.

"Hold it right there!" yelled one of the men. "You ain't goin' any farther!"

CHAPTER 22

Denny recognized one of the men from the previous confrontation at the Bluejay Mine, but she didn't recall his name. As she and Conrad reined in, she moved slightly ahead and lifted a hand. "Hold your fire! We're not here to cause trouble."

The man she had seen before lowered his rifle a little. "Miss Jensen," he said, proving that he recognized her, too, "you'd better get outta here. This ruckus don't have anything to do with you."

"I don't want good men getting hurt. That's plenty of reason for me to be involved."

The other cowboy said, "There ain't any good men gonna get hurt, miss. Just them blasted miners!"

"Listen, you men," Conrad said as he urged his mount forward. "I'm the owner of that mine, so if you have a problem, it's with me, not the men working there. They're just as innocent of wrongdoing as you are for trying to protect the ranch where you work. Both sides need to stop shooting. We can figure out what to do about this."

"There ain't no figurin' it out. You're tryin' to ruin the Bluejay spread! That's plain as day!"

Conrad shook his head. "That's not true. What

happened this morning was just an unfortunate accident. I've seen the creek, and we'll make it right."

The young cowboy Denny had seen before said to his companion, "Maybe we ought to listen to him, Hutch. He's the boss of that bunch."

"Yeah, and because of that, he's lucky I don't blow him out of the saddle!" Hutch responded.

Denny asked sharply, "Does Mr. Campbell know what you're doing? Did he send you up here to attack the mining camp?"

Neither of the cowboys answered right away, and that was answer enough. Denny knew they were acting on their own.

Conrad must have sensed their hesitation, too, because he said, "Come with us and tell your friends to call off the attack. I'll ride to Mr. Campbell's ranch and settle things with him. No one has to get hurt."

Anger and resolve stiffened Hutch's features. "Too late for that!" he yelled. "I saw a couple of my pards get shot already. Somebody's got to pay for that!" He jerked the rifle up and aimed at Conrad, obviously having worked himself up to the point that he could pull the trigger.

Denny drew the Lightning and fired in less than the blink of an eye. The .38 slug struck the ground right at Hutch's feet, kicking up dirt around his legs and making him jump backward. The Winchester in his hands cracked, but the barrel was pointing skyward already and the bullet sailed high, doing no harm. Hutch lost his balance and sat down hard, dropping the rifle.

Denny swung the gun to cover the other cowboy and told him, "Toss that rifle away. Now!"

"Take it easy, Miss Jensen," the man said as he lowered his Winchester. He set it on the ground and stepped away from it, lifting his hands to elbow level to show that he wasn't going to make a try for the weapon.

Conrad had pulled his Winchester from its scabbard. He levered a round into the firing chamber and covered Hutch. "Don't even think about reaching for that rifle," he warned.

Hutch muttered some curses, but he kept his hands well away from the fallen rifle as he climbed to his feet. Conrad motioned with the Winchester for him to step over next to the other cowboy.

"What's your name?" Denny asked that man.

"Denton, ma'am. Jack Denton."

"All right, Mr. Denton. You seem to have some common sense. Where are your horses?"

Denton jerked his head toward the trees. "Tied up over yonder."

"Fetch them, and we'll all ride on up to the mine together."

"Blast it, Jack—" Hutch began.

"She could have drilled you through the heart,

and you know it," Denton interrupted him. "She's Smoke Jensen's daughter. Just be glad you ain't dead right now."

Hutch muttered some more but did look relieved that Denny hadn't killed him.

"Unbuckle that gunbelt before you go and leave it here," Conrad told Denton. "You, too, mister."

Both cowboys unbuckled their gunbelts and set them aside. Denton went into the trees and returned a minute later leading two saddle horses. They mounted up, and with Denny and Conrad following them, guns drawn, they rode up onto the bench and headed for the mining camp where shots still blasted up ahead.

Conrad looked over at Denny and said, "I really do wish you would stay back. Wild shots are coming this direction, and one of them could hit you."

"That's true for you, too," she replied. "I'll take my chances."

Conrad looked like he wanted to argue more, but after a second he nodded as if starting to realize that arguing with Denny Jensen was a waste of time.

Riding closer, they could see that the Bluejay hands had taken cover in clumps of brush and behind wagons and mining equipment. Thin, drifting clouds of powder smoke marked their location.

On the other side, some of the miners had used

the big water tank and pump as shelter, and some were inside the tunnel. A few shots came from those places, as well, although clearly the miners were outgunned.

With all the gunfire, the men might not have noticed the shots fired by Denny and Hutch. None of them seemed to be paying attention to the approaching riders.

Conrad said, "Denton, call out to your friends and tell them to hold their fire."

"The miners are still shootin' at them," Denton objected.

"If they keep their heads down, they should be all right. I'll get my men to stop, too, but they probably will as soon as the others hold their fire."

Denton looked dubious, but he reined in and raised his hands to cup them around his mouth. He shouted, "Hold your fire! Hey, Bluejay, hold your fire! Stop shootin'!"

The reports dwindled, then halted.

Conrad raised his voice and called, "You men at the mine! Hold your fire! This is Conrad Morgan! Hold your fire!"

Silence that echoed from all the gun-thunder fell over the bench. After a moment, one of the cowboys yelled, "Jack, Hutch, what in blazes is this? You're supposed to be standin' guard!"

"These two got the drop on us," Hutch answered with a surly scowl. "That yellow-haired witch—"

"Best tread lightly, Hutch," Denton broke in. "You know who the gal is."

Denny laughed humorlessly. "Don't let that stop you if you've got something to say, Hutch."

"No, ma'am," the cowboy replied through clenched teeth. "I got nothin' to say."

Conrad told them, "Move on closer, but don't get in any hurry."

As the riders approached, several of the Bluejay punchers stepped out from the places where they had taken cover. They held their guns ready, but they looked like they were willing to listen, rather than fight.

Without taking his eyes off the cowboys, Conrad said to Denny, "Will you be all right with this bunch? I'd like to check on my men."

"Don't worry about me," Denny said. "They're not going to try anything."

"Because they know you're Smoke Jensen's daughter?"

"Because they know I'll shoot their ears off if they do."

Conrad chuckled and sounded genuinely amused. He didn't say anything else as he rode around Denton and Hutch and headed toward the mine.

One of the Bluejay punchers, a grizzled older man, frowned at Denny and said, "Your pa's a cattleman, girl, and has been for more 'n twenty years. Why are you throwin' in with these dang miners? Didn't Smoke teach you nothin'?"

Another man said, "I heard she spent most of her time in *Europe*." The way he said it, the name must have tasted pretty bad in his mouth.

"My pa taught me just fine," Denny snapped, "and I'm not throwing in with anybody yet. I just don't want to see anybody getting killed for no good reason . . . even muleheaded hombres like you."

"We got a good reason," declared the old cowboy. "We ride for the brand, and these mud muckin' sons o' perdition are foulin' up Bluejay water and range! Only thing worse they could do is start stealin' our cows!"

Hutch growled, "Don't give 'em any ideas, Linc."

Denny said, "Call all your men in. I want you where I can keep an eye on you."

Linc narrowed his eyes at her. "You know there's only one o' you, girlie, and nearly a dozen of us. You're outnumbered."

"And I have five rounds in this Colt. That means if you crowd me, there'll be five less of you. You feel like taking your chances on *those* odds?"

The man looked intently at her for a couple of long seconds, then grinned. "Doggone if I don't think you mean it."

"You'd better believe I mean it."

He looked around, waved an arm, and called, "All right, boys, gather up here, and pouch those irons. Looks like the fracas is over."

"Has anybody been hurt?" asked Denny.

"A couple of our fellas got grazed, but nothin' serious." The old cowboy made a contemptuous sound. "Those fellas are miners. They got hams for hands and sausages for fingers. They ain't made for shootin'. Never seen a miner yet who could hit the wall of a barn with a gun—from the inside!"

Denny let that pass, and although she kept most of her attention focused on the ranch hands, from time to time she let her gaze stray to the mine for a second. She saw some of the men gather around Conrad when he rode up. He dismounted, talked to them for a few moments, and then strode inside the tunnel.

When he came back out after several minutes, he had his arm around the waist of an obviously wounded miner, supporting him on one side while another man held him up on the other side. The injured man's arms were around the shoulders of the ones assisting him.

Conrad and the other man took the wounded miner to a tent and helped him inside. Conrad came back out and walked toward Denny and the Bluejay cowboys.

"How badly is that man hurt?" she asked him.

"Bad enough, but I think there's a good chance he'll live. He was shot through the body. With any luck, the bullet missed any major organs. He's lost a considerable amount of blood, though. One of the men has some experience at patching up bullet wounds. He's going to do the best he can for now, then they'll make the wounded man as comfortable as possible in a wagon and take him to Big Rock so he can get proper medical attention."

Conrad turned to look at Seth Campbell's cowboys. His eyes were like chips of ice. "I want you to know that if that man dies, I'm going to consider it murder and act accordingly. My men told me you just rode up and opened fire without giving them any warning."

Hutch said, "But you don't care if you murder our ranch!"

"What happened was an accident."

Denny could tell that Conrad barely had his temper under control.

"I told you that before. I regret it, I take responsibility for it, and I intend to make it good. But that accident was no excuse for a savage attack on my men. *They're* not responsible for what happened."

"So what you're sayin'," grated Hutch, "is that next time we need to come after *you*. Hell, maybe we shouldn't wait until next time."

"If you feel like pushing your luck, go ahead," said Conrad.

"I don't have a gun. You made us throw ours away, remember?"

"I'm sure you can borrow a gun from one of your friends."

Conrad's voice was a lazy drawl, but Denny heard the menace in it. She saw the fires burning in his eyes, too, and in that moment, she knew she had gotten Conrad Morgan all wrong. He was handsome and easygoing, with a quick smile and sense of humor, but underneath all that was the cold steel of a gunfighter, a man who could kill in the blink of an eye, without a split second of hesitation, if he was pushed.

She knew that look. She had seen it in her own father, her uncles Luke and Matt, her cousins Ace and Chance, and in men such as Monte Carson and Pearlie and Louis Longmont. Men who knew what it was like to live by the gun.

At times she had looked within and seen it in herself, too. It wasn't something limited to the male of the species. Some women could be just as deadly.

The old cowboy called Linc and Jack Denton knew that Hutch was treading on dangerous ground.

Denton put a hand on the cowboy's arm and said, "You better let this go, Hutch."

"He's not even wearin' a gun," Hutch blustered. "He's just got that rifle. He's a big man as long as he's holdin' it, but I ain't afraid of him."

"If you're worried about this rifle, we can take of that." Conrad stepped over to his buckskin and shoved the Winchester back in its saddle sheath. As he turned toward Hutch, he went on. "We can either borrow some handguns, or we can settle this hand to hand—"

Hutch piled out of the saddle in a diving tackle, catching Conrad around the waist and driving him into the ground with terrific force.

CHAPTER 23

Denny winced at the savage, treacherous attack. Hutch was bigger and weighed more than Conrad. Crashing to the ground with Hutch on top of him could have broken Conrad's ribs or other bones.

He seemed to be uninjured, though, as he twisted and shot a punch upward into Hutch's face. The blow landed with enough power to knock the cowboy to the side and away from him.

Conrad rolled the other direction, giving himself more room and coming up on one knee. He paused there long enough to rake back the hair that had fallen in his face when his hat flew off. On his feet, he braced himself just in time to meet Hutch's charge when the cowboy surged back up.

Hutch bulled in, throwing wild, looping punches. Conrad ducked and weaved and avoided the fists that whistled toward his head. He held his ground, snapped a right jab that landed squarely on Hutch's nose and rocked his head back, then followed that with a left hook that found the cowboy's jaw and made him stagger a step to his left.

While Hutch was off balance, Conrad hooked a boot toe behind his right knee and jerked that leg out from under him. Hutch went down like a falling tree, landing heavily, and lay there breathing hard for a long moment. Conrad stepped back instead of rushing in.

Hutch pushed himself up on an elbow and shook his head groggily. His nose was swelling, and blood leaked from both nostrils.

Fists still cocked and ready, Conrad said, "You should let that be the end of it."

Hutch growled a curse, said, "Not hardly," and shoved himself back to his feet. He went at Conrad again, but it wasn't a wild, out-of-control rush. He must have figured out that he wasn't going to overpower his opponent with sheer size and strength. His punches were more deliberate, but not lacking in impact.

Conrad's superior quickness still allowed him to avoid most of the blows. However, Hutch was more cunning than he'd appeared at first. He feinted, and Conrad bit on it, putting him in perfect position for Hutch's fist to explode in his face. Conrad flew backward and landed in the dirt.

Denny caught her breath and leaned forward in the saddle as Hutch rushed Conrad again and drew back a leg to kick him. For a second, she thought about shooting the cowboy but knew Conrad would be upset with her for interfering. She kept her finger off the Lightning's trigger.

The kick aimed at Conrad's head never

landed. Conrad recovered just in time to catch the cowboy's foot and heave upward, throwing Hutch over on his back. Conrad scrambled up, dived, and landed on top of him. Digging a knee into Hutch's midsection and pinning him to the ground, Conrad hammered a couple of punches into his already bloody face.

Perhaps realizing that Conrad was about to beat him senseless, Hutch bucked wildly, threw his slightly smaller opponent to the side, and rolled away. He slapped his palms against the ground and tried up push himself upright again. He didn't make it, slumping back onto his belly.

By that time, the rest of the cowboys and most of the miners had gathered and formed a circle around the combatants to shout encouragement. Denny sat just outside that circle on horseback, with Jack Denton near her.

The puncher looked at her and shook his head ruefully. "I'm sorry about this, Miss Jensen. I hope your fella don't get hurt."

"Conrad Morgan isn't *my fella,*" Denny snapped, "and I'm not taking sides in this."

"Well, I appreciate that, anyway," Denton said glumly. "I'm just glad Chip ain't here today. He's even more hotheaded than any of these boys."

That didn't seem possible, but Denny remembered how Chip Runnels had attacked the mining camp a few weeks earlier. It was looking more and more likely that cowboys and miners sharing the valley peacefully might not work out.

Conrad had gotten back to his feet. A bruise was starting to appear on his face where Hutch had landed that powerful punch, and he seemed a little winded. Other than that, he was in much better shape than his opponent. Hutch's face bore a resemblance to raw meat, and he couldn't seem to get his breath.

"Let it go," Conrad advised him again. "It was a good fight. You've nothing to be ashamed of."

"You can just . . . go to blazes," Hutch panted. With a groan of effort, he climbed to his feet and started forward again, but weaved back and forth. When he tried to raise his fists, his arms sagged. He didn't have the strength to hold them up.

"This is over," said Conrad.

"The hell . . . it is!"

Hutch lunged forward and launched a punch. Conrad stepped aside and avoided it easily. Hutch stumbled past him for a couple of steps and then pitched forward. He landed face-first and didn't move again, although his back rose and fell. As silence descended on the bench, the raspy, bubbling sound of air passing through his bloody, broken nose could be heard. He was alive, just out cold.

Conrad looked at the other cowboys and said, "That fight was his choice, and his choice to continue it, as well. But whether you believe it or not, I hope he's all right."

"I believe it," Denton said. "You took it easy on him there at the end, mister. We're obliged to you for that."

A few of the other men muttered agreement with that sentiment. Most of them just glared at Conrad, clearly still hostile.

"All of you go on back to the ranch now," he continued. "Tell Mr. Campbell I'll be riding over there to see him later today to discuss a settlement for the damages, just as soon as I get cleaned up. In the meantime, we'll shut down operations here so as not to add to the problem."

"We'll tell him," Denton said. "I got a hunch that this ain't over, though, Mr. Morgan."

Conrad shook his head. "No, I don't expect that it is."

After the cowboys had lifted a still mostly unconscious Hutch onto his horse, mounted up themselves, and ridden off, Conrad made a quick check on all his men. Despite what the old-timer called Linc had said, it didn't appear that the cowhands were any better shots than the miners. The wounded man was the only one who had been hit.

Heavily bandaged around the middle and groggy from the whiskey that was poured down his throat for medicinal purposes, he had been loaded in a wagon. It was rolling away with one man handling the reins and another man beside him on the seat with a rifle to serve as guard, when three men on horseback topped out from the trail onto the bench and rode toward the camp.

Denny recognized the burly shape and mostly bald head of Axel Strom as he led the trio. He seldom wore a hat, despite his lack of hair. His scalp gleamed in the sun. The other two men wore caps and the rough work clothes of miners.

Strom's face was dark with anger as he rode up and reined in. He barely glanced at Denny, then concentrated his wrath on Conrad. Waving a thick arm, he asked, "Why aren't the pumps running?"

Conrad had picked up his hat and was brushing it off. He took his time putting it on, then said, "I ordered them shut down because of an accident."

"Mechanical failure? Impossible! All the equipment is inspected regularly."

"Structural failure. The retaining wall on that pond gave out and flooded a lot of Campbell's range. Fouled his creek, too."

"So?" Anger made Strom's voice harsh, and his accent came through a little more, so the word sounded like *Zo* to Denny. "It's water and mud and rock. All natural things. It does no lasting harm."

"If we keep it up, though, it'll turn parts of Campbell's ranch into a swamp for as long as the mine's operating, and it might stop that creek from flowing entirely and flood even more of the range."

Strom's brawny shoulders rose and fell. "His cows can eat grass and drink water somewhere else."

The man's callousness and arrogance made Denny's blood run hotter. She said, "That range down below is the best grazing land Mr. Campbell has, and if the creek's cut off, the rest of his spread won't be worth much."

Strom glared at her for a second, then forced an insincere smile onto his face. "Miss Jensen," he began, "you are not a mining engineer—"

"No, but I know what it takes to raise cattle, and your mine is interfering with that."

Strom turned away from her, coldly, dismissively. That put an even bigger burr under her saddle.

"We will build another retaining wall," he said to Conrad, "but in the meantime the pumps should continue to run and the mine should be in operation. Every hour we are shut down is that much gold we do not take out of the mountain."

"We can't build another wall if the water is running through there constantly," Conrad pointed out. "And I'm not going to order that the pumps be restarted if it's just going to make the situation worse."

For a long moment, the two partners looked at each other, their two stares dueling intently.

Then Strom shrugged again. "Of course. I'm only in charge of seeing that the equipment is set up properly and functioning as it should. You are responsible for everything else."

"We'll get the mine back into operation as quickly as we can."

"Certainly." Strom changed the subject by saying, "Some of our men passing by in the valley reported hearing gunshots coming from up here. Is that true?"

"Several of Campbell's men got mad when they saw what had happened and came up here to start a fight, but it's all over now."

"Did they kill any of our workers?"

Denny thought Strom's question sounded like he would expect Campbell to compensate them for the dead men if that were the case.

Conrad said, "No, one man was wounded, that's all. You passed the wagon taking him to the doctor in town when you rode in."

"I see. You will notify the authorities, of course, and have the men who attacked us arrested and jailed?"

"I hadn't thought that far ahead yet. I want to get things settled with Campbell. But yes, I expect there'll have to be a report made."

"But no arrests?"

"I don't know. I'll leave that up to the sheriff."

Strom's face was grim as he said, "You leave too much up to others, my friend. When a man is

210

attacked, he should fight back with every weapon at his disposal."

"I'm trying to do the right thing here—"

"The right thing is to get that gold out of the mountain and deal harshly with anyone who tries to interfere!" Strom yanked his horse around, sawing brutally at the animal's mouth and giving Denny one more reason—not that she needed any more—to dislike him intensely. He jerked his head at the men who had ridden in with him, and they all turned to leave the camp.

"Where's he going?" she asked.

"Back to one of the other properties, I suppose," Conrad said. "Right now, I don't much care."

"And *he* doesn't care about anything except making money."

"Yeah, I'm starting to get that impression, too." Conrad sighed. "But we're partners, so I guess we're stuck with each other, at least for now. Even so, I call the shots when it comes to everything but the equipment, so I'm not going to let Axel stampede me into doing anything I don't want to."

"I hope you can back that up."

Conrad looked over sharply at Denny. "You think I can't?"

"I think Axel Strom is the sort of man who doesn't stop at anything to get what he wants . . . even if it means destroying anybody who gets in his way."

• • •

When Strom and the two miners who had ridden up to the Bluejay camp with him reached the bottom of the trail, the big man reined in and signaled for the others to do likewise. They sat there while Strom dismounted and dug around in his saddlebags until he found a piece of paper and a stub of pencil.

In bold, blunt letters, using his saddle as a desk, he printed a message on the paper and then handed it to one of the men, along with some coins. "Ride to Big Rock and send that message at the telegraph office," he ordered. "Make certain it goes through before you leave."

"Sure, boss," the man replied. "You want me to wait for an answer?"

"No, it may take a while for the message to catch up to the man it's intended for. But he'll get it, and when he does, he'll be here." Axel Strom smiled. "And once he is, a lot of people in this valley will find out that things are going to be very different from then on."

212

CHAPTER 24

Three nights later, five men led horses up the steep trail to the bench where the Bluejay Mine was located. They had ridden part of the way up, then stopped and dismounted so they wouldn't make as much noise while they climbed the rest of the trail.

As they neared the top, one of the figures whispered to the man beside him, "Blast it, Chip, I still say this is a big mistake."

"Jack, you know good and well those varmints will just do something else to ruin things for the old man unless we put a stop to their devilment once and for all."

"I don't know if anything's gonna stop what they're doin' short of blowin' up that mine entirely," Jack Denton said.

The old puncher called Linc grunted and said, "Don't give the boy any ideas."

"By doin' this, they'll see we mean business," Chip Runnels insisted. "That Morgan fella may be a dandy, but I'm thinkin' he ain't a plumb fool. He'll see that it's gonna cost him more money to keep that mine runnin' than he'll ever make out of it, because we ain't ever gonna let them ruin the old man's range without fightin' back."

"Morgan promised he'd clean up the mess and keep it from happenin' again," said Denton.

"Hombres like that will promise anything. They don't care about nobody but their ownselves."

"But he's already been to see Mr. Campbell, and from what the cook overheard 'em sayin', they reached some sort of agreement."

Runnels made a disgusted sound. "That'll last until Morgan breaks his word again. You know it's bound to happen."

"And Morgan fought dirty against me, so whatever we do, the varmint's got it comin'," blustered Hutch, the fourth man in the group.

Linc and the fifth man, a vaquero from down New Mexico way who called himself Polo, knew that claim wasn't true. They had been there for the brutal battle between Hutch and Conrad Morgan. Denton was well aware of the real facts, too. But if Hutch wanted to tell himself that Morgan had fought dirty, they weren't going to waste time and energy arguing with him.

The group stopped just below the bench.

Denton said, "I'm not gonna help you with this loco plan. I only came along to try to talk you out of it."

"Yeah, you made that pretty clear, Jack," said Runnels. "But here's what we'll do. We need somebody to hold the horses. Are you willin' to do that?"

"There's no way I can stop you from goin' ahead?"

"Nope."

Denton sighed. "All right, then, I'll hold the horses."

"And if a ruckus breaks out, you'll ride in leadin' our mounts so we can light a shuck out of there?"

"Yeah, I will," Denton said. "I may not agree with what you're doin', but I won't stand by and do nothin' if you fellas are in trouble."

Runnels clapped a hand on his shoulder. "I knowed you was a good pard, Jack. Everybody, give your reins to Jack."

The others passed the reins over, then untied double-bit axes they had strapped to their saddles.

Denton said, "You don't even know those axes will chop through the hoses."

"Those hoses are made out of canvas," said Runnels. "I saw that much when we were at the camp before. We can chop 'em up, all right. And those big pumps won't be worth a thing without the hoses."

"You're just mad because the boss had you off on another part of the range when that last ruckus happened and you didn't get in on it," Denton said. "That's the only reason you're doin' this."

"No, I'm doin' it because I ride for the brand. We all do." Runnels looked around. "Ain't that right, boys?"

He got an enthusiastic nod from Hutch and slightly more reluctant ones from Linc and Polo. But none of the men put the axes back on their saddles or turned back as Runnels led them on foot toward the camp.

Denton sighed as he watched them disappear into the shadows. If nobody got themselves killed tonight, he was going to be mighty surprised.

A man named Rufus Chandler was the superintendent of Bluejay Mine now that Seamus Burke had moved on to one of the other properties Conrad Morgan and Axel Strom owned. He was an experienced miner who had worked on many different operations during the past twenty years, including a number that had used hydraulic mining techniques.

The pumps and the separating equipment designed by Strom were the best and most efficient Chandler had ever seen. Strom was a hard man to get along with, but he was a top-notch engineer; Chandler had to give him that.

At the moment those pumps were silent. They had been shut down for several days while the men in Chandler's crew built up the earthworks around the overflow pond and braced it with a new retaining wall made of thick logs.

Strom himself had supervised the construction of the first wall, and Chandler hadn't been surprised when it collapsed. In his hurry to get the equipment operative, Strom had cut too many corners on it and should have known that problems were inevitable. Burke should have realized that, too.

Chandler suspected that both men had known perfectly well the wall wouldn't hold up. They were just hoping it would last a while, and in the meantime they would be taking gold out of the mine every day.

That hadn't worked out very well, and now that Chandler was in charge of rebuilding the wall, he was determined to do a much better job of it. Pride in his workmanship, no matter what the job was, wouldn't allow him to do any less.

When the pumps had been running, they operated twenty-four hours a day, but the men couldn't do the construction work in the dark, so they were all in their tents, asleep. It was what Chandler should have been doing—sleeping—but for some reason he was restless tonight.

After tossing and turning in his bedroll for a while, he finally decided he would get up and have a look around the camp. Sometimes seeing for himself that everything was all right settled his mind enough for him to doze off. If that didn't work, he would go to the mess tent, stir up the fire in the stove, and put a pot of coffee on to boil.

A slight chill in the air made him stick his hands in his pockets as he walked around the camp. At that elevation, the nights were cool even during the summer. As he strolled past some of the tents, unexpected sounds drifted to his ears and made him stop to listen.

He couldn't figure out what those sounds were. Somebody was hitting something, but the series of impacts had a muffled quality to them.

One thing he was sure of—the sounds came from the direction of the mine tunnel, and nobody was supposed to be up there. Chandler took his hands out of his pockets and walked quickly in that direction.

The noises got louder as he approached. He saw shapes moving around the big, ungainly pump and the massive water tank. Long dark objects rose and fell, and each time they did, he heard another *chunk!*

Rufus Chandler's eyes got big in the darkness as he realized what he was seeing. The shapes were men using axes to chop up the hoses leading from the water tank and the pump!

"Hey!" he shouted without thinking. "Hey, stop that, you sons of—"

He broke into a run toward the tunnel as the yell erupted from his throat. He never paused to consider the fact that he was alone and unarmed, and several intruders were vandalizing the equipment. All he thought about was the threat to the operation he was in charge of, a threat that had to be stopped as quickly as possible.

Startled curses came to Chandler's ears. One of the men by the equipment dropped his ax and whirled toward the mine superintendent. The realization that he might be rushing straight into danger burst in Chandler's mind, but not in time to prevent what happened next.

A spurt of orange flame ripped the darkness apart. What felt like a sledgehammer struck Chandler's right leg and knocked it out from under him. As he fell, his momentum caused him to tumble forward. He was so stunned that he only vaguely heard the crash of more gunshots.

He had the presence of mind to flatten himself out on the ground, belly down, to make himself a smaller target. Startled shouts came from the direction of the tents as the workers, jolted awake by the gunfire, thrashed out of their bedrolls and stumbled into the night.

"Stay back!" Chandler bellowed at them as he raised his head. "Hunt cover!"

At first, the bullet's impact had numbed his leg. He knew he'd been shot but couldn't really feel it. The pain was starting to well up inside him, and it was bad enough to make him gasp. He reached down to his leg and felt blood soaking into his trousers.

Rapid footsteps slapped the ground nearby. Chandler rolled onto his side and looked around, fearing that the intruders would shoot him again as they ran past him.

But the men were angling off to the right. Hoofbeats pounded somewhere in the darkness.

More attackers, Chandler wondered, or was someone bringing them their horses so they could get away?

Rifles began to crack from the tents. Handguns boomed a ragged return fire from the intruders. The hellish glare of muzzle flashes from both sides lit up the night.

With all that racket going on, Chandler didn't know if anybody would hear him, but he called, "Hey! Somebody in the camp! Come help me! Edison! Richmond! Scott! Somebody!"

A wave of dizziness threatened to engulf him. He forced his muscles to work and dragged himself toward the tents by using his arms and his uninjured leg.

Figures loomed up in front of him, and a man shouted, "Boss! Mr. Chandler! Are you out here?"

"Here!" Chandler responded, and a moment later a couple of men appeared beside him, grasped his arms, and lifted him to his feet. "Careful!" he exclaimed. "The varmints shot me in the leg!"

"Pick him up!" ordered one of the men. "Carry him back to his tent. Careful!" He leaned closer to Chandler. "Which leg is it, boss?"

"The right one," he replied. He had to grit his teeth against the pain as they lifted him and carried him toward the tents. He heard the dwindling sound of running horses and asked, "Did the no-good skunks get away?"

"Yeah, I'm afraid so. I don't know if we winged any of them or not. I sure hope we did!"

"So do I," Chandler said. Then his voice trailed off in a groan. He was barely aware of it when the men gingerly laid him on his cot.

A match rasped to life, and the man who'd struck it held the flame to the wick of a lamp sitting on a small folding table. The wick caught and the yellow light from it spread as the man lowered the lamp's chimney.

Another man knelt beside the cot and used a folding knife to cut away the leg of Chandler's trousers. Chandler gasped as the man probed at the wound with experienced fingers.

"I think it busted the bone, boss," the man reported grimly. "You've lost a lot of blood, too. I'll clean the wound and wrap it up, maybe strap some splints on it to keep it stable, and then we'll need to put you in a wagon and take you to Big Rock so a real doctor can tend to you."

"Bouncing in a wagon . . . is gonna . . . hurt like blazes," Chandler forced out.

"More than likely," agreed the other man. "And because of the damage to the bone, there's a good chance that leg'll be a little shorter than the other one, once it's healed up."

"Meaning I'll never walk normally again," Chandler said bitterly.

"No use gettin' ahead of ourselves, I reckon." The miner looked up. "Bardwell, get me some whiskey. That'll clean out that bullet hole as good as anything else."

"I wouldn't mind . . . having a slug of it . . . to drink, too," panted Chandler.

"I think we can do that."

Chandler had several slugs of whiskey during the next half hour. He was in and out of consciousness from loss of blood and the shock of being shot, but it seemed like every time blessed oblivion claimed him, pain jerked him right back out of it.

Finally, the man who had been patching him up straightened to his feet and declared, "I've done all I can do. A couple of the boys have gone to hitch a team to one of the wagons."

"Thanks," Chandler said in a husky whisper.

Another man pushed aside the flap at the tent's entrance and stepped into the yellow lamplight. He tugged his cap off and said, "Got some news, boss."

"Can't it wait?" asked the amateur medico.

"I think Mr. Chandler's gonna want to know this."

"Go ahead," Chandler managed to say.

"We found out what those damned cowboys were doin' here," the newcomer said. "It looks like they took axes to all the hoses connected to the mining equipment."

"I already . . . figured that out . . . before they . . . shot me," Chandler said. "How bad . . . is the damage?"

"They did a hell of a job on those hoses. Most of 'em are flat-out ruined."

Chandler closed his eyes and sighed. "That means we can't start mining again . . . even when that new retaining wall . . . is finished."

"I reckon not. Not until the hoses are replaced. And it'll take a while for new ones to get here, won't it?"

"Yeah. Maybe . . . weeks." Chandler felt too bad to think very deeply about this development, but he knew one thing that he didn't even have to think about. Axel Strom wouldn't take sabotage lying down. He would strike back at whoever was responsible, and once he figured out exactly who that was . . . Strom would bring hell raining down on them.

Rufus Chandler was sure of that.

CHAPTER 25

By the time the five cowboys got back to the bunkhouse at the Bluejay spread, Polo had passed out from losing so much blood.

"Let's get him inside on his bunk," ordered Linc as the other men swung down from their saddles, except for Jack Denton, who sat his horse close beside Polo's and gripped the vaquero's arm to keep him from falling.

Hutch, Chip Runnels, and Linc reached up to take hold of Polo and lift his unconscious form from the saddle. Because Hutch was the biggest of the bunch, he got his arms under the wiry Polo's shoulders and knees and carried him into the bunkhouse.

A rifle slug had screamed out of the night as they were fleeing from the mining camp and blasted through Polo's torso. In the darkness, the others hadn't been able to see how badly he was hurt. He had insisted that the wound wasn't bad and he could still ride, and so they'd lit a shuck out of there. They didn't slow down except when they had to as they weaved back and forth along the trail down the slope.

By the time they were back out in the valley, headed for home, Polo had been swaying wildly in the saddle. Denton had seen that and grabbed hold to steady him as he called out in alarm to the others.

They paused long enough to discover that the vaquero was hit pretty bad and was only half-conscious. They headed on to the ranch as quickly as they could.

As they stepped back from the bunk and looked down at their friend's pain-twisted features, frozen that way when he'd passed out, bitter curses exploded from Runnels.

"I'll kill 'em," he swore. "I'll kill 'em all!"

The front of Polo's shirt from the middle of his chest down below his belt was dark and sodden with blood. They could see the hole where the bullet had gone in, low on the left side, and blasted through his guts at an angle. The exit wound was around on the right side of his back, a couple of inches higher.

No man could survive a wound like that. It was a miracle that Polo had made it back to the ranch alive.

"I'd better go get the boss." Denton turned toward the door.

Linc gripped his arm. "There's nothin' Mr. Campbell can do for him," the older cowboy said. "Polo's done for. The rest of us gettin' in trouble ain't gonna help him."

Denton stared at him for a second then demanded, "You mean we're just gonna let him die?"

"Ain't any lettin' about it. He's gonna die."

"Linc's right," said Hutch. "There's no sense in the rest of us landin' in more trouble if it won't help Polo . . . and it won't."

Denton looked at Runnels. "Are you goin' along with this, Chip?"

Runnels shrugged and said, "Linc and Hutch are makin' sense, Jack, whether we like it or not."

Denton stared around at the others, then asked, "What do you think we should do?"

"Polo's not hurtin' anymore since he passed out," said Linc. "Once he's crossed the divide, Hutch and me will take him up into the hills and find a good place to lay him to rest. The two of you can stay and clean up, so that it won't look like a wounded man's been in here. After that . . . we keep our mouths shut and go on with our work."

"Like nothin' happened," Denton said scathingly.

"Like nothin' happened." Linc's tone was hard and flat.

"And when the boss asks where Polo is?"

Linc shrugged. "We tell him that Polo decided to ride on."

"Without drawing his time?"

"You know how shiftless Mexicans are," Hutch said.

Denton glared at him and shook his head. "It's a hell of a thing to do. Polo was our pard."

"Sure," said Linc. "But once he's gone, nobody

can prove it was us up there tonight at that mining camp. Morgan and Strom might suspect it, but they can't prove it. Monte Carson's not gonna arrest anybody without proof."

What the others were saying made sense. Denton hated to admit that, but it was true. Slowly, he nodded. "All right. I guess you're right. But until the time comes, we need to make Polo as comfortable as possible—"

"No need to worry about that," Hutch said. "He's gone."

It was true. Polo's eyes had opened in his last seconds, and he stared at the bunkhouse ceiling without seeing it. He had died while the others argued about what to do.

Denton couldn't help but wonder if he had heard them talking about burying him in a lost, lonely grave, up in the hills.

Conrad paced back and forth in the room in the doctor's house where Rufus Chandler sat propped up in bed. Chandler's bullet-broken leg was splinted, wrapped, and stretched in front of him.

Conrad was so furious it took quite an effort to control his anger. "You didn't get a good look at any of them?" he asked as he paused in his stalking.

"I didn't get much of a look at all, let alone a good one," replied Chandler. "And the other men didn't even really see them, just some moving shadows in the dark and a bunch of muzzle flashes. That's what they were aiming at."

"But none of the saboteurs were hit bad enough to keep them from getting away."

Chandler shook his head. "I couldn't say if any of 'em were hit at all, boss."

Conrad sighed. "I know, Rufus, and I know we've already been over this. It's just so blasted frustrating."

Sheriff Monte Carson appeared in the room's open door. He nodded to Conrad and said, "I got word of what happened, Mr. Morgan. Sorry you had trouble up there at your camp."

Conrad turned toward him and snapped, "What do you intend to do about it, Sheriff?"

"I'm here talking to you, aren't I?" Monte responded with an edge in his voice. "I came to get the story from your man here." He nodded toward Chandler.

"I'm afraid I can't tell you much, Sheriff," Chandler said.

For the next few minutes, the mine superintendent went over the events of the previous night, as well as he could.

When Chandler finished, Conrad said, "It must have been those cowboys from Campbell's ranch, the ones who caused the trouble before."

Monte didn't respond to that accusation. Instead, he asked Chandler, "Could you identify any of the men?"

"You mean could I swear to it in a court of law?" Chandler shook his head. "No, sir, I'm afraid I couldn't. I never got anywhere near a good enough look for that."

"But Sheriff—" Conrad began.

Monte held up a hand to stop him. "I'll ride out to the Bluejay and have a talk with Seth Campbell and his punchers," the lawman said. "Maybe if it was them, they'll admit it."

Conrad snorted in disbelief.

"I'll try to do some tracking, too," Monte went on, "but I wouldn't hold out much hope of that turning up any real evidence. You have to understand, Mr. Morgan, in a situation like this, there's not a whole lot I can do."

"And you're friends with all these cattlemen, too."

Monte's expression hardened even more. "I'm going to overlook that because I know you're upset right now. But I do everything in my power to uphold the law, Mr. Morgan. You don't know me very well, but I can give you my word on that."

Conrad glared at him for a couple of seconds, then sighed and nodded. "My apologies, Sheriff. Like you said, I'm upset. One of my men was hurt, and he could have been killed. Several of them could have, the way the bullets were flying around out there. And I don't even know yet how bad the damage to the equipment is. My partner has gone up there to check on that and ought to be back soon."

"Well, I hope it's not too bad and that your man here heals up fine." Monte jerked his head in a curt nod. "I'll be in touch."

The sheriff left.

Chandler said, "When Mr. Strom gets back to town, boss, he's going to tell you the damage is pretty bad. It'll be a week or more, probably more, before we can get the mine in operation again."

"And you'll be laid up for several weeks, Rufus, so it's not your worry right now." Conrad squeezed the man's shoulder. "I'll be taking care of all the medical expenses, and you'll still have a job when you're up and around again, no matter how long that takes."

"I appreciate that, Mr. Morgan. I wish I could have stopped those fellas from raising so much hell."

"I know, Rufus. So do I."

Conrad left the doctor's house, too, after making sure the physician knew he was to spare no expense in taking care of the injured man. He walked up the street to Longmont's, figuring he would get a cup of coffee while he waited for Axel Strom. He had told his partner to meet him there after he finished inspecting the damage at the Bluejay Mine.

The first person he saw when he walked in was Denny Jensen.

She was sitting at a table with Longmont. Both had coffee cups in front of them. Denny spotted Conrad and lifted a hand in a gesture that was both a greeting and an invitation to join them.

Conrad was glad to do that. Even though he was upset, he felt a surge of warmth when he saw Denny, and a certain sense of calm spread through him in her presence.

As he pulled out an empty chair and sat down, Denny said, "I heard what happened at your mine. I'm sorry about the man who was hurt."

"What about the damage to the equipment?" he asked.

"That can be fixed, can't it?"

"I don't know for sure yet. Axel's gone up there to have a look. But I'm sure it can, with enough time and expense. That doesn't excuse the destruction."

"No, it doesn't," Denny agreed. "Whoever was responsible for it needs to be held accountable. I was worried about the injured man."

"He's going to be all right. I'll see to that."

Longmont asked him, "Would you like some coffee?"

"That would be good."

Longmont signaled to a waiter, who brought a cup and filled it from the pot he carried.

Gratefully, Conrad sipped the strong brew and then said, "I suppose what happened is the talk of the town."

231

"It's news," said Longmont, "and most folks are interested."

Conrad looked steadily at him and asked, "Are most folks on my side . . . or the side of the men who attacked my mine?"

"The valley and the town rely on the ranches for most of the business around here. Raising cattle helps everyone. Those mines help only you and your partner."

"We've brought money into the valley and into Big Rock," Conrad objected.

"Yes, you have," Longmont allowed. "But it's not the same. For one thing, cattle will be here forever. Those mines could play out tomorrow."

"Or they might produce for the next ten years."

Longmont shrugged. "Only time will tell, I suppose."

Conrad looked over at Denny and asked, "What do you think? Although I have a hunch I already know the answer."

"I already said that whoever it was shouldn't have attacked your camp," she replied. "Even so, I don't like what your mines have brought to the valley."

"What have they brought?"

"Trouble. Destruction. Bloodshed." Denny shook her head. "It's starting to look like hydraulic mining is going to ruin the range around here. You can't expect people to accept that without fighting back, all so you can get richer."

232

The warmth and calm he had felt when he first came in vanished in the face of her obvious scorn. He said, "There's nothing wrong with hydraulic mining if it's done properly—"

"As long as Axel Strom's in charge of things, it won't be done properly," Denny interrupted him. "Because that costs more money and would cut into Strom's profits. If the man wasn't your partner, you'd be able to see that." She paused. "Unless you're the same way and don't care who gets hurt as long as you rake in plenty of money."

Anger surged up inside Conrad. "I never—" He stopped short as he noticed Louis Longmont looking toward the entrance.

The saloon owner leaned forward a little in his chair, and his hand drifted toward his coat. Conrad saw that and knew it meant Longmont was moving his hand closer to the pistol he carried in a shoulder holster. It was the instinctive reaction of a gunman to a possible threat.

Conrad recognized the gesture because it was the same reaction he had felt, too many times to count.

He turned his head toward the door and saw that Axel Strom had just come in. He wasn't alone. A man Conrad had never seen before was with him.

The stranger was medium height and stocky, with a blunt, unhandsome face. Rusty brown hair showed from under a black hat. He wore a dark

233

suit, a white shirt, and a string tie. A black-butted revolver rode in a holster attached to the gunbelt strapped around his hips.

Conrad glanced at Longmont. "You know that man who just came in with Axel?"

"I do," Longmont said, "and he's a killer."

CHAPTER 26

Denny had noticed Louis Longmont's reaction, and also knew what it meant. She didn't like Axel Strom to start with. The man he had brought with him into the saloon strengthened that feeling.

Strom came straight to the table without waiting to be invited. The stranger trailed him.

"I just got back from the Bluejay," Strom said without preamble as he came up to the table. "It's bad, Morgan. They ruined all the hoses except one, and one doesn't do us a damned bit of good."

"They can't be patched?" asked Conrad.

"With the kind of pressure they have to stand up to?" Strom snorted. "You know better than that."

"Do we have any extra hoses at the other camps? Surely there are a few. We could take them to the Bluejay and hook them up."

Strom rubbed his blunt chin as he frowned in thought. "That's a possibility," he said after a moment. "We'd be without spares at the other camps if we did that, but at least all the mines would be operating while we're waiting for new hoses to arrive. It'll take a couple of days to make a circuit of all the camps and find out what's available, but I'd rather have the equipment at the Bluejay be silent for two days instead of two weeks . . . or more. The important thing is making sure that nothing like this happens again."

"How do you plan to do that?"

Strom inclined his head toward the stranger. "With our new employee. This is Mace Lundeen."

The name meant nothing to Denny. Judging by Conrad's blank look, he had never heard of the man, either.

Louis Longmont knew him, though. He said coolly, "Hello, Lundeen. I didn't know you were still in the business . . . or still alive, for that matter."

"Very much alive," Mace Lundeen replied. Even though he smiled when he said it, his eyes seemed to Denny as cold and humorless as the gaze of a rattlesnake. "As long ago as you hung up your guns, Longmont, I figured you'd have died of boredom by now."

"I enjoy my life," said Longmont. "It's killing people all the time—and having them try to kill you—that gets tiresome."

Lundeen shrugged. "Whatever you say."

Conrad leaned forward in his chair. "You didn't say anything to me about hiring a new man, Axel."

"I'm just taking the necessary steps to prevent more trouble," snapped Strom. "And it's not just one man. Mace has several associates who'll be arriving over the next few days, too."

"Are Ennis Desmond and the Kinch brothers still riding with you?" Longmont asked.

"That's right," Lundeen said. "And Pat Carr, Jed Nevins, Tom Clute, and several others you'd know. Some new blood, too, that I reckon you've never heard of, stuck in this backwater as you are."

"You're talking about hired guns," Conrad said.

"Men who can stand up to trouble," Strom corrected him. "Our crews are good miners, but they're not equipped to handle attacks all the time."

Denny saw the corners of Conrad's mouth tighten. *He doesn't like this,* she thought.

But hiring guards for the mining camps was a reasonable reaction to the trouble they'd had. At least, Strom would see it that way.

"All right," Conrad said after a moment. "I suppose we can give it a try. But I wish you'd talked to me about this first, Axel."

Strom's burly shoulders rose and fell. "I didn't think we had any time to waste. And that was *before* this latest trouble."

"I've talked to the sheriff about it—"

"Is he going to do anything?"

"There's probably not much he can do," Conrad admitted.

"That's right. The law isn't any good before trouble happens. They won't do anything until it's too late. That's why we have to take steps of our own to protect our interests. And right now we need to see about getting those spare hoses from the other camps."

Conrad swallowed the last of the coffee in his cup and got to his feet. "I'll go with you. You're right. We need to get the Bluejay operating again as soon as possible." He nodded to Longmont. "Thanks for the coffee—"

Longmont held up a hand to stop Conrad as the younger man reached for his pocket. "It's on the house."

"Obliged to you."

Conrad and Strom started for the door, but Mace Lundeen lingered.

He pinched the brim of his hat as he nodded to Denny. "We weren't introduced, miss, but it was a pleasure anyway."

"This is Miss Denise Jensen, Lundeen," said Longmont.

The gunman cocked a rusty eyebrow. "Jensen," he repeated. "As in . . . ?"

"Smoke is my father," Denny said.

"Well, then, it's a *real* pleasure to meet you," Lundeen said. "Tell your pa I said hello."

"The two of you know each other?"

"I know *of* him. I expect most hombres in my line of work do. But we never crossed trails."

"Probably be best for you if you don't," Longmont said.

"We'll see." With that, Lundeen turned and followed Conrad and Strom out of the saloon.

Denny looked at Longmont and said, "This isn't good, is it?"

Longmont shook his head slowly. "I suppose we'll have to wait and see . . . but no, I don't believe it is."

A few evenings later, Brice Rogers swung down from his saddle and looped the horse's reins around the hitch rack in front of Blaise's Place.

He hadn't visited the saloon in a couple of weeks, through no fault of his own. Chief Marshal Long in Denver had sent him a big stack of federal warrants to serve, so he had spent the time riding all over that part of Colorado and even on up into Wyoming. As it turned out, the chore hadn't been a dangerous one, just time-consuming and tedious.

He had gotten back to Big Rock earlier in the evening and checked in with Sheriff Carson to find out what had been going on in his absence. Monte had filled him in on the recent trouble at the Bluejay Mine.

Brice wasn't surprised that the friction caused by Conrad Morgan's operation hadn't settled down yet. Morgan was trouble. Brice had thought that the first time he'd laid eyes on the man.

Monte was worried that sooner or later all-out war would erupt between the cattlemen and the miners. Brice figured that was a definite possibility—especially since, according to Monte, Morgan and Strom had brought in hired guns to protect their camps.

It was a local matter, of course, and didn't fall under federal jurisdiction. However, if it came to a showdown of some sort, Brice would stand with Sheriff Carson. One star-packer didn't turn his back on another in times of trouble.

For now, though, Brice wanted to get a beer, relax for a while, then head to his rented room for a good night's sleep after spending too many nights out on the trail in the past two weeks.

Earlier, he had thought that if he got back to town in time, he would ride out to the Sugarloaf and say hello to Denny. To be honest, he probably still had time to do that, but it could wait, he decided. Paying a visit to Blaise's Place seemed more appealing at the moment.

He pushed through the batwings. The atmosphere in the saloon was slightly smoky and smelled of liquor and unwashed human flesh, but it wasn't as bad as some of the dives he'd been in recently.

The scenery was definitely better. Several young women in low-cut, spangled gowns delivered drinks to the tables as they talked and laughed with the customers. All of them had a fresh, unspoiled look about them, very unlike the faded doves a fella usually encountered in saloons. Brice wasn't sure where Blaise had found them, but she had done a good job recruiting such talent. As a result, the establishment was busy, even on a weeknight. Most of the places at the bar were taken, and there were no vacant tables.

Nearly all the customers wore rough work clothes. They were miners, not cowboys—with a few notable exceptions playing poker at one of the tables. Three of the four men who sat there wore range clothes. The fourth man was dressed in a dark suit and black Stetson.

As Brice looked closer at the men in range clothes, he realized they weren't cowboys, despite their garb. Each sported at least one holstered revolver. A couple wore two guns apiece. Their hard-planed faces looked familiar. For a second, he wondered if he had seen them on wanted posters.

No, he decided, he didn't actually recognize any of them as individuals.

But he knew their type. They were gun-wolves, men who made their living hiring out to fight and kill. He had seen plenty of their breed in the past.

Having them gather in Blaise's Place was a mite disturbing.

But he didn't have time to think more about that.

A familiar, slightly husky, enthralling voice said from beside him, "Why, Marshal Rogers, I was about to decide you'd fallen off the face of the earth. Where have you been lately?"

Brice turned his head and looked down a little to meet the impudent gaze of Blaise Warfield. The gown she wore was slightly more modest than those of the working girls, but still it revealed mostly bare shoulders and a couple of intriguing inches of the cleft of her bosom. Her rich brown hair was loose, tumbling around her shoulders in thick waves. She rested the fingers of her left hand lightly on Brice's right forearm.

He felt the warmth of her touch through his sleeve. "I've been out of town on law business," he told her.

"Chasing desperadoes?"

Brice chuckled. "More like embezzlers, swindlers, and frauds. It wasn't very exciting. On the other hand, nobody shot at me." He glanced around the room. "Have you had any more trouble?"

"Not here in the saloon."

"Well, that's good, but I reckon I know what you mean. I talked to Sheriff Carson. He said tensions are still running high all over the valley because of the mining."

"That's right. I hear the customers talking about it."

Brice said, "It looks like this place has become the miners' home away from home."

"I just take care of whoever comes in the door," Blaise said with a trace of crispness in her voice. She took her hand away from his arm. "I didn't set out to support either side over the other."

"I understand that," Brice assured her. He'd felt a little pang of loss when her fingers no longer touched him. "It's good that you're trying to stay neutral."

Blaise smiled again. "Come on back to my table," she invited. "You look like you could use a drink."

"And some pleasant company."

"I can provide both," she said.

Over the next half hour, Brice slowly drank a couple of beers and chatted with Blaise. He felt his weariness evaporating.

Every so often he experienced a twinge of guilt because he enjoyed spending time with this beautiful young woman and hadn't gone to see Denny Jensen. But even though he and Denny had shared danger *and passion* in the past, it didn't mean they were meant to be together.

That very question of their future together had cropped up in Brice's mind during several of those nights he had spent out on the trail, but he was no closer to having an answer than when he'd set out on the job for Marshal Long.

Suddenly, Blaise sat up straighter and a small frown creased her forehead.

Brice saw that and asked, "Is something wrong?"

"Could be," Blaise replied as she looked toward the saloon's entrance.

A young man pushed aside the batwings. He didn't come all the way into the saloon but stood on the threshold with one hand resting on each of the swinging doors. His range garb marked him as a cowboy, and he looked familiar to Brice.

After a moment, the lawman recognized him as the puncher from the Bluejay spread who had picked a fight with Seamus Burke, the ramrod of Morgan and Strom's crew.

Runnels, that was his name. Chip Runnels.

"Appears that boy is on the prod," murmured Brice.

"He's looking for trouble, all right," agreed Blaise. "I've seen that look too often."

Brice scraped his chair back. "I'll see if I can steer him out of here."

Before he could get to his feet, Chip Runnels shoved the batwings back and strode into the saloon. A slight unsteadiness in his step told Brice he might have been drinking some before he got there.

Raising his voice, Runnels said, "Any of you stinkin' polecats work at the Bluejay Mine?"

A couple of men at the bar turned to face him.

One of them said, "We do. What business is it of yours, cow nurse?"

Runnels jabbed his left index finger toward them. "You killed a pard of mine," he accused. "Killed poor Polo."

"You're crazy," the other miner said. "We don't know what you're talking about."

"Three nights ago," said Runnels. "You shot him. He died."

244

The two miners looked at each other.

One of them exclaimed, "He must've been part of the bunch that wrecked the equipment!"

The other miner said to Runnels, "*You* attacked *us,* you damn troublemaker. And your bunch started the shooting. But if you want to confess to causin' the damage out there, we'll be glad to take you to the sheriff—"

Runnels put his hand on his gun butt. "Nobody's takin' me anywhere," he declared. "But you got to pay for killin' poor Polo—"

One of the poker players—the stocky man with rusty brown hair who wore a dark suit—stood up. "Hey, kid, if you've got a problem with the men from that mine, then your problem's with me."

Runnels stared owlishly at the man and demanded, "Who are you?"

"My name's Mace Lundeen. I'm in charge of protecting all the mines belonging to Strom and Morgan, and that goes for the men who work for them, too. So if you're looking for a fight—"

"Not lookin' for a fight," Runnels broke in.

For a second Brice thought the young cowboy might have decided to be reasonable.

But then Runnels yelled, "Lookin' to settle the score!" as he clawed at the gun on his hip.

CHAPTER 27

Runnels never had a chance.

He had barely moved to get his gun out of its holster when a Colt appeared in Lundeen's hand in a blur of speed. The gun blasted. Flame spurted from the muzzle. The slug smashed into Runnels's chest and knocked him back a step.

He let go of his gun and it thudded to the floor at his feet.

Runnels turned as if he were about to walk out of the saloon. He even lifted his hands to push the batwings aside then toppled forward through them and landed facedown. The upper half of his body lay on the boardwalk outside. The lower half was still inside the saloon.

The batwings swung back and forth a couple of times above his body, set in motion by the violence of his fall. They slowed and soon stopped.

Brice was on his feet, having drawn his gun as he stood up. He raised the Colt and said in a clear, powerful voice, "Hold it right there, Lundeen. Put that gun on the table and step away from it."

Lundeen turned his head to look over his shoulder. "Who are you to be giving me orders, mister?"

"Deputy U.S. Marshal Rogers," Brice replied.

"Lawman, eh? Well, unless you're blind, you

saw that stupid cow nurse draw first. This is a clear case of self-defense."

"You'll have to take that up with Sheriff Carson. There'll need to be an inquest—"

"I'm not giving up my gun," Lundeen said as he shook his head. "And you won't be very smart if you try to force me to."

Brice knew what the man meant. The other three hombres at the table had shifted around so they were watching him. If they were the sort they appeared to be—hired gunmen—he wouldn't stand a chance against that many of them. In a shoot-out, he might be able to kill Lundeen and maybe one of the others, but the remaining two would drill him.

Blaise was in the line of fire, too, making Brice hesitate.

But a lawman couldn't back down, couldn't allow men such as these to buffalo him. The story would get around and ruin his reputation. He might as well turn in his badge if that happened.

Before he could decide what to do, a man outside the saloon yelled, "Chip! Oh, hell, Chip!"

Running footsteps slapped the boardwalk. A man appeared and dropped to his knees beside Runnels's body.

Two more cowboys leaped over the fallen Runnels and bulled inside. They had guns in their hands and looked around wild-eyed, as if they were searching for somebody to shoot.

"Get 'em!" Mace Lundeen called to the other men at the poker table.

Faced with the new threat, the men at the poker table ignored Brice. They leaped to their feet. Guns sprang into their hands. Before the two cowboys realized what was happening, the gun-wolves opened up with a thunderous barrage of shots.

Bullets slammed into the cowboys and knocked them back. They stayed on their feet for a moment and managed to get off several shots in return. They were too badly hurt to aim, and their slugs went wild and slammed into the wall near Brice and Blaise.

It was too late to stop the violence. Brice protected Blaise instead. He grabbed her, dived to the floor, and dragged her down with him.

Gun-thunder continued to roll for several seconds. As it came to a stop and the echoes died away, Brice raised his head to look around. The two cowboys who had charged into the saloon were both down, riddled with bullet holes. A pool of blood spread around each man. The legs of one man twitched a couple of times, then stilled.

Mace Lundeen and the other three gunmen lowered their smoking weapons. Lundeen looked around the saloon with an eager expression on his face, as if he dared anybody else to challenge them.

Brice heard Blaise gasping for breath and

realized that he had sprawled on top of her. He pushed himself up and came to his feet. He didn't think about the fact that his Colt was still in his hand until Lundeen whirled toward him. The man was so fast, Brice didn't stand a chance of stopping him from firing.

Lundeen held off on the trigger. His lips pulled back from his teeth as he half smiled, half grimaced. "Still plan to arrest me, Marshal?"

From the saloon's entrance, a new voice said, "I don't know about Brice, but I'd be happy to fill you full of buckshot, Lundeen. Give me a reason, why don't you?"

Lundeen turned his head in that direction. "Howdy, Monte. I heard you'd pinned on a star. Hard to believe, but I can see it for myself."

Sheriff Monte Carson went into the saloon with a double-barreled shotgun held level in front of him. He stepped around the two dead cowboys and approached the table where Lundeen and the other gun-wolves stood. Without taking his eyes off them, he asked, "Are you all right, Brice?"

"Yeah. None of those shots came very close to me or Miss Warfield."

Now that Monte had taken control of the situation, Brice turned to Blaise and bent to help her to her feet.

She brushed her hands over her dress and straightened it, then said softly to him, "Thank you."

"I wasn't going to let anything happen to you if I could help it."

Another cowboy followed Monte into the saloon, pointed at Lundeen and the others. "They murdered Chip Runnels, Sheriff, and then they slaughtered Linc and Hutch!"

"Nobody murdered anybody," Lundeen responded. "That young fool drew on me. I didn't have any choice but to defend myself." He laughed. "Ask the marshal, there, if you don't believe me. He saw the whole thing. So did everybody else in here."

Monte glanced at Brice.

Brice hesitated, then said, "Runnels drew first, Monte. No doubt about that."

Lundeen nodded toward the cowboys called Linc and Hutch. "And those two charged in here with fire in their eyes and waved guns around. What were we supposed to do? Wait for them to shoot us full of holes before we fought back?"

Most of the miners in the saloon looked shaken by the massacre they had just witnessed, but one of them spoke up and said, "He's tellin' the truth, Sheriff. Those two came in here lookin' for blood."

Brice couldn't dispute that, either, even though a part of him wanted to.

Disgust warred with determination on Monte's face. Disgust won out. "Maybe it was self-defense, but you're still going to have to come to my office and make statements, and there'll be an inquest. For now, holster those guns. You're making me nervous."

"You heard the sheriff, boys," said Lundeen. That mocking tone was back in his voice. "Holster 'em. Sure, we'll come with you, Monte. We're peaceable, law-abiding men. Aren't we, fellas?"

The other three laughed. They pouched their irons and went out of the saloon as Monte trailed behind them with the shotgun. Before he went out, he glanced over his shoulder at Brice and said, "You'll have to testify at the inquest, too."

Brice nodded. "Just let me know when."

"Sheriff?" Blaise said.

"What is it, Miss Warfield?"

"You'll send the undertaker for those men, won't you?"

"Yes, ma'am, if he's not already on the way." Monte grimaced. "Be kind of hard for anybody in town to have missed all that shooting."

Brice motioned to the young puncher who had survived the battle and summoned him over to the table. "I want to talk to you."

"Figured you might, Marshal."

"What's your name?"

"Jack Denton." The cowboy looked around at all the miners in the saloon. "This isn't the friendliest sort of place for a fella like me."

251

"Nobody's going to bother you," Brice promised. "Sit here with us until the undertaker has come and gone."

Blaise said, "Actually, he can sit with you, Brice. I don't feel very well. I'm going up to my room for a bit."

"You're all right?" Brice asked with concern suddenly on his face and in his voice.

"I'm not hurt, if that's what you mean. Just, well, shaken."

Brice nodded. "That's understandable, having something like that happen right in front of you."

Blaise put her hand on his arm again and said, "If you'd like to wait a while . . ."

"I'll be here," he told her.

When Blaise was gone, Denton sat down on the other side of the table. He was careful to keep his back turned so he didn't have to see the bloody shapes of his dead friends sprawled amid the sawdust.

Brice sat down and said, "Runnels was drunk when he came in here, wasn't he?"

"I don't know that he was *drunk,* exactly," Denton replied. "He'd had a few at the Brown Dirt Cowboy, though. Enough to make him start broodin' about what had happened. He started ravin' about settlin' the score for Polo. We tried to stop him from comin' over here . . ." Denton shook his head. "But he got away from us."

"Sheriff Carson told me earlier that somebody

attacked one of the mining camps and damaged a lot of equipment a few nights ago, as well as wounding one of the men who worked there. That was you and your friends?"

"I was there. I just held the horses, though. I didn't have anything to do with damagin' equipment or shootin' anybody." Denton made a rueful face. "I'm not tryin' to make excuses. Like I said, I was there."

"Who's Polo?"

"He was a friend of ours, another hand who rode for the Bluejay. Those miners . . . well, they took some shots at us while we were tryin' to get out of there, and one of 'em hit Polo." Denton sighed. "He made it back to the ranch with us but died a little while after we got him in the bunkhouse."

"I'm sorry for your loss. But now three more men are dead because of what happened that night."

"Because of that blasted mine, you mean," Denton said with heat in his voice. "Morgan and Strom are gonna ruin the whole valley if they keep this up. There's gotta be a law against that, doesn't there, Marshal?"

"They're responsible for any damage their operations cause, but as long as they reach agreement with the ranchers to resolve any disputes, there's really nothing the law can do. And when men like you and your friends take the law into your own hands"—Brice sighed—"it leads to things like what happened tonight."

A man wearing a suit and an old-fashioned stovepipe hat appeared on the boardwalk in front of the saloon. He peered at the body of Chip Runnels, then gestured to someone. Two burly men set a stretcher on the planks beside Runnels, picked him up, and placed his body on it. They positioned themselves at the stretcher's front and rear and carried it off into the night.

The undertaker poked his head into the saloon and announced, "I'll be back for these other two shortly."

Jack Denton asked, "Is it all right if I go with 'em, Marshal? I . . . I'd like to see to it that they're treated properlike."

"All right," Brice told him. "When you're finished with that, head back out to the ranch and stay there, in case the sheriff wants to talk to you."

"I expect he'll want to," Denton said, his face glum. "I may be facin' charges for what happened at the mine. I'm the only one left who had anything to do with it."

"That'll be up to Sheriff Carson."

Denton nodded and left the saloon. Several of the miners gave him hostile glares as he left. Hard feelings still ran high. Brice didn't see any way to stop that. He hoped the friction wouldn't erupt into more violence, but he didn't feel confident in that happening.

A few minutes later, one of the saloon girls, a tall, sultry redhead, angled over to the table where Brice sat. He was about to tell her that he wasn't interested in any company when she said, "I have a message from Miss Blaise for you, Marshal."

"You do?" He hadn't seen Blaise come downstairs or contact anyone, but obviously, she had a way of doing so.

"That's right. She wants you to go up to her room. Do you know where it is?"

Brice bristled. "Of course not."

She looked amused by that straitlaced response. "Go upstairs and down to the end of the hall. That's where Miss Blaise's living quarters are."

"All right." Brice didn't have a reason not to be polite. "Thank you."

The redhead smiled at him and headed back to the bar.

Brice put his hands on the table and pushed himself to his feet. He felt a little uncomfortable, but he went to the stairs and climbed them to the saloon's second floor. Blaise was a different sort of young women, he reminded himself. Not . . . proper . . . like Denny Jensen. Although *proper* wasn't the best word to describe Denny, either.

He went to the door at the end of the hall and knocked.

From inside, Blaise answered, "Come in."

Brice opened the door and stepped into a sitting

room. She sat on a divan next to a table where a lamp burned but had been turned down low. Its light made Blaise's skin seem like burnished gold where it showed through the thin wrapper she wore.

"I didn't feel like going back downstairs after all," she said as she smiled at him. "But I still felt the need of company. I hope it's all right that I invited you up here."

"Sure," said Brice. His voice sounded strange in his ears, almost like it belonged to somebody else.

"You can hang your hat there beside the door, and then come over here and sit with me." She gestured toward two snifters that sat on the table with the lamp. "I poured some brandy for us."

"I'm obliged to you."

"Well, if you're truly grateful, you can show it." She said again, "Come over here and sit with me. Unless . . . you don't want to."

Brice wanted to. Heaven help him, he surely did.

So he hung up his hat and went to her.

CHAPTER 28

After listening to the testimony of Brice and the other men who had been in Blaise's Place that night, the coroner's jury at the inquest had no choice but to find that Charles Runnels, Philo Hutchinson, and Lincoln Pragnell had met their deaths at the hands of men acting in lawful self-defense.

"It was the right decision, according to the evidence," Monte Carson said later as he sat in Louis Longmont's saloon and restaurant with Smoke, Sally, and Denny. "But it's sure not going to help matters around here."

Smoke nodded. "The other cattlemen in the valley aren't going to take it well. Most of Seth Campbell's crew is dead, and he blames himself for what happened."

"It's not his fault at all," Denny said. "None of it would have happened if Conrad Morgan hadn't brought in all that blasted mining equipment and started ruining the range."

"It's not Conrad as much as it is that partner of his," Smoke said. "Strom cuts too many corners. That's obvious to anybody who knows much about hydraulic mining."

Sally said, "How much do *you* know about the process, Smoke?"

He shrugged. "I've read up on it. Conrad should have, too, before he threw in with Strom."

"Maybe he did," said Denny. "Maybe he doesn't care about anything except money, like Strom." She had accused him of that very thing, and even though he'd denied it, she didn't know whether to believe him.

The important thing was that the trouble in the valley threatened to spiral out of control. As the sheriff had said, the recent shooting in Blaise Warfield's saloon would make the situation even worse. Denny wasn't surprised that was where violence had erupted. That woman seemed like the type to attract trouble.

Sally asked, "Is there any way the men who sold those mines can void the contracts and force Mr. Morgan and Mr. Strom to shut down?"

"I don't see how," Smoke said. "From what I know of Conrad, he's a pretty savvy businessman. I'm sure his lawyers saw to it that the contracts are ironclad as long as he abides by them."

"I'm glad you didn't sell him your mine, Pa," Denny said.

"So am I. I never even considered it."

Despite that, Smoke was worried that sooner or later the growing unrest in the valley would reach out and touch the Sugarloaf. Denny felt the same way.

They hadn't come into town to attend the inquest. In fact, they hadn't even known it was taking place. Sally had driven the wagon in to pick up a few things at various stores. Smoke and Denny had ridden along to keep her company and pass the time. Smoke sometimes lamented that Cal and the rest of the crew did such a good job with the Sugarloaf, he didn't have much to do anymore. He had to fill his days somehow.

Once they were in Big Rock, they had run into Monte Carson, and the sheriff had filled them in about recent events. They had adjourned to Longmont's to discuss the situation over coffee.

Monte said, "Brice was there that night, you know." He was looking at Denny when he said it.

She responded. "You mean at the Warfield woman's saloon?"

"That's right. When I came in, he was at one of the tables with Miss Warfield. From the looks of it, they'd been sitting together before the trouble broke out."

"You know, Sheriff," Denny said, "I wouldn't have taken you for a gossip."

"Denise!" Sally exclaimed. "That was a rude thing to say."

Monte chuckled. "I reckon Denny's right. I was gossiping a mite. I've been a little surprised, though, to see how much attention Brice has paid to Miss Warfield since she came to town."

Denny shrugged. "It's his business who he pays attention to."

259

Smoke sipped his coffee. "You haven't seen much of Brice lately, have you?"

"He knows where I live."

"I thought the two of you—"

"A lot of people think a lot of things," said Denny. "That doesn't mean they'll work out that way."

"Nope, I suppose not." Smoke nodded toward the door. "Speaking of which . . ."

Denny looked in that direction and saw Conrad Morgan come into the saloon and restaurant.

He paused and looked around the room. When he spotted the Jensens and Sheriff Carson sitting at one of the tables, he started toward them.

"Wonder what he wants," Smoke said under his breath.

Denny didn't want to talk to Conrad, but she supposed they would have to be polite, especially since her mother was there. Sally wouldn't settle for anything less than common courtesy unless someone gave her a good reason *not* to be courteous.

Then she could be hell on wheels, if she was pushed to it.

Conrad took off his hat as he came up to the table and nodded to the ladies. "Mrs. Jensen. Denny. It's a pleasure to see you again."

"Hello, Mr. Morgan," Sally said. "How are you today?"

"Not too good, to be honest." He gestured at

the empty chair with the hand holding the hat. "Do you mind if I sit down?"

"Please," Sally said.

As Conrad sat, Louis Longmont sauntered over to the table from the bar where he had been standing. "Something to drink, Mr. Morgan?"

"Coffee would be fine."

"I'll have someone bring it over."

Smoke asked, "What can we do for you, Conrad?"

He set his hat on the table and clasped his hands together in front of him. "I want to ask you about the men my partner has hired recently. I have some doubts about them."

"As well you should. Mace Lundeen is a hired killer. The men riding with him aren't any better."

"I thought you might know them," Conrad said. "Or at least you'd have heard of them."

Smoke grunted. "Yeah, I've heard of 'em. I've even met a few of them. I wouldn't call any of them a friend." He paused, then added, "I'm sure your father would say the same thing if he was here."

"I wish he was," said Conrad with a sigh. "I could use his advice." He looked across the table at Smoke. "I was hoping maybe I could get some from you instead."

That blunt statement surprised Denny. She figured Conrad Morgan was so sure of himself, he wouldn't ask for advice from anybody. He sounded sincere, though.

Smoke shook his head. "I'm no mining tycoon

or business magnate. I wouldn't know what to tell you."

"I'm not asking you about that . . . although I happen to know that you *are* a very successful businessman with a lot of varied interests, Mr. Jensen, not just cattle. I'm asking because you used to travel in the same circles as my father . . . and Mace Lundeen."

"That was a long time ago."

"I don't think Lundeen has changed."

Monte Carson said, "No, he hasn't. Not from what I've seen so far."

Smoke studied Conrad for a moment, then asked, "What is it you're worried about?"

"Protecting the mines is one thing. I think Lundeen is liable to go beyond that. I think Axel hired him to frighten the ranchers into going along with whatever he wants to do . . . and the ranchers aren't going to stand for that."

"Which could lead to open war between the two factions." Smoke nodded. "Sounds to me like what you need to do, Conrad, is rein in that partner of yours and make him understand that he can't run roughshod over folks around here."

"I'm not sure I can do that anymore. Axel's seen the gold we're taking out of those mines."

Denny couldn't resist putting in a comment of her own. "And that's all he cares about."

Conrad made a face, but he didn't argue the point.

Smoke leaned back in his chair and gave Conrad a long, cool, calculating look. "Seems to me that sooner or later you're going to have to make a choice, son. Go along with what your partner wants, or do the right thing. Maybe you'd better give some thought to what your pa would do."

Clouds had drifted in and thickened during the evening. They obscured the moon, which was only a quarter full to begin with, meaning the night was even darker than usual . . . the perfect sort of night for what Mace Lundeen and his friends were up to.

Instead of protecting any of the mines in the valley, the men rode across range that was part of one of the ranches. It was called the Slash P, Lundeen recalled, and belonged to a man named Jock Pemberton.

Under the guise of providing protection for the nearby Spanish Peso Mine, Lundeen had done enough scouting to know that the Slash P herd was a good one. He knew where the cattle grazed and that Pemberton didn't have any guards watching them at night.

He knew, too, that another canyon a short distance up the valley past Hammerhead Canyon, where the mine was located, led into the hills and offered a good route for stolen stock to be moved out. Tom Clute had found a small basin in the hills. They could hold the cattle there and take a few at a time to be sold off to contacts Lundeen had. Such an operation took patience, but it could pay off very well over the long haul.

He intended to strip the whole valley before he was finished. Axel Strom was paying decent wages, but with a nice little rustling scheme on the side, Lundeen and his men could really clean up.

Tonight was the first step. A test, of sorts, to see how things would go.

Lundeen reined in. The other men gathered around him.

"All right, spread out and start your gather. Push them north. Tom, you ride ahead to the mouth of that other canyon and whistle when you hear the fellas approaching, so they'll know where to go."

"What if anybody tries to stop us, Mace?" asked the gunman called Jubal Kinch.

"I don't think anybody will . . . but if it happens, I expect you'll know what to do. We're not going to be caught. Be as quiet as you can about it, though."

Kinch chuckled. "Just wanted to be clear on that."

"Let's get to it," ordered Lundeen.

The group split up. They weren't only hired guns now; rustling made them outlaws, plain and simple.

Lundeen didn't care. He had been in the game for a long time and had far outlived the span that most gun-wolves managed. He wanted one last big payoff, and then he would leave that life behind and spend the rest of his years soaking up the warm Mexican sun somewhere below the border.

He was thinking about young, dusky, willing señoritas and bottles of tequila when a figure on horseback suddenly loomed out of the shadows in front of him.

A man called, "Hey! Who's that?"

Actually, from the way the voice cracked, the rider was more of a boy than a grown man.

That's too bad, thought Lundeen.

"Reckon I'm lost," he said as he urged his horse closer. "I'm looking for the Spanish Peso Mine."

"You're one of those dirt diggers?" Scorn was evident in the young cowboy's voice.

"No call to be rude about it, friend," said Lundeen as he went closer. The cowboy was right beside him, barely visible in the darkness . . . but visible enough for what Lundeen needed to do next.

"Sorry," the kid muttered with the natural politeness of a Westerner. He shifted in the saddle and lifted his left arm to point. "You just go on up the valley a ways—"

Lundeen leaned over and drove the knife he had slipped from its sheath under his coat into the cowboy's side. The blade went in under the youngster's arm, scraped over a rib, and pierced the heart. Lundeen could tell his thrust had gone home from the way the cowboy jerked and gasped. He left the knife where it was— less blood that way—and grabbed the kid as he sagged toward him.

They would take the dead cowboy and the horse with them, Lundeen decided. The body would go in an unmarked grave somewhere. Maybe when he was discovered missing, along with the cattle, he would be blamed for the rustling. Probably not, but it was worth a try.

Still holding the cowboy in the saddle, Lundeen dismounted, then took the kid's rope and lashed him in place with it. The smell of blood and the deadweight on its back made the cow pony skittish, but Lundeen managed the grim chore without much trouble.

Then he mounted up again and led the horse away from there. Running into the cowboy unexpectedly wasn't the best break in the world, but Mace Lundeen would figure out a way to turn it to his advantage.

He always did. That was one reason he was still alive after so many years.

CHAPTER 29

The disappearance of Bodie Kendall, a young puncher who rode for Jock Pemberton's Slash P, along with a couple of hundred of Pemberton's cows, puzzled and outraged the people who lived in the valley.

The rest of Pemberton's crew searched every foot of the range and never found Kendall or his horse. They found hoofprints indicating that several men had driven the cattle northward, but the trail disappeared on rocky ground in the hills.

Monte Carson speculated that Kendall had thrown in with stock thieves and helped them run off Pemberton's cows, then went with them when they left the valley. The irascible Pemberton refused to believe it, stating that Bodie was a good boy and wouldn't have done such a thing, but he didn't have any other explanation to offer.

That was just the first of several such thefts. Quite a while had passed since an organized rustling ring had plagued the area, but that appeared to be the case.

"The answer's obvious," Smoke said one evening at the supper table. "Mace Lundeen is behind it."

"Lundeen and his men are busy riding around

intimidating all the ranchers so they won't complain about the mines," Denny said.

Smoke snorted. "From what I know about Lundeen, he could do that and still find time for rustling and murder." He shook his head. "Monte's been out trailing nearly every day, looking for proof, but so far he hasn't had any luck. I told him I'd be glad to help him, but he says it's not my job." Smoke shrugged. "He's right about that."

Denny said, "That never stopped you from getting mixed up in things in the past. Of course, most of what I know about that is hearsay."

"You're right, though," Sally said. "Your father never let little things like the law stop him from doing what he knew was right."

Some women might have sounded scornful when they said something like that, but not Sally. Her voice was full of admiration for the man she had married and the direct way he had of dealing with problems.

Inez Sandoval appeared in the dining room doorway. "Señor Jensen, Pearlie wishes to speak with you but hesitates to interrupt your supper."

"Nonsense," said Smoke. "Pearlie must think it's important, and I trust his judgment. Bring him in here."

"Set a place for him, if he'll stay and join us," Sally suggested. "And you, too, Inez."

"He seems too bothered to sit and eat," said Inez. "I will fetch him."

Pearlie came into the dining room a moment later with Inez following him. He had his battered old hat in one hand. "Beggin' your pardon for bustin' in like this, Miss Sally. Smoke, one of the crew members who was ridin' in late just now saw somethin' off to the northeast that bothered him. He said there was a reflection on the clouds. An orange reflection like you see sometimes when there's a big fire."

Smoke set his napkin aside and scraped his chair back. "Seth Campbell's spread is in that direction. I can't think of any reason why he'd have a big fire burning."

"No *good* reason," said Pearlie. The former foreman's face was set in grim lines.

"We'll go take a look. Have four men saddle horses and get ready to ride with us."

Pearlie nodded.

Denny came to her feet at the same time as her father and declared, "I'm coming with you."

"That's not necessary—"

"Maybe not, but I'm doing it anyway."

Smoke glanced at Sally.

She said, "Don't look at me. She gets her stubborn streak from you."

Smoke grinned briefly and jerked his head at Denny. "Come on. I reckon if there's trouble, you're usually handy to have around."

"Thanks," Denny said dryly.

Sally stood up as well. "Inez, let's put the food away, so it can be warmed up later."

As frontier women, they were used to dealing with such things.

Smoke and Denny paused in the foyer to take down gunbelts from the pegs where they hung near the front door. In the new, modern century, not everybody kept their guns handy like that, but Smoke wouldn't know any other way to live. They buckled on the gunbelts as they headed for the barn with Pearlie.

Smoke asked, "Where's Cal?"

"That's another reason I'm a mite worried. He was workin' off in that direction today, accordin' to the crew, and he ain't come in."

Smoke looked over at him, then increased his pace toward the barn. Denny had to hurry to keep up with the two long-legged men.

Ten minutes later, seven riders galloped away from the Sugarloaf and headed northeast across the valley. Smoke and Pearlie led the way, with Denny right behind them. The four members of the Sugarloaf crew brought up the rear.

They hadn't been riding for long when Denny spotted the faint orange glow in the sky. It painted the bottoms of the clouds and grew brighter as the group headed in that direction.

Smoke said with a note of worry in his voice, "Looks like a big fire, all right."

"Can't be anything good," said Pearlie.

"I'm afraid you're right about that."

Denny had been back from Europe and

living at the Sugarloaf for long enough that she knew the valley well. Not nearly as well as Smoke and Pearlie, though, who had ridden over every foot of it many times during the past quarter century. They knew exactly where they were going and when they had crossed invisible boundaries.

"We're on Bluejay range now," Smoke announced after a while. "Look around, Pearlie. Notice anything odd?"

"Hard to be sure in the dark, but I don't think I've seen any cows since we crossed the line."

"That's right. Some of them should have been grazing in these pastures. It's like somebody swept the range clean of cattle."

Pearlie cursed, then glanced guiltily over his shoulder at Denny.

"Don't worry about me," she told him. "I feel the same way."

"It's them rustlers," Pearlie said. "Has to be the same bunch that's been operatin' around here. They've cleaned out Seth Campbell now."

"Let's hope they haven't done worse than that," Smoke said.

The same thought was in Denny's mind. The outlaws might have gone from stealing cattle to attacking ranches. She hoped they hadn't hurt Mr. Campbell and the few hands he still had working for him.

She couldn't forget that Cal might be in the

271

area, too. If Cal had realized the Bluejay spread was under attack, he would have gone to help Seth Campbell without hesitating. Denny had heard stories about how reckless the foreman had been when he was a young puncher on the Sugarloaf. Cal was older now and not as rash, but he would still plunge headlong into danger if he believed it was the right thing to do.

The riders had covered another mile or so when faint popping sounds came to their ears.

Smoke reined in and said, "Those are gunshots."

"Sounds like a battle," Pearlie agreed.

Smoke turned to look at Denny. "Head back to the ranch and round up the rest of the crew," he told her. "Send them this way in a hurry."

"Blast it, Pa, send one of the men. I'm coming with you."

"No, you're not," he said in a flat, hard tone that allowed for no disagreement. "And you're wasting time that could be important."

"Oh!" Denny blurted the angry exclamation but didn't argue after that. She wheeled her mount and rode toward the Sugarloaf, pushing the horse to get as much speed as she could from the animal. Her father was right. Minutes, even seconds, could be important in a gun battle.

One of these days, though, Smoke Jensen was going to learn that she was a grown woman and couldn't be bossed around anymore!

"That gal's pretty put out with you," Pearlie said as he, Smoke, and the four Sugarloaf punchers rode hard toward Bluejay Ranch headquarters.

A grim laugh came from Smoke. "You're not telling me anything I don't already know, Pearlie. And honestly, she's as tough and as good a fighter as most men I know. Better than a lot of them, as she's proven many times. Still, she's my little girl and always will be, so I'm always going to feel like I have to keep her out of harm's way if I can. She'll do a good job of fetching help from the ranch, too, in case we need it."

"You reckon Cal's mixed up in that fracas?"

"He's always had a knack for finding trouble."

The gunfire got louder as they approached the fight. From the sound of the shots and the way they were spaced, Smoke estimated that two or three men were battling against a somewhat larger group. The fact that the shooting continued was actually a good thing. It meant that the defenders hadn't been wiped out.

The orange glow in the sky had begun to dim. The fire was dying down. Hard to say whether that was good or bad.

A few minutes later, the riders topped a hill and looked down at what had been Seth Campbell's ranch house. The roof and three of the outer walls had collapsed. One wall still stood, but it was on fire. Flames leaped up inside the ruins of the house.

Off to the side, a blaze consumed the long, low bunkhouse. Another pile of burning rubble marked the place where the barn had been. The attached corral hadn't been destroyed, but the beams of which it was constructed were charred black. The flickering glare from the burning house and barn gave the whole scene a hellish, nightmarish aspect.

Muzzle flashes came from a smaller, squat, thickly walled building. Smoke recognized it as the ranch's blacksmith shop. Judging by the flashes, two men were holed up in there.

They were shooting at men who had taken cover behind a wagon, a big watering trough, and a storage shed. Tongues of flame licked out from their guns as they poured lead into the blacksmith shop. The shop's walls were sturdy enough to stop most bullets, but some slugs were bound to be getting in through the open door, the window, and gaps between boards.

Smoke, Pearlie, and the Sugarloaf hands had stopped at the top of the hill instead of charging in blindly.

After watching the battle for several seconds, Pearlie said, "We can't see any of those fellas. They're all behind cover. How do we know which side is which?"

"And how do we know who to throw in with?" Smoke said. "That's the important question." He frowned in thought. "There are two men in that blacksmith shop and at least half a dozen shooting at them."

"Go with the underdog, eh?" said Pearlie. He pulled his Colt from its holster. "That's fine with me!"

The other men were eager to get into the action, too.

Smoke drew his gun and said, "Fire over their heads since we don't know for sure who they are. Maybe we can force them out into the open."

"It's that varmint Lundeen," Pearlie said. "Got to be!"

At a nod from Smoke, the men urged their horses into motion again and swept down the hill.

Smoke saw one of the men attacking the blacksmith shop stand up behind the wagon he was using for cover. Smoke threw a shot over the man's head, high enough to miss, close enough for him to hear the bullet whistle through the air. The attacker ducked wildly.

Pearlie and the other Sugarloaf hands opened fire as well. They sprayed lead around the ranch yard where the attackers had taken cover. For a long moment, the air was full of flying bullets as muzzle flashes lit up the night.

The attackers broke from cover and fled, running around the burning house and firing up the hill at Smoke and his companions. He knew they probably had their horses waiting back there.

He tried to get a good look at the men, but

in the shifting mix of light and shadow, it was impossible. They vanished from sight on the other side of the flames.

"Are we goin' after 'em?" Pearlie called.

"We don't want them doubling back on us," Smoke said. "Keep the pressure on them!"

With their guns still booming, the group from the Sugarloaf charged around what was left of the ranch house. The raiders—Smoke was sure that's what they were—had reached a stand of trees. A few scattered shots came from them, but for the most part they were concerned with getting in their saddles and lighting a shuck out of there.

Smoke's men saw fast-moving shapes darting through the trees and heard hoofbeats pounding as the shots died away. Smoke waved and called out for his men to stop.

"We can run 'em down, I'll bet," Pearlie said.

"I want to find out who's in that blacksmith shop," replied Smoke. "Remember, we haven't found Cal yet."

"Dadgum, that's right! Reckon I was so caught up in the fight that I forgot for a minute." Pearlie wheeled his horse. "Come on, boys!"

As they hurried back around the house and rode toward the blacksmith shop, the only wall left standing in the house finally collapsed, sending a huge cloud of sparks boiling up into the night sky.

In the light from that, a lean figure stepped out of the blacksmith shop with a gun in his hand.

CHAPTER 30

Instead of shooting, the man called in a surprised voice, "Smoke? Pearlie? Is that you?"

"Cal!" cried Pearlie. With a flurry of hoofbeats, he urged his horse forward. "It's mighty good to see you, son. Are you all right?"

Calvin Woods holstered his gun, took off his hat, and scrubbed a weary hand over his face as Smoke, Pearlie, and the other men from the Sugarloaf rode up and dismounted.

"It's mighty good to see you fellas," Cal said. He put his hat back on. "I'll tell you the truth. For a while there I thought I wasn't going to make it out of this little fandango."

"What happened?" Smoke asked.

"I was over at the edge of our range, about to call it a day and head for home. It was already getting dark, so I was able to see the glow from a fire in this direction. It looked too big to be anything good, so I figured I ought to check it out, make sure Mr. Campbell and the other Bluejay hands were all right." Cal gazed grimly at their surroundings. "You can see for yourself, things weren't all right. Not hardly."

"The house was already on fire when you got here?"

Cal nodded. "The house, the bunkhouse, the

barn, all of them. The raiders were shooting at the house, so I could tell somebody was still in there. I knew they wouldn't have a chance where they were, so I charged in shooting hard and fast and scattered the varmints enough for the two men still inside to make a dash for the blacksmith shop. I got here right after them."

Pearlie said, "You picked a good place to fort up. Those walls are pretty thick."

"Yeah, but we were outnumbered more than two to one, and Mr. Campbell was hit when he and Denton made the dash from the house."

Smoke nodded toward the blacksmith shop. "That's who's in there? Seth Campbell and one of his men?"

"Yeah." Cal's voice took on an even grimmer note. "Mr. Campbell was hit pretty bad. We'd better go see if there's anything we can do for him."

Smoke told the four Sugarloaf hands to stand guard in case the raiders came back. He didn't think that was likely, but he couldn't rule it out completely. Then he and Cal and Pearlie walked into the blacksmith shop. Some light from the fire seeped in, but thick shadows made it difficult to see much.

Cal fished a match from his pocket, muttered, "I think I saw a lantern hanging over here somewhere . . ." and snapped the lucifer to life with his thumbnail.

The match's glare revealed the lantern hanging on a nail. He took it down and lit it. Wavering yellow light welled up and revealed the young puncher Jack Denton sitting against one of the shop's walls with his legs stretched out in front of him. He had pulled Seth Campbell's body up so that the rancher was half sitting, half lying against him.

One look at Campbell's sightlessly staring eyes was enough to tell Smoke that the man was dead.

"He didn't make it," Denton choked out. "He was shot through the body three times. Never had a chance."

"I'm sorry, son," Smoke said as he stepped closer. "There's nothing we can do for Seth, but how about you? Are you hit?"

Denton shook his head. "I'm all right. They missed me somehow. But I'd rather it had been me instead of the boss! He was a good man. Always treated all his hands decent, whether we deserved it or not."

Smoke hunkered on his heels, thumbed his hat back, and said, "I know. I was acquainted with Seth Campbell for a good number of years, and he was a fine man. Let's get you out of here so we can take a look and make sure you're all right."

For a second, Denton looked like he was going to argue, but then he nodded and allowed Smoke to take hold of Campbell's shoulders. Smoke eased the cattleman's body to the ground.

Cal extended a hand to Denton and helped the puncher to his feet.

As they all stepped outside, Smoke heard the swift rataplan of hoofbeats in the distance. That would be the rest of the Sugarloaf crew summoned by Denny, he thought, as the sounds grew louder.

Not surprisingly, she was in the lead when the group of riders swept up to what was left of the ranch headquarters a few minutes later. No one at the Sugarloaf would have been able to hold her back from returning with the men.

By that time, Smoke had assured himself that both Cal and Jack Denton hadn't been wounded in the battle. That was the way it happened sometimes. Hundreds of rounds filled the air, but none of them found a target.

Except that three of them *had* found Seth Campbell. He had died as he lived, defending his range.

Denny swung down quickly from her saddle and hugged Cal. "You're all right?" she asked him.

"Yeah. What are you doing here, girl?"

She stepped back and glared at him. "What do you think I should be doing? Sitting in the parlor with my needlework?"

"Well . . ."

Denny ignored that and turned to Smoke. "Where's Mr. Campbell?"

Solemnly, Smoke said, "He didn't make it, Denny."

"Oh, no," she said as her eyes widened. "He was such a nice man. Who . . . who did this?" She gestured vaguely at the destruction surrounding them.

"We don't know. A small gang was laying siege to the blacksmith shop when we got here. That's where Cal and Denton were holed up, along with Seth Campbell."

"It was that man Lundeen," snapped Denny. "You know that, Pa. It had to be."

"More than likely," Smoke agreed, "but Cal and Denton never got a good look at any of the raiders, and neither did the rest of us when we rode in."

"So there's no proof," Denny said with a bitter edge in her voice. "And that means the law can't touch them."

"I'm afraid that's right."

"You didn't wait for the law to go after Stratton and Richards and Potter," she said, naming the men responsible for the death of her grandfather, as well as the murder of Smoke's first wife and child. "I've heard *that* story plenty of times."

"It's not a pretty story, either."

"No, but it ends with justice being done."

Smoke knew his daughter was right. He had never regretted his actions in those long-ago days.

But like it or not, the world was different now.

Monte Carson would be upset if he took the law into his own hands. Out of respect for his old friend, if for no other reason, Smoke wasn't going to hunt down Mace Lundeen and kill him.

Yet.

But that day might still come . . .

With all the mines now operating, Conrad had rented a vacant storefront from Jasper Dunlap and established an office in Big Rock. The dislike most people in town felt for Conrad was like a physical thing, a slap in the face when he walked down the street and everyone turned away from him. He was sure most of them wouldn't have rented to him. However, Dunlap was quick to make the deal.

Conrad had had desks brought in for himself and Axel Strom, along with chairs and filing cabinets, and a picture of President Theodore Roosevelt to hang on the wall. The Prussian engineer was at his desk, working on what looked like plans for more modifications on the mining equipment, when Conrad came into the office.

Strom glanced up, then went back to what he was doing. After a long moment of silence, he lifted his gaze again and frowned at Conrad, who stood just inside the door with a grim expression on his face.

"What?" Strom demanded. "Is something wrong?"

"Have you heard what happened at the Bluejay last night?"

Strom set his pencil aside. "More problems with that blasted retaining wall?"

Conrad shook his head. "Not the mine. The ranch."

Strom snorted and waved a hand in dismissal. "I don't care what happens on somebody's ranch. That's none of my business."

"Rustlers stole all of Seth Campbell's cattle, then attacked his headquarters and burned down the ranch house, the bunkhouse, and the barn. Campbell was killed, and three men died in the fire when the bunkhouse burned."

Strom didn't express any shock or sympathy. "Again, that's none of—"

"It *is* our business, Axel, because most people in the valley believe that Lundeen and his men are responsible . . . and Lundeen works for us." *For you,* Conrad actually wanted to say. He never would have hired the gunman. But he and Strom were partners, so he considered himself equally responsible, whether he liked it or not.

Strom shoved his chair back and stood up. "Are you saying they think *I* ordered Lundeen to carry out an atrocity like that?" he demanded.

"They blame both of us, actually," said Conrad. "I got some pretty hostile looks while I was walking over here from the hotel." He let out a grunt of humorless laughter. "Usually folks just pretend that I'm not there."

Strom's brawny shoulders rose and fell. "The hell with what they think. I'm not going to worry about the opinions of a bunch of backwater bumpkins."

"Maybe you should. We're relying on those backwater bumpkins, as you call them, for the supplies we need to keep the mines operating."

"They'll sell us what we need. All they care about is the money they can gouge from us."

"That's exactly what they say about us," Conrad pointed out bluntly. "And Seth Campbell was a very well-liked man. I wouldn't count on people overlooking his death just because we're in business here. In fact, I can guarantee they won't."

"What do you want from me, Morgan? I have work to do."

Conrad strode over to the desk and looked squarely across it at Strom. "Fire Lundeen. Send him and his men away from here."

Strom scoffed at the idea. "That would be foolish. Mace has let the troublemakers in the valley know that if they interfere with our operation, they'll pay a hefty price for their foolishness. He's been well worth the money we're paying him. As for the insane idea that I ordered him to steal Campbell's cattle and kill the man . . ." Strom slapped a hand on the desk. "Bah! I never did any such thing."

"Well, I'm glad to hear you deny it, anyway," said Conrad. "But whether you ordered it or not, that doesn't mean Lundeen and his men are innocent. From what I've heard, a lot of rustling has been going on in the valley recently, and they could be responsible for it, acting on their own."

"Is there any proof of that?"

Conrad shook his head. "Not that I know of."

"All right." Strom looked at the papers on his desk. "I need to get back to work. My advice, Morgan, is to ignore all the gossip and innuendo. Let's go about our business . . . *gold*."

The greed that practically dripped from Strom's voice told Conrad everything he needed to know. Strom might not have ordered the attack on the Bluejay Ranch; probably hadn't, in fact. But he didn't care about it, either. He would be perfectly content to allow Mace Lundeen and the other gunmen to run roughshod over the valley, stealing cattle and killing anybody who got in their way—as long as the mines were protected and operating.

"All right, Axel," Conrad said. "You can get back to work."

Strom's eyes narrowed. "What are you going to do?"

"I don't know yet."

"What do you mean by that?"

Conrad didn't answer. He pushed through the door and stalked out of the office.

The only solution was for him to buy out Strom's share of the partnership. Then he could fire Lundeen and run the mines the way they should be run. He lacked the hydraulic mining experience Strom had, of course, but he wasn't a total novice when it came to such things. And there were other experts, other engineers, out there who he could hire.

Next time, they would be employees, and they would conduct the business the way he ordered.

Conrad sighed. It might not be too late to build up some trust with the people in the valley, but it wouldn't be easy. Nor would it be easy to convince Strom to sell out to him. But he had one advantage—enough money to keep throwing it at Strom until the man agreed to a deal.

Upset, Conrad hadn't paid any attention to where he was going. Realizing the course of action he had to take, he calmed down enough to look around him. He wasn't far from Longmont's. The idea of a cup of the restaurant's excellent coffee appealed to him, and his steps turned in that direction.

Unfortunately, he didn't know Big Rock well enough to realize that his route took him in front of the Brown Dirt Cowboy Saloon until he was walking past the watering hole.

"Hey!" someone inside shouted. "There goes that hombre who's caused all the trouble!"

Footsteps rushed toward the door. Somebody slapped the batwings aside and half a dozen men bulled out of the saloon onto the boardwalk behind Conrad. At that time of day, they were men who didn't have regular riding jobs, but they considered themselves cowboys anyway.

"Hold it right there, mister!"

Conrad stopped, but not because of the angry shout. He had known the men were back there as soon as they stepped onto the boardwalk. He wasn't going to ignore them and keep walking, and he certainly wasn't going to run.

He turned toward them with a cool, calm indifference and asked, "Something I can do for you?"

"Yeah," one of the men replied. "You can get the hell out of this valley, you damn murderer!"

"You have me mixed up with someone else," said Conrad. "I haven't murdered anyone."

"I'm talkin' about Seth Campbell, and you know it! Three other good men died with him at the Bluejay, too."

Conrad shook his head. "I'm sorry that happened, but I had nothing to do with it."

Another cowboy shook a clenched fist at him and said, "Runnin' him outta town ain't enough! We oughta string the varmint up!"

"We've all got lassos on our saddles," said a third man, "and I'll bet we can find a tall enough tree!"

Whooping and cursing, the cowboys suddenly lunged toward Conrad with lynch mob fury burning in their eyes.

CHAPTER 31

Conrad's gunbelt and Colt were back in his hotel room. He tended not to carry a gun while he was in town.

That might have been a mistake. A fatal mistake . . . but he didn't just stand there and allow the cowboys to swarm him. It was nearly always better to take the fight to the enemy.

Conrad leaped forward to meet their charge and slammed his right fist into the jaw of the man closest to him. The impact sent the cowboy flying back against his friends.

That took them by surprise. Legs tangled. A couple of men fell and sprawled on the boardwalk. The one Conrad had punched reeled to the side and fell against the saloon's front wall, half stunned.

The other three were able to continue the attack. One of them threw a big, looping right that Conrad ducked easily. He stepped in and hooked a left to the man's belly, then tagged him with a right cross when the blow made the man bend forward.

One of the other men closed in to whip a fist at his head. From the corner of his eye, Conrad saw the blow coming, and he jerked his head away.

He was only partially successful. The cowboy's

bony knuckles scraped his skull just above his left ear with enough force to make Conrad take a step closer to the building.

That put him within reach of the third man, who drove a fist into his ribs on the right side. Pain shot through Conrad's body as the punch jolted the air out of his lungs.

He snapped a backhand into the face of the man who had just hit him and reeled back to put himself out of reach as he gasped for breath.

The men who had been tangled up and tripped had made it back to their feet, as did the cowboy Conrad had hit in the jaw. He had recovered to a certain extent, too, although he still shook his head groggily.

The three of them rushed him again. Crowded together on the boardwalk to reach him made it more difficult, but Conrad knew that if he'd been out in the street, they could have surrounded him and he wouldn't have stood a chance against them.

He wondered fleetingly where Monte Carson was. Surely some bystander had already run to fetch the sheriff.

But would they? Or did everyone in Big Rock hate him so much that once they saw who the mob was after, they wouldn't interfere?

He stood his ground stubbornly. Trading punches with the men crowding around him, he blocked the blows he could, and absorbed the punishment from the ones he couldn't. His hat had fallen off. He tasted blood in his mouth.

A hard punch to the solar plexus rocked him for a second and made him drop his guard. With a wild yell, one of the cowboys launched himself into a flying tackle. He caught Conrad around the waist and drove him off the boardwalk. Both of them rolled in the dust of the street. The cowboy hung on to Conrad as they went over and over.

Conrad finally got a chance to lift a punch under the man's chin as they rolled. The blow jarred the cowboy's head back and made him loosen his grip. Conrad tore free, scrambled away, and surged to his feet.

Exactly what he hadn't wanted to happen. He was out in the open. The five cowboys still on their feet leaped from the boardwalk and charged him. They spread out so he had nowhere to go.

"A couple of you get behind him!" called one of them. "Grab his arms! We'll teach him a lesson before we string him up!"

Some of the townspeople had to have heard that shout, thought Conrad. They were talking about lynching him. How could the citizens ignore that?

Did they really hate him that much?

A glance told him that the boardwalks were strangely deserted. Everybody had retreated inside the buildings to watch the lopsided battle.

Yeah, he thought, *they really do hate me that much.*

But that didn't mean he was going to give up.

He feinted at one of the men trying to circle around him, then whirled instantly and kicked a man on the other side in the stomach. That man staggered back, doubled over in pain.

Another cowboy managed to land a punch to Conrad's chest that paralyzed him for a second. Strong hands grabbed his arms. He was pinned between two of his enemies. One of the other cowboys sprang at him, face twisted with hate, fist raised to strike.

Taking the men holding him by surprise, Conrad drew his knees up, then snapped his legs out and drove both boot heels into the chest of the man attacking him. The double kick was powerful, lifting the man off his feet and sending him flying ten feet backward in the air. He landed in a limp sprawl, too stunned to move.

Conrad was still held tight by two men, and two more cowboys were ready, willing, and able to beat the hell out of him. They wouldn't fall for that knees-up trick a second time, either.

"Hang on to that son of a gun!" one of them panted. "Time we get through with him, he ain't even gonna look human!"

Conrad was afraid they might be right about that.

As one of the cowboys drew back a fist to crash it into Conrad's face, another figure came flying out of nowhere, tackled him, and drove him off his feet.

Conrad caught enough of a glimpse of the newcomer to recognize him as Brice Rogers. With no love lost between them, he was surprised to see the deputy U.S. marshal coming to his aid. But Rogers was a lawman. Evidently he couldn't stand by and watch while a man was beaten and lynched—even a man he didn't like.

Rogers had his hands full with the man he had tackled. That left the others free to continue their attack on Conrad. Unable to pull loose from the cruel grip on his arms, he couldn't avoid the punches as a man slammed a right and a left into his belly. Sickness rose inside Conrad like a tidal wave.

He kicked again. That was all he could do. The toe of his boot found a cowboy's groin and sank into it. The cowboy reeled back, yelling in pain and clutching himself as he doubled over.

A few yards away, Brice Rogers sprang lithely to his feet. The man he'd been struggling with tried to get up, too, but he ran right into Rogers's fist. The blow, and all the power of the lawman's lean body behind it, landed cleanly. The cowboy went over backward and hit the ground with his arms outflung. He looked like he'd been knocked cold.

Rogers whirled and charged into the fray again. He lowered his shoulder, rammed it into the back of a man who was hammering Conrad with punches, and knocked all of them sprawling like ninepins.

Conrad tore loose, jabbed an elbow to the face of one of the men who'd been holding him, then rolled clear.

Rogers came back up on his feet at the same time. Their gazes locked for a second, long enough for Conrad to jerk his head in a slight nod and Rogers to understand what he meant. That brief exchange was all a couple of fighting men needed.

They put their backs together, and punches began to fly again as the would-be lynchers crowded in on both sides.

For several long moments, the wild melee was a blur of fists striking flesh and bone, grunts of effort and pain, a haze of dust in the air from the shuffling feet of the combatants, and the salty taste of sweat and blood intermingling.

Conrad hit everybody who popped up in front of him until no one was there. Panting for breath, he held up his bloodied and swollen fists, blinked sweat out of his eyes, and looked around for another enemy. He was aware that Brice Rogers was still behind him, but the deputy marshal didn't seem to be punching anybody, either.

"Are . . . are they all down?" asked Conrad.

"That's what it . . . looks like," replied Rogers, equally breathless.

Both men slowly lowered their arms and looked at the limp bodies surrounding them. A couple of the cowboys groaned and shifted. They weren't out cold, but they wouldn't be getting up and continuing the battle any time soon.

Conrad lifted a hand and dragged the back of it across his mouth. The gesture left a smear of blood on his skin. "Pretty good . . . fight."

"Yeah, I was . . . thinking the same thing," Rogers agreed.

From the boardwalk, Monte Carson said, "Yeah, so was I."

Conrad looked over at him. "I see you finally . . . got here, Sheriff."

"Following you around and waiting for trouble to break out isn't my only job, Mr. Morgan," Carson said as he stepped down from the boardwalk. He had a shotgun tucked under his left arm. He looked at the battered cowboys lying in the street. "Appears you didn't actually need my help, anyway."

"And Seth Campbell was a friend of yours, I'll wager."

"He was," Carson snapped, "but that doesn't mean I won't do my job. For example, if you started this fight, I'll haul you off to jail and charge you with disturbing the peace."

"Do you really think I'd start a fight knowing I'd be outnumbered six to one?"

"I don't really know what you'd do," said Carson. He shrugged. "But I'll admit, it's unlikely." He looked at Rogers. "You know anything about this, Brice, other than you got mixed up in it?"

"I don't know who threw the first punch, no," Rogers answered. "But when I came along, Mr. Morgan had his hands full. Somebody told me those cowboys were talking about lynching him."

The sheriff's mouth tightened. "Not in my town, they're not," he declared. "That's enough for me to give you the benefit of the doubt, Mr. Morgan. You're free to go."

"I appreciate that," Conrad said dryly.

"You and your partner might want to talk about moving your headquarters somewhere else, though. Neither of you are very popular in Big Rock . . . and I don't expect that feeling to change any time soon."

Conrad walked over to the boardwalk, picked up his hat, and slapped it against his thigh to get some of the dust off it. "I'm not in the habit of running away from trouble, Sheriff. Nor do I intend to start."

Carson shrugged again. "Just giving you some friendly advice, that's all."

Conrad doubted very much that the advice was all that friendly, but he nodded and put his hat on.

Brice Rogers had retrieved his Stetson, as well. "Where are you headed, Morgan?"

"What business is that of yours?"

"I thought I might walk along with you, if you planned to stay here in town for a spell. That might keep any more trouble from breaking out."

"I don't need your protection," Conrad said.

"I'm not worried about protecting you. I just figure it's best to maintain peace and quiet, if possible." Rogers paused. "Besides, I'd like to talk to you."

That took Conrad by surprise. As far as he knew, they didn't have anything to talk about.

Other than . . . maybe . . . Denny Jensen.

"All right," Conrad said. "I was going to get a cup of coffee at Longmont's."

"Sounds good to me," said Rogers.

CHAPTER 32

Brice Rogers was aware of the hostile looks he got from Big Rock's citizens as he walked along the street with Conrad Morgan, but he couldn't blame them for being upset with the mine owner. Seth Campbell had been a popular man in the valley. His death, along with those of the three hands who had perished in the bunkhouse fire, had upset everyone for miles around.

Louis Longmont raised an eyebrow in surprise when Brice and Conrad walked in together. He nodded and said, "Gentlemen, what can we do for you?"

"Coffee," Conrad said.

Brice nodded agreement.

"Of course. Sit anywhere. I'll have it brought to you."

The place wasn't busy at the moment. The two men sat at a table with no one else close by. They didn't say anything until the bartender had brought their coffee and each man had taken a sip.

"All right, Marshal," Conrad said. "What is it you want to talk to me about?"

"To start with . . . do you know if your partner had anything to do with what happened at the Bluejay Ranch last night?"

297

"You're not going to accuse *me* of being behind the attack? That's what most people around here seem to be doing."

Brice regarded him intently for a moment, then said, "No, I'm not. I've been a lawman for a while now. I'd like to believe that I'm a pretty good judge of character *and* that I can spot an owlhoot when I see one. I think you're an honest man, Morgan."

"Well, I'm obliged to you for *that,* anyway, I guess." Conrad took another sip of coffee. "For the record, I was just as surprised and appalled to hear about what happened at Campbell's ranch as anyone else was. It's a tragedy and a heinous crime."

"And you haven't answered my question about your partner."

Conrad sighed. "I've spoken to Axel. He claims that he knows nothing about it other than what I told him this morning."

"Do you believe him?"

"I don't have any reason to think he's lying." Conrad leaned forward. "You say that you can spot an owlhoot. Is that what you think Axel Strom is?"

"I think he's a man who doesn't give a damn who he hurts as long as he gets what he wants." Brice studied Conrad again and added, "I have a hunch that you feel the same way about him."

Conrad made a face and pushed his coffee cup

away. "Let's just say that not everything about this enterprise has turned out the way I expected it to . . . or wanted it to. In fact, I've been debating with myself what I need do about that."

"What conclusion did you come to?" asked Brice.

"I'm going to buy out Strom's interest in our partnership."

"You reckon he'll go along with that?"

"I don't intend to give him any choice." Conrad smiled ruefully. "I have a great deal of money and the best lawyers in the country. Those things have to be worth *something*. I can usually find a way to get what I want."

"Does that include people, too?"

The sharply voiced question made Conrad raise his eyebrows. "Are you referring to anyone in particular? Denny Jensen, maybe?"

"Seems like you might think the two of you are a good match. Her father's a famous gunfighter, and so's yours. You both have lots of money—as you just pointed out—and were raised in luxury. She's got a lot more in common with you than with . . ."

"A deputy United States marshal?" asked Conrad when Brice's voice trailed off.

"Well, it's the truth."

Conrad considered for a moment, then said, "Having a common background in some respects doesn't mean that two people are a good match or will get along at all. I'll make no secret of the fact that I have a great deal of admiration for Miss Jensen, though."

"So do I."

"If that's the case," Conrad said coolly, "I have to wonder why you're spending so much time in the company of Blaise Warfield these days."

Anger welled up inside Brice. "I don't know what you're—"

"I hear some of the gossip that goes around town," Conrad interrupted him. "You've been a frequent visitor to Miss Warfield's saloon."

"The miners drink there, and I like to keep an eye on things to make sure trouble doesn't boil over."

Conrad chuckled. "That's Sheriff Carson's job, isn't it? Not that of a federal marshal."

Along with the anger, Brice felt an unexpected twinge of embarrassment, as well as a flush of guilt. Then he shoved that away. He didn't have a blasted thing to feel guilty about, he told himself. He and Denny had never made any promises to each other.

Brice left half his coffee in the cup as he got to his feet. "I just wanted to talk to you about Strom and Lundeen and what you're going to do about them. It'll be to your benefit if you get yourself clear of them, Morgan. You saw what happened out there today. I'm not sure those saddle tramps would have strung you up like they threatened, but it could have been pretty bad for you anyway. Most of the people around here don't like you."

"I didn't come to Colorado to make friends," Conrad said.

"Maybe not, but you've made plenty of enemies, and it's liable to get worse. I probably won't be around next time to give you a hand."

"I'm obliged to you for your help," Conrad said coldly, "but I didn't ask for it."

"Just remember what I said." Brice started to turn away.

"Anything you want me to tell Denny the next time I see her?"

The mocking question made him stop. He looked back, *this close* to throwing a punch at Conrad Morgan himself, but then he suppressed the impulse and walked out of Longmont's.

Louis Longmont strolled over to the table and commented, "You know, it's not a good idea to have the law carrying around a grudge against you."

"I'm not worried about Marshal Rogers," said Conrad. "I haven't broken any federal statutes."

"Perhaps not, but you might need him as a friend someday. From what I've heard about the trouble earlier, he was quite helpful today."

"I can stomp my own snakes."

Longmont raised an eyebrow. "That's not an

expression I'd expect a business tycoon from Boston and San Francisco to use."

"I've been other places in my life," said Conrad, "and done other things."

Axel Strom was still working on the technical drawings he'd made when the office door opened again. He looked up, expecting to see that his partner had returned. Morgan might be looking for another argument.

Strom was tired of such confrontations, but he wasn't going to allow Morgan's ridiculous scruples to interfere with taking as much gold out of the mountains as they possibly could.

Instead of Conrad Morgan, a woman—a very *attractive* woman—stood there a step inside the door. She wore an elegant green gown, not really the sort of thing a respectable woman would wear but not as gaudy and revealing as a typical saloon girl's dress. Blond curls were piled atop her head in an elaborate arrangement.

"Mr. Strom?" she said as she eased the door closed behind her.

"That's right." He set the pencil aside and leaned back in his chair. "What can I do for you?"

"My name is Maureen. I work for Louis Longmont."

"Ah."

That explained the outfit. Strom had been in Longmont's several times and had seen the women the gambler had working for him. They were all beautiful, and they dressed and conducted themselves with more grace and gentility than, say, the soiled doves at the Brown Dirt Cowboy or Blaise's Place.

Strom didn't say anything else. He waited for her to go on.

After a moment, she said, "I was there just now, and a few minutes ago I happened to overhear a conversation between two of the customers. You might be interested to know who they were."

"I *might* be . . . or you think I'll be willing to *pay* you to find out what you're talking about."

She looked a little put out with him, probably because he had spoken in such a blunt fashion, but she said, "It's something you'll want to know about, I can promise you that."

Strom grunted, dug in a pocket with his blunt fingers, and pulled out a double eagle. He set the twenty-dollar gold piece on its edge onto the desk and spun it. Seeing the way Maureen's eyes followed it, he chuckled.

With a thump from his finger, he knocked the double eagle into the floor. It bounced to a stop near her feet.

"Pick it up," he told her. "That way, even if I don't like what you have to tell me, I'll have gotten *something* for my money."

Her jaw tightened. She glared at him.

She was angry and offended, he thought . . . but

303

she bent forward and picked up the coin anyway. Her gown wasn't as low-cut as some, but still low enough to give him an intriguing view for a second.

She straightened with the double eagle clutched in her hand and said, "It was your partner, Mr. Morgan, I overheard talking with Deputy Marshal Rogers."

A frown creased Strom's forehead. "The federal lawman?"

"That's right."

Strom shook his head. "Those two don't like each other." A bark of laughter came from him. "They're jealous of the same girl, the young fools."

"Maybe so, but they were sitting in Longmont's having coffee together and talking about you."

Strom drew in a sharp breath and stood up. He balled his hands into fists and rested the knuckles on the desk as he leaned forward. "Talking about me, you say?"

"You, Mace Lundeen, the killings that happened out at the Bluejay Ranch."

Strom lifted a hand and waved that away. "Bah. Nothing to do with me."

"I don't know one way or the other about that, but I can tell you Morgan's worried enough he's ready to buy out your share of the partnership."

Strom straightened. He shook his head and said, "I know nothing about that, either. There has been no discussion about dissolving our partnership. It will never happen!"

"He came right out and told the marshal that's what he intends to do." Maureen smiled. "He seemed pretty confident, too. He said he has enough money and lawyers to get whatever he wants."

Fury boiled up inside Strom. That sort of arrogance coming from Conrad Morgan sounded completely believable. Strom had been able to tell from their first meeting that Morgan believed he was superior to a mere mining engineer.

Strom's teeth ground together in rage for a few seconds before he said, "So he believes he can force me out, eh? When those mines wouldn't even be in operation now if not for my genius?"

"I told you it was something you'd want to know," said Maureen. "Seems to me that might be worth a little more than what you gave me."

Strom felt the urge to step around the desk, go to the woman, grab those blond curls, and smash that mocking smile off her face. He suppressed the impulse. Greedy and grasping she might be, but an unexpected ally who had come out of nowhere. And she was right—the information was valuable.

He stepped around the desk, but instead of striking her, he took another double eagle from his pocket. Her eyes lit up. He handed it to her, then moved his fingers so they closed around her bare forearm.

"Take it easy," she told him. "You're not paying for anything except what I told you."

"Of course," murmured Strom. "But I'm grateful to you, and I like to express my gratitude."

She held up the hand in which she had the second double eagle. "You've already done that."

"Consider this a bonus."

He moved his hand to the back of her neck and pulled her toward him. His mouth came down hard on hers. She struggled, but not too strenuously and only for a moment.

She would learn—just as Conrad Morgan would learn—that Axel Strom was the one who always got what he wanted.

CHAPTER 33

No matter how many times he got on the back of one of the cursed animals, Strom would never grow accustomed to riding a horse. Nor would he ever enjoy the experience. His legs and backside already ached from the saddle.

Sometimes, however, such unpleasantness and discomfort were necessary. Tonight was one of those times.

Strom let his mount pick its own way as he approached Hammerhead Canyon. The horse could see better than he could. Strom had ridden all over the valley with Conrad and had a pretty good idea where he was going, but he trusted the horse more. He didn't want to rush things, either.

When he believed he was getting fairly close to the canyon, he heard a man call softly to him.

"Whoever's there, rein in and stay right where you are. Don't make any sudden moves."

Strom followed the order, although he had never liked having anyone tell him what to do. He recognized Mace Lundeen's raspy tones.

"It's me, Mace. You got my message?"

Lundeen loomed out of the shadows, a bulky shape on horseback. "Yeah, or I wouldn't be here. If you wanted to see me, boss, I'm not sure why we couldn't get together in Big Rock, at the hotel or one of the saloons."

"Neither of us are very welcome in Big Rock right now."

Lundeen snorted. "You reckon I care about that? It's been a long time since I gave a damn what anybody thinks of me, unless they're paying my wages."

"Even so, I plan to be operating here in this valley for a while yet, so I can't afford to have a mass uprising against us." Strom paused. "Nor can I afford to have my own partner stab me in the back."

Even though he couldn't see Lundeen well in the shadows, he could tell that statement made the gunman's interest perk up.

"What do you mean by that?" Lundeen wanted to know.

"Conrad Morgan plans to force me out of our partnership and take over everything himself."

"Are you sure?"

The question forced Strom to consider. All he had to go by was the word of that saloon doxy Maureen. It was possible she had made up the whole thing in order to weasel some money out of him.

He didn't believe that. She had seemed sincere, and what she had told him sounded *exactly* like the sort of thing Conrad Morgan would say. Strom always trusted his instincts. They hadn't let him down yet.

"I'm certain," he snapped in reply to Lundeen.

"That wouldn't be good. For either of us. I reckon Morgan would fire me and my boys first thing."

"He would, indeed."

"He might even try to set the law on us."

"That's why we need to make sure he never gets an opportunity to do so."

Lundeen brought his horse closer and asked, "Exactly what do you mean by that, boss?"

"I think you have a pretty good idea," said Strom. "Our partnership isn't officially dissolved yet, so the standard clauses in the agreement we signed all still apply, including the right of survivorship. If anything happens to one of us, his share in the enterprise goes to the remaining partner. If something happened to Morgan, I would be in sole charge of the mining operation."

"And all the profits would go to you, too," Lundeen said. "That sounds like a pretty good deal for you, Mr. Strom . . . *if* something was to happen to Morgan."

"Yes, I'm counting on that."

"Is there any deadline for this to happen?"

"It needs to be soon," said Strom, "before Morgan can take any steps to cut me out. I wouldn't presume to tell you how to handle such a matter. You're the one who's made that your business."

"So I have." Lundeen rubbed his chin. "There's

one other thing we need to talk about, though. You know who Morgan's father is?"

"I've heard him mentioned. Some sort of notorious figure from your ridiculous American dime novels, isn't he?"

"Frank Morgan's one of the deadliest gunfighters who ever buckled on a six-shooter," said Lundeen. "If something happens to his boy, I don't know how he'll take it."

"You're well paid to take risks," Strom said, unable to keep the sneer completely out of his voice.

"Not well enough." Lundeen's voice was flat and hard as he went on. "If there's even a chance I'll have to tangle with Frank Morgan somewhere down the trail because of this, I'll need ten grand more. Five thousand for me and five thousand to split among my men."

"You can't handle Morgan by yourself?"

"I reckon I can, but why take that chance? If it's as important as you say it is, we'll all be better off by making sure, won't we?"

For a long moment, Strom considered what Lundeen had said. He felt as if the gunman were trying to take advantage of him, but unfortunately, what Lundeen had said was correct. Getting rid of Conrad Morgan was important, and Strom didn't want to take any unnecessary chances.

"All right," he said. "Ten thousand. Five tomorrow, when I've had a chance to get it from the bank, and five when Morgan is no longer a problem."

"Done and done," said Lundeen. "And I think you'll see that it's the best ten grand you've ever spent, Mr. Strom."

It had better be, thought Strom.

Or Mace Lundeen would be answering to him.

The funeral for Seth Campbell and the three men who had worked for him had been well-attended. The church was packed, in fact. Campbell had been well-liked among his fellow cattlemen and the townspeople alike.

Much of the talk among the men who'd gathered outside the church after the service centered around the rustling that had been going on in the valley. Since the outlaws responsible for it had been bold and ruthless enough to wipe out the Bluejay, no telling what they might do next.

Denny would have liked to be right there among the discussion with Smoke, but Sally had steered her away. In the sober black dress and veil she wore, Denny knew the men probably wouldn't have talked as freely around her, anyway. She would get her father to fill her in on the conversation later, she decided.

Denny and Sally sat in the buggy Sally had driven into town. Smoke's saddle horse was tied to the hitch rack beside the buggy horse. As they waited for him to finish talking and join them, Denny looked around the street.

A somber atmosphere hung over Big Rock. Folks were on the boardwalks and going in and out of the businesses, but most wore grim expressions. It almost seemed like the town and the surrounding valley were at war.

That was what it felt like, mused Denny. Invaders had come in and declared war on everybody.

And there was one of those invaders now, she thought as she spotted Conrad Morgan on the other side of the street. She didn't know where he was bound, but the citizens of Big Rock gave him hostile looks and a wide berth as he moved along the boardwalk.

Acting on impulse, Denny said to her mother, "I'll be back in a minute," and stepped down from the buggy before Sally could stop her.

She walked across the street, angling to intercept Conrad. He saw her coming toward him and slowed so she didn't have any trouble meeting him.

"Are you sure you want to have anything to do with me?" he asked as she stepped up onto the boardwalk in front of him. "Associating with me will make you a social pariah."

"I've never cared that much what folks think of me," she said coolly. "That's why I ride horses and wear trousers and shoot guns."

"Yes, but now you're talking to a murderer. A man who wants to destroy the way of life in this valley."

"Are either of those things true?" asked Denny.

Conrad shook his head. "Not at all. What happened at Mr. Campbell's ranch shocked and saddened me as much as it did anyone else around here. I never would have bought those mines and opened them up again if Axel hadn't assured me we could do so without harming the range and the water and the cattle business. Every study he did supported that claim."

"But *he* made those studies, and he wants that gold. Anyway, you signed off on all of it, didn't you?"

"I'm not trying to make excuses and blame him for everything," Conrad said. "Yes, I certainly bear my share of the responsibility. That's why I want to make things right."

"How are you going to do that? You can't bring Mr. Campbell and those other men back from their graves."

Conrad shook his head. "No, I can't. But I can make sure all the damage the mines have created is cleaned up, and that they're operated in the future in a manner that won't cause more trouble. I can cooperate with Sheriff Carson and help him put a stop to the rustling and killing."

"Rustling and killing that's being done by men who work for you and your partner."

"There's no proof of that—" Conrad held up a hand to forestall the argument that was about to come out of Denny's mouth. "But for what it's worth, I believe you're absolutely right. Mace Lundeen is behind the raids. As soon as I've dealt with Strom, Lundeen won't be working for Browning Holdings anymore."

Denny frowned. "What do you mean, as soon as you've dealt with Strom?"

"I'm going to buy him out and dissolve our partnership."

"You can do that?"

"It'll take some legal maneuvering"—he smiled—"but yes, I can do that. I'm *going* to do that."

"He won't like it," Denny warned.

"There won't be much he can do about it. I'm not going to wait until it's official to start taking steps to improve my standing around here, either. Starting tomorrow, I'm going to visit each of the mines and inspect them. I've been studying hydraulic mining even more, and if there's anything that isn't being done to protect the rangeland, I'm going to order the crews to put those practices into effect immediately, even if it decreases our production. If Axel doesn't like it . . ." Conrad shrugged. "Soon enough, he won't have any say in the matter."

"You're going to get a lot of arguments about this," Denny predicted.

"I don't care. There's no reason we can't get that gold out without ruining things for the cattlemen."

Denny nodded slowly. "Maybe I was a little too quick to judge you, Conrad. If I didn't know better, I'd say you almost sound like you mean it."

"I do mean it, and I'll prove it to you."

"How are you going to do that?"

"Tomorrow morning, before I ride up to the Spanish Peso, I'll stop by the Sugarloaf. You can ride with me and see for yourself that I'm serious. You can help me inspect the mine and listen while I give the orders to the crew."

Denny wasn't sure she needed that confirmation, but what he proposed sounded interesting. The idea of spending a few hours with him held some appeal, too. Despite the anger she had often felt toward him, Conrad Morgan possessed some admirable qualities. He was smart, tough, and had plenty of ambition. He was very good with a gun. Given Denny's background, that was important to her. And he wasn't exactly repulsive to look at . . .

She shoved that thought away. Without getting bogged down in too many mental wanderings, she said, "All right. I'll take you up on it. I'll be ready to ride when you come by."

He smiled. "Good. You'll see, things are going to be different around here from now on."

Denny would believe that when it actually happened, but she was willing to give him the benefit of the doubt.

And maybe taking a ride with him tomorrow would be fun.

CHAPTER 34

"If you're riding up to Hammerhead Canyon with Conrad Morgan, you'd better take your guns," Smoke said the next morning at breakfast, after Denny had explained her plans for the day.

"I don't ever ride out on the range without my carbine," Denny replied.

"Take your Lightning, too," said Smoke.

Sally put down her coffee cup. A concerned frown creased her forehead. "Do you really think it's that dangerous, Smoke? We may not agree with everything Conrad has done, but I just don't believe he would ever act improperly toward Denny. He was raised to be a gentleman."

Smoke grunted. "An Eastern *gentleman* isn't exactly the same as a Westerner. But that's not what I meant. With rustlers and outlaws running loose in the valley, there's no telling what they might stumble into. And emotions are running pretty high against Conrad among the ranch hands around here."

"That's true," said Sally. She turned her frown toward Denny. "I don't think you should go."

"I'll be well-armed," Denny assured her. "More than likely, Conrad will be, too." She laughed. "If he's not packing iron when he gets here, he can always borrow a Colt."

317

"I think it'll be all right," Smoke told Sally. "Anybody foolish enough to tackle those two"— he smiled—"would be in for a mighty big surprise. I can probably get Pearlie to ride along with them, though, if that will make you feel better."

"That's not necessary," Denny said quickly. "We'll be fine."

"All right," Sally said, although not without a note of reluctance in her voice. "I suppose we're long past the point where I should be worrying all the time about where you are and what you're doing. When you're a parent, though, it's hard not to do that. You'll understand someday."

Denny understood what Sally meant, but she thought maybe her mother was being a mite too optimistic about the prospect of her having kids of her own someday. That wasn't really in her plans the way running the Sugarloaf was.

She finished her breakfast and drank the rest of her coffee, then went upstairs to buckle on her gunbelt. She wore jeans, a faded red shirt, and a buckskin vest. She paused in front of the dressing-table mirror long enough to tuck her hair under her dark brown Stetson and make sure it wasn't going to escape.

Smoke was waiting in the barn when Denny came in to saddle her horse.

"Going to give me some more advice?" she asked. She patted the Lightning's ivory grips.

"I'm packing a gun. My Winchester's in its saddle boot."

"I don't talk about it like your ma does," Smoke said, "but I worry about you, too. You're a grown woman and I know that, but you'll always be—"

"Your little girl." Denny smiled and came up on her toes to brush a kiss across his deeply tanned cheek. "I know that, Pa. And it makes me feel mighty good, too. Don't ever change."

"As old and set in my ways as I am, I don't expect to," Smoke said gruffly. As he watched Denny walk toward Rocket's stall, he went on, "Are you riding that black devil today?"

"He's learned how to be a good horse," she said. "He hasn't given me any trouble for a long time, and I don't expect him to today."

"That's the bad thing about trouble. Sometimes we don't expect it."

Denny smiled to acknowledge his point, but she went on to Rocket's stall and saddled the stallion.

By the time she finished, she heard hoofbeats outside in the ranch yard and suspected that Conrad Morgan had arrived. She led Rocket outside and found that was the case. Smoke stood over by the porch, talking to Conrad, who was mounted on the sturdy buckskin he'd rented from the livery stable in town.

Conrad greeted her with a smile. "Good morning. Are you ready to go take a look at some of those mines with me?"

Denny noted that Conrad wore a holstered Colt, as well as having a sheathed Winchester strapped to his saddle. Smoke would be happy that he was well-armed, too.

"I'm ready," she said as she tugged her hat down a little tighter on her head.

"I asked your father if he'd like to come along with us, but he said he has too many other things to do today."

"Yeah, that's my pa," Denny said with a glance at Smoke. "He's a busy man."

As far as she knew, Smoke didn't have anything in particular that had to be done today, but if that was what he'd told Conrad, it was fine with her. She didn't believe for a second that Smoke was playing matchmaker. He just wasn't going to interfere either way. Denny put her foot in the stirrup and swung up into the saddle.

Conrad reached behind him and patted a bundle lashed on behind his saddle. "I brought some food, in case we decide to eat out on the range somewhere instead of at the mess tent at one of the mining camps," he explained.

"Smart thinking," said Smoke. "You never know when you'll need some supplies." He lifted a hand in farewell. "Be careful, you two."

"Say good-bye to Ma for me," Denny called to him, then she and Conrad rode out of the ranch yard and headed across the valley, angling northeast toward Hammerhead Canyon.

It was a beautiful day with plenty of sunshine, blue sky, and puffy white clouds, but the air also held a tang of high-country coolness. Rocket reacted to that, stepping along briskly and tossing his head. Sensing the stallion wanted to run, Denny had to hold him in a little.

If she hadn't been with Conrad, she would have been tempted to give him free rein.

However, Conrad noticed Rocket's actions, too. "He's full of spirit today, isn't he?"

"He likes to stretch his legs, especially on a nice day like this."

"Then let him," Conrad suggested. "In fact, I'll give him something to test himself against." With that, he dug his heels into the buckskin's flanks, and the horse leaped forward into a gallop.

Denny exclaimed, loosened her grip on Rocket's reins, and jabbed her own heels into the stallion's sides. Rocket took off, breaking into a run with smooth, breathtaking speed.

Conrad's buckskin was strong and ran well, but Rocket caught up to the other horse quickly and seemingly without much effort. Denny didn't try to slow him down. They flashed past Conrad and the buckskin.

Denny threw a laugh over her shoulder. She knew it would drift back to Conrad as they left him and the buckskin behind and continued toward a stand of trees on the far side of the wide meadow they were crossing.

By the time Conrad reached the trees, Denny and Rocket were resting at the edge of the shade, waiting for them. Rocket wasn't even breathing hard.

Denny grinned at Conrad. "What kept you?"

Instead of answering directly, he said, "That's quite a horse you have there. High-spirited and mighty fast. Let him have his head and he'll run all day, won't he?"

Denny nodded. "That's right."

"Sort of like the girl riding him," drawled Conrad.

Denny nudged her horse closer to him. "Are you saying we should get down from these saddles and run a footrace?"

"That wasn't exactly what I was suggesting."

"I didn't think so." With a toss of her head, she tightened up on Rocket's reins and turned the stallion. As she kneed him into motion again, she continued. "Come on. You promised to show me those mines."

"All right." He added under his breath, "I'll show you some other things, one of these days."

"What was that?" she asked, although she knew good and well what he had just said. Her hearing was pretty good.

"Nothing," Conrad replied. "Let's go. We'll be at Hammerhead Canyon and the Spanish Peso in less than an hour."

• • •

Jubal Kinch lowered the field glasses from his eyes, turned his head to spit, and said, "Yeah, that's them, Mace. They're still at least half a mile away, but they're comin' this direction steady-like."

His brother Early said, "We shoulda jumped Morgan earlier when we had the chance, afore he got together with that Jensen girl."

Mace Lundeen put his hand on the butt of his gun. "If you want to complain about the decisions I make, Early, you know the best way to do that."

Early Kinch held up a hand and shook his head. "No, no, I ain't meanin' to complain, Mace," he said quickly. "You know that. Jubal and me have been ridin' with you for a good long time now, and you ain't ever steered us wrong. You know what you're doin'."

"Damn right I do," Lundeen grunted. Inside, though, he cursed himself.

Early Kinch was right. They should have struck sooner, while they were following their quarry from Big Rock. Now they had to deal not only with Conrad Morgan but with Denny Jensen as well. From everything Lundeen had heard about her, she was no shrinking violet. She would fight if threatened, and she was good at it.

Even worse, her pa was Smoke Jensen. If anything happened to his girl, Jensen would go on the vengeance trail. Nobody in his right mind wanted Smoke Jensen coming after him with blood in his eye.

Lundeen planned to take advantage of the confusion following the deaths of Morgan and the girl to grab what he could and shake the dust of this country off his heels. He wanted that other five thousand dollars Axel Strom had promised him, but he figured on getting his hands on more than that. Strom had money in the bank in Big Rock. He was going to draw it out, every bit of it, and turn it over to Lundeen.

Maybe . . . maybe there was an even bigger payoff to be had, mused Lundeen as he stood at the edge of the cliff looking out at the valley. Big Rock would be in an uproar when word of the killings got there. That would be a good time to hit the bank and clean it out completely. He and his men had never indulged in bank robbery . . . but hell, there was a first time for everything, wasn't there?

While that was going on, a couple of the men could push the rest of those rustled cows on out of the canyon in the north and drive them over into eastern Colorado to sell them. They could bring the profits from that down to the rendezvous in Mexico.

Yeah, a quick strike on two fronts, decided Lundeen. That would garner them the biggest payday.

And the ambush of Conrad Morgan and Denny Jensen would be the first step.

Lundeen, the Kinch brothers, Ennis Desmond, and a half-breed everybody called Crowbait were gathered atop the cliff not far south of where Hammerhead Canyon cut into the palisade. Tom Clute and the others waited on horseback inside the canyon's mouth. Once the shooting stopped, they would come out and make sure Morgan and the girl were dead.

Might be a good idea to take the girl's body with us, Lundeen thought. Her disappearance would confuse the issue even more. It had to be well-established that Morgan was dead, otherwise Strom wouldn't be able to claim his share of the partnership.

Strom was a fool. Everybody would blame him for Morgan's murder, even without any proof. He'd never be able to operate effectively in the valley with such a cloud of suspicion hanging over him. Strom's greed and arrogance blinded him to that fact.

But it didn't matter to Lundeen. He and his men would get their money, regardless of what happened to Axel Strom.

The Kinch brothers, Desmond, and Crowbait all knelt behind the rocky knobs of the rim. All were excellent shots and had their rifles ready. Lundeen watched the approaching pair of riders for a moment longer. Morgan was on that big buckskin he normally rode. The Jensen girl straddled a magnificent black stallion.

Lundeed wouldn't mind having that horse for himself . . . if they were able to catch it. One more thing he'd come out with.

"All right," he said to his men.

In response, they lifted their rifles and rested them on the rocks.

"When I give the order . . . *cut 'em down!*"

CHAPTER 35

Conrad had stopped flirting so shamelessly as he and Denny continued across the valley toward the Spanish Peso Mine. It was a relief in one way. She was having a hard time sorting out her feelings regarding Conrad, Brice Rogers, and Blaise Warfield.

It felt like one of those stupid plays she had seen in England where folks sat around fancy drawing rooms and uttered brittle, witty dialogue. Denny preferred things to be simple and direct. She knew that wasn't the way most ladies acted, but she couldn't help it.

Conrad spent most of the time talking about hydraulic mining. He told her all about the changes he intended to make in the way they used the heavy equipment at the mines. She understood most of it—many of the precautions were just common sense, after all—but found her mind wandering anyway.

During one of those intervals, she idly lifted her gaze to the rimrock ahead of them as they angled toward the mouth of Hammerhead Canyon a few hundred yards to the north.

The flash of reflected sunlight from the top of the cliff lasted only a fraction of a second, but that was enough.

Denny acted instantly, without thinking about it. She dug her heels into Rocket's flanks, hauled hard on the reins, and drove the stallion against Conrad's buckskin. Slightly larger and heavier, Rocket's shoulder rammed into the buckskin's shoulder, and the buckskin stumbled to the right and almost fell.

Conrad yelled, "Hey!"

At the same instant the surprised exclamation left his mouth, something whipped between his head and Denny's, closely enough for both of them to hear the flat *whap!* of a passing bullet.

"Go! Go!" Denny called to him. "Head for the canyon!"

The same instinct that had told her the flash of reflected light came from a bushwhacker's rifle barrel made her certain that the ambush wasn't over. More shots would come from up on the rimrock. Probably more than one rifleman was hidden up there, too.

Denny leaned forward in the saddle to make herself a smaller target as she galloped toward Hammerhead Canyon. She turned her head to glance over her shoulder and saw that Conrad wasn't far behind, just a short distance to the right. He had regained control of the buckskin and was urging all the speed he could muster from the animal.

Over the drumming of hoofbeats, she heard the irregularly spaced whipcracks of rifle shots and felt the heat of a slug practically kissing the back of her neck. Part of her wanted to stop and fight back. It wouldn't take but a moment to rein in, yank the Winchester carbine from its saddle sheath, and start throwing lead back at the ambushers.

In that moment, though, she might be drilled half a dozen times. It made more sense to keep moving. She'd be harder to hit that way.

Once they reached the canyon mouth, the bushwhackers wouldn't have an angle to shoot at them anymore, not without changing position. Denny felt like she and Conrad could reach the Spanish Peso before that happened.

She realized that she was holding Rocket back. If she hadn't, they would have run away from Conrad and the buckskin, but she wasn't going to abandon him. They would escape from this ambush together—or not at all.

He drew almost alongside and called, "Denny! Are you all right?"

"Yes!" she replied. "How about you?"

"I'm not hit! I'd sure like a shot at those men up on the rim, though!"

She felt exactly the same way.

"Who do you think they are?" he went on.

"How in blazes would I know? You're the one they're trying to kill! I'm just in the wrong place at the wrong time!"

"How do you figure that?"

329

"Nobody's got any reason to want me dead!"

"But nobody—" Conrad stopped short in what he was saying.

Denny knew he had figured out the same thing that had occurred to her just now.

Plenty of men in the valley had grudges against Conrad Morgan—but only one had a group of hired killers at his command. Only one stood to lose a great deal if Conrad carried out his plans. And that same one would gain half a potential fortune if Conrad was dead.

If Axel Strom had found out somehow that Conrad intended to force him out of their partnership—

Dust flew in front of Rocket as a bullet struck the ground, breaking into Denny's thoughts and made her veer the stallion to the left. They needed to be zigzagging to make themselves harder targets while they tried to reach Hammerhead Canyon.

The thought of the canyon made Denny look toward it. As she did, her heart fell. Half a dozen riders spurred from the entrance and raced toward them. Denny knew without having to think about that those horsebackers were more of the enemy.

Conrad had spotted them, too. He shouted, "They've got us cut off!"

Denny kept turning the stallion toward the center of the valley. "We have to get around them!"

330

Another bullet whistled past her ear. They couldn't turn and race away at right angles to the cliff, she realized. The bushwhackers up there would have easy shots at them. The fact that they had been moving from north to south, parallel to the cliff, had made them more difficult to hit.

Still, if they could angle toward the center of the valley enough to get around the men on horseback, without getting blown out of the saddle . . .

Denny knew this valley better than Mace Lundeen and his men, she told herself. If she had just half a chance, she could give them the slip. She was sure of it. "Follow me!" she called to Conrad.

She eased off on the reins a little. Rocket picked up speed and pulled farther ahead, but she didn't let him leave Conrad in the dust.

The riders waiting in the canyon opened fire. Denny saw the puffs of smoke from their guns. The range was too long for handguns, so she wasn't worried about them hitting anything unless they got closer.

She didn't intend to let that happen.

"Over there!" she called to Conrad as she pointed at a line of trees. She knew a broad wash, dry eleven months out of the year, lay just on the side of those trees, and figured on a good chance the men pursuing them didn't.

Not only that, she also knew where to find the

trail that would let her and Conrad descend into the wash without breaking their horses' legs. "Be ready for a sharp turn to the right up here!"

They flashed through the trees with Denny in the lead, weaving Rocket back and forth around the trunks. The buckskin responded beautifully to Conrad's knees and his touch on the reins, so they navigated through the band of growth without slowing too much.

Fifty yards later, Denny emerged from the trees and hauled hard on Rocket's reins. The stallion took the turn deftly and raced along the bank, which dropped an almost sheer dozen feet to the dry bed of the wash.

Denny looked back, half afraid that Conrad's horse wouldn't be able to make it. Seeing him about twenty feet behind her, relief surged through her.

She hoped the pursuers wouldn't see the wash in time to slow their horses. She hated to think about the poor animals piling off into the wash, but those men wanted to kill her and Conrad, so she was going to pull every trick she could think of to get away from them.

Ahead, part of the bank had caved in and formed a gentle slope for horses to handle. Denny pointed to it and called over her shoulder, "Up there!"

Conrad jerked his head in a nod of understanding.

She had to slow the stallion again in order to make the turn onto the slope. As they clattered down into the wash, rocks flew from under Rocket's hooves until they reached the bottom and Denny reined in long enough to look back and see the buckskin half leaping, half sliding down the slope. The rough descent jolted Conrad back and forth, but he clung to the saddle expertly.

Then he was beside her. "Where are we headed now?"

"This wash runs mostly northwest, but it twists and turns enough they shouldn't be able to get a clear shot at us, even if they follow us."

"Is there any place we can give them the slip?"

"Another canyon north of Hammerhead. Once we leave the wash, we'll head that way. It leads up into some badlands where it'll be harder for them to find us."

"Sounds good. Let's go!"

Denny heard hoofbeats not too far away and knew the would-be killers were closing in on the trees. Conrad was right. It was time for them to light a shuck.

A minute later, she heard horses screaming and men shouting behind them. Some of the pursuers had emerged from the trees at a full gallop and been unable to stop before their horses plunged into the wash. Again, she hated to think of the fate of those poor animals, but that ought to slow down the pursuit.

It didn't bring the chase to a complete stop, though. Hoofbeats still sounded back there. Lundeen's men were still after them.

As they neared the first big bend in the wash, Conrad pulled alongside her again. "I'm sorry I got you into—"

A rifle cracked behind them. He grunted, twisted, and leaned forward sharply in the saddle. His left hand clutched the horn.

"Conrad!" Denny cried. "You're hit!"

"Keep going!" he told her through clenched teeth. "I'll be all right!"

Moving that fast, she had no way of knowing if he was telling the truth. She couldn't see any blood on his clothes but didn't have any doubt that a bullet had struck him. She had heard the thud of lead against flesh. It was a sound she knew too well.

They swept around the bend as more shots blasted behind them. The straightaways ahead were shorter, Denny knew, which would make it more difficult for the gun-wolves to draw a bead on them.

"Can you make it?" she called to Conrad.

"Just . . . keep moving!"

She heard the strain in his voice and spotted a dark stain on his shirt and trousers, low down on his left side. From the looks of it, a bullet had just clipped him, but that was enough to hurt like blazes, especially on top of a galloping horse.

He was right. They had to keep moving. If they stopped, they would have to shoot it out with the men pursuing them. That was a bad idea. They didn't know how many killers were back there, or what kind of shape they were in.

An idea occurred to Denny. She and Conrad had ridden into an ambush; maybe it was time to return the favor.

She slowed Rocket slightly and said, "Follow this wash for another half mile. There'll be a trail to the right that leads to the top. Ride out and head a little bit north of east, and you'll come to that smaller canyon leading into the badlands. Follow it until you find a good place to hole up!"

"What do you think you're going to do?" he asked.

She grasped her carbine and pulled it from the sheath. "I'll give them a hotter reception than they're expecting! That'll slow them down some!"

"You're loco! You'll just get yourself killed!"

"No, I won't. I know what I'm doing—"

"We fight them together or not at all!"

Even though they were riding at nearly top speed, trying to stay ahead of the men who wanted to kill them, for a moment their eyes met and locked. Denny saw the same fierce determination she had felt when she refused to leave him behind.

Those locked gazes didn't last long, but it was

long enough to form a bond that would never be broken. A bond of comrades in arms, facing danger together . . . and maybe something more.

"All right!" she said. "We'll make a run for the canyon. Come on!"

CHAPTER 36

Conrad did his best to ignore the pain radiating out from his left hip. It wasn't the first time he'd been shot. He knew how to set aside the discomfort and concentrate on what had to be done.

Somehow, it was harder to do when he had Denny to worry about. If anything happened to her . . .

If anything happened to her, he wouldn't just force Axel Strom out of their partnership, Conrad vowed. He would kill the Prussian son of a—

"There!" Denny cried, pointing. "There's the trail out!"

It was steeper than the one that had brought them into the wash. Denny's black stallion took it at full stride anyway, lunging and driving up the slope.

Conrad was close behind her. With every jolt, a fresh stab of pain went through him. He gritted his teeth and hung on.

The short climb seemed longer than it really was, but eventually they were out on level ground again. The stallion appeared tireless, a sleek, black machine in the guise of horseflesh. However, Conrad felt the buckskin beginning to labor beneath him. The horse had sand and plenty of it, but not an unlimited supply.

Neither do I, thought Conrad wryly.

Although Denny had offered to stay behind and slow down the pursuit, Conrad had refused, of course. That was something *he* ought to be doing, not her. He called to her, "As soon as we find some good cover, I'll fort up there and teach those rannies a lesson!"

She looked back over her shoulder at him. Her hat had come off and hung behind her shoulders by its chin strap. The wind of their galloping pace whipped her blond curls around her face.

Conrad thought she had never looked lovelier.

"You're a loco coyote!" she responded to his suggestion. "What happened to 'We'll fight them together or not at all'?"

"My horse can't keep this pace up, and neither can I. If I can give you a chance to get away—"

"Forget it! They might not kill me. I'm Smoke Jensen's daughter, after all. But you . . . they're bound and determined to kill *you,* Conrad!"

She's right about that, he thought. Although he didn't believe Lundeen would allow her to live, whether she was Smoke Jensen's daughter or not. Too much lead had flown around their heads already for Conrad to believe that. Clearly, Lundeen didn't care about Denny's life.

Conrad did care. The thought that Denny might die because of Strom's grudge against him gnawed at Conrad's guts and hurt as much as his hip where the bullet had slammed against it.

"Another mile!" she urged him. "Another mile and we'll be in that canyon! We can get away from them!"

Conrad nodded and weakly waved her on. He hoped he wasn't riding the valiant buckskin to death.

He hadn't heard any shots behind them for a while. When he looked back, he thought he saw some riders in the distance, but he wasn't sure. Out on the flats, Denny's stallion could outrun any of the gun-wolves' horses. The buckskin could hold his own as long as he didn't wear out.

The pursuers had to worry about riding their mounts into the ground, too, Conrad reminded himself. They couldn't catch up to their intended quarry if they were set afoot.

He wondered what had happened to the bushwhackers who had been on top of the cliff. They had had time to make their way into the valley and join the chase, but had they?

Or were they lurking somewhere ahead of him and Denny, hoping to spring another trap?

"Better keep an eye out," he called to her. "Some of them might have gotten ahead of us."

"I know. I've been watching for them."

She rode with her carbine across the saddle in front of her, ready to whip it to her shoulder and open fire. Conrad would have pulled his Winchester from the saddle scabbard, too, if he hadn't needed both hands to hang on since he'd been wounded. He was starting to feel weak. He knew that was due to the blood he'd lost. He didn't believe he was in any danger of bleeding to death, but he might pass out, and under the circumstances, that was almost as bad.

Time became meaningless. He didn't know how long they had been fleeing from the killers. It seemed like hours, perhaps even days. The world was hazy in front of him, as if a fog bank had moved into the valley. He knew that wasn't true; it was his vision that was going.

His strength was gone, too. He could no longer jab his heels into his horse's flanks to keep it moving. The buckskin began to slow as its own exhaustion claimed it.

"Blast it!"

Conrad heard Denny's frustrated exclamation. He lifted his head and saw that she had gotten farther ahead of him. Realizing that she was leaving him behind, she stopped and wheeled the stallion to hurry back toward him.

She stopped alongside him and reached over to take the reins out of his hands. "Just hang on. I'll get you out of here!"

Conrad nodded, mumbled, "Thanks . . . Denny . . . I'm obliged—"

"Shut up and hang on!" She got the stallion moving again and tugged on the reins to lead the buckskin.

Conrad swayed back and forth in the saddle

and tightened his grip until the horn felt like he was going to crush the jutting piece of leather-covered wood.

Everything faded around him, but somehow he hung on.

The thought of saving herself never occurred to Denny, but she *was* a mite annoyed with Conrad Morgan. If he hadn't trusted an obvious varmint like Axel Strom, they wouldn't be in this mess right now, with a bunch of kill-crazy hired guns after them.

The past couldn't be changed, though. The best a person could do was fight to make the future as good as possible.

Used to fighting with bullets and occasionally fists, she also had to fight with grit and determination and cunning.

Her spirits leaped as she spotted the narrow mouth of a canyon up ahead. That was her goal. She had never really explored the badlands that lay at the other end of that canyon, but she knew they were there. A rugged trail led into them. She and Smoke planned to ride all through there someday, but they hadn't gotten around to it yet.

It was never a good idea to put things off too much, mused Denny. You never knew when you might not get another chance to do what you really wanted. That thought made her glance back at Conrad. He looked like he was just about out, but had managed somehow to stay in the saddle.

He couldn't die, she told herself suddenly. He just couldn't! She hadn't figured out yet what to do about him and Brice Rogers!

"Hold on, Conrad," she said softly, knowing that he probably couldn't hear her—but hoping that the sentiment would get through to him anyway.

The cliff loomed up. They rode through the canyon mouth, which was about twenty yards wide. As soon as they were beyond it, shadows cast by the high walls closed around them and the temperature seemed to drop considerably. That was all right with Denny. The cooler air felt good after the hot, sweaty, desperate ride they had made.

And it wasn't over yet, she reminded herself. She had no idea how much of a lead they might have over the men chasing them, determined to end their lives. They had to keep moving.

The horses were just about played out, even Rocket. She slowed their pace.

Conrad lifted his head. "Wha . . . where . . . where are we?" he asked.

"We made it to that canyon I told you about," said Denny. "Now we're going to give those varmints the slip and find a place to hole up long enough to see how bad you're hurt."

"I'm . . . fine . . . Don' worry . . . 'bout me . . ."

Yeah, you look and sound just fine, thought Denny. He was starting to remind her of death warmed over.

The canyon ran mostly straight for nearly a mile, then it took a sharp, almost ninety-degree turn to the left. Denny felt a little better once that bend was behind them, although she had no doubt that the gun-wolves would be able to follow their trail and would know that they had gone into the canyon. There hadn't been time to conceal their tracks.

After a couple more bends, they came to a place where the canyon forked. Denny reined in and said, "What do you think? Right or left?" It was a gamble either way.

When Conrad didn't answer, she looked quickly over her shoulder. What she saw made her exclaim and call his name. He had sagged forward against the buckskin's neck.

As she slipped out of the saddle and let Rocket's reins dangle, hoping he would stay ground-hitched, she prayed that Conrad had just passed out and was still alive.

He was, she saw to her great relief as she sprang to his side and grasped his arm. He roused a little at her touch and opened his eyes.

"D-Denny . . . ?" Amazingly, he smiled. "You sure are . . . pretty . . ."

"Oh, shut up," she whispered. "This is no time for compliments. Tell me how pretty I am some other time. Can you ride? Do I need to tie you in the saddle?"

"N-no . . . I can make it." He drew in a deep

breath and seemed more alert. "Feel better now. Jus' needed . . . a lil' nap."

"All right. *Don't you fall off that horse.*"

She went back to the stallion and quickly swung up in the saddle. They moved out, following her instinct and taking the right-hand branch of the canyon, but she kept a closer eye on Conrad, glancing back often to make sure he wasn't swaying and in danger of toppling from the saddle.

At the same time, she listened for sounds of pursuit and watched closely ahead of them for any signs of another ambush. As far as she could tell, they were alone in the canyon. She saw birds and small animals and knew that they hadn't been disturbed recently. That was a good sign.

After a little while, she began to worry that she had made the wrong choice at the fork. The stone walls closed in on both sides and the canyon shrank until it was a narrow cleft no more than fifteen or twenty feet wide. If it choked down to a point and ended, they would have to turn around and retrace their steps . . . and that would take them closer and closer to the men who were after them.

Then the canyon widened slightly. A ledge ran up the left-hand wall and curved around out of sight.

That might be a trail leading out of here, she thought. It was so narrow they would have to ride single file, and she would have to rely on Conrad to stay mounted. If he toppled off the buckskin, the fall might be fatal.

The ledge looked like it climbed pretty high. She found herself wanting to chance it.

She stopped again, and despite his objections, lashed him into the saddle. He couldn't fall to his death—not without taking the horse with him.

"Where are we . . . going?" he asked.

"Up there," she said, pointing.

"You mean . . . Heaven?" He laughed. "I don't . . . think so . . . not after . . . some of the things . . . I've done . . . You might . . . make it . . . though . . . You already . . . look like . . . an angel."

"There you go again with the compliments," she said gruffly. "We're going up that one-way trail and see what we find at the top. I'll lead your horse. All you have to do is ride."

"I can . . . do that."

She hoped so. Grasping the buckskin's reins, she mounted the stallion and started up the ledge. She knew Rocket was fast. It would be a good thing if he was sure-footed, too.

She trusted the stallion's instincts and let him pick his own way and set his own pace. That allowed her to hip around in the saddle and watch Conrad as he rode behind her. She thought about trying the buckskin's reins to her saddle horn. That way, if Conrad and his mount went over, Denny and Rocket would be pulled along, too. *Together or not at all,* she told herself.

But she wasn't quite bold enough to do that. She wanted to survive this encounter with the men who were after Conrad. She wanted to help pay them back for what they had done.

Rocket followed the trail higher, around the curving canyon wall. As they came out on another straightaway, Denny let out a gasp of surprise. At the top of the slope, tucked away at another spot where the canyon bent sharply about a hundred yards away, was a small, brush-covered bench, no more than twenty yards long. With that thick growth, it might offer a decent hiding place.

However, that was where the ledge ended. There was no way out from there, so if Lundeen and his men trailed them here, they would be stuck. The gun-wolves couldn't advance up the ledge to the bench; with the Winchesters and plenty of ammunition, Denny could pick them off one by one, easily.

But Lundeen could starve them out, and she had to worry about Conrad's wounded hip, too.

Maybe the pursuers wouldn't spot their sign. The ledge was too rocky to take hoofprints. Maybe Lundeen and his men would ride right past it.

Denny couldn't make herself believe that would happen, but she had to hold out hope. It wasn't in her nature to give up.

"Hold on, Conrad," she muttered. "We're almost there."

At the very least, they could stop and she could check out his wound, maybe patch it up and stop the bleeding.

Once that was done, they could prepare to fight for their lives.

CHAPTER 37

Because Denny was still being careful ascending the narrow ledge, several minutes passed before she and Conrad reached the bench. Denny dismounted and led both horses, following a narrow game trail through the thick growth.

"Almost there," she told Conrad.

"I'm . . . fine," he said. "Jus' fine."

Denny knew that wasn't true, but she didn't waste her breath arguing with him. She hoped to find a clearing in the brush where she could get Conrad off the buckskin and they couldn't be seen from below. What she discovered was even better.

At the back of the brush, mostly screened off by the growth, was the mouth of a cave about five feet tall and that same distance wide. Denny left Conrad and the horses where they were and went to the opening. She bent to peer into the shadows. She couldn't see very far, but she had matches in a small tin container in the pocket of the faded work shirt, so she took one of them out and snapped it to life with her thumbnail the way Smoke had taught her when she was seven years old.

The light from the match penetrated far enough to reveal that the cave's ceiling rose to a height of seven or eight feet. Denny stepped inside and held the match up. The space widened, too, spreading out to a dozen feet wide and maybe twenty deep.

Something on the walls caught Denny's attention. She stepped closer and caught her breath as she saw faded drawings of stick figures, crudely rendered animals, and shapes that probably represented the sun, the stars, and several geographic features such as mountains and rivers.

She was familiar with cave drawings. Some had been found in Europe that were estimated to be tens of thousands of years old. The Indians who had left behind these drawings probably hadn't lived here *that* long ago, but they were still ancient.

From the looks of it, the cave hadn't had any regular occupants since then except maybe some animals. A bear or two might have denned up for the winter in there. The litter of dead, dusty leaves from the brush outside that had blown inside looked like it hadn't been disturbed in a long time. Denny kicked through it, anyway, just to be sure no rats or snakes were lurking.

Satisfied that it would be safe to bring Conrad inside, she pushed together a pile of leaves, then stepped out of the cave, shook out the match, and dropped it on the rock to grind it with her toe, making certain it was extinguished. She grabbed the rolled-up blanket she always carried behind the saddle and returned to the cave to spread it on the leaves, making a bed of sorts.

She went to the buckskin. Conrad's head had drooped forward and his eyes were closed, but he was breathing. He lifted his head as she started to untie the ropes holding him in the saddle.

"Are we back at the hotel?" he asked in a clear, strong, but uncomprehending voice. "I think we should go to dinner, don't you?"

"Sure."

He really was disoriented and didn't know where they were or what was going on.

She reached up to take hold of him and went on. "Let's get you inside."

As Conrad tried to dismount, he lost his balance and fell.

Denny had her legs braced, and caught him, managing to get his feet on the ground without both of them toppling over. "Come on," she told him. "You'll have to walk. I can't carry you." She could drag him, though, and she would if she had to.

Conrad managed to hobble along, wincing every time he put any weight on his injured left side. "What . . . what happened to me? What's wrong with me?"

"You got shot. You just don't remember right now."

"A . . . a gunfight? Some young firebrand . . .

trying to make his rep . . . as the man who killed Kid Morgan?"

"Kid Morgan?" Denny repeated. "Who . . . I don't know . . . Never mind that now! Come on, bend down a little. We're going in this cave . . ."

"This isn't the hotel!"

"No, but you'll be all right." She maneuvered him to the pile of leaves with the blanket spread over it and helped him lie down. He groaned as he stretched out.

"Stay right there," she told him. "I'll tend to the horses, and then I'll be right back." She tied their reins to some sturdy branches so they couldn't stray and would unsaddle the horses later.

At the moment, she took the saddlebags off Rocket. She had things in there that would help her deal with Conrad's injury. Nobody with any sense rode the range without taking along some rudimentary medical supplies.

Conrad had brought along some food, too, she recalled, and their canteens were full. They would be able to hold out for a while, even if Lundeen and his men laid siege to the cave.

And once some time passed and she didn't return to the Sugarloaf, Smoke would come looking for her. She didn't doubt that for a second. She didn't doubt that he would find her, either, and then Mace Lundeen would wish he'd never been born.

She put those thoughts aside to deal with more

pressing problems. She needed light if she was going to check Conrad's wound. She gathered some dead branches from the brush outside, used dried leaves for kindling, and soon had a small fire going. Some of the smoke drifted out the cave mouth. The air inside would get foul if she left the fire burning too long, but she thought they could stand it long enough for her to examine the wound.

He lay on the blanket with his head turned to the side and his eyes closed as if he were asleep. Denny knew he had passed out again. She took her clasp knife from her pocket, opened it, and started cutting away the blood-soaked shirt.

Conrad stirred a little.

Denny whispered, "Shhh. Just lie there and rest. I'll take care of you."

"Rebel?" Conrad murmured without opening his eyes. "Rebel, is that you?"

Who in blazes is Rebel?

He turned his head and opened his eyes. As he peered up into her face, he said, "Rebel! It *is* you. I thought I was dreaming, but you . . . you've come back . . . to me . . ."

His strength was already deserting him again. To keep things simple and to prevent him from using more of his reserves, Denny said, "That's right, it's Rebel. I'm here, Conrad, and I'll take care of you. Just rest and don't worry about anything."

352

His eyelids lowered slowly.

"Rebel," he breathed again. "I thought I'd never . . . never see you . . ." With a sigh, his head fell back to the side.

Once again, Denny had a bad moment, thinking that he might have died, but his chest continued to rise and fall, easing that concern.

She bent to her work . . . but she still wondered who Rebel was.

She didn't have to cut away his trousers, although she eased them down a little. The wound was more than a deep graze; the bullet had penetrated his side and bored a tunnel a short distance under the skin before blasting out through an exit wound. She studied the bloody holes, calculated angles in her head, and decided there was a good chance the slug had missed the hip bone. Conrad had lost some meat and blood, but although it was messy, the wound shouldn't be life-threatening.

That depended on her getting it clean enough to keep blood poisoning from setting in. Grunting with the effort, she turned him onto his right side. His lean build was deceptive; he was a good-sized man. He didn't wake up, which she was grateful for. He would regain consciousness soon enough.

She cut a piece from his shirt that wasn't sodden with blood and wet it with water from one of the canteens. Carefully, she swabbed blood from around the bullet holes. They were still oozing crimson, but for the most part, the bleeding had stopped.

She delved into the saddlebags again and came up with a silver flask Pearlie had given to her, explaining that a wise cowboy always carried some whiskey with him.

"Purely for medicinal purposes, you understand," he had said.

That was exactly how she intended to use it—although after she'd unscrewed the cap, she took a tiny sip from the flask. Just enough to feel the warmth going down and draw some strength from it then carefully began trickling the fiery stuff into the bullet hole closer to Conrad's front.

His eyes snapped open, and he let out a strangled cry.

Denny clapped her free hand over his mouth, leaned closer, and whispered, "Quiet! We don't know how close Lundeen and his men are. I'd rather them not find us right away."

Conrad groaned against her palm.

"I know, it hurts like the devil. But it's got to be done."

He nodded. His lips moved, and when Denny took away her hand, he whispered, "Go ahead." He sounded like the pain had shocked him back into an awareness of the situation.

She took one of the broken branches she hadn't

354

fed into the fire and slipped it between his teeth. "Here. Bite on this."

"All . . . right."

She went back to cleaning the wound with whiskey from the flask. He groaned softly now and then but didn't make any more loud noises.

Even though she was concentrating on what she was doing, Denny kept one ear cocked for noises of horses or men outside. She thought that sound would carry well enough in the narrow canyon to give her some warning if Lundeen and his men approached. If she heard them coming in time, she could hurry out of the cave and clamp her hands on the noses of Rocket and the buckskin to keep them from calling out to the other horses.

A great quiet hung over the canyon, however. Maybe the gun-wolves had lost their trail somehow. Denny would have to see proof of that to believe it, but she could hope, anyway.

Sure she had saturated the wound with whiskey from one end to the other, she cut more cloth from Conrad's shirt and fashioned thick pads that she also soaked with the liquor. She bound those in place, one on each bullet hole, with strips of cloth from the shirt.

He had spat out the branch, which was covered with teeth marks and nearly bitten in two. "Looks like . . . you've pretty well used up . . . the part I didn't bleed all over."

"I figured you can afford another shirt." She sat

back on her heels and managed to smile despite how bone tired she felt and the tension that pulled at her nerves.

"Yeah, I'll be all right. What's the . . . verdict? Will I live?"

"I never had any doubt about that," Denny said. "You're too stubborn and full of yourself to die."

"I reckon you'd know . . . about things like that." Conrad licked his lips. "Have you got . . . any of that whiskey left? You should have . . . given me a slug of it . . . before you started . . . gouging out my insides . . . you know."

"I needed it myself to steady my nerves." She held one of the canteens to his lips. "Here, drink this instead. It'll help with all that blood you leaked out."

Conrad gulped down water. She was careful not to give him too much. When she took the canteen away, he let his head fall back on the blanket and sighed.

After lying there quietly for a moment, he said, "Thank you, Denny. You saved my life. I never would have made it this far without you." His voice sounded considerably stronger. His face was still very pale and drawn, and his eyes seemed sunken in deep pits.

But any improvement was welcome. She looked at him. "I wasn't going to let you die before you'd had a chance to deal with Strom and Lundeen. After all the misery they've caused in this valley, whatever happens to them, they've got it coming."

"Most people around here . . . think that I'm just as responsible . . . for the misery . . . as they are . . . and that I've . . . got it coming, too. Nobody's going to . . . shed any tears . . . over me dying."

Denny wasn't so sure about that. "The only things you did wrong were trusting Strom and trying to work it all out so that everybody was happy. Nobody can blame you for that, especially when you've tried to make it right. And once Strom is gone and the law has dealt with Lundeen, I'm sure you *will* make it right."

"You think anybody will ever listen to me again?"

"They will if my father listens to you," Denny declared. "And I'll see to it that happens"—she shrugged—"as long as we get out of here alive. Speaking of which, if you're all right, I'd better go fetch in the supplies and the rifles and make sure the horses are out of sight."

"I'm fine," he told her.

Denny carried the supplies and rifles into the cave, then led the horses deeper into the brush, unsaddled them, and left them where they could graze on the sparse grass growing amid the bushes. She wasn't sure if the animals could be seen from down below, but it was the best she could do. The cave wasn't big enough for them, too.

By the time she was finished with that, Conrad's eyes were closed and his chest rose and fell in a steady rhythm. He was sound asleep. The rest would do him good.

She didn't disturb him.

Breaking out the supplies he had brought, she realized the food was more like what somebody would pack for a picnic—fried chicken, a loaf of bread, corn on the cob . . . even an apple pie—rather than provisions for a camping trip. If they rationed it out, they could make it last a couple of days. She didn't expect to be there any longer than that.

Her father would come looking for her before then.

She let the fire go out, knowing that she could start another without any trouble. That allowed the lingering smoke to drift away. Her eyes had adjusted to the shadows inside the cave, so she didn't have any trouble seeing Conrad as she sat a few feet away with her back propped against the wall.

After a while, he started stirring again. She was about to scoot closer to him when he said again, "Rebel . . ."

Denny stayed where she was. She knew she didn't have any right to feel jealous, but her curiosity was about to get the best of her. A few more minutes went by, but he didn't say anything else.

Then he opened his eyes, lifted his head a little, and turned it to look at her. "Denny . . . I . . . I guess I was dreaming . . ."

She looked straight at him and blurted out, "Who's Rebel?"

CHAPTER 38

He drew in a sharp, surprised breath, and from the way he winced, it hurt. But the pain in his eyes came from more than just the bullet holes in his side. "Where did you hear that name?"

"You've been saying it, off and on, ever since we got here. You thought *I* was Rebel. I let you believe it, because you cooperated better when you believed she was here with you."

"How did you know . . . Rebel was a woman?"

Denny snorted. "I may not fish for compliments as much as some girls do, but I'd like to think you wouldn't mistake *me* for a man."

"No, I don't reckon anybody would ever make that mistake . . ." He lay there, seemingly looking at something far in the distance, as several seconds dragged by. Then he said, "I'm not surprised I mistook you for Rebel. She was a lot like you. Blond, beautiful . . . a crack shot . . . rode like the wind . . . could fight like a wildcat when she was cornered . . ."

"Sounds like you were pretty impressed with her."

"I was more than impressed with her. I loved her. I married her."

That startled an exclamation out of Denny. "You're married?"

Conrad shook his head. "I was. She died . . . several years ago." He swallowed hard. "She was murdered . . . by enemies of mine."

"Oh, Conrad," Denny murmured. "I'm sorry. I didn't mean to . . . to stir up a bunch of old, bad memories. You just rest, and we'll forget—"

"No, I'll never forget. I don't want to forget." He pushed himself up until he was sitting with his back braced against the wall. The effort deepened the haggard lines on his face and put a fine sheen of sweat on his brow, but he was determined. "I don't want to forget all the good times with Rebel and how much I loved her . . . and I don't want to forget what her death turned me into."

Denny frowned and shook her head. "What are you talking about?"

"Did you ever hear of Kid Morgan?"

"You mentioned the name earlier. Is that . . . *you?*"

Conrad nodded. "When Rebel died, I set out to avenge her death, but I didn't do it as myself. I let the world believe that Conrad Browning was dead. I changed the way I looked and dressed and became a gunfighter. I called myself Kid Morgan, after my father. That way I could take the men I was after by surprise.

"But when that was done . . . when I'd gotten vengeance for Rebel . . . I was still left with the knowledge that I hadn't brought her back. I was still hollow inside, and I found that . . . I liked being Kid Morgan. I liked being a drifter, roaming around and getting into trouble, helping people whenever I could . . . I think that for a while, I actually forgot who Conrad Browning was. It was like Conrad was the myth, and Kid Morgan was the reality, instead of the other way around.

"Maybe it was easier that way . . . to hide from all the things that had hurt me."

Silence reigned in the cave after Conrad finished.

He was still staring off into his memories when Denny said, "I don't think you were hiding."

Slowly, his gaze moved over to her. "What?"

"I don't think you were hiding," she repeated. "You said you helped people, didn't you?"

With a grim smile on his face, he said, "The Kid had a habit of poking his nose into things that were none of his business. Sometimes folks needed a hand from somebody who was fast with a gun."

"That was a lot more fun than sitting in an office, wasn't it?"

"It was a lot more *dangerous,* I can tell you that." Conrad paused, then chuckled. "But yeah, there were some things I liked about roaming around like that, acting like sort of a . . . knight errant, I guess you'd say. When I stop and think about it . . . my father was a lot the same way."

"So was mine, at times in his life," said Denny.

"He lost his first wife and child to killers, too."

Conrad shook his head. "I didn't know that."

"I'll tell you the story sometime, after we get out of here. He doesn't like to talk about it."

"I can understand why."

Denny felt a pang of guilt. "And then there I went, forcing you to talk about Rebel."

"No, that's all right," Conrad said quickly. "I would have told you about all that, sooner or later, even if this trouble today had never happened. I don't want there to be any secrets between us, Denny."

"You don't?"

"No. For some reason, I . . . I feel like it's important that we be honest with each other . . ."

She moved onto her knees beside him and leaned closer. "You want honesty, Conrad Morgan, I'll give you honesty." Her head was spinning, and her actions seemed somehow beyond her control. And yet, at that moment, she was doing exactly what she wanted to do.

She leaned down and kissed him hard on the mouth.

He couldn't have been more surprised if she had hauled off and punched him. In fact, he probably would have been *less* surprised if she'd punched him.

Despite that, and despite his injury, he responded. He couldn't help but feel the blood coursing hotter and faster through his veins.

Being careful not to twist his torso too much, he reached up with his right hand and cupped the back of her head as he returned the kiss. His fingers sank into her luxuriously thick blond curls. Time stretched out.

Finally, Denny lifted her head and leaned back. "I'm sorry if I hurt you—"

"You didn't," Conrad told her. "You couldn't."

"I mean . . . well, you have a bullet hole in your side. *Two* bullet holes."

He laughed. "And I might have bled to death from them if not for you. The way I see it, I owe you my life, Denny, so anything you want to do is all right with me."

"I don't want to do anything except—" She got up and moved around to his right side, away from the wound, and sat down close beside him. She leaned against him, and rested her head on his shoulder.

He put his right arm around her shoulders and held her.

"That's really nice," she murmured. "Plus, if you start to run a fever from that gunshot wound, I might be able to feel it."

Conrad laughed. "I'm glad your emotions haven't completely overwhelmed your practical side."

"There are still men out there looking for us, men who want to kill us. I'm not likely to forget that, and you shouldn't, either."

364

"Not likely," Conrad said with a grim note in his voice.

It would have been nice to just sit there and enjoy the unexpected closeness with Denny, but reality wouldn't allow him to do that. At least, not for more than a few minutes . . .

Without meaning to, he dozed off. His body was still exhausted and oblivion claimed him.

He had no idea how much time had passed when something caused him to lift his head. He blinked, frowned, and looked around. Slowly, he realized where he was and remembered everything that had happened.

Everything . . . including that kiss.

Denny was still huddled against him with her head on his shoulder. He felt her deep, regular breathing and knew that she was asleep, too. For a moment, he just sat there, reveling in the closeness.

There had been other women in his life since Rebel, but none had he been drawn to as much as he was to Denny Jensen. They were kindred spirits.

Another realization burst on his brain and stiffened his muscles. *Something* had roused him from sleep. He listened intently, thinking he might hear hoofbeats or men's voices outside in the canyon. Maybe even sneaking up the trail toward the cave. Nothing. Everything seemed as quiet and peaceful as it had been earlier. He was about to relax and decide that maybe he *hadn't* heard anything, when a very faint *clink* drifted to his ears.

A horseshoe striking rock. He was sure of it. Someone *was* moving around out there, after all.

He slipped his arm from around Denny's shoulders as gently as he could, then braced her so he could slide away from her. She stirred a little but didn't wake up as he eased her down onto the blanket spread over the pile of dried leaves. They crackled under the movement, and she muttered something Conrad couldn't make out. Then her breathing settled back into the same steady rhythm.

He rolled onto hands and knees, then rested his hands on the cave wall as he climbed carefully to his feet. The wounds in his side twinged a little as the motion pulled at them, but the pain wasn't too bad. Denny had wrapped the makeshift bandages tightly around him, which helped. A little light-headed, he stood for a moment with one hand on the wall until his senses and equilibrium settled down.

When he felt stable enough, he walked slowly toward the irregular blob of light that marked the cave's entrance. The sun had moved around and no longer shone directly into the opening, but the afternoon was still bright outside. He had to squint against the glare until his eyes adjusted.

Pausing just inside the entrance, he listened

again. Not having heard anything since that *clink,* he rested his hand on the butt of his holstered gun and stuck his head out. He was in no shape for a gunfight, but if Lundeen and his men were trying to sneak up on the cave, he would give them a hot lead welcome.

The ledge curving around the canyon wall was empty.

A man's voice made Conrad hold his breath. He couldn't make out the words, but as another man replied, equally unintelligible, Conrad realized the voices weren't coming from the canyon but rather were drifting in from somewhere else.

His memories of the ride he and Denny had made were blurry and confused, but he knew they were in some sort of badlands, an area riven with canyons and buttes and ravines. Sound might do strange things in a place like that. There was no telling how far away the riders were.

"Conrad," Denny whispered, "what is it?"

He'd been listening so hard to what might be outside that he hadn't heard her slip up behind him. He glanced around and saw her standing there with a wary expression on her face. Her Colt Lightning was held next to her head with the barrel pointing up at the cave roof. She was ready for trouble, even though she had been sound asleep only a few moments earlier.

"I heard horses and men," he told her.

She looked impatient. "Well, get out of the

way. You're in no shape to fight. You should have woken me when you realized they were sneaking up on us!"

"But they're not. No one is out there on the ledge. I don't think they're even down there in this canyon. The sounds are coming from somewhere else." For a second, he thought she was going to argue with him.

But then she frowned and said, "Let me take a listen." Still holding the gun, she moved up beside him and cocked her head slightly in intense concentration. Long, silent moments went by.

Conrad was about to decide the men were gone—which might make Denny believe he had imagined the whole thing—when he heard a voice again, fainter than before.

But not so faint that Denny failed to hear it. She looked quickly over at him and nodded. "They're out there, all right, and I've got a pretty good idea where. Do you remember where the canyon forked?"

"Well . . . not really."

"I'm not surprised. You were pretty much out of your head from losing so much blood. Take my word for it, the canyon forked a ways back, and we took the right-hand branch. No particular reason. It was just a hunch on my part."

"A good hunch," said Conrad. "It led us here."

"Yeah. But what if Lundeen and his men took

368

the other fork? I don't know how close it runs to this one. Sounds can take some odd bounces in rugged country like this."

"I was thinking the same thing. About the odd bounces, I mean. I suppose the important thing is that they appear to have lost our trail."

"Maybe," said Denny. "But I wouldn't mind knowing how many of them are left . . . and where they're going."

Conrad stared at her, then shook his head. "I don't see how you can find out."

"I have an idea." Denny stepped boldly out of the cave and turned, then tipped her head back to stare up at the canyon wall above them. "If I climb up there, I might be able to cut across and find that other branch of the canyon."

"You'd have to be a mountain goat to climb that wall!"

She smiled at him. "I'm a tomboy, remember? I'm good at climbing things."

"That's loco," Conrad insisted. "You couldn't make it."

Her smile widened into a grin. "You really don't know me very well yet, do you? Telling me I can't do something is the best way in the world to get me to try."

"Wait, I didn't mean—" He lifted a hand and reached toward her, but another wave of light-headedness came over him at that moment, and he had to lean on the canyon wall.

By then it was too late. Denny had moved to the side of the cave mouth, found some foot- and handholds, and started pulling herself up toward the rimrock.

CHAPTER 39

Denny wished she'd had more time to talk to Conrad and make sure he was all right. He had seemed stronger and a lot more coherent during their brief conversation at the cave mouth. He struck her as the sort who would bounce back quickly from an injury. The best fighting men had that ability. She had seen it in Smoke, her uncles Luke and Matt, and her cousins Ace and Chance.

And in herself, if she was being honest.

Conrad Morgan seemed cut from the same cloth.

The canyon wall was very steep but not sheer. Enough rocks jutted out to provide good footholds and handholds, although in some places Denny had to stretch precariously to secure her next grip.

She kept her eyes fixed on the rock a few inches in front of her face and was careful not to look down. She didn't have a great fear of heights, but she didn't want to risk getting dizzy. At the same time, she knew her actions were a little reckless. The smart thing would be for her and Conrad to hole up in the cave until the next morning. By then, Lundeen probably would have called off the search for them. They could slip out, follow the canyon back to the valley, and light a shuck for the Sugarloaf. Then she and Smoke could get Conrad to Big Rock for some actual medical attention.

Instead, she had given in to her curiosity. She wanted to find out if Mace Lundeen and his men had some other reason to be in these badlands, other than chasing her and Conrad.

The climb didn't take long, although the strain of the ascent made it seem longer. Denny pulled herself over the edge and rolled onto the relatively flat rock.

The area was a large, irregular butte several miles wide, cut into crazy patterns by time and the elements. Sandstone spires jutted up, and ravines dropped dizzyingly, but a person could navigate through it carefully on foot. Denny did that, heading generally northward. She knew sooner or later that ought to take her to the other canyon that had branched off. She made sure not to kick any rocks. The clatter might have been heard for a good long distance, just as she and Conrad had heard the horses and the men's voices.

Every few minutes, she stopped to listen, hoping to hear something to tell her she was going the right direction. She didn't hear anything, but something else happened.

She smelled smoke.

Certain it was wood smoke, like from a campfire, she told herself nobody would have a reason to be camping in the badlands unless they were up to no good. That made her even more determined to find them, and the best way to do that was to follow her nose.

She did so for the next half hour. Estimating she'd covered nearly a mile in that time, she came to the canyon's other branch. It stretched as far as she could see right and left and was a good twenty yards wide. Denny turned and followed it northeastward. She could still smell the campfire somewhere ahead of her.

After another half mile, she heard the familiar sound of cattle lowing. Remembering all the stock that had been rustled in the valley recently, she was sure she had stumbled on the place where the wide-loopers were keeping the animals cached until they could move them out and sell them.

She crept closer and finally came to a spot where she could crouch behind a rock slab and peer down into a wide, grassy basin that opened unexpectedly in the middle of the badlands. Several hundred head of cattle grazed there. The rustlers had pitched tents for themselves and built a crude pole corral for their horses.

Half a dozen horses were in that corral at the moment. Denny spotted a few men moving around the tents. Among them was the stocky, unmistakable shape of Mace Lundeen. This hideout was all she needed to prove that Lundeen was behind the rustling. Denny also didn't have any doubt some of those cattle wore Seth Campbell's Boxed B brand, proving that Lundeen and his men were responsible for the raid on the Bluejay Ranch that had caused the deaths of Campbell and his men.

She was confident she could find this place again. All she had to do was get back to Conrad, and the two of them could head for the Sugarloaf. Once she told Smoke what she had discovered, he and Monte Carson could round up a posse and put an end to Lundeen's depredations.

She wouldn't have minded being in on that cleanup herself. With Conrad wounded, maybe it was more important to make sure a doctor tended to his injury.

She watched the outlaws' camp a while longer. Lundeen stomped around and seemed to be angry about something. His voice was loud enough she could hear him talking but wasn't able to make out the words. Once he waved his arms animatedly as he talked to a couple of the gun-wolves. Lundeen made a sweeping gesture toward the cattle.

Was he telling the men to move out the stolen stock? That was possible. Lundeen could have been planning to leave this part of the country once he bushwhacked and killed Conrad Morgan.

But not without collecting what Axel Strom owed him, mused Denny. Strom was too canny to have given Lundeen the whole payoff. He would insist on knowing that Conrad was dead before he turned over the rest of the money.

And Conrad *wasn't* dead, so what was Lundeen going to do? As far as Denny could see, the man's only option was to continue searching for Conrad and try to finish the job.

Suddenly she wanted to get back to that cave as quickly as possible.

Conrad wished he could have stopped Denny from leaving, but in his condition, that hadn't been possible. She had moved too quickly, and he was still too weak.

He watched until she vanished over the rimrock. At least he knew she had made the climb without falling. He had that to be thankful for, anyway.

Deciding that food might help him regain some of his strength, he went into the cave, sat down carefully on the makeshift pallet, and ate a piece of fried chicken from the supplies he had brought with him. He followed it with a small piece of corn on the cob and washed everything down with swigs of water from one of the canteens.

The food unsettled his stomach a little, but in a while he felt better. He leaned back and rested his head on the rock wall again, giving himself stern orders to remain alert.

Unfortunately, he wasn't completely successful at that. He didn't go to sleep, but he did drift off into a kind of twilight stupor.

When he roused from that state, he found that it actually was twilight outside, with shadows gathering in the canyon. His heart began to slug a little harder in his chest. A look around the cave told him that Denny hadn't returned. He would have thought she'd be back already.

Being careful not to rush because his wounded side had stiffened up considerably, Conrad climbed to his feet and hobbled toward the cave mouth. He was almost there when he heard a soft scraping sound outside and recognized it as boot leather on rock.

He almost called Denny's name but stopped himself in time and drew his Colt, pressing his back against the rock wall a few feet from the opening. Whoever was out there would have to step into the cave mouth to see him.

A shadow moved. He knew from experience how quietly Denny could move. It might be her approaching the cave—although it seemed she would have the sense to call out and let him know, rather than just waltzing in.

He heard some whispered words in a male voice: "Jubal . . . horses back there . . . holed up . . . Mace thought . . ."

That confirmed the skulkers as Mace Lundeen's men. Conrad didn't know how many of them were out there. Two, at least.

"Hush . . . blasted fool . . . warn 'em," replied another man.

That caution came too late. Conrad already knew they were there.

And an idea had just occurred to him. Moving quickly but quietly, he hustled back over to the blanket and sat down on it with his legs stretched in front of him and his back against the wall.

He kept the Colt in his hand, down along his right thigh where it wouldn't be noticeable. If the men came in shooting, he would have the advantage on them because his eyes were adjusted to the gloom and theirs weren't. They would be shooting blind, but he would be able to pick them off as they were silhouetted against the fading light outside.

Of course, they might get lucky, and a lucky bullet could kill a man just as dead as a well-aimed one. He was willing to take that chance.

And if they *didn't* start shooting right away, they might be tempted to gloat over their apparent triumph and spill some important information.

Seconds ticked by.

With a sudden rush of footsteps, two men charged through the entrance into the cave and stopped short as they swung their guns back and forth, looking for a target.

Conrad sat up straighter. In the apparent confusion of a man just jolted out of sleep, he said, "What . . . who . . . who are you men?"

"Hold it right there, Morgan!" one of them yelled. He hadn't actually spotted Conrad yet, which was obvious from the way he jerked his head back and forth. "Don't you move!"

"There he is, Early!" exclaimed the other man. "Over there by the wall!"

Both of them pointed their revolvers at Conrad. It was a nerve-wracking moment, but neither man appeared to be in a rush to shoot.

The first one laughed. "We got you, you slippery son of a gun!"

"Don't shoot." Conrad made his voice sound weak and helpless. "I'm hurt. I'm no threat to you."

"You may not be a threat, but you're worth money to us."

"Only if you're dead, though," said the other man.

"Wait . . . wait a minute. Whatever you're being paid to kill me, I'll double it. No, I'll triple it! If you know who I am, you know I have plenty of money."

That proposition actually made the two gun-wolves exchange a quick glance.

They're actually considering it, thought Conrad.

Then one of them said, "Mace 'd kill us, Jubal. You know how he feels about double-crossers."

The other gunman lifted his hand and rubbed his rocklike, beard-stubbled chin. "Yeah, you're right, Early. No matter where we went, as long as he was drawin' breath he'd be huntin' us. I don't want him on my trail, no matter how much this fella offers us." He nodded toward Conrad.

"I can understand why you'd worry about Lundeen," Conrad said. "But if he was dead, he couldn't come after you, could he?"

"The others would," said Jubal. "Desmond or Clute or that 'breed Crowbait. They're loyal to Mace."

"Anyway," added Early, "we're gonna make plenty of money off this deal just the way it is. By the time Clute sells off all those cows we rustled and the rest of us collect from your partner and then clean out the bank in Big Rock—"

"Quit flappin' your gums, blast it!" Jubal interrupted him. "You've done gone and told him the whole plan. Now we're gonna have to . . ." His voice trailed off as he nodded slowly. "Oh, yeah, we're supposed to kill him anyway, aren't we?"

"Yeah, but since he's already shot up and helpless, maybe it'd be better if we took him back to Mace as a prisoner. Mace could turn him over to that German fella, and Strom could do whatever he wants with him."

"Strom don't want to get his hands dirty. That's why he hired Mace and the rest of us, remember?"

"That's true," Early said.

These two weren't the smartest outlaws ever to come down the pike. Conrad remembered them.

They were the Kinch brothers. He didn't know anything about them except that they rode with Mace Lundeen and looked like brutal, ruthless killers—which they undoubtedly were.

But they had revealed that not only was he in danger, so were the people in Big Rock if Lundeen intended to rob the bank. Innocent folks often got hurt in crimes like that. Conrad remembered everything that had almost happened the day he first met Denny Jensen . . .

"Wait a minute," Early Kinch suddenly exclaimed. "Where's the girl?"

"She's dead," Conrad answered quickly. If, by some chance, they succeeded in killing him, he wanted them to believe that Denny was dead, too, so they wouldn't continue looking for her. "I threw her body in a ravine back up the canyon a ways."

A familiar voice came from behind the two gun-wolves. "Aw, isn't that sweet of you?"

The Kinch brothers yelped curses and tried to swing around toward Denny. Before their guns could come in line with her, Conrad raised his Colt and shot Jubal in the head.

An instant later, Denny's Lightning cracked twice and Early staggered back. He fought to stay on his feet and raise the gun that had sagged when Denny's bullets struck him.

Conrad didn't give him a chance to do that, and neither did Denny. They fired at the same time.

Conrad's slug went between Early's shoulder blades into his heart. His head snapped back from the impact of Denny's bullet as it bored into his forehead. His knees buckled, and he dropped onto the floor of the cave next to his dead brother.

CHAPTER 40

"Looks like I got here just in time," said Denny as she stepped deeper into the cave.

"I had it all under control, whether you showed up or not," Conrad said. "But I'm obliged to you for lending me a hand."

"I think it was the other way around." She thumbed fresh cartridges into the Lightning, replacing the rounds she had fired. Then she pouched the iron and lost her nonchalant, bantering air and hurried over and knelt at his side. "Conrad, are you all right?"

"I'm fine," he assured her.

She looked at the makeshift bandages wrapped around his torso. "I don't see any fresh blood."

"I was careful not to do any running and jumping and fistfighting while you were gone." His voice turned serious as he went on. "I'm glad you're back. I was worried about you. Did you find anything?"

Denny sat back on her heels. "More than I expected to. Less than two miles from here, Lundeen and his men are keeping what looks like most of the stock they've rustled. It's a nice little hideout basin tucked away in these badlands. I didn't know it was there."

"We need to let Sheriff Carson know about that as soon as we can."

"I agree," Denny said.

"But there's more you don't know unless you overheard those two gloating." He nodded toward the bodies of the Kinch brothers.

Denny shook her head. "I got here just a few seconds before I spoke up. I only heard enough to know you were in trouble." She laughed softly. "I didn't realize you had set a trap for them and used yourself as bait. But that's what happened, isn't it?"

"Pretty much," said Conrad. "They confirmed that Axel paid Lundeen to kill me. That's all the proof I need that he found out somehow I planned to force him out of the partnership. He figured he'd better act first . . . and his solution was a more permanent one.

"However, Lundeen's not satisfied with that. He wants all the money Axel has, and everything that's in the bank vault, as well."

"He's going to rob the bank?" Denny exclaimed.

"That's the plan."

"I saw what looked like him giving orders for some of his men to move those rustled cattle out of the basin. Are the rest of his men heading for Big Rock?"

"That would be my guess," said Conrad.

"Then we've got to stop them." Denny came to her feet. "Or rather, I've got to stop them. I'm sorry, Conrad, but I'm going to have to leave you here. I need to ride for the Sugarloaf tonight, so there'll be time to get ready for Lundeen's raid."

Conrad shook his head. "You're not doing that without me."

"You're in no shape to ride." Denny made a face. "You've got a couple of bullet holes in your side, remember?"

"Yes, and you did an excellent job of patching them up. A hard ride might make them start bleeding a little again, but it's not going to kill me."

She gave him a dubious frown and said, "You lost a lot of blood earlier. I'm not sure you can afford to lose any more."

"That's my risk to take, isn't it?" He reached up, extending his hand toward her. "Help me to my feet, and let's get out of here. I'd like to get back down that ledge before it's completely dark out there."

Denny hesitated. He was right. The descent would be easier while a little daylight remained. She drew in a deep breath, then clasped his wrist as he clasped hers.

Axel Strom had ridden into Big Rock late that afternoon, worked for a while in the office he shared with Conrad Morgan, then locked up and left an hour or so after nightfall. He was hungry and decided to go to Longmont's for supper, even though he knew Louis Longmont didn't like him.

Strom had long since stopped worrying about

whether people liked him, as long as he got what he wanted from them.

He hadn't reached Longmont's yet when a man stepped out of the dark mouth of an alley in front of him. Strom had to stop or run into the man. He tensed in wariness. The man might be a would-be robber—

"Hello, boss." The familiar voice belonged to Mace Lundeen.

Strom relaxed. "What are you doing here?" he snapped. "You're supposed to be, ah, dealing with that problem for me."

"You mean your business partner problem?" asked Lundeen. "I've got a couple of men out looking for Morgan right now. They'll find him and take care of him."

Strom made a sharp slashing motion with his hand and hissed through clenched teeth, "Stop that! There's no need to talk of it. We both know what has to be done."

"Yeah, we do, and I'm confident my men can take care of it. So confident that I've come for the rest of my money."

"When the job is done," Strom said coldly. "You know the terms, Lundeen."

"Well . . . the terms have changed." Lundeen's arm moved.

The shadows were too thick for Strom to see the gun in the man's hand, but he heard the metallic click when Lundeen eared back the hammer.

"You're going to go ahead and pay me that other five thousand," said Lundeen. "And not only that, we're going back to your office and getting any other money you've got stashed there."

"Why . . . why, you're insane!" Strom blustered. "I'll do no such thing. Put that gun away and stop threatening me, or you'll find yourself without a job."

"I'm already not working for you, mister. Things have gotten too hot to risk staying around here." Lundeen paused, then went on. "There's a chance Smoke Jensen will be getting mixed up in this, and I want to be long gone from these parts before that happens."

"Jensen! I'm not afraid of Smoke Jensen."

"That just goes to show what a fool you are." Lundeen moved closer and jabbed the gun barrel in Strom's belly. "Now turn around and head back to your office."

Strom thought about making a grab for the gun, but Lundeen stepped back quickly away from him. The mining engineer hadn't acted swiftly enough.

"So you're abandoning me," he said with scorn heavy in his voice. "I'll make sure the word gets around, Lundeen. No one will ever trust you again."

Lundeen laughed. "I don't care about that. I'm done after this job. I plan to head somewhere I can spend the rest of my days in peace. Now, are you going to do what I told you, or do I have to pistol-whip you for a while first?"

If Lundeen came close enough to do that, Strom thought he could overpower the man. But Lundeen had the gun and probably wouldn't hesitate to pull the trigger. Perhaps it would be best to play along with him for the moment and wait for a better chance to strike.

"All right," Strom said. "We'll go back to the office."

"Unless you don't have enough money there to pay me. Do we need to go to the hotel?"

"No, no. Our ready cash is locked in a strong-box in the office."

"How much is in it?"

Strom hesitated, then told the truth. "Almost nine thousand dollars."

"So only four more than what you already owe me? That's disappointing. I thought you were a high roller, Strom."

"I am a prudent businessman," Strom said stiffly.

"You're about to be a poorer one. Move."

Strom needed only a few minutes to retrace his steps to the office, with Mace Lundeen close behind him. Strom could almost feel the barrel of Lundeen's gun prodding him on, although that actually didn't happen.

"Where are you going to go when you leave here?" Strom asked over his shoulder.

"No need for you to know that. If you're thinking about sending the law after me, that wouldn't be a good idea. I can always testify that you wanted Conrad Morgan dead bad enough to pay me ten grand to take care of it."

"Enough! We will speak no more of it."

"Now you're getting smart."

No, if he'd been smart, he would have killed Conrad Morgan himself, instead of hiring the treacherous snake to do it.

They stopped in front of the office door. Strom got out the key, unlocked the door, and led the way into the darkened room.

"Draw the shades and then light the lamp," Lundeen ordered.

Strom did so. As he lowered the lamp's glass chimney and its yellow glow welled up, Lundeen's face became visible above the gun he held. A malevolent grin creased his heavy features.

"Where's that strongbox you talked about?"

"Here in the bottom drawer of the desk."

That was also true, but what Strom hadn't mentioned was that a loaded pistol lay in the metal box, on top of the banded bundles of cash he had gotten from the bank. He went behind the desk and sat down as he took the strongbox key from his vest pocket. It was a natural enough move, but it also served to put the heavy piece of furniture between part of his body and Lundeen's gun.

As Strom pulled the large bottom drawer open

and started to bend so he could unlock the box, Lundeen said, "Hold it! You think I'm a damn fool?"

"I'm sure I don't know what you mean," Strom said.

"Put that strongbox key on the desk, stand up, and move back."

Strom held in the curse that tried to well up his throat. Lundeen wasn't trustworthy, so of course he wouldn't trust anyone else. With the gun menacing him, Strom had no choice but to set the strongbox key on the desk. He stepped back.

Lundeen circled the desk. Greed shone in his eyes. He reached for the key with his free hand and looked down into the drawer at the strongbox. As soon as Lundeen took his eyes off him, Strom put his foot on the chair and shoved it against Lundeen's legs as hard as he could.

The unexpected attack made Lundeen stumble. His gun hand sagged, and Strom leaped at him. As Lundeen tried to straighten to meet the attack, his legs got tangled in the chair legs, and he fell forward.

Strom got both hands on the wrist of Lundeen's gun hand and shoved it upward. Even though Lundeen was off-balance, he managed to ram his other hand into Strom's belly. Strom doubled over in pain.

Lundeen's Colt blasted, deafeningly loud in the office's close confines.

Something slammed against the side of Strom's head. He had been in plenty of fights in his life, but nothing had ever hit him that hard. He toppled backward with agony and thunder filling his skull. He was too stunned to feel it when he crashed to the floor.

"You fool." Lundeen's voice sounded muffled and far away after that close-range shot had assaulted Strom's ears. "I would have let you live . . . maybe. Now you can lay there while your brains leak out." Lundeen grinned. "And you can die knowing that Conrad Morgan's still alive. It's not worth the trouble of hunting him down now. I was only doing it to hedge my bets. But I've already *got* your money, and you've got nothing . . . nothing . . . *nothing* . . ."

That word echoing in his ears was the last thing Axel Strom heard as black oblivion rose and washed over him.

Knowing Strom was either dead or next thing to it, Lundeen holstered his gun and grabbed the strongbox key off the desk, but watched him from the corner of his eye anyway. He didn't want to be taken by surprise so close to the final payoff.

He wasn't surprised to see the gun in the strongbox when he opened it. He had expected some sort of trick from Strom. He picked up the pistol and stuck it behind his belt. Might as well get some use out of it.

Then he stuffed the bundles of money inside his

shirt. No time to waste. He didn't think the single shot would attract much attention. The office's walls would have muffled it to a certain extent. His men were waiting to move on the bank, and he wanted to bust in there, blow the vault, and get out of Big Rock while everybody was still running around like chickens with their heads cut off, asking what had happened.

Lundeen blew out the lamp and hurriedly left the office. He closed the door behind him. It wasn't likely anybody walking by would look in and see Axel Strom's bleeding body sprawled on the floor halfway behind the desk, but no need to attract attention by leaving the door open.

Nobody was moving around on the street or the boardwalks near the office. A few men drifted in and out of the Brown Dirt Cowboy Saloon, a couple of blocks away. Looked like the shot hadn't roused the town, Lundeen decided. He walked quickly toward the bank but didn't run.

Ennis Desmond, Crowbait, and six other men were waiting in the alley behind the imposing redbrick building. Crowbait, for an uneducated 'breed, had a surprising number of talents, one of which was handling dynamite. He could blow open the vault door without damaging any of the contents.

"I thought I heard a shot a little bit ago, boss," Desmond whispered when Lundeen came up and identified himself.

"That was me," said Lundeen. "Strom tried to get tricky. He won't ever do that again." He turned to Crowbait. "You ready to blow that door down?"

"Ready, boss," the half-breed replied.

"Let's get in there, then. A couple of you boys bust that door down. Don't make any more racket about it than you have to."

Two men went to work with the pry bars they had brought with them. Wood splintered around the lock on both door and jamb, but the noise didn't amount to much. Then they were in. Desmond pulled the door up behind them, although it wouldn't latch anymore because of the damage.

Lundeen snapped a match to life with his left thumbnail and held it up so Crowbait would have enough light to work by. He didn't want to light a lamp, since that might be noticed from outside.

The match's flickering glow spread out and touched a grim-faced man standing in front of the tellers' cages, arms loose and ready at his sides. Seeing him like that was such a shock that for a second Lundeen couldn't do anything except suck in a breath and stand there.

"Hello, Lundeen," Smoke Jensen said. "I was about to decide you weren't coming."

CHAPTER 41

Lundeen dropped the match and clawed at the gun on his hip. Before the still-burning match could fall all the way to the floor, his Colt was out of its holster and rising.

Smoke had drawn, too, and his gun thundered a split second before Lundeen's. The killer rocked back as Smoke's slug smashed into his chest. His mouth dropped open in shock and pain. He triggered a second shot into the floor at his feet and struggled mightily to raise the gun higher.

Smoke fired again, the shot striking Lundeen in almost exactly the same spot as the first one. Lundeen crashed to the floor but didn't feel it. He was dead already when he landed.

As that fierce exchange had taken place in little more than the blink of an eye, the rest of Lundeen's men were trying to get their guns out and spitting flame, too. Smoke was outnumbered.

Or he would have been if he had been alone. Sheriff Monte Carson, Pearlie, Cal, and several other members of the Sugarloaf crew stood up behind the tellers' cages and other places around the room where they had been concealed and opened fire. Lundeen's match had gone out when it hit the floor, but Colt flame lit up the bank lobby as it geysered back and forth from the two groups. The floor shivered from the thunderous roar of gunfire, and the acrid tang of powder smoke filled the air.

After a long moment, the shooting stopped abruptly and Monte Carson shouted, "Hold your fire! If any of you men are still alive and want to give up, now's your chance. Your only chance!"

The only answer was an echoing silence.

As soon as he had gunned down Mace Lundeen, Smoke had stepped swiftly to the side and crouched behind the free-standing marble counter where bank customers could fill out deposit and withdrawal slips. He straightened, moved over to a desk, thumbed a match to life, and lit the lamp there.

Pearlie let out a low whistle as the yellow glow spread across the lobby. "We shot 'em plumb to doll rags, didn't we?"

"They were trying to do the same to us," Cal said.

Holding his gun ready, Monte Carson moved among the fallen outlaws to check on them. Smoke went with him.

"Looks like they're all dead," Monte announced a few moments later.

"Maybe not all," Smoke said with a nod toward the bank's front door, which stood open. "That was closed when the shooting started. One of them might have ducked out and gotten away."

Monte did a quick count of the riddled corpses

and said, "Couldn't have been more than one. I didn't get a chance to see exactly how many of them came in here, but I think this is pretty much all of them."

"Pretty much," agreed Smoke. If one of the would-be bank robbers had gotten away, more than likely he would jump on his horse and light a shuck away from Big Rock, not stopping until he had put a lot of miles behind him.

"That fella Strom's not with them," Monte commented.

Smoke shook his head. "I didn't expect him to be. According to what Denny and Conrad said when they showed up at the ranch earlier this evening, Lundeen planned to double-cross Strom, take all the money he had, and then rob the bank. Strom's probably in his office or at the hotel . . . unless Lundeen killed him."

Monte grunted and said, "I'll need to check on that . . . when I get around to it. I'm not going to worry overmuch about Strom, seeing as he's the one who brought all the trouble here to start with."

The young cowboy named Jack Denton stepped up and gazed at the bodies with a solemn expression on his face. "I appreciate you letting me in on this showdown, Mr. Jensen. I feel like I helped avenge Mr. Campbell and Chip and the other fellas who died at the hands of these varmints. It's not that satisfying, but it's better than nothing."

Smoke clapped a hand on Denton's shoulder. "You did all you could, Jack, and that counts for something. It counts for a lot."

Denton nodded. "I'm obliged to you for letting me stay at the Sugarloaf, too."

"You can do more than that. You're welcome to ride for the brand if you want."

"Thank you, sir. I'll sure think about it."

Cal holstered his gun and said, "For now, we'd better see about getting the undertaker busy. If we all pitch in, we can haul these bodies down to his place."

"You give Monte a hand with that," said Smoke. "Pearlie and I will head back out to the ranch. I want to make sure the doctor got there all right to tend to Conrad."

"What about all that rustled stock?" asked Pearlie.

"We'll get on the trail of it first thing in the morning," Smoke told him. He slid his Colt into leather. "Nothing left now but the cleaning up."

The customers in Blaise's Place gasped at the bloody apparition that reeled in. With blood smeared over most of his face and still trickling from the wound on his bald scalp, Axel Strom was almost unrecognizable.

As he had slipped into darkness, lying on the floor of his office, he had figured he was dying. When he had regained consciousness a short time earlier, he had been shocked to realize he was still alive.

But despite the gory mess and the unholy throbbing that threatened to blow his skull apart, he'd lived. And somewhere deep inside him, he had found the strength to climb to his feet and stagger out of there.

The sounds of battle had penetrated his half-stunned brain and led him toward the bank. He'd been vaguely aware of the lean figure of a man slipping out through the open door and disappearing into the alley beside the building. Strom didn't know who it was and didn't care. He had stood there on the boardwalk breathing hard as the men inside spoke into the echoing silence following the gun-thunder.

One name exploded through his consciousness. *Conrad.*

Morgan was at the Jensen ranch, wounded but alive. And from the sound of it, Smoke Jensen and most of his men were in Big Rock at the bank.

Morgan had ruined everything. He had taken a plan that would have made a great deal of money for both of them and utterly wrecked it.

For that, he had to pay.

Strom had turned and stumbled away from the bank. Instinct had led his steps to Blaise's Place.

As he stood just inside the saloon, holding onto the batwings to keep from falling down, he peered around through a bloodred haze and finally recognized the man he was looking for, standing at the bar staring at him. "Burke," rasped Strom. "Burke, come with me."

The big miner shook off his surprise and hurried across the room. Several other burly members of the crew followed him.

Burke grasped Strom's arm and said, "Boss, what the hell happened to you? You look like you've been shot!"

"It's . . . nothing," Strom forced out. He lifted a trembling hand and gingerly touched the wound on his head. "A mere . . . graze . . . nothing more."

"I don't know, boss," said Burke. "You could have a busted skull or worse."

"You fool! If it was worse . . . would be I standing up . . . walking around . . . talking? I can do . . . what must be done . . . but I need your help."

Burke nodded. "Sure. Whatever you say, Mr. Strom."

"We're going after . . . Morgan. It's time to . . . settle things . . . with him."

Burke's lips drew back from his teeth in a savage grin. "I like the sound of that. After all the trouble he's caused, whatever happens to Morgan, he's got it comin'."

The other men muttered in profane agreement.

"He's at . . . the Sugarloaf Ranch. That's where . . . we're going."

One of the other men said, "I don't know, boss. That's Smoke Jensen's place. From what I hear, Jensen's not a good man to mess with."

"Jensen is here . . . in Big Rock," grated Strom. "That's why . . . we need to move quickly. Any man who comes with me . . . helps me get Morgan . . . I'll pay five hundred . . . dollars."

That took care of any objections the others had.

Seamus Burke said, "Let's go, boss. But are you sure you don't need a doctor first?"

"Killing Conrad Morgan . . . will take care of everything . . . that's wrong with me," Strom declared. With Burke's help, he turned and stalked out of the saloon, followed by the other miners.

Blaise Warfield stared at the batwings as they swung slowly back and forth for a moment and then came to a stop. Strom, Burke, and the others were gone, but she had heard enough of what they said to know where they were going.

To the Sugarloaf to kill Conrad Morgan.

Blaise wasn't sure what Conrad was doing at the Jensen ranch, but she was certain Denny Jensen had something to do with it. Jealous anger welled up inside her. But she had no call to be jealous, she reminded herself. Conrad didn't belong to her . . . yet.

But he never would if Strom succeeded in killing him. She couldn't let that happen. She had to find somebody to help her.

Drawing more astonished stares from the saloon's customers, Blaise rushed out into the night. She wasn't sure where she was going or who she was looking for, but she hadn't gone very far when someone abruptly called her name.

She stopped and turned around to see Brice Rogers striding toward her. Her breath caught in her throat. She hurried to meet him, rushed into his arms, and hugged him as she said, "Oh, Brice, thank goodness you're here!"

"What is it?" he asked as he held her. "What's wrong?" He took hold of her shoulders and moved her back a little so he could look down into her face. "Just tell me what you need me to do, Blaise."

The lone rider quickly drew his horse off the trail and into the shadows of some trees where he wouldn't be seen. He'd heard hoofbeats sweeping up behind him from the direction of Big Rock and figured it would be a good idea to get out of sight. Anybody coming from town right now wasn't likely to be his friend.

Enough light came from the moon and stars for him to make out five horsemen galloping west from the settlement. The one in the lead was Axel Strom. The sight of him sent a shock through the watcher in the shadows. Lundeen had said Strom was dead, but clearly that wasn't the case. That blocky, mostly bald head was unmistakable. The watcher thought the men riding with Strom were some of the miners who worked for him.

The man in the trees waited until Strom and the others vanished around a bend in the trail before he moved his horse back out of the shadows. He didn't know where they were going, didn't know and didn't care. He wanted nothing more to do with this valley. He was going to move on, put it far behind him, and look for work elsewhere.

A man with his talents could always find work.

Crowbait nudged his horse into motion and rode off into the night.

Conrad leaned back against the pillows propped behind him and sighed. Clean sheets, a soft bed, freshly disinfected and bandaged wounds, and some excellent brandy to help dull the pain . . . After everything that had happened, it was exactly what he needed.

Dr. Enoch Steward, who had come out from Big Rock earlier in his buggy, snapped his medical bag closed and told Denny, "I'll come by tomorrow to check on the patient." The sandy-haired physician smiled at Conrad. "But I'd say that Mr. Morgan has the sort of vitality necessary to make a speedy and full recovery."

"It helps that I had such good medical attention right from the start," Conrad said.

Denny frowned. "I didn't really do much—"

"On the contrary," Dr. Steward told her. "Under

the circumstances, you couldn't have done much better. I'd say this young man owes you a great deal."

"This young man agrees," said Conrad.

Denny blushed prettily. "Well, I'm just glad he's going to be all right."

"Don't take anything for granted," Steward advised. "But I'm sure you and your mother and Señora Sandoval will do an excellent job of caring for him." The doctor picked up his hat from the dressing table where he had placed it earlier and put it on his head. "I'll see you tomorrow."

Steward turned toward the door of the spare bedroom on the ranch house's second floor, but it opened before he could get there. Sally Jensen stood in the doorway.

Conrad knew right away that something was wrong. Her face was pale and showed lines of strain.

Denny saw that, too. She said quickly, "Mother, what is it?"

"Mr. Strom is downstairs," said Sally. "He wants to see you, Conrad."

Dr. Steward said, "I wouldn't advise anything too stressful—"

"He's not alone," Sally broke in. "He has a man named Burke with him, and some of the other miners. They're all armed, and Mr. Strom is holding a gun to Inez's head."

That news shocked a curse out of Denny's mouth.

Conrad sat up straighter. "He wants to see me?"

"That's right."

"Blast it!" said Denny. "I heard horses earlier, but I figured it was Pa and Pearlie and Cal getting back from Big Rock. I never expected it to be Strom."

"He's been hurt," Sally went on. "His head is bloody, like he's been struck hard, and he's acting like he's half-mad."

"Mad with hate and greed," said Conrad. "Maybe he's got the crazy idea that if he can get me out of the way, he can still take over the company and operate those gold mines the way he wants to."

"That'll never happen," said Denny. "The law will come after him because of his connection with Lundeen."

"He may be too far gone to think about that." Conrad pushed the sheet back. "I need to deal with this."

Dr. Steward reached out quickly and put a hand on his shoulder. "You're can't do that, Mr. Morgan. You're in no shape—"

"It's my responsibility," Conrad said. "Now, if you ladies don't want to watch me put my pants on . . ."

"Wait a minute," Denny said. "Mother, does Strom know I'm up here?"

403

Sally frowned. "He didn't mention you, and I didn't, either. So I really don't know."

Denny nodded toward the window. "I'll go out that way and circle around so I can come up behind them and get the drop on them. Maybe we can get out of this without anybody being hurt."

Conrad figured she really meant she didn't want to miss out on any action that took place. But he couldn't argue with her plan. "Give me a few minutes before you move in, Denny. Mrs. Jensen, Doctor, go to one of the other rooms and stay up here . . . no matter what you hear."

"You underestimate me, Conrad," Sally snapped. "I'll go to my bedroom, all right . . . because my Winchester is there."

He grinned. "All right, but stay out of it unless things go to hell."

"Strom brought hell with him to this valley," said Denny. She eased up the window pane and threw a leg over the sill.

Conrad looked at her and thought what she'd just said was true. Strom hadn't been alone in bringing hell to the valley. Conrad had played his part, too, although that had never been his intention.

It was time to put an end to this, so he could make a start on repairing the harm he had done.

CHAPTER 42

It wasn't the first time Denny had climbed out of a window in the ranch house. She hung from the sill by her hands for a second and then dropped to the ground below, landing lightly on the carpet of grass that grew around the house. She had to take a step to keep her balance, then caught herself. The landing had been almost silent.

Slipping her Lightning from its holster, Denny quickly checked the cylinder and thumbed a cartridge into the chamber she usually kept empty under the hammer. She didn't pouch the iron as she stole toward the front of the house.

She heard horses stirring and figured those were the mounts Strom, Burke, and the others had ridden, the ones she had mistaken for her father and the Sugarloaf crew returning home.

Smoke would be there before too much longer, she was sure, but with Strom acting loco and threatening Inez Sandoval, they might not be able to wait.

Denny was passing a tree near the front of the house when someone stepped out from behind the thick trunk, wrapped an arm around her waist, and clapped a hand over her mouth.

• • •

Wearing his boots and trousers and a shirt borrowed from Smoke's wardrobe, along with the gunbelt buckled around his hips, Conrad paused at the second-floor landing and looked down into the big foyer.

Seamus Burke stood there with a rifle in his hands. He gave Conrad an ugly grin and said, "Come on down, Morgan. Somebody wants to see you."

"Don't do this, Burke," Conrad said quietly. "You've always been a roughneck, but you're not a criminal."

"There's a lot of money to be made in this valley, but not the way you want to go about it. I've thrown in with Mr. Strom. I'll back his play."

"Then you're a fool," Conrad said coldly, "and you deserve whatever happens to you."

"So do you." Burke motioned with the rifle barrel. "Now get down here, unless you want something happening to that Mexican servant."

"I'm coming. There's no need for anyone else to be hurt."

Conrad started down the stairs. He wondered where Denny was and when she would make her move. He hoped he could convince Strom to let Inez go before any shooting started. He would take his own chances, but she didn't deserve to be in danger.

Burke backed off into the parlor, covering Conrad every step of the way.

When he stepped into the room's arched entrance, Conrad saw Strom standing over by the fireplace with an arm around Inez Sandoval's waist and a gun in his other hand pointing at her head. The other miners, also armed, were spread around the room and had their guns pointing at Conrad.

The sight of Strom's bloody head shocked him. "What in the world happened to you, Axel?"

Strom's mouth twisted in a snarl. "I learned that a man can't trust anyone but himself to take care of what needs to be done," he said. "That's why it's come down to this, Morgan. Time for the two of us to settle things."

"That's right," Conrad said. "So let Señora Sandoval go."

"Not just yet. This knock on the head addled my brain for a while, but I had time to do some thinking on the way out here. You're going to write out a paper deeding your share of our partnership to me, Morgan. That way no one can claim I murdered you in order to get my hands on the company."

Conrad stared at him for a moment before saying, "You really have lost your mind. There are witnesses who can swear to everything you've done, every crime you've committed. You paid Mace Lundeen to try to kill me! You're finished, Axel, can't you see that? Don't make things any worse than they have to be."

He looked around at the miners. "That's even more true for the rest of you men. Put down those guns and leave. Go back to your jobs. The law won't bother you, I swear it."

Burke shook his head. "I think we've come too far to turn back now, Morgan. You've got to die, and so does everybody else in this house."

"That's right." Strom laughed. "I have money and lawyers, too, you know! By the time I'm through, the law will never be able to touch me!"

Conrad drew a deep breath and said bleakly, "You realize you're not giving me any choice, don't you?"

"No choice but to die!" Strom frowned suddenly. "Wait. What do you mean by—"

"Have you ever heard of Kid Morgan?" Conrad interrupted him in a soft voice. Without waiting for an answer, he drew and fired.

It took every reserve of strength and determination he had within him, but he had never made a faster draw or fired a more accurate shot. The bullet struck Axel Strom in the throat, ripped through flesh, and shattered his spine. No nerve impulses could travel from his diseased brain to his muscles. He couldn't pull the trigger of the gun he held, couldn't do anything except drop the weapon and collapse like a carelessly thrown-aside rag doll.

Inez Sandoval, free of Strom's grip, dived behind a heavy sofa as Burke and the other miners opened fire on Conrad.

He wasn't facing them alone anymore. Denny appeared on his right side, Brice Rogers on his left, and both held Colts that spat flame and death. They had leaped into the parlor from the foyer just in time to join the battle.

The house seemed to rock from the storm that raged inside the room. Peals of gun-thunder slammed the ears. The Colt in Conrad's hand roared and bucked and he saw Seamus Burke's face turn into a red smear from the bullets that smashed into it. Slugs sizzled past Conrad's head, so close he felt as much as heard them. Clouds of powder smoke filled the parlor.

Then the shots died away and an eerily echoing silence took their place. Conrad, Denny, and Brice covered the fallen miners, but none of the huddled, bloody shapes moved.

Sally Jensen rushed into the room with a Winchester carbine in her hands. "Inez!" she called. "Inez!"

"Here, Señora Sally," Inez replied from behind the sofa as she pulled herself up.

Sally hurried to her side to help her. "Are you all right?"

"Sí. The shot Señor Morgan made"—Inez shook her head in awe—"it would have done Señor Smoke proud."

Automatically, Conrad reloaded his Colt. He looked over at Brice and nodded. "I'm obliged to you, Marshal. I'm not sure where you came from, but I'm glad you're here."

"He just about scared me to death when he grabbed me outside," said Denny. "He just didn't want me giving anything away."

Brice thumbed fresh rounds into his revolver's cylinder, as well.

"You can thank Miss Warfield for me being here, Morgan," he said. "She's the one who told me Strom and those other varmints headed out here to kill you. She didn't want that to happen." Brice added coolly, "And I didn't want her upset, so . . ."

"Well, I appreciate the help, no matter how it came about."

A gurgling sound interrupted the conversation. Conrad looked around and saw Axel Strom staring at him in a mixture of hate and horror. Blood welled from the hole in the man's throat. Clearly, he didn't have long to live, but he was trying to form words anyway.

Conrad holstered his Colt. "I'm sorry it had to come to this, Axel. You really were a brilliant engineer, if your greed hadn't gotten the better of you."

Strom choked out a couple more incoherent sounds. Then the effort died along with the life in his eyes. The sightless orbs began to glaze over.

As a swift rataplan of hoofbeats came from outside, Denny smiled and said, "My father's not going to be happy that he got here too late for this fight."

"He shouldn't worry about that," said Sally as she rolled her eyes a little. "I'm sure there'll be more shoot-outs in the future!"

Denny reined in alongside Conrad. They had just topped the trail up to the bench where the Bluejay Mine was located. The mine was in operation again, the engine that powered the big pumps thumping again in the high country air.

Down below, the range was recovering well since the minor flood several weeks earlier. In time, it would be back to normal. So would all the other places in the valley that had been damaged by the hydraulic mining.

Conrad had already recovered, Denny knew. He had mentioned earlier, while they were riding out there, that he could barely tell he'd been shot.

"I suppose, now that you've got everything running the way you want it, you'll go back to San Francisco or Boston or somewhere," Denny said as she leaned forward a little in the saddle on Rocket's back. "Don't you have businesses all over the country to run?"

"The Browning Holdings have interests all over the world," said Conrad. "But that doesn't mean I have to keep up with all of them, all the time."

He thumbed his hat back. "No, as long as I have the telegraph, I can take care of what I need to do from right here. So . . . I may be staying around for a while."

"I'm sure Blaise Warfield will be happy to hear that. She was so worried about you that night Strom came out to the ranch, you know."

"What about Marshal Rogers?" asked Conrad. "How do you think he'll take the news?"

"I'm sure that's none of my business," Denny responded without hesitation, but if she were being totally honest with herself . . . she *did* wonder how Brice was going to feel about Conrad staying around the valley.

It was too nice a day to worry a great deal about such things. One way or another, they would sort themselves out in the future. For today, Denny was just going to enjoy this ride with Conrad Morgan.

They were on their way back across the Bluejay spread when they spotted a rider coming toward them. Instinctively, they reined in and watched warily as the man approached. Denny relaxed when she recognized him as the young cowboy, Jack Denton.

"Howdy, folks," Denton said as he came up to them and brought his mount to a stop. "Miss Denny, Mr. Morgan, good to see you."

"How are you doing, Jack?" asked Denny. "My father told me you're taking care of the Bluejay until the authorities can locate Mr. Campbell's heirs."

A posse led by Smoke had recovered nearly all the rustled stock before it could be sold and scattered, so the Bluejay herd was back where it belonged.

"I got some news about that today, as a matter of fact." Denton looked vaguely embarrassed. "Sheriff Carson rode out from Big Rock and told me that when he was going through Mr. Campbell's things, he found a will saying that because Mr. Campbell didn't have any blood relatives left alive, he wanted the ranch to go to the crew. And . . . well . . . I'm the only one left."

"Wait a minute," Denny said as a smile broke across her face. "You mean *you* own the Bluejay now?"

"The court had to go through it and make sure everything was done properlike, but . . . yeah, I reckon I've got myself a ranch now. Not sure what I'll *do* with it, mind you."

"I know exactly what you'll do," said Denny. "You'll be a good neighbor to the Sugarloaf and keep the Bluejay one of the best spreads in the valley."

"And you'll be a good neighbor to the mine, too," Conrad added. "I just hope the mine will be a good neighbor to you. I'll do everything I can to make sure of that."

"Reckon I know that, Mr. Morgan."

Conrad stuck out his hand and grinned. "Call me Conrad."

"Yes, sir . . . Conrad." Jack Denton leaned over from the saddle and clasped his hand.

They parted company a few minutes later, with Denny and Conrad continuing on toward the Sugarloaf.

Denny looked over at him and mused, "What with you talking about being a good neighbor and all . . . you sound almost like you're at home here in these parts."

"You know," said Conrad, "maybe I am."

ABOUT THE AUTHORS

WILLIAM W. JOHNSTONE is the *New York Times* and *USA Today* bestselling author of over 300 books, including the bestselling series Smoke Jensen, the Mountain Man, Preacher, the First Mountain Man, MacCallister, Flintlock, and Will Tanner, Deputy U.S. Marshal, and the stand-alone thrillers *The Doomsday Bunker*, *Tyranny*, and *Black Friday*.

Being the all-around assistant, typist, researcher, and fact-checker to one of the most popular western authors of all time, J. A. JOHNSTONE learned from the master, Uncle William W. Johnstone.

The elder Johnstone began tutoring J.A. at an early age. After-school hours were often spent retyping manuscripts or researching his massive American Western History library as well as the more modern wars and conflicts. J.A. worked hard—and learned.

"Every day with Bill was an adventure story in itself. Bill taught me all he could about the art of storytelling. *'Keep the historical facts accurate,'* he would say. *'Remember the readers—and as your grandfather once told me, I am telling you now: Be the best J. A. Johnstone you can be.'*"

Visit the website at www.williamjohnstone.net.

Center Point Large Print
600 Brooks Road / PO Box 1
Thorndike, ME 04986-0001 USA

(207) 568-3717

US & Canada:
1 800 929-9108
www.centerpointlargeprint.com